UNDER DOG

KERRY KAYA

Boldwood

First published in 2018. This edition first published in Great Britain in 2022 by Boldwood Books Ltd.

Copyright © Kerry Kaya, 2018

Cover Design by Colin Thomas

Cover Photography: shutterstock

Every effort has been made to obtain the necessary permissions with reference to copyright material, both illustrative and quoted. We apologise for any omissions in this respect and will be pleased to make the appropriate acknowledgements in any future edition.

A CIP catalogue record for this book is available from the British Library.

Paperback ISBN 978-1-80162-963-8

Large Print ISBN 978-1-80162-962-1

Hardback ISBN 978-1-80162-961-4

Ebook ISBN 978-1-80162-964-5

Kindle ISBN 978-1-80162-965-2

Audio CD ISBN 978-1-80162-956-0

MP3 CD ISBN 978-1-80162-957-7

Digital audio download ISBN 978-1-80162-960-7

Boldwood Books Ltd
23 Bowerdean Street
London SW6 3TN
www.boldwoodbooks.com

For my mum Lynda, and my niece Kaya. With love to you both, always.

1

Nineteen-year-old Tommy Carter punched his fist in the air. Not only had he just done a deal, but he'd done the deal of the century. He'd practically skipped out of Davey Abbott's office at the back of his betting shop in Barking, East London. He was that pleased with himself.

He shook a cigarette out of its packet, popped it into his mouth, and puffed on it happily, drawing the smoke deep into his lungs.

'Well, how did it go?'

Tommy turned to his younger brother Jimmy. 'It went pukka, bruv. You are now looking at an employee of Davey Abbott.'

Jimmy's eyes widened and he glanced back at the betting shop. 'What, and he took you on, just like that?'

'Yep, I'm telling you Jim, this is the start of things for us. And I told Davey that I want you coming with me when I collect the debts. I told him I can only trust you.' He winked.

'Cheers, Tommy.' Jimmy beamed from ear to ear as his brother ruffled his dark hair. 'Did you really say that to him?'

'Course I did, you're my brother. I trust you, and I know for a fact you wouldn't try to get one over on me.'

They began the short walk back towards Thames View Estate on the south side of Barking, chatting away as they did so. This was to be a big break for them, after Tommy had finally managed to get himself noticed by Davey Abbott.

He was a big lad and tall for his age, not to mention strong. He could look after himself. His old man had seen to that. From an early age Frank Carter had taught all of his sons to box. It'd been his dream to have a boxing champion in the family, and with six sons, he was determined to make at least one of them a professional.

'You wait and see Jim, this is only the beginning for us Carters.'

Davey Abbott was a shrewd man. More than once he'd heard the name Tommy Carter mentioned, and after watching the boy box at Golds Gym, he'd known the young lad would make a great asset to his team of debt collectors. In fact, the only stipulation he had, was that the young Tommy Carter wouldn't be averse to breaking a bone or three if the need should arise – if the debts owed to himself weren't paid up on time.

He puffed on his cigar and almost laughed out loud as he recalled the lad telling him he would only work with his brother, Jimmy.

'I only trust me brother,' he'd told Davey, his face deadpan. 'And I can only work with people I trust.'

Davey shook his head as he smiled. He could see he would have his work cut out for him with this one.

He leaned back in his chair and closed his eyes. Yes, he could see Tommy Carter going places. He certainly had a lot of front, if nothing else. Not many people spoke to him the way the boy had and lived to tell the tale.

* * *

Stacey Williams was getting herself dolled up. She applied a coat of mascara, before standing back and inspecting her appearance in the mirror.

Tommy was due to come and see her soon. They'd been courting for six months, and she still had to pinch herself at times. She couldn't believe he was actually her fella.

With a mop of thick dark hair and piercing blue eyes, her Tommy was easily the best-looking lad on the council estate where they both lived. He had a smile to die for – the type of smile that made her swoon and go weak at the knees.

She applied a slick of pale pink lipstick across her lips, before rubbing them together. Well, he wouldn't be smiling tonight, she knew that much. She gave a little shudder. Not when she told him she was pregnant.

* * *

As they reached Bastable Avenue, Tommy leant against a wall. 'I'm gonna go and meet my Stace,' he said, glancing down the street towards his girlfriend's house. 'Wait here for me, and if you see anyone, keep schtum about Davey Abbott. I don't want our old man to find out I'm working for him yet. You know what he's like. He'll only try and put a stop to it.'

Jimmy nodded. He didn't need telling twice. He always did as Tommy asked of him. 'I still don't get why you're knocking about with Stacey Williams,' he stated, wrinkling his nose. 'They're trouble, that family. Always have been.'

Tommy shrugged. He knew the Williams family had a bad rep, but Stacey was different. She wasn't like her brothers, and he'd fallen for her hook, line and sinker. 'She's all right, you just have to get to know her.'

'I suppose so.' Jimmy didn't mention that he thought the family was scum. In fact, that was what everyone thought of the Williams family, and they were given a wide berth by the locals. They couldn't be trusted, that was their problem. They thieved from their own, and it was an unspoken rule, you never thieved on your own doorstop.

* * *

Stacey ran down the stairs, her kitten heels clip-clopping down the bare wooden staircase. Flinging open the front door, she jumped into Tommy's arms, kissing him on the lips as she did so.

'She's been like a cat on a hot tin roof, waiting for you to arrive.' Mary Williams grinned from the kitchen doorway.

'Mum!' Stacey exclaimed, her cheeks blushing.

'Are you stopping here for your tea, Tommy?'

Tommy glanced at Stacey, before turning to look across at her mother. 'No thanks, Mrs Williams. I can't stop. I've got a bit of business to do with me brother.'

'What? I thought we were going out tonight?' Stacey's smile froze.

'Sorry darling, I've made plans with our Jimmy.'

'But I had something important to tell you,' Stacey said, leaning in towards him, her voice low.

'Can't you just tell me now?'

Chewing on the inside of her cheek, she grabbed hold of his hand and dragged him outside of the house.

'Well come on then, what's so important that it couldn't wait?' Leaning against the outside wall, Tommy lit a cigarette and squinted down at her through the curling smoke.

'Oh Tommy,' she cried, wringing her hands together, 'what are we going to do? I'm pregnant.'

The colour drained from Tommy's face and he brought his hands up towards his head. He couldn't believe this was happening to him, not now, not when he'd only just started to work for Davey Abbott. He was about to go places and having a kid hanging around his neck wasn't in his plans, at least not yet anyway.

'Well, say something,' Stacey urged him.

Tommy continued to puff on his cigarette, his mind going into overdrive. Finally, he flicked the cigarette butt to the floor and stamped on it with his heavy boot. 'I don't know what you want me to say, Stace. I don't think I want a baby yet.'

Two pink spots appeared on Stacey's cheeks and she placed her hands on her hips. Tommy had annoyed her with his carefree attitude; it was all right for him, he could walk away, but what about her? She couldn't turn her back on her own flesh and blood. 'Well, that's tough, isn't it? Because this baby, our baby, is already growing inside of me. You don't get the choice to put it back, Tommy Carter.'

Shamefaced, Tommy looked down at the floor. He supposed she was right; the baby was already here. He jerked his head towards the house. 'Have you told anyone?'

'Do you really think you would still be standing here in one piece if I had?'

Tommy raised his eyebrows at the veiled threat, and immediately he saw her shoulders drop.

'I'm sorry,' she said, beginning to cry. 'I didn't mean that, you know I didn't.'

'Come here.' Wrapping his arms around her, Tommy stroked her hair. 'Don't worry babe, we'll sort this out.'

'I'm not getting rid of it,' Stacey stated, sniffing back her tears.

Tommy nodded. He'd already known she would say that, and

he swallowed deeply before speaking. 'I suppose we'll have to get wed then, won't we?'

Even as he said the words, he wasn't so sure it was the right thing to do. They were still young, only just old enough to vote or get served alcohol in a boozer, and here they were talking about marriage and babies.

Flinging her arms around him, Stacey kissed his cheek. Already, she was planning the perfect wedding. All they needed to do first, was break the news to their families. Instinctively, she knew it wouldn't go down well.

'My dad's gonna go ape shit.' Stacey's lips curled down at the corners.

Tommy glanced back towards the house. 'Let me take care of that,' he said, his voice a lot more confident than he actually felt.

* * *

'What's with you? You've got a face like a smacked arse. Did you have a row with Stacey?'

Tommy ignored his brother. They were on their way to the Heathway, in Dagenham, to collect the first debt for Davey Abbott.

'Well?' Jimmy demanded.

'Keep your nose out of my business, Jimmy,' Tommy snapped. As close as he was to his brother, he wasn't in the mood to answer what felt like a hundred questions from him.

Jimmy raised his eyebrows but kept schtum all the same. Obviously, something was troubling his elder brother.

They climbed the stairs to a block of flats. Taking the steps two at a time, they carefully watched their tread, avoiding the puddles of urine.

'They live like animals,' Tommy said before thumping hard on a front door on the fourth floor.

'We're here to collect the money you owe to Mr Abbott,' Tommy stated once the door had been flung open.

Craig Masters sniggered at the two young lads in front of him. Was this some kind of joke? Was Davey Abbott sending out kids to do his donkey work now? 'I don't owe no money,' he began.

Shoving his foot inside the door in a bid to stop Craig from closing it in their faces, Tommy grabbed the man by the throat. 'I'm gonna say this one last time before I break your fucking arm. We're here to collect the money you owe to Mr Abbott.'

'All right, bleeding hell.' Shaking from head to toe, Craig had clearly underestimated the boys in front of him. Handing over the cash, he breathed a sigh of relief once they'd left, and he'd firmly closed the door behind them.

Tommy counted out the money he'd collected, then shoved the cash into his jacket pocket.

'Well that was easy.' Jimmy grinned.

Tommy nodded. 'I'm getting married,' he stated, before jogging down the concrete steps.

His mouth falling open, Jimmy stared after his brother's retreating back. 'Married?' he shouted out.

'You stupid, stupid boy.' Janet Carter was livid. She knew exactly who the Williams family were, she'd even pitied Mary Williams when her eldest boy had been sent to Borstal for the third time in as many years. And now, her own flesh and blood, her first-born, was planning to marry into the family. Well, over her dead body, would he.

'Sorry Mum, it just happened.'

'What do you mean it just happened?' Janet roared as she gave her son a clout around his ear. 'Nothing just happens. I thought you knew better than to get caught out by the first girl who fluttered her eyelashes at you.'

Tommy rolled his eyes. 'You'll like her Mum, honest. In fact, you're gonna love her. Think of her as the daughter you never had.'

'Don't you roll your eyes at me, Thomas Carter,' Janet yelled, using her son's full name as further proof of just how angry she was with him. 'And I'll decide who I do and who I don't like, thank you. As for treating her like a daughter, don't you think I've got enough on my plate looking after you lot?' She held onto the kitchen sink for support as she tried to get her head around the news her son had given her. 'And how are you going to look after this baby? They don't come cheap you know; they need clothes, nappies, somewhere to sleep.'

'I've got a job.' Biting down on his lip, Tommy averted his gaze.

Janet's grip on the worktop tightened. 'What do you mean you've got a job? What about your boxing?'

Tommy sighed. What was boxing ever going to bring him? There were hundreds of kids out there trying to make it as a professional, what made him any different? Yeah he was good, admittedly; in fact, he had a cabinet full of trophies to prove just how good he was, but in the grand scheme of things, that meant nothing, it didn't mean he would make it. 'I've got a job working for Davey Abbott, and he pays well Mum, this could set me up for life.'

Janet was aghast; she knew exactly who Davey Abbott was, everyone did – the man made his living from skulduggery. 'This is going to break your poor dad's heart; he's got high hopes for you. You're on your way to making it as professional Tommy, you can't throw all that hard work away.'

'I don't want it Mum. All I've done ever since I was a kid is live and breathe boxing. I've had enough, I want this job, I want to earn money.'

Janet sighed. 'And where will you live, eh? Have you thought about that?'

Tommy shrugged. 'With Stacey's family, I suppose.'

Janet's mouth fell open. 'Over my dead body, you will. No son of mine will go and live with that family.'

'Well, we'll have to live here then, won't we?'

Nodding her head, Janet remained silent as she tried to think through the sleeping arrangements. They were already cramped as it was, what with the six boys, plus her and Frank. 'That's easy for you to say, where will I put yous, eh?'

'I don't know, Mum, but we'll sort something out.' Tommy hugged his mother to him. From the get-go he'd known that he would be able to win her around in the end. As her eldest son he'd always been her blue-eyed boy. And he also knew the moment she held her first grandchild in her arms, her heart would melt and all would be forgiven.

* * *

Standing in the middle of Stacey's parents' front room, Tommy cleared his throat. He could feel the eyes of her parents and her brothers on them in the crowded room, and he gently squeezed his girlfriend's hand in his.

'Well, spit it out,' Jack Williams barked. He was a large man, with a shaven head, and tattooed arms the size of hams. Every inch of him screamed out thug.

Tommy glanced nervously towards the Williams boys. He didn't think it was going to go down too well, when they learnt he'd knocked up their only sister.

'Well, come on, we ain't got all night.'

'I'm pregnant.' With that, Stacey darted from the room in tears, leaving Tommy alone to deal with the backlash.

'Do fucking what?'

Standing his ground, Tommy held his head high. The last thing he needed to do was show them that he felt intimidated; Stacey's brothers would tear him apart at the first sign of weakness. 'That's right. Stace is having a baby and I'm gonna stand by her, so we're getting married.'

Jack held up his hand, warning his sons to stay back. In his eyes, it took a lot of courage for the boy to stand in front of them and tell them what he just had. He thrust his hand forward. 'You'll do boy.' He grinned. 'It's about time the girl settled down, and she won't go far wrong with you beside her.'

Relieved, Tommy shook the proffered hand. He had to admit he hadn't been expecting this at all, in fact, he'd been thoroughly prepared to take a kicking, it was the least he deserved in the circumstances. Taking the can of lager which had been shoved towards him, he snapped open the ring pull and drank deeply. He guessed this meant he'd officially been welcomed into the Williams family.

2

'C'mon, Stace, it's my stag do.'

Stacey was sulking. She knew exactly what went on at stag dos, and with both Tommy's brothers and her brothers attending, it was bound to get messy. Besides, she herself hadn't been able to have a hen party, not a proper one anyway. Hers had consisted of sitting in Tommy's parents' front room, with her mum and Tommy's mum shooting daggers at each other. The highlight of the night had been when the cheese sandwiches had been passed around.

'I didn't have a hen night.'

Tommy laughed as he came to stand behind her. He rubbed his hand over her ever growing bump. 'What did you expect, eh? You're cooking our baby in there. You could hardly go out partying, could you?'

'I know.' Stacey sighed. 'It's just... it would have been nice to have had a few of me mates over at least.'

'There'll be plenty of time for all of that at the wedding.'

Turning around, Stacey smiled. She couldn't wait to become Mrs Carter. Immediately, her thoughts went to her wedding dress. Beautiful, it was. She'd found the design in a wedding magazine and fallen in love with it. Her Tommy had paid for a dressmaker to make it for her. She'd felt like a princess when she'd stepped into the ivory Organza gown with huge puff sleeves and a lace bow at the back. She couldn't wait for Tommy to see her when she walked down the aisle towards him.

Tommy kissed his wife-to-be on the lips. 'C'mon then, Stace. Let me go now, otherwise they'll end up killing each other down there.'

With one last peck on his cheek, Stacey let Tommy walk from the room. He was right, their brothers were likely to kill one another without him there to referee.

* * *

Pint after pint Tommy had downed, and he swayed unsteadily on his feet. 'I'm getting married tomorrow,' he told all and sundry, with a wide lopsided grin spread across his face.

They were in The Short Blue public house on Thames View Estate and pulling out a large wedge of cash from his trouser pocket, Tommy paid for a round of drinks. He'd have a hangover in the morning, he knew that much, but luckily, the wedding wasn't until midday, so he would have plenty of time to recover.

'She's a smasher ain't she, my Stace?' he slurred, slinging his arm around Jimmy's shoulder.

'She is.' Jimmy nodded, grinning.

'Here, hold this. I need a piss.' Handing over his pint glass, Tommy walked unsteadily towards the men's toilets.

He'd barely made it through the door when a blow to the back of his head sent him flying. Sinking to the floor, he was out cold as his pockets were rifled through.

'Give him a few kicks for good measure,' a voice said, before the assailants fled the scene.

* * *

Stacey had burst out crying when she'd seen Tommy. Not only was it unlucky to see the groom before the wedding, but her Tommy looked as though he'd just gone ten rounds with Mike Tyson. 'Who did this?' she demanded through her tears.

Tommy shrugged before wincing as his mum dabbed TCP on the cut above his eye. 'I don't know, babe. I was out cold.'

Janet Carter pursed her lips. She'd put money on one of the Williams boys having a hand in this. She wouldn't say anything just yet, though. Not today of all days. But after the wedding, she would voice her opinion on who she thought was responsible. She turned to her second eldest son. 'You must have seen who did this. You and Tommy are usually joined at the hip.'

Jimmy shook his head. 'I didn't see anything. The boozer was packed solid. It wasn't until I went looking for our Tommy that I even knew anything was wrong.'

Tommy lit a cigarette and blew the smoke out noisily. It wasn't exactly the money that they'd pinched that bothered him. It was his dented pride that hurt the most. In any normal circumstances, whoever it was wouldn't have got the better of him, and they'd had to resort to dirty tactics by hitting him from behind to get one over on him.

'Well, we won't let it spoil our day.' Stacey sniffed back her tears. 'But you'll have to stand at an angle for the photos Tommy, otherwise the cuts and bruises will show.'

'Yeah, I'll do that,' Tommy answered, studying his reflection in a hand mirror. They'd done him over good and proper, and as a result, he was livid. He would find out who'd done it though. People always talked, and someone was bound to brag that they'd got one over on Tommy Carter.

* * *

Frank Carter took one look at Davey Abbott and turned up his nose. He couldn't stand the man, and everything he stood for. He'd swallowed the fact that his eldest son worked for him, but he wasn't happy about it one little bit. Even the fact that Davey had paid for a large portion of the wedding hadn't softened his mood towards him. Why would the man pay for the wedding? That was the question he'd kept asking, but that no one seemed to want to answer. What did Davey Abbott have to gain by stumping up the cash?

He grabbed hold of his son's arm, bringing him to a halt beside him. 'What's he doing here?' he hissed.

Looking towards Davey, Tommy kept his voice low. 'He's me boss, Dad. And besides, he's paid for most of today. I had to invite him.'

Frank shook his head. If he knew anything about Davey, it was that he didn't do anything for nothing. He had a feeling his son was getting in over his head, and his protests were falling on deaf ears. He watched as Davey strutted around as though he owned the place, and he decided that after the wedding, he would have a serious word with his boy.

* * *

Davey felt a sense of pride as he watched Tommy Carter take his vows. He'd become fond of the young man, and he'd taken his place in the front pew, as was his given right, considering he was not only Tommy's boss, but he'd also paid for the day. Tommy was fast becoming one of his greatest protégés. The boy was a fast learner. In fact, he reminded him of himself when he'd been the same age.

Having had no children, Davey had begun to see Tommy as the son he'd never had, and like an overprotective father, he was furious about the beating the boy had suffered. He would keep his ears to the ground and find out who was responsible, and when he did get a hold of them, they were going to wish they'd never been born.

* * *

'Are you happy, babe?' Tommy asked as he spun his bride around the dance floor.

Stacey grinned. She was so happy, she felt giddy with it all. 'It's been a fantastic day, Tommy.' The three-course meal Davey Abbott had paid for was delicious and must have cost a fortune, that was without the finger buffet that was to come later on in the evening. Everything from jellied eels to sausage rolls would be laid out for them. It was a proper East End wedding, and one that people would always remember. She looked across to her family; even her dad and brothers were behaving themselves, which was a first.

Beaming, Tommy held Stacey close. 'This is just the start for us, Stace,' he whispered in her ear, 'you just wait and see.'

Stacey rested her head on her new husband's shoulder as he whirled her around. She knew he may not be everyone's cup of tea, but her Tommy was perfect in her eyes.

* * *

After a short honeymoon in Blackpool, Tommy and Stacey returned home to his parents' house. They'd been given the back room, or the dining room as it had been formally known, and peering inside the dark room, Stacey smiled before coming to sink down onto the double bed. It wouldn't take her long to make the place feel like home. Tommy had promised she could decorate however she wanted to, and she'd already decided on a pink and grey colour theme.

'So, you're back then?'

Tommy turned towards his mother and grinned. 'Yep.' He caught Jimmy's eye and lowered his voice. 'How's everything been here?'

Jimmy shrugged. 'It's been okay, our Gary was a natural.'

Impressed, Tommy ruffled his younger brother's hair. At just sixteen, Gary was a big lad for his age and could easily pass for someone a lot older. Right from the start he'd had a feeling that Gary would be able to handle working with Jimmy, collecting the debts in his absence.

'Davey said to remind you he wants a word, when you're back,' Jimmy said, keeping his voice low.

Nodding, Tommy was thoughtful. He'd already known that Davey would want to speak to him; he'd pulled him aside towards the end of the wedding and said as much. 'I'll go and see him in a bit.'

Overhearing their conversation, Stacey looked up. 'You're not going out already, are you? We've only just got home.'

Tommy sighed. He wasn't used to explaining his comings and goings. 'I have to, Stace, it's to do with work' – he nodded towards her bump – 'and we're gonna need all the money we can get once the baby's born.'

'What am I supposed to do then, while you're out?'

'My mum's here. You can keep each other company.'

Hiding her annoyance, Janet walked through to the kitchen. It wasn't her place to keep the girl company. As much as she liked Stacey, she would always be a Williams in her eyes, and if she was being perfectly honest, she didn't think she would ever fully take to the girl, or any girl her sons brought home for that matter.

'You'll look after Stace, won't you Mum?' Tommy called out.

Rolling her eyes, Janet swallowed down the irritation. The girl was about to become a mother herself; she didn't need babysitting.

'It's okay, I'll be fine,' Stacey answered quickly, her lips curling down at the corners. 'I'll go and see me mum.'

After kissing his wife's forehead, Tommy left the house. 'They'll be okay, won't they?' he asked Jimmy for reassurance. 'I mean Mum and Stace, they'll get on eventually?'

Jimmy shrugged. He didn't know what to say. It was nothing to do with him.

* * *

The two brothers walked the short distance to Davey's scrap yard on River Road. It was here that the majority of Davey's business was carried out – the more illegal business anyway.

Tommy pushed open the office door. In one corner, sat a tattered grey filing cabinet. On top of it piled high, was a precarious stack of paperwork. Blu-Tacked to the walls were posters of topless page-three models, and in the far corner was a rickety wooden desk cluttered with even more paperwork, a telephone, and a mug full of biro pens and pencils. Tommy almost gasped at the sight that met him. Stacey's elder brother, Pete, had been tied to a chair in the middle of the small room.

'What's going on?' Tommy asked, narrowing his eyes.

'My sources have told me this is the bastard responsible for robbing you, or at least his name was put forward anyway,' Davey answered. In his eyes, it was the same thing. After all, there was no smoke without fire as the old saying went.

Spotting the gun in Davey's hand, Tommy's eyes widened. 'Fucking hell Davey, what are you planning to do with that?'

'Little lesson for you, Tommy. It's the easiest and quickest way to make them talk,' Davey stated as he smacked the gun around the side of Pete's head.

'Did you know about this?' Tommy demanded as he rounded on his younger brother.

'Well, yeah,' Jimmy admitted, 'but I could hardly say anything in front of Stacey, could I? Not exactly a good welcome home present, is it?'

Stunned, Tommy wiped his hand across his face. He could hardly believe what he was seeing and hearing. Surely, it wasn't his own brother-in-law who'd robbed him. Stepping inside the office, he rounded on Pete.

'Did you do this?' he demanded.

'I swear on our Stacey's life, it wasn't me, Tommy.'

'I can't fucking believe this is happening. I've only just come home from me honeymoon.'

'Of course it was him. He's a fucking Williams. They're all thieving bastards.'

As the enormity of the situation kicked in, Pete's eyes became wide with fear. 'Honest, Tommy, I didn't do anything. You have to believe me.'

'Look Davey, he said he didn't do it,' Tommy argued.

'Don't be so fucking wet behind the ears. If you let this cunt get away with it, you'll be finished in this business. Every other bastard out there will think they can get one over on you,' Davey stated, his steely grey eyes hard.

Faced with a dilemma, Tommy stood thinking through his next move. The truth was, he had no idea who'd attacked him on his stag night, and they only had the word of Davey's source that it was Pete who was responsible. What if the source was wrong?

'I didn't do it, Tommy. I swear to you.'

The metal shaft of the gun hit Pete full on in the face and his head rolled to the side with the force of the whack.

'You need to sort this fucker out once and for all, brother-in-law or no brother-in-law,' Davey bellowed.

'Let's just think this through, eh? We all need to calm down.' Tommy's day was beginning to turn into a complete nightmare. How could they even let his brother-in-law go now, after this? Stacey was bound to find out, and he knew all hell would break loose when the rest of the Williams family knew what Davey and Jimmy had done.

'There's nothing to think through,' Davey said, smashing the butt of the gun into Pete's face. The little shit wouldn't get away with what he'd done to Tommy, and on his stag night of all days, too. In fact, they would teach him a lesson he wouldn't forget in a hurry. The quicker Pete learned that no one – and he meant no one – fucked over one of his men, then the quicker they would let him go.

The sudden gun explosion was deafening to their ears. Startled, Tommy ducked for cover. 'Fucking hell,' he cried.

Shocked himself that the gun had accidently gone off, Davey leapt backwards and stared down at the gun in his hand. How the fuck had that happened?

Crawling out from underneath Davey's desk, Tommy immediately looked towards his younger brother. Jimmy was covered in blood splatter, but very much alive. He turned to look towards Davey. One of them had been hit, he knew that much, and with the three of them still standing, it only left one other person. His heart in his mouth, he slowly turned his head towards Pete.

The sight which met him had Tommy retching on the floor. It was obvious Pete was dead. His brains were splattered across the far wall and ceiling.

3

Stacey was going out of her mind. Her brother Pete had been on the missing list for more than seventy-two hours. She squeezed her mum's hand tightly and fought down the urge to cry.

'Maybe he's done a runner,' Steven Williams stated.

Jack dismissed his son's words. 'Our Pete wouldn't do that. When have you ever known him to run before?'

Their dad was right. Even when he'd known he was going to be sent to Borstal for the third time, Pete hadn't run.

'Well, he's got to be somewhere,' Stacey chirped in. She looked across to her husband, hoping he would have a suggestion as to where her elder brother could be.

Leaning against the door frame, Tommy kept his face neutral. How he was able to face both his wife and her family after what he'd done, he had no idea. He could still smell the scent of Pete's blood on his hands. He felt sickened to the core by the sheer thought of what had taken place in the aftermath of his brother-in-law's death. It had taken them hours to saw through the flesh and bone, before burning his remains in an oil drum.

'Well, someone, somewhere, must know where he is.'

The Williams nodded at Jack's words.

'Where should we start looking?' asked Jack Junior.

Jack tapped the side of his nose. 'We'll have to start by retracing his steps. Someone must have seen him.'

Tommy cleared his throat, worried in case Jimmy's name came up in their enquiries. 'Maybe he just wants a bit of time out, a bit of space, and will turn up when he's good and ready.'

All eyes turned towards him, before they burst out laughing. 'A bit of space,' Jack laughed, holding onto his stomach. 'Fuck me, Tommy. Who do you think our Pete is, some kind of la de fucking da? He can just about write his own name.'

His cheeks flushing red, Tommy shrugged. 'It was just a suggestion,' he mumbled.

Catching her husband's eye, Stacey gave him a gentle smile. You could trust her Tommy to lighten the mood.

* * *

'I could fucking kill you for this,' Tommy roared as he held his brother, Jimmy, up against the wall by his throat. 'How am I meant to keep this a secret from Stace and the rest of her family? They're gonna find out. I know they are, and then what, eh?'

Jimmy gasped for breath. It hadn't even been his idea to nab Pete. It was Davey Abbott who'd done it. He'd just happened to be there at the time.

Tommy threw his brother away from him. He was worried. His Stacey meant the world to him, and if she ever found out about what they'd done, he knew she would never forgive him.

'Take it up with Davey; it's nothing to do with me.'

Jimmy's nonchalant attitude was like a red rag to a bull, and chasing his brother through the house Tommy's fists were curled into balls and his feet were heavy, as he charged up the stairs after him. Jimmy may be able to run, but he couldn't hide in the tiny council house.

'What's going on up there?' Stood with her hands on her hips, Janet Carter bellowed at the top of her voice. When she received no reply, she raced up the stairs after her two sons. 'Stop, stop!' she screamed, as Tommy's fist was ready to connect with Jimmy's face. 'What's going on, eh?'

'It's him,' Tommy spat. 'Get him away from me, Mum, before I end up killing him.'

Leading Jimmy out of the room, Janet bit down on her lip. Ever since he'd begun working for Davey, Tommy had changed, and it wasn't a change for the better. Until now her boys had always been close. Of course, they had their spats, all brothers did, but since he'd returned from his honeymoon, she could sense that something had shifted between them. She could feel the animosity, the anger that followed her eldest son around like a thick black cloud. It wasn't like them to be at loggerheads, with just eleven months between them they'd always been so close in the past.

'What's going on between the two of you?' she demanded.

'Nothing,' Jimmy spat, shrugging his mother away from him. He wasn't a baby; he didn't want her fussing over him. He could take care of himself, and he didn't need her to protect him from his brother.

To hell with Tommy. He kicked out at the door frame in frustration then slammed the door to the bedroom he shared with his younger brothers shut.

* * *

Davey Abbott rubbed at his tired eyes. He was becoming bored with explaining himself to young Tommy Carter. If it had been any other man questioning him, they would have felt the force of his fist by now. 'How many times do I need to tell you it was an accident? Do you honestly think I planned to shoot the fucker with all three of us in the office? Think about it logically, Tommy.'

Tommy blew out his cheeks. He didn't know what to think any more. The only thing he knew for certain, was that he couldn't work with his brother for the foreseeable future, not when he felt like he wanted to kill him stone dead every time he looked at him.

'So, what am I meant to do with you both, eh?' Davey had recently taken Jimmy onto his payroll for the sole purpose of working alongside his brother.

Sitting forward in his seat, Tommy looked Davey in the eyes. 'It's bad enough I have to live with him. I can't work with him; I'll end up murdering him.'

Davey nodded. 'Okay, I'll have to send you out with Mad Dog Harris instead then.'

Satisfied, Tommy smiled. Working with the mad Scotsman had to be better than working with Jimmy.

* * *

Mad Dog Harris had grey, cropped hair, and a saddlebag moustache. He reminded Tommy of an older version of Charlie Bronson; the prisoner that was, not the actor.

A man of few words, Mad Dog had barely said two words to him on the short drive towards East Ham, and if he was being totally honest, that suited Tommy down to the ground. He wasn't in the mood for small talk.

They stopped outside a Turkish restaurant, and Tommy looked across at the premises. He'd been warned by Davey to tread carefully. You didn't mess with the Turks, apparently. They were all a bunch of mad bastards.

Tommy stepped out of the car and adjusted his clothing before crossing the road and pushing open the door to the restaurant. 'Mehmet Ali?' he enquired.

Mehmet Ali turned towards the young man in front of him. 'Who are you?' he asked in broken English.

'I'm here to collect the money for Mr Abbott.'

Mehmet eyed Tommy suspiciously. He'd never seen this boy before in his life. 'I don't know you,' he answered with a dismissive flick of his hand.

'Don't piss me off, mate. I want Mr Abbott's money.' Tommy knew he needed to take control of the situation, and fast, before he was laughed out of the restaurant. He also knew for a fact that Mad Dog Harris would relay how he'd handled the situation back to Davey, and he didn't want to lose face with his boss.

'I said, I don't know you.'

'I heard what you said,' Tommy said, moving forward. 'And like I said, I'm here to collect Mr Abbott's money. Now, you do as I say, otherwise you're going to find yourself going head-first along that bar of yours.'

Mehmet began to laugh at the threat; he wasn't concerned in the slightest, in fact, he was more than capable of taking care of himself. 'Tell Mr Abbott I will deal with him personally, not with some little boy.'

Tommy lunged forward, grabbed a handful of Mehmet's shirt in his fist, and as promised, hurled him head-first across the length of the bar. Once the man had fallen to a crumpled heap on the floor, Tommy stood over him. 'Money, now.'

'Okay, okay, I'll get the money.' Scrambling to his feet, Mehmet hastily opened the till and counted out fifty pounds in crisp ten-pound notes. 'Here take it.'

Taking the money from the man, Tommy passed it across to Mad Dog. 'I'll be back next week,' he warned, stabbing his finger forward. 'Make sure you have the cash ready for me.' He didn't wait around for a reply, and with his head held high, he left the restaurant.

Out on the street, Mad Dog burst out laughing. 'The boss said you were a live wire – he wasn't wrong.'

Tommy shrugged. He'd only just started.

* * *

Stacey stood back and inspected her handiwork. She was impressed with herself. Hers and Tommy's room was coming along nicely. He'd bought them new furniture and a lovely grey carpet, which her toes sank into.

She began unpacking a box of their clothes, placing them into the white chest of drawers Tommy had bought. She'd never had such a lovely bedroom before and couldn't stop admiring the plush furniture and matching double bed. Tommy had been right when he'd told her it would only be the best for them from now on.

Once she was finished, Stacey cast her eyes across the room before straightening out the bedspread. She wanted everything to look perfect, before her Tommy came home from work. She was about to leave the room, when something poking out from underneath the bed caught her eye.

Crouching down, Stacey sat back on her haunches then shoved her hand underneath the bed and fished the object out.

In horror she recoiled. Her eyes were wide, and her heart was beating ten to the dozen. It was the first time she had ever seen a gun before, and in her panic, she fell backwards, kicking the firearm back underneath the bed.

Why would her Tommy have a gun? She kept asking herself that same question, over and over again. She needed to know the answer, she decided, and there was only one way of doing that. She would have to ask him.

* * *

Tommy's eyes flickered towards where he'd hidden the gun.

'Well?' Stacey demanded. 'What's it doing here?'

Even as he shrugged, he knew Stacey was no fool. There was only one person who could have put the gun underneath their bed, and that was him. He took her hand in his and guided her towards the bed, giving him a few moments to think through an explanation. 'It's for protection.' He could see confusion spread across her face and continued talking, unable to look her in the eyes, a sure sign that he was lying. 'I need it for work, Stace. Davey Abbott insists we all carry one, just in case we come across any trouble.'

Biting down on her lip, Stacey thought the explanation through. 'But it was underneath the bed. You didn't take it to work.'

Tommy paused. He should have known she would catch him out on the lie. The truth was, this had been the gun used to shoot and kill her brother. Davey had shoved the firearm into his hand, and ordered him to dispose of it, but instead he'd panicked, and brought it home. He wished now he'd just thrown it into the Thames. 'Yeah, you're right. I just don't feel comfortable carrying it around, Stace, but I'll get rid of it soon. I promise.'

'But if Davey said you should keep it with you for protection, then shouldn't you do that? I don't want anything to happen to you, Tommy.'

Tommy kissed his wife's forehead and pulled her close. 'Don't you worry about me, Stace. I can look after myself.'

When he felt her arms curl around him, Tommy wanted to curse himself. He hated the fact he was lying to her, but what other choice did he have? He couldn't bear the thought of Stacey knowing the truth, of seeing the hurt and hatred she felt for him in her eyes; he loved her too much for that, and he knew for a fact that she would never forgive him, how could she? Pete had been her brother and he knew if it had been one of his brothers, he wouldn't have been able to easily forgive. Maybe his mum was right all along, and he was stupid. He had to be if he thought he could brush Pete's death under the carpet, that he could pretend he knew nothing about his disappearance, when all along he'd not only been there when Pete had been killed but he'd also helped to dispose of his body.

4

Stacey smiled at Jimmy as she followed him through to the kitchen. They were alone in the house, and it was on the tip of her tongue to ask him about the gun. Something just wasn't ringing true with Tommy's explanation. As much as she wanted to believe her husband, the problem she had was that she knew him, and she also knew when he was lying.

She busied herself making a cup of tea. 'Would you like one?' she offered Jimmy, her hand hovering over the small round tin that contained the tea bags.

Jimmy shook his head, feeling awkward. He'd never felt completely comfortable around Stacey, or any female come to that, not that he would ever let on to his family.

'I'm glad I caught you, actually. I wanted to ask you something.'

Alarmed, Jimmy stared at his sister-in-law.

Stacey could feel Jimmy's shyness and continued to make her tea, pouring the hot water over the teabag. 'It's about the gun.' She looked up and watched his reaction. 'The gun Mr Abbott makes you all carry.'

Confused, Jimmy racked his brains as to what she meant.

Laughing, Stacey shook her head sadly. 'You don't even know what I'm talking about, do you?'

'Yeah, I do. You mean the guns.' Jimmy stumbled on his words. The problem was, Stacey was right, and he didn't know what she meant. There was only one gun he'd seen, and that was the one Tommy was supposed to have gotten rid of. The one that had been used to kill her brother.

'It's okay, Jimmy, stop trying to protect him, I know everything.' Picking up her mug, Stacey walked from the kitchen.

'I'm sorry, Stace, it was an accident, honest to god it was.'

Coming to a halt, Stacey's stomach flipped over. 'Was it?' she asked, calling his bluff.

'Yeah and Tommy was gutted, please don't blame him for it. He didn't even know we had him, not until you came back from your honeymoon. Honestly, we didn't mean for him to die. It was an accident. The gun just went off. And even if it was him who'd robbed our Tommy, I know what Tommy's like, he would have made Davey let him go. I know he would have done.'

The colour drained from Stacey's face. Was Jimmy trying to tell her they'd killed someone? 'Yeah, he would definitely have let him go,' she said, playing along. 'The trouble is' – she shrugged – 'you know what Tommy's like; he doesn't like to talk about it.'

'He doesn't want to upset you. I think he's worried you'll tell your dad and brothers.'

Stacey's chest began to tighten and she had a horrible feeling Jimmy was talking about her brother, Pete. 'Who did you kill, Jimmy?'

'What?'

'Who did you kill?' Despite the hysteria she could feel building up inside of her, her voice remained calm, controlled.

'I thought you knew.' Cold beads of sweat began to break out across Jimmy's forehead. He thought she'd known about the shooting, that's what she'd said, wasn't it?

'Who did you kill?' she began to shout, taking a step towards him, her fist raised in the air, ready to thump him if he didn't tell her. 'Tell me.'

'I dunno. Just forget I even said anything, Stace.'

'Tell me!' she screamed.

'Pete!' Pushing Stacey away from him, Jimmy ran from the house. He was terrified, and knew Tommy was bound to go ballistic when he found out he'd told Stacey.

Collapsing in a heap on the cold linoleum floor, Stacey felt as though her world had shattered before her eyes. How could Tommy do this to her? He was supposed to love her, wasn't he? Tears spilled down her cheeks as she lay on the floor and sobbed her heart out.

* * *

Davey clapped Tommy on the back. He was more than impressed with the lad. He'd sent him to the Turkish restaurant as a little test, knowing from experience just how hard it was to prise money from Mehmet Ali's hands, and he'd wanted to see how Tommy handled the situation. By all accounts, the boy had done well. He'd started to gain a name for himself had young Tommy, and on more than one occasion he'd heard him referred to with a mixture of fear and respect.

'You'll do, Tommy, and I think it's about time I promoted you to the strip clubs and protection rackets. Mad Dog here will show you the ropes.'

Beaming, Tommy grinned from ear to ear. His hard work had paid off and he definitely had a step on the ladder now. 'I won't let you down.'

'I know you won't, young Tommy.' Davey grinned, raising his glass towards him.

* * *

Tommy was in high spirits as he returned home. He let himself into the house, whistling as he did so. 'Stace,' he called out. 'I'm gonna take you out tonight.' A night on the town was exactly what they needed to celebrate his promotion.

Walking through to the lounge, he looked at the faces staring back at him. 'What?' he asked, feeling a sense of panic.

Janet Carter nodded towards the bedroom he and Stacey shared. 'You'd better see for yourself.'

With one last glance towards his mother, Tommy gingerly pulled down on the door handle.

With only the bedside lamps switched on it took a moment or two for his eyes to adjust to the dim lighting, but once they had his blood ran cold. Standing in the middle of the room was Stacey; her eyes were red-rimmed, her hair in disarray, and in her hand, she held the gun.

Closing the door gently behind him, Tommy's arms were outstretched as he cautiously took a step towards her. 'Stace,' he began, 'what's going on babe?'

'Did you do it?' Her voice was low as she spat out each word.

His heart in his mouth, Tommy narrowed his eyes. 'Did I do what?'

'Did you do it?' she screamed. 'Did you murder my brother?'

The colour drained from his face. 'No.' And it was the truth; he hadn't been the one holding the gun; he hadn't pulled the trigger.

Stacey vehemently shook her head. She'd fully expected him to lie; she didn't even know who he was any more. This wasn't the man she'd married, the man she'd wanted a future with.

Taking a step forward, Tommy eased his arm towards his wife. 'Give me the gun, babe, and then we can talk about it.'

'You mean, you'll lie to me again?' Stacey stabbed the gun towards him, her hands shaking.

'No, I'll tell you the truth, I promise, darling.' He watched with bated breath as the hand holding the gun lowered to her side. He lunged forward, half twisting her wrist until she dropped the weapon. 'Fucking hell, Stace,' he said, kicking the firearm across the bedroom floor, 'what were you planning to do, shoot me?'

She began to cry and instinctively he pulled her into his arms. 'Is Pete dead?' she asked, her breath coming in short little bursts.

Tommy closed his eyes, wishing more than anything that he could turn back time. If only he hadn't gone to the scrap yard, if only he hadn't helped to dispose of Pete's corpse. 'It was an accident, babe.' He felt her body stiffen and he held her to him even tighter. 'We didn't mean to kill him, I swear we didn't. The gun just went off.'

* * *

Janet Carter's eyes were wide with fear as Tommy came out of the bedroom. An hour earlier she'd ushered the rest of her sons out of the house. The less they knew, the less they could repeat, she decided.

'Did you do it son?' she asked, not sure she really wanted to know the answer.

'Please Mum, not now.'

Following her first-born through to the kitchen, Janet was scared. It could mean life in prison, if Tommy was ever caught and found guilty.

Tommy sat down heavily at the kitchen table. His eyes were red-rimmed and he looked as though he had the weight of the world piled on top of his shoulders.

Janet sat down opposite him and, reaching across the table, she grasped his hand in hers. 'Please son, tell me the truth.'

Tommy sighed. He looked as though his heart had been shattered into tiny little pieces, and all Janet wanted to do was hold him close to her, like she had when he'd been a little boy. Only, he wasn't a child any more. He was a married man and about to become a father himself.

'It was an accident, Mum. And to answer your question, no I didn't do it, but I was there. Me and Jimmy were both there.'

Janet gasped. Not both of her boys! An ice-cold chill ran down her spine, making her shiver. 'Where is our Jimmy?'

Tommy shrugged. 'I don't know, and I don't really care, but when I get my hands on him, I'm gonna kill him. It was him who told Stacey.'

The calmness of Tommy's words chilled Janet to the bone. 'He's your brother, son, not some stranger you've just met down the pub. You can't go around killing one another.'

Tommy's eyes flashed dangerously. 'Then he should have kept his fucking mouth shut, shouldn't he?'

* * *

Jimmy was scared. It wasn't often he and Tommy fell out, and this was by far the worst the situation had ever been between them. In fact, he wasn't so sure that things could ever go back to being normal again.

He was hiding out in Davey's scrap yard on River Road, and knew it was only a matter of time until Tommy found him. The problem was if Tommy did turn up, there was actually no place he could run and hide. He was completely blocked in.

He chewed on his thumbnail as he crouched down beside the filing cabinet. His eyes were trained on the office window, looking out towards the scraps of metal piled high across the yard floor and side fences. There was no escape. Maybe coming here hadn't been such a good idea after all.

Every little noise outside had him jumping out of his skin. He should have kept his mouth shut, that's what he should have done, but Stacey had tricked him into talking. Somehow though, he didn't think Tommy would see it that way. In his brother's eyes, he would be a grass, and if there was one thing he knew for certain about his brother, it was that Tommy loathed people who told tales.

* * *

Tommy was on the war path. He stormed into Davey's yard, ready to have a tear up. 'Jimmy,' he bellowed. 'I know you're fucking in here.'

Standing stock still, Tommy looked around him, his eyes missing nothing. He knew Jimmy was in here somewhere, he had to be, where else would he go?

From the corner of his eye, he caught a flicker of movement from the office window, and without even pausing he ran towards it. Throwing open the office door, he curled his heavy fists into balls. 'I fucking knew it,' he spat. 'I knew you would be the one to tell Stacey about Pete, you no-good grassing cunt.'

His heart in his mouth, Jimmy scrambled to his feet. 'She tricked me into telling her.'

'What and you're so fucking stupid that you fell for it? No, you knew what you were doing, you're not that thick bruv. You did this out of spite and jealousy, because you don't like the fact I've actually got someone in my life other than you following me around everywhere I go like a fucking dog.'

Tommy didn't wait around for a response. Slamming his heavy

fists into Jimmy's body, weeks of pent-up anger came to the fore as he beat the living daylights out of his younger brother.

It was Davey who finally pulled him away. 'Enough,' he yelled. 'What are you trying to do, kill him?'

Out of breath, Tommy stabbed his finger forward. 'Make sure you stay out of my way. From now on you're no brother of mine, you're dead to me.'

Wide-eyed, Davey watched as Tommy walked from the office. He could see now he had underestimated the boy. Tommy Carter was clearly a dangerous individual. He looked down at Jimmy to inspect his injuries. Tommy had done him over good and proper, but he would live. He heaved the boy to his feet. 'Go home,' he told him. He had a feeling their mother may well be the only person who could stop Tommy from killing the boy, if he should decide to come back and try to finish off what he'd started.

5

Despite her threats to leave her husband, Stacey couldn't bring herself to actually see it through. How could she? Her family would want to know the reason she was leaving him, and she would have no other choice but to tell them the truth. She couldn't put her mum through the added pain of losing her eldest son, it was bad enough that Pete was missing.

Not only that but she still loved Tommy; she was having his baby, and her child deserved to have his or her father in their life. If she opened her mouth, Tommy would end up in a shallow grave or in prison. Either way, her baby would be fatherless.

As for her in-laws, they were beginning to make her feel claustrophobic. Everywhere she turned they were there, watching her every move. She knew they thought she held all the cards regarding both Tommy's and Jimmy's freedom. After all, all it would take was one word from her and the Old Bill would be all over them like flies around shit. But she wouldn't talk. From an early age, it had been drummed into her that you didn't grass.

Determined that Tommy would always remember what he'd done to her brother, she hoped the baby was a boy. She'd already decided she would call the baby Peter if it was, and every time Tommy looked at their son, he would remember he'd been involved in her brother's death. In fact, her husband had no say in the matter. She'd already made up her mind. The baby would be named Peter, whether he liked it or not. It may have been a small victory, but it brought her some satisfaction, nonetheless.

* * *

Lillian Chambers patted her peroxide blonde hair, before popping a cigarette between her scarlet painted lips. She waited for Mad Dog Harris to light her cigarette for her, then slowly exhaled the smoke.

'And who's this?' She had a little soft spot for the Scotsman, and she gave him a wide grin before nodding towards Tommy.

'Tommy Carter, one of Mr Abbott's new boys.'

'Well, you're a handsome fella. Where's Davey been hiding you, eh?'

'He's here to learn the ropes... see how the clubs work.'

'Is that so? Well, it's always nice for the girls to have a bit of eye candy to look at while they're working.' Lillian laughed at her own wit, before leaning in towards Tommy. 'If only I was twenty years younger.'

'And if only I wasn't a married man.' Tommy winked back.

Lillian laughed at Tommy's reply. 'You'll do.' She grinned. The girls would see him as fair game, and it was always good to let them know where they stood early on. It saved her dealing with the drama months down the line.

* * *

Tommy's eyes were wide as he walked through the club doors. The heady scent of sweat and stale cigarette smoke immediately hit his nostrils. The heavy beat of the music vibrated underneath his feet as girls in all different stages of undress danced seductively. Some danced across the laps of punters, others gyrated up against floor-to-ceiling length poles on a stage in the middle of the vast room.

'When you work here, you make sure the punters pay up, and that they don't start any trouble with the girls,' Mad Dog shouted above the music.

Tommy nodded. He gave the scene before him one last glance before following Mad Dog back through to the foyer.

And down here, we keep these, just in case of trouble.' Leaning over the reception desk, the Scotsman pulled out a baseball bat. 'You'll probably not need to use them that often. Usually your fists or boots are enough to get your point across.'

'And you'll probably find it's the girls causing the most trouble. They're a fierce bunch, that lot in there. Don't let their pretty looks deceive you. They'd stab you in the eye as quick as look at you,' Lillian said.

Tommy glanced at the door leading to the club and nodded, taking the warning on board. He had a feeling his Stace wouldn't like him working here, and it would be yet another secret he had to keep from her. In fact, the list of things he was keeping from his wife seemed to be growing by the day. Stacey was meant to be able to trust him; she was his wife, not some bird he was knocking off. Before he'd started working for Davey he'd never lied to her, well, maybe the odd tiny white lie every now and again but that had only been if he'd wanted to have a night out with Jimmy instead of seeing her. He'd never told her any whoppers, had never tried to actively deceive her, and now here he was lying to her on a daily basis; it just didn't sit right with him. The fact she believed every lie he told made him feel sick to his stomach, and his shoulders were heavy from having to keep up the pretence.

* * *

It was a week after the beating, and although Jimmy's face wasn't as swollen, he was still sporting yellowy-green bruises over his body and face. He'd spent most of that week locked up in the bedroom he shared with his younger brothers, trying to keep out of Tommy's way.

'Come on, love, why don't you come down and have your tea with us?'

'I'm not hungry.' Jimmy ignored his mother's pleas. He wasn't stupid. He knew Tommy would go ape shit if he was to walk in and catch him sitting with the rest of the family as though nothing had happened.

Janet bit down on her lip. The situation had gone on for too long between her sons. 'Don't make me get your dad up here to drag you out, Jimmy,' she threatened. Despite what Tommy may think, her Frank was still the head of this house, and for as long as they lived under their roof, the boys would have to toe the line. And that meant all of the boys. Tommy wasn't excluded from that, just because he so happened to work for Davey Abbott. 'I mean it, Jimmy.'

'Just leave me alone.'

Janet sighed before making her way wearily down the stairs. She would need to have a word with Tommy about this. However angry he may be with his brother, enough was enough. And if that didn't work, then she would go and see Davey Abbott herself. She knew her sons would listen to him.

* * *

Tommy's reputation had begun to precede him, and he knew people were wary when he walked onto their premises. He'd quickly grasped the context of protection racketeering. Small businesses, such as pubs and restaurants, paid Davey money to make sure they had no trouble from other firms or wayward punters. And if they were stupid enough to choose not to pay up the cash on a weekly basis for protection, then they themselves would smash up the premises.

He strolled into The Brewery Tap public house in Barking with an air of confidence and knew his arrival had been duly noted by more than one person.

Simon Wilson was standing behind the bar. He'd been the landlord for more than ten years. With a cheerful disposition and a friendly face, his good nature had been taken advantage of on more than one occasion. Just two nights ago, his pub had been smashed up for the third time that month. He'd always paid Mr Abbott on time, and now wanted answers as to why nothing was being done about the situation.

Tommy nodded towards the landlord and indicated for him to join Mad Dog and himself at a corner table.

Grabbing a bottle of scotch and three glasses, Simon followed the two men. He unscrewed the bottle and poured out their drinks before taking a seat.

Tommy took a sip of the scotch. It wasn't his usual tipple, and if he was being honest, he would have preferred a pint of lager, but seeing as both the landlord and Mad Dog had gulped theirs down, he followed suit, before wiping the back of his hand across his lips as the alcohol burned at the back of his throat.

'Another?' Simon offered, the bottle already raised in his hand.

Tommy nodded. He would take his time with this glass he decided. 'So,' he said, looking around at the obvious damage. 'Who was it causing trouble in here?'

Simon shrugged. He was hoping they would already know the answer to that question. 'I don't know who they were, but I heard Mr Abbott's name mentioned once or twice.'

Tommy raised his eyebrows before looking across to Mad Dog. 'Are you sure they definitely mentioned Mr Abbott?'

'As plain as day.'

Intrigued, Tommy sat back in his seat. He couldn't get his head around this. Why would someone come into a packed boozer, smash it up and mention Davey's name? There was only one explanation. Whoever was responsible, wanted it to get back to Davey.

'It's the third time this month, Tommy. Now, I pay Mr Abbott for protection without fail every week.'

Tommy held up his hand, cutting Simon off. He got the picture. In other words, they weren't keeping up their end of the bargain. 'Let me speak to Mr Abbott. Don't worry, we'll get this sorted out.'

Simon nodded before gulping down his drink. It was what he'd expected them to say, and he felt a shiver of fear run down his spine. The men responsible for smashing up the pub had forced him to organise this meeting. They'd said they would hurt him and his family if he didn't. He kept his eyes on the door, waiting for the men to burst in at any moment.

Glancing over his shoulder, Tommy turned his attention back to Simon. 'Are you expecting trouble, guvnor?' Not one to miss a trick, Tommy's body was suddenly tense. Beside him he could feel Mad Dog also stiffen.

'He's fucking set us up.'

Simon jumped up from the table. 'He said he'd hurt me kids if I didn't get you here.'

'Who did?'

'Dean Johnson.'

The name meant nothing to Tommy and he turned to Mad Dog. 'Who the fuck is Dean Johnson?'

Mad Dog paled at the name and groaned, before wiping his hand across his face. 'No time to explain, Tommy lad. If I were you, I'd get yourself tooled up. You're gonna need it.'

Stunned, Tommy looked around him. How the fuck was he meant to get tooled up? Thinking on his feet, he walked behind the bar and grabbed a beer bottle, then smashed it against the bar top. The jagged remnants made the perfect weapon.

'Are you ready, lad?' Mad Dog asked, not taking his eyes from the doors.

Tommy puffed out his cheeks. 'As I'll ever be,' he reluctantly answered. He had to be. He had Stacey and his unborn child to think about.

6

Tommy glanced across at Mad Dog. Beads of cold sweat broke out across his forehead. In his fist, he held the broken bottle. He could barely believe this was happening. He didn't even know who the fuck Dean Johnson was.

The packed boozer had turned deathly silent. The last few remaining customers, too intoxicated to have picked up on the vibes, continued supping their pints.

'Get them fucking out,' Tommy screamed towards Simon. The last thing he wanted was their blood on his conscience.

His face deathly pale, Simon ushered the customers out of the pub, before running out of sight.

'Give me the low down,' Tommy snapped.

Not taking his eyes off the doors, Mad Dog quickly filled Tommy in. 'Years ago, Davey and Dean Johnson were partners, this was before they had a major falling out. Dean's brother, Chrissy, was killed in the crossfire. Dean has wanted revenge ever since. I'm guessing this is it.'

'You've got to be fucking kidding me? How the fuck do we get out of this?'

Mad Dog glanced across at Tommy, his lips remaining set in a straight line. 'We don't get out of it, lad. All we can do is just hope for the best, and pray we get to go home at the end of the night.'

Tommy swallowed deeply. He didn't like the sound of this one little bit.

* * *

Returning home from the corner shop, Janet turned the key in the lock, and was faced with pandemonium.

'Where have you been, woman?'

Janet's mouth fell open. It wasn't like her Frank to take that tone with her. 'I only popped out to the shop. What the hell is going on in here?' she demanded.

'It's the baby. It's coming. Get in there and sort her out.' Frank nodded towards the bedroom Tommy and Stacey shared.

Not needing to be told twice, Janet raced towards the room. 'Someone go and fetch her mother. And where is our Tommy? He needs to be here.'

Frank shrugged, his expression serious. 'Who knows where that boy is. He stays out until all hours.'

Rolling up her sleeves, Janet called out to her youngest son, 'Jonny, go to the Williams' house and fetch Stacey's mum.'

Wide-eyed, twelve-year-old Jonny did as he was told and raced out of the house.

'I'll bleeding well clout our Tommy one when he finally turns up. He knows the girl is near her time, and he should have been stopping close by,' Janet stated before pushing open the bedroom door.

Hanging onto the bed sheet, Stacey twisted the thin cotton material in her fists as a contraction ripped through her. 'I want Tommy and I want me mum. It hurts.'

'I know it hurts girl. I had six of me own. Now, when that contraction finishes, you need to get yourself dressed, so we can get you down to the hospital. Our Jonny has gone to fetch your mum.'

'Where's Tommy?'

Janet wanted to curse her eldest son. Where was he indeed? That was the question on everyone's mind. 'I'll get Jimmy and Gary to go out searching for him. Don't you worry, he'll be there.'

* * *

Jimmy wasn't happy, but did as his mother asked of him anyway, and went out looking for Tommy. He could only hope and pray it would be Gary who actually found him. He didn't want another run-in with his brother.

'Where do you suppose he is?' Gary asked as he lit a sneaky cigarette.

Jimmy shrugged. They were making their way towards the centre of Barking. 'Gawd knows. But I'm guessing Davey Abbott must have an idea where he is, so we should start there.'

'Are you and our Tommy ever gonna make up?'

Ignoring the question, Jimmy carried on walking in silence.

'It was a pretty shitty thing to do to Tommy, grassing him up like that.'

Jimmy came to a halt. Staring at his brother, he grabbed hold of his arm in a vice-like grip. 'What do you know about any of that, eh?'

'We're not stupid. We all know what you did. Did yous really kill Stacey's brother?'

Shocked, Jimmy tightened his grip. 'You need to learn when to keep your mouth shut, Gary. Look at what our Tommy did to me. Do you want him doing the same to you?'

Shamefaced, Gary looked to the floor.

When his brother didn't answer, Jimmy continued. 'No, I didn't think so. Keep your nose out of things that don't concern you.'

'All right.' Puffing on his cigarette, Gary decided to keep his own counsel. He and his brothers had heard the hushed conversations and knew exactly what Tommy and Jimmy had done. 'I hope we find him,' he said, changing the subject.

Jimmy rolled his eyes in annoyance. He was starting to think it would have been better if he'd come alone.

* * *

Tommy's eyes were wide as Dean Johnson and his henchmen entered the pub.

'Mad Dog.' Dean nodded his dark head in a greeting. 'It's been a long time. I see you're still running around for Davey.'

'Aye, and this business is between you and Davey, not me and the lad.'

Turning to look towards Tommy, Dean smirked. 'So, this is the famous Tommy Carter I've been hearing so much about.'

Tommy glanced across at Mad Dog and, taking his lead, kept quiet.

'Cat got your tongue, boy?'

'Come on now, leave the lad out of it,' Mad Dog said.

Dean held up his hand. 'If he's old enough to run around for Davey, then he's old enough to speak up for himself.'

Tommy cleared his throat. 'I don't even know who you are.' He shrugged.

'Now, I am insulted. Surely Davey must have mentioned me. We go back years, isn't that right, Mad Dog?' Taking a seat, Dean lit a cigarette and noisily blew out the smoke. 'Well, I've heard of you, Tommy Carter. In fact, a couple of my men had a run in with you, in the gents' toilets, of all places.'

'You mean that was you?' Tommy was so shocked his mind was reeling. Pete had been telling the truth; all along he'd been innocent. Bile rushed into Tommy's mouth and pressing the back of his hand across his lips he swallowed the vomit down in one large gulp. Not only had Pete died for nothing, but he could have lost everything too; his marriage had almost been destroyed, Stacey's heart was broken, he'd even risked his freedom, and for what? For Dean Johnson to use him as way to get even with Davey? 'You dirty bastard.'

'So, where is that old wanker Davey?' Dean asked, ignoring Tommy's words.

'He's not here. It's just me and the boy,' said Mad Dog.

'I can see that. Hiding out somewhere, is he?'

'What is it you want, Dean?'

Standing up, Dean took a step towards them. 'What I'd like to see, is both of your heads on spikes, but seeing as we're in this lovely boozer, and it would be a shame to ruin the decor, it'll have to be plan B.'

'Which is?' Tommy asked, barely able to keep the anger from his voice.

Dean turned his attention to Tommy. 'He's a cocky one this one, isn't he? Plan B, son, is to see the both of you on the floor begging me not to end your sorry lives.'

Tommy felt his heart sink. This wasn't looking good for either Mad Dog or himself.

* * *

Davey Abbott was about to close up shop, when the two Carter brothers burst through the door.

'We need to find our Tommy,' Gary stated. 'His wife's having the baby.'

Davey's eyes widened. He knew young Tommy was out with Mad Dog, but where exactly was anyone's guess. Sliding the bolt across the shop door, Davey gestured for them to follow him through to the office.

He knew they were due to visit the strip clubs in the West End, and from there, they were going to The Brewery Tap. 'Let me make a few calls, lads, and see if I can locate him.'

A few minutes later, Davey replaced the phone into its cradle, his face ashen. He looked at the two boys in front of him. 'Your brother is in a spot of bother.' Having just come off the phone with the landlord of The Brewery Tap, he rubbed at his temple as he tried to think. He needed more manpower, that's what he needed.

Jimmy and Gary glanced towards each other, before turning back to Davey.

'What sort of bother?' Jimmy asked, concerned. They may have fallen out, but no matter what, Tommy was still his brother.

'The sort of bother that'll get him killed if he doesn't think fast on his feet.'

'Fucking hell.' Gary's eyes were wide. 'We need to go and help him.'

Davey held up his hand. 'And we will do, once back-up arrives.'

'Yeah, but our Tommy needs us now.'

'And unless you want to end up getting yourself killed son, you'll wait. Now, listen up, this is the plan.'

'Get on your fucking hands and knees and beg.'

Tommy swallowed deeply. His mouth was dry, and he felt as though he was swallowing sandpaper. Every instinct inside of him, told him to do as Dean Johnson had ordered, yet his pride wouldn't let him.

'Do as he says, lad,' Mad Dog said as he began to get down on his knees.

Before he had the chance to, the doors opened, and Jimmy walked through. Tommy didn't know whether to laugh or cry.

Dean turned to look behind him. 'Get the fuck out,' he began, before pausing. Looking towards Tommy, he then turned back to Jimmy. 'What's this?' he asked. 'Brothers? Twins?'

'Go home, Jimmy,' Tommy begged of his brother.

Dean pointed his finger towards Tommy, a sly grin creasing his face. 'No, he's older. So we have Tommy Carter's little brother added to the mix. Now this could get interesting.'

'Jimmy, please just go home,' Tommy said a second time. The authority in his voice brooked no arguments.

Backing towards the door, Jimmy spoke. 'Davey knows you're here.' With those parting words, he turned on his heels and ran outside.

* * *

Out on the street, Davey raised his head as Jimmy raced out of the pub. 'Well?'

'There's about six of them in there.'

Davey nodded. 'Are they tooled up?'

'I don't think so, but I couldn't really tell.'

Davey pondered this over. He knew for a fact Dean was no fool. He wouldn't have brought anything heavy, just in case the Old Bill was sent for at the same time, though he'd want to protect himself. Maybe he'd have a few knuckle dusters, or even a cosh, but that would be the extent of him carrying any weapons. 'Okay, well, we'd better get this over with then, eh?'

'And what if he's tooled up, boss?' asked Mickey Brown, not taking his eyes off the pub entrance.

'If there's one thing I know about Dean, he's no idiot. He wouldn't have brought tools to a boozer. Muscle yes, maybe even a baseball bat but certainly no knives or firearms.'

A large man with close-cropped hair, Mickey sighed. 'I hope you're right about this.'

'Trust me, when it comes to Dean Johnson, I always am,' Davey replied confidently.

Seeing Davey walk through the doors, Tommy sighed with relief. All he wanted to do was go home to Stacey, and when he saw her he was going to give her the biggest cuddle going and beg for her forgiveness, he'd even get down on his hands and knees if that's what it took.

'And here he is my old mucker, Davey.' Dean's voice was loaded with sarcasm.

Tommy waited for Davey's response. He knew how the man answered would be crucial to them getting out of the boozer in one piece.

'What do you want, Dean? I thought all of this old bollocks had been put behind us.'

Dean shook his head. 'Do you know what today is?'

Davey shrugged.

'Ten years today it was, that my brother Chrissy was shot down and killed. You remember Chrissy, don't you? He looked a bit like me.'

'You know full well that I remember him. And you also know I didn't mean for that to happen.'

Dean nodded. 'That's right, and so you should remember him, seeing as you were the bastard who murdered him.'

Knowing Dean from old, Davey knew there was no point in trying to talk sense into him. Besides, Dean was right. He had been the one responsible for Chrissy's death, and with this knowledge,

Dean should also know he had regarded the man like a younger brother and would never have willingly harmed him. Chrissy had just so happened to be in the wrong place at the wrong time.

'So, the question is, Davey, what do I do about this now?' Walking towards Tommy, Dean took a gun from the waistband of his trousers and pointed it towards Tommy's head. Not once did he take his eyes off his adversary. 'You took one of mine, I take one of yours.'

'Whoa.' Tommy held up his hands, his eyes wide, clearly terrified.

'Don't do that.' Jimmy took a step forward. 'His wife is in the hospital having a baby.'

Tommy's eyes widened. Was Jimmy telling the truth?

A father himself, Dean looked down at Tommy. 'Looks like your wife just saved your bacon.' With that, Dean pointed the gun towards the ceiling, and fired a single bullet. 'I'm coming for you Davey, and slowly, bit by bit, I will break you down,' he stated, before indicating for his henchmen to follow him out of the pub.

Tommy's hands were shaking as he got to his feet and breathed a sigh of relief. 'Fucking hell, that was a close call.' He pulled Jimmy towards him and hugged his brother as if his life depended on it. All of the hard feelings between them were gone. Jimmy had just saved his life. With his brother's face clasped between his hands, Tommy kissed Jimmy's forehead. 'I owe you one, bruv.'

'It's true, Tommy,' Gary said, 'Stacey is in the hospital. Mum sent us to get you.'

Astounded, Tommy looked towards Davey.

'Go.' Davey flicked his hand towards him.

Not needing to be told twice, Tommy raced from the pub with his two brothers hot on his heels.

Flagging down a black taxi, the three brothers jumped inside. 'Upney Hospital mate, and as quick as you can. I'm about to become a father.'

* * *

Janet's expression was stern as her sons charged down the hospital corridor towards her. 'Where the effing hell have you been?' she shouted. 'You're too bloody late, the baby's already here.'

Scooting past his mother, Tommy dodged the clout around the ear, which he knew was coming. A beaming grin was spread across his face as he hastily opened the door to the delivery room.

In her arms, Stacey held their newborn baby. Seeing Tommy, she promptly burst into tears.

'Hey, what's all this?' Tommy asked concerned, his gaze instantly going to the bundle in her arms. 'The baby is okay isn't it,' he choked out. He'd never forgive himself if something had gone wrong. He'd put Stacey through so much stress over the past few months, what if his actions had somehow harmed the baby?

Stacey swiped at her tears. 'It's a girl,' she sobbed.

Letting out a shaky breath, relief flooded through Tommy, and inching closer to the bed, he watched in awe as his daughter kicked away the blanket she'd been wrapped in. He'd almost died and if it hadn't been for Jimmy's quick thinking, he would have never got the chance to meet his little girl. He still couldn't believe it, he was actually a dad. 'She's beautiful,' he whispered. Tears filled his eyes, and unashamedly he allowed them to slip down his cheeks. His heart melted; she looked like Stacey but had his dark hair. She was actually theirs; they had made her. 'She's perfect Stace.'

'But I wanted a boy.'

Laughing, Tommy kissed Stacey on the lips. 'Next time,' he said as he gently lifted the bundle from his wife's arms and held it towards his chest. 'The next one will be a boy.' He grinned as he looked into his daughter's eyes. 'I promise, babe.'

7

Amid nappies and night feeds, Tommy and Stacey adjusted to becoming parents. They had decided to call their daughter Karen, and despite his early reservations that he wasn't ready to be a father, Tommy was besotted with his little girl.

Bleary-eyed, Tommy pressed snooze on the alarm clock beside the bed. The baby had had them up for most of the night with her constant crying. Colic, his mum had said, nothing a bit of gripe water wouldn't fix, she'd added gently, seeing their worried expressions.

Rolling onto his side, he pulled Stacey into his arms. 'I could stay here all day,' he murmured into his wife's ear.

'And you know full well with a baby in the house, that'll never happen, Tommy Carter.' As if on cue, Karen let out a shrill cry. 'See, what did I tell you?' Stacey grinned.

Rolling onto his back as Stacey climbed out of the bed and padded across to the baby's cot, Tommy sighed. 'I have to get up anyway. I've got a busy day today. Davey wants me working up Soho in the clubs.'

After gently picking up the baby and placing her against her shoulder, Stacey narrowed her eyes. 'What sort of clubs?'

Tommy closed his eyes before telling yet another lie. 'Gentlemen's clubs. You know, where men can go to drink or gamble.'

Stacey pursed her lips. 'I hope you're not gambling in there too, Tommy. You know we need all the money we can get, so that we can save up for our own place.'

'Of course I'm not.'

Satisfied, Stacey sat on the edge of the bed and lifted Karen towards her breast for a feed.

Taking this as his cue to get up, Tommy jumped out of bed. He needed a quick bath and then some breakfast before he had to leave. The truth was, he didn't want Stacey asking any more questions about the clubs. He knew instinctively she would go mental if she found out it was a strip club he was working at.

Lillian Chambers smiled as Tommy walked through the club doors. 'Hello, darling. Have I got you working here today?'

Tommy gave a wide grin. 'Indeed you do, Lil. Let's hope it's a good one, eh?'

Lillian nodded. She stood chewing on her lip and, as Tommy was about to walk past her, she grabbed hold of his arm. 'One of the girls, Kitty Mae, she's been asking one too many questions about you. Now, I wouldn't normally get involved, but I know your wife's just had a baby, and well, I think you should be careful. Don't get involved with the girls, Tommy. You're still a young man, and it wouldn't be fair on your wife.'

Stunned, Tommy stared at Lillian. 'What are you talking about? What do you mean, get involved?'

'Look, the girls talk, that's all I'm saying, and Kitty Mae has been talking a lot about you.'

Disgust was evident across Tommy's face. 'Do I look like I go out shagging behind my wife's back? I've done fuck all wrong with this Kitty bird. I don't even know who she is.'

Lillian was taken aback. She'd expected him to laugh off her warning. That's what most of the men who worked here did.

'Well, do I?'

Looking around her, Lillian tried her best to keep Tommy's voice down. The last thing they needed was for the punters to hear him shouting. 'No, of course you don't. Ignore what I said, Tommy. My mistake.'

'No, c'mon, spit it out. If someone's spouting shit about me, then I want to know about it.'

'It was obviously just talk, darling. You know what they're like. She probably wanted to get one over on the other girls, and I, like a silly old fool, took it as gospel, that's all.' Realising Tommy wasn't going to leave until she told him everything, Lillian patted her blonde hair before continuing. 'She was asking around, wanting to know where else you worked other than here. She said you and her had been out a few times, and so I wrongly assumed you were shagging around. A lot of the men who work here do that. Sorry, Tommy, like I said, my mistake.'

Tommy was fuming. All he could think about was his Stace catching wind of something like this. He was already skating on thin ice, thanks to the Pete incident. 'Where is she, this bird?'

'In there.' Lillian nodded towards the club doors.

'Well, seeing as I haven't got a clue who she is, don't you think you'd better point her out to me?'

'Oh, of course.' Leading the way through the doors, Lillian weaved her way through the crowd of girls and punters. 'That's her up there, on the stage.'

Tommy looked up at the girl in question. He had to admit, she was beautiful. He swallowed deeply, before turning back to Lillian. 'Okay, I'll take care of it now.'

With one last look at Kitty Mae, Lillian made her way back to the reception. She could kick herself for having such a big mouth. She should have known better and kept schtum. Davey would go ballistic, if all because of her and her big gob, Tommy started trouble in the club.

* * *

Tommy waited for Kitty Mae to finish her routine before beckoning her over. She reminded him of a cat as she shimmed up and down the pole. Her moves were both seductive and powerful, and he could see why a lot of men would find her attractive. With thick dark hair and green eyes, she certainly knew how to use her assets to her best advantage. She smiled at Tommy as she climbed down from the stage.

'I saw you watching me,' she breathed, leaning closer towards him.

Tommy took a step away. 'And I've heard you've been spreading a lot of shit about me.'

Kitty laughed. 'Let me guess, Lillian?'

Nodding, Tommy couldn't help but smile. He hated to admit it, there was something about her that he liked, really liked, and for the briefest of moments he felt like hiding his wedding band from her view. 'I'm married,' he began, willing himself to shut up. He bit down on his lip and glanced over his shoulder to check that Lillian wasn't loitering around. 'I mean if I wasn't married...' He looked from her face to her ample cleavage then back up to her face again and swallowed deeply. 'I mean if—'

Kitty brought a finger up to his lips, silencing him. 'Hold that thought handsome,' she said, turning to walk away. Glancing back over her shoulder she flashed him the most beautiful smile he had ever seen. 'You're still watching me.' She winked before sashaying her way across the dance floor.

Watching her, Tommy smiled. He was intrigued by her and that was an understatement; he'd never seen a more beautiful woman. As far as he was concerned she was the whole package. He turned to walk away, all the while unable to wipe the interaction from his mind, and with one last lustful glance at the dance floor he pushed through the door that led to the foyer. It was only then that the guilt hit him. He was a married man, he shouldn't have been thinking about another woman, and he certainly shouldn't have been tempted to want to do more than just watch Kitty Mae dance on stage. He loved Stacey, he would always love Stacey, wouldn't he?

Kitty Mae, also known as Bethany Johnson, tottered down the street in her high heels towards a waiting car. Her dad always had the same driver come to collect her, and at one time she would have thought of him as quite attractive, but that was before she'd clapped her eyes on Tommy Carter. Now, she couldn't get him out of her mind.

Silently, she slipped into the back seat, kicking off her heels as she did so.

'Good night, Miss?' asked Brian, her driver.

Bethany smiled as she recalled Tommy's startling blue eyes staring into hers. 'One of the best,' she answered, barely able to conceal the excitement from her voice.

The situation with Dean was causing Davey concern. He still couldn't get his head around why his old business partner had waited ten years to drag up the past.

He stared down at the documents on his desk. The sense of foreboding inside of him was strong, and he couldn't shrug the feeling of dread away. Taking his pen, he quickly signed along the dotted line, before folding up the sheets of paper and passing them across to his solicitor. 'Is that it?' he asked.

Bernard Cohen nodded. 'That's it. In the event of your death, your businesses and assets will be passed over to a Mr Thomas Carter.'

Satisfied, Davey sat back in his chair. He'd grown close to Tommy over the months and with no known relatives of his own he could think of no one else who he would like better to inherit his formidable fortune and businesses. Tommy had become like the son he'd never had, and if he looked closely enough he could even see a bit of himself in Tommy; they were both risk takers, they didn't take fools gladly, and they both had a mind for business, however illegal that business might be. In fact, Tommy had taken to the life like a duck to water and with his personal guidance he'd flourished. He knew the score and knew not only how to play the game but to also win. 'Oh and before I forget.' Davey passed across a key. 'If and when the time comes, I want you to give Tommy this key to the safe. He'll know what to do with it.'

Bernard nodded. It wasn't his place to ask what the contents of the safe were, but he took a wild guess that it would be something illegal.

* * *

That evening, Tommy was quiet. The truth was, he was feeling guilty, even though he hadn't done anything physically wrong. The fact he had spent the rest of his shift at The Soho Club thinking about Kitty Mae, sat heavily on his conscience.

He glanced across at Stacey as she cradled their daughter in her arms. He knew for a fact he would never cheat on her, so why was he feeling so guilty? It was the temptation, he guessed, and the fact Kitty Mae, if that was even her real name, had let it be known she was more than interested in him.

He smiled as Stacey looked towards him, and he grabbed hold of her hand, giving it a little squeeze as he did so. No, he would never cheat, he reassured himself. He only wished his conscience felt as confident.

* * *

Dean Johnson was a wealthy man. Although he had made his money illegally, as long as he and his family were okay, then screw everyone else. That was his motto.

He glanced up as his daughter walked into the room. Scrubbed of all that makeup she covered her face in, his Bethany looked like his little girl once again.

'How did it go? Did you find out any information?'

Taking a seat on the sofa next to her father, Bethany smiled. 'He works in a few clubs. That's all I managed to find out, Daddy.'

Dean grinned. 'Well done, baby. Just a few more weeks, and I'll pull you out of the club.'

Bethany chewed on her fingernail before looking up at her father. 'You're not going to hurt him are you, Dad?'

Dean laughed out loud before throwing his arm around his daughter. 'First lesson in this business, is you get rid of anyone or anything that stands in your way.' His expression became serious. 'And Tommy Carter is in my way.'

Bethany nodded. It was exactly what she'd expected him to say.

She blinked away the tears that glistened her eyes. The problem was she liked Tommy, really liked him. She'd fancied him like crazy from the very moment she'd laid her eyes on him and no matter how much she'd tried she couldn't erase him from her mind. She thought about him night and day and even dreamt about his blue eyes looking into hers. She'd tried telling herself that this was business and nothing else, that she was working for her dad and giving him the information he desperately needed to bring down his onetime business partner Davey Abbott. But it went deeper than that; she wanted to get to know Tommy better, wanted to see if the spark between them was real or if she'd just imagined it.

The next morning, Tommy rose early. Without waking his wife, he crept out of bed, washed and shaved. Then, after eating a slice of toast, he quickly dressed and left the house. He knew he should have woken Stacey and said goodbye, but he was eager to get to the club before the girls arrived, mainly Kitty Mae. The plan was to remove the club's takings from the safe, and get back to Davey, without having to see anyone. Well, that was the theory. The reality was proving to be a lot different.

Already, the club was a hive of activity, and walking through the doors, Tommy kept his head down.

'Couldn't keep away, eh?'

Startled, Tommy looked up and locked eyes with Kitty Mae. He groaned inwardly before answering. 'I'm not stopping.'

'That's a shame.' Bethany forced herself to sound a lot happier than she felt. The fact Tommy was leaving again so soon, disappointed her.

'Excuse me,' Tommy said as he brushed past. When he felt her hand clasp hold of his, he looked down at their entwined fingers in alarm. 'Stop, I've already told you I'm married.'

Bethany smiled. Ever since she was a little girl, she'd got what she wanted, and Tommy Carter wasn't about to become the exception. 'Listen,' she said, pressing her breasts against his chest. 'I like you, really like you, and I've got a feeling you like me, too. So, where's the harm in what we're doing?'

Tommy could feel her hot breath on his neck and the sweet scent of her perfume filled his nostrils. Before he could stop himself, he pushed her into one of the offices. 'You need to leave me alone,' he warned.

Placing her finger on his lips, Bethany silenced him. 'I know you're married,' she said, her voice husky, 'but I don't care. I want this, I want you.'

For a moment Tommy just stared. Talk about give him the green light. He felt his erection straining against his trousers and looking over his shoulder he hastily reached out to lock the office door. His mind and body fought against one another and as she flashed him a smile, he gave in to temptation, pressed his lips against hers, and teased his fingers through her hair. 'I can't do this,' he mumbled, tugging at the waistband of her shorts, 'I'm—'

'Shh,' Bethany breathed, her fingers expertly unbuttoning his trousers, 'no one will ever know.'

Lust spurred him on and as he thrusted inside Kitty, all thoughts of Stacey were gone from his mind.

Ten minutes later he was fastening his trousers. He hated himself for what he'd just done; he'd always sworn he would never cheat on his wife, he wasn't that kind of man. He'd prided himself on the fact that he didn't have a wandering eye and it wasn't as though he didn't love Stacey because he did, more than he could love any other woman, so why had he just potentially fucked up his marriage? It had to have been a moment of madness, he told himself, the fact she had handed it to him on plate. Still, it was no excuse. Plagued by guilt, he was silent as he tucked in his shirt.

'My real name is Bethany.'

Tommy looked up. 'What?'

'My name' – Bethany laughed – 'isn't Kitty Mae, it's Bethany, and seeing as we're more than just friends now, well you should at least know my name.'

Alarm filled Tommy. He had no intention of seeing her again, at least not like this. He couldn't; what if Stacey found out what he'd done, what if Stacey left him and took Karen with her? The mere thought was enough to bring him out in a cold sweat. Oh, he might see Bethany in the club from afar, but from now on that was as far as it could ever go.

Checking that no one else was in close proximity, Tommy slipped out of the office.

'I'll see you around.' He forced himself to smile.

'You will.' Bethany grinned back. 'I'm looking forward to it already.'

After collecting the takings, Tommy left the club. He would have to tell Davey he could no longer work the clubs. It had to be a lot safer than the alternative, he decided. For all his intentions not to see Bethany again, he didn't trust himself around her; all she would have to do was flash him that beautiful smile of hers and he would want her again and again.

'What do you mean, you don't want to work at the club any more?' To say Davey was surprised was an understatement. 'You don't get to pick and choose, Tommy. You work where I send you, lad.'

'For personal reasons, I don't want to work there.' Tommy stood his ground.

'What the fuck are you talking about, personal reasons? What personal reasons?'

Tommy sighed. 'There's this girl' – he rubbed his hand over the back of his neck, his cheeks flushed – 'and she keeps putting it on me.'

Davey burst out laughing. 'Well, you need to stop thinking with your cock, lad, and tell the girl to piss off. You're there to work, nothing more.'

'She's persistent,' Tommy answered, careful not to let on that he'd already fallen for her charms and broken his wedding vows. 'She doesn't take no for an answer.'

This caused Davey to laugh even harder. 'Do I need to tell Lillian to put the hard word on her?' he asked, once he'd managed to get his breath back.

Shamefaced, Tommy looked to the floor. He would look a right pillock if Lillian had to fight his corner for him. 'No,' he said, 'don't say anything to Lillian.' He'd have no other choice but to deal with the situation himself.

As Tommy left his office, Davey shook his head. He'd seen it all now. In all the years he'd owned the strip clubs, young Tommy was the first of his men to complain about one of the girls putting it on him.

* * *

Safety in numbers was the best way to handle the situation, Tommy decided. And so he dragged Jimmy along to the club with him. Pulling up beside the kerb outside The Soho Club, Tommy switched off the engine to the car Davey had kindly supplied him with.

The feud between the two brothers was long forgotten, and Tommy ruffled Jimmy's hair before they climbed out of the car.

'Oi, watch it,' Jimmy complained as he patted his dark hair back into place. 'Leave it out, Tommy.'

Grinning, Tommy opened the car door. There was a method to his madness. With just eleven months between them, the two brothers looked so similar they were often mistaken for twins. Hopefully Bethany would take a shine to Jimmy instead and leave him alone.

'Lillian, this is my brother, Jimmy. He'll be working here with me for a bit.'

As she made her way from behind the counter, Lillian eyed the two young men in front of her with interest. 'Well, I never. Another handsome fella. What do they put in the water where you two are from, eh?' she asked with a twinkle in her eye.

Jimmy's eyes widened, causing Tommy to laugh. 'Come on,' he said to his younger brother as he pushed him through the entrance doors leading inside the club. 'He's a bit wet behind the ears,' he whispered towards Lillian.

Lillian placed her hand across her heart. God love him, she thought to herself. The girls would eat him alive.

Despite himself, as Tommy showed Jimmy around he couldn't help but look around him, on the lookout for Bethany. As quickly as he could, he explained the workings of the club, before weaving his way back through to the reception to show his brother where they kept the baseball bat.

'Here. Where's Mad Dog been keeping himself? I haven't seen him around for a few weeks,' Lillian enquired.

Leaning against the reception desk, Tommy took his cigarettes from his pocket. 'He's been at the betting shop with Davey.'

Lillian raised her eyebrows before taking the cigarette Tommy offered her. Popping it into her mouth, she waited for him to offer her the use of his lighter, before blowing out a small cloud of smoke. 'Not been any trouble, has there?'

'Nothing we can't handle,' Tommy answered before quietening down as Bethany walked through the doors. He could feel his cheeks redden and averted his eyes. He couldn't look at her, didn't want Jimmy to see his blushes.

Not one to miss a trick, Lillian picked up on the vibes, and ushered Bethany through to the club. 'You have to have eyes like a hawk where they're concerned,' she said to Jimmy, nodding after Bethany, trying to lighten the mood.

Tommy smiled his gratitude. 'Come on then, our Jimmy. We best get on our way to the other clubs. See you later, Lil.'

'See you later boys,' Lillian replied, returning behind the desk.

With a smile upon her face, Bethany climbed up onto the stage. It had been over a week since her and Tommy had had their fun in the office; it had even crossed her mind that he could be avoiding her. She couldn't lose him, not now, not when they were just getting to know one another. If she played her cards right, she may even be able to string it out a little bit longer at the club. If she told her father there was more information to come, then he would let her stay, wouldn't he?

Happier now that she had a plan in place, Bethany gyrated to the music, her lithe body curling around the pole. In fact, she would do anything she could to keep a hold of this job, if for no other reason than to keep seeing Tommy. No matter what her father thought about him she was determined he would be hers.

8

Stacey counted out her change, then passed it across the shop counter to Rose Lyon, who owned the newsagents.

'How's your Tommy?'

Stacey beamed. She loved it when people referred to Tommy as hers. 'He's doing well, just been promoted at work.'

'Tell him I said hello.'

'I will do.' Backing up the pram, Stacey accidently bumped into the woman behind her. 'I'm so sorry' – she smiled apologetically – 'I still can't get the hang of this thing.'

Bethany Johnson returned the smile. 'That's okay. She's beautiful. What's her name?' she asked, leaning over the pram.

'Karen. She's six weeks old now.'

Straightening up, Bethany smiled again and held out her hand. 'I'm Beth.'

'I'm Stacey, Stacey Carter. Nice to meet you.'

'I was just about to go and have a coffee over the road. Do you fancy one? My treat.'

Stacey glanced across to the café. She barely knew the woman, but she seemed friendly enough. 'Okay then.' She grinned. 'Why not? It's nice to get out of the house for a bit if I'm being honest.'

Once they were seated at a table with frothy coffees in front of them, Bethany nodded towards Stacey's wedding ring. 'So, are you married then?'

Taking a sip of her coffee, Stacey quickly swallowed the hot liquid down. 'Yes, me and Tommy have been married for just over six months now.'

Bethany took a sip of her own coffee. 'What's he like, your husband?'

'Oh, he's lovely. Everyone loves my Tommy.'

Bethany swallowed her irritation down. She couldn't, for the life of her, think of what Tommy saw in the girl in front of her. She wasn't even that pretty, and if she was being honest, she thought her to be quite plain looking; she certainly wasn't what she was expecting. 'Maybe one day I'll get to meet him, that's if you ever want to meet up for coffee again? It must be hard work having a baby, and you must get lonely if your husband is out all day working.'

Stacey nodded. 'That would be nice. I do get lonely sometimes. I've only got my mum, or mother-in-law, for company. All of me mates are out working in the day time. What is it you do for work?'

'I'm a dancer.'

Stacey smiled. A dancer, she thought to herself. Her new friend was so glamourous.

Tommy ate heartily. After eating a plateful of eggs and chips, he mopped up the egg yolk with thick slices of buttered bread. 'That was smashing, Stace,' he said, once he'd finished eating. It was the first meal his wife had cooked the family, and it felt good to see his

Stace more like her old self, just how she used to be, before the sorry business with her brother, Pete.

'I made a new friend today.'

'That's good, babe. That's exactly what you need, some new mates your own age.' He gave his mum a surreptitious glance before mouthing, 'Instead of the old fogies.'

Stacey giggled. Her Tommy could be so funny when the mood took him. 'Her name's Beth and she's a dancer.'

Immediately, Tommy sat up in his seat. He tried to keep his voice neutral, even though, to his ears, it sounded more strained than usual. 'Where did you meet her, babe?'

'In the newsagents. Oh and by the way, Mrs Lyons said to say hello.'

Alarmed, Tommy nodded. Beth and Bethany couldn't be the same person, could they?

'There's a good film on the box at eight, shall we watch it?'

'I can't.' Tommy cleared his throat. 'I have to go into work, babe.'

At this, Jimmy's ears pricked up. 'I thought we had the night off?'

'You do. I just need to pop into The Soho Club and get the takings for Davey. It shouldn't take me long, then I'll be home.'

'I'll come with you,' Jimmy offered.

Tommy shook his head, refusing Jimmy's offer. He didn't want anyone else to hear what he had to say to Bethany.

Lillian was surprised to see Tommy back at the club. 'What are you doing back here?' she asked through narrowed eyes. 'I thought it was your night off, that's all you've been talking about all week.'

'I just want a word with Kitty Mae,' Tommy replied, pushing his way through the entrance doors.

He spotted Bethany as soon as he walked through to the club, and he strode purposefully towards her. Grabbing hold of her arm, he half-dragged her out to the back office.

'Ow, you're hurting me,' Bethany protested once they were in the office and the door had been closed shut behind them.

'Did you go near my wife today?' Tommy raged.

'Why would I go near your wife?' Bethany lied, knowing full well she had.

'Don't play games with me. Answer the fucking question. Did you go near my wife?'

Watching the man in front of her warily, Bethany swallowed before answering. 'Of course I didn't. What's this all about?'

Wiping his hand across his face, Tommy sunk into a chair. 'I'm sorry,' he apologised, 'I just thought... oh it doesn't matter,' he said, shamefaced.

Bethany crouched down beside him. She placed her hand on his arm and caressed it gently, her fingertips teasing his skin. 'No need to apologise.'

In a moment of weakness, he pulled her to her feet and leaned in closer. God, he wanted her. Without even realising what he was doing, he was unfastening his trousers. Then he was kissing her and she tasted of minty toothpaste, and as his tongue explored hers, he spread open her legs and pushed his fingers through the lacy thong she wore.

'I'm sorry. I shouldn't have done that,' he muttered once he was finished and refastening his trousers. 'We can't do this again.' Tommy felt ashamed of himself. He should never have come here tonight. It was a big mistake putting himself into a room with Bethany, just the two of them alone together. He should have known this would happen; he couldn't keep his hands off her no matter how much he didn't want to. It was sex, that was all, nothing more than that; they weren't about to walk off into the sunset hand in hand, it was no love story. Admittedly, he found her attractive but that didn't mean he actually wanted her in his life. How could he? He was married. And that was when it hit him; he'd cheated on Stacey. It would break her heart if she ever found out; she trusted him, she loved him, she'd given him a daughter. How could he have been so stupid? He'd betrayed her.

In amazement, Bethany watched as the man she wanted more than anyone else in the world raced out of the office. She couldn't help but smile to herself. She'd obviously been doing something right after all. Tommy Carter wouldn't be able to deny there was definitely a spark between them.

* * *

'You all right, Tommy? You've been a bit quiet lately.'

Silently, Tommy nodded. He had a few things on his mind... things he couldn't talk to anyone about, even Jimmy. Mainly the situation with Bethany. He'd managed to avoid her ever since their last interaction in the office, but still he was plagued with guilt. He just couldn't, for the life of him, understand what had made him do what he'd done. He loved his wife and always would. He must be weak, he decided. It was a sobering thought.

They were on their way to collect a debt for Davey, and Tommy felt a sense of relief that he was once again doing what he did best. Sod the clubs, it was debt collecting that he excelled in.

Stepping on the brakes, Tommy pulled the car up outside a house in Barking. Sat directly opposite Barking Park, the houses were large and grand, nothing like the council houses on Thames View Estate where they had just come from.

They climbed out of the car and made their way up the path.

'Get a load of these houses.' Jimmy whistled through his teeth.

He was clearly impressed. 'Must have a bit of dough to own one of these.'

'One day, I'll have a house like this,' Tommy answered confidently, before knocking heavily on the front door.

When the door was opened, Tommy took one look at the man in front of them and felt an instant dislike towards him. Without the man even speaking, Tommy knew he would be a pompous old bastard. The type of geezer who would look down his nose at them, all because they weren't so well off or educated.

'Yes?' Malcom Davies squinted at the two young men in front of him.

'We're here to collect the money you owe to Mr Abbott.' After slamming his foot inside the front door, so it couldn't be closed in their faces, Tommy leant nonchalantly against the door frame.

Malcom looked towards his neighbouring houses before answering. He was a man of good stead within the local community and having riffraff on his doorstep was bound to give the gossip mongers something to talk about. He wanted to curse himself. A secret gambling addiction had caused him to go to Davey Abbott for a loan. He knew he should have repaid the man months ago, and he swore before God he would have done it, if the horse he'd backed had won the race instead of coming in third.

'Give me a week or so, and I will have the money for Mr Abbott.'

Tommy shook his head. 'Sorry pal, but that's not good enough. Mr Abbott's expecting the money today. Right now, in fact,' Tommy replied, pushing his way past Malcom, and walking through to the lounge. Looking around him, Tommy couldn't help but feel impressed. So, this was how the other half lived? The entire contents of the lounge would have cost more than everything his parents had worked all of their lives for to own.

'I don't have that kind of money now,' Malcom stated as he

chased after Tommy. He didn't take his eyes off the boy. He didn't trust him to not try and steal something.

'Looks like we've got a bit of a dilemma then, doesn't it? Because we're not leaving here until you've handed over the cash.'

'Like I said, I can get you the money by next week. Now, could you please kindly leave before my wife comes home and finds you both here,' Malcom stated, snatching a silver figurine out of Jimmy's hand, and returning it back to the marble mantelpiece where it belonged.

Tommy raised his eyebrows. Clearly this prick didn't understand the reason for them being there. He lunged forward; his hand clasped around Malcom's throat and he pushed him roughly up against the wall. 'Now, I don't care. In fact, to be more precise, I couldn't give a shit if you have to beg, steal, or borrow to get what you owe, but we are not leaving this house until we have the cash. Am I making myself understood?'

Malcom nodded profusely. He could feel his bowels loosening, and he clenched his buttocks tightly together. The last thing he wanted to do was mess himself in front of these two louts, and especially not over the cream carpet he'd paid a small fortune for.

'So,' Tommy said as he released his grip, chop, chop. Go and get the money. We haven't got all day.' Winking at Jimmy, he took a seat on the high-backed sofa and kicked his legs out in front of him, making himself comfortable.

Near to tears, Malcom raced out of the room. He would have to raid his wife's jewellery box. He had no other choice. How he would explain to Margaret why her gold and diamond rings were missing, he had no idea.

Returning to the room, Malcom handed over the gold. 'Here, take this, there is more than enough there to cover what I owe.'

Tommy took the proffered goods and weighed them up in his

hand. The gold weighed a fair bit, he had to admit, but all the same, it wasn't the cash Davey was expecting.

'Please just take it. This jewellery will sell for over one thousand pounds.' Malcom could see the young man in front of him faltering. Clearly the boy knew nothing about gold and its worth.

In a quandary, Tommy looked across at Jimmy, who shrugged in return. He knew nothing about gold either. 'Okay. We'll take it, but if Mr Abbott isn't happy, we'll be back.'

Relieved, Malcom blinked his eyes rapidly. 'Mr Abbott will be more than happy. I can assure you of that.'

'He'd better be.' With one last look around the lounge, Tommy indicated for Jimmy to follow him out of the house.

'Jumped up fucking ponce,' Jimmy growled, once the front door had been slammed shut behind them.

'You can say that again, bruv. Come on, let's get this over to Davey, and I swear to God, if that old bastard has had us over, I'm gonna go ape shit.'

Davey was more than pleased with the haul the two brothers brought back to him. 'Well done boys,' he said as he clapped them on the back. 'You both did good.'

Tommy grinned. It was to be his first lesson in the value of gold.

Taking Tommy to one side, Davey leaned towards him to speak in private. 'Has there been any problems, in the clubs, or while out collecting?'

Shaking his head, Tommy shrugged. 'Nah, no trouble at all. Why? Are you still expecting comebacks from Johnson?'

Davey shrugged. 'Just keep your ears and eyes to the ground lad, okay?'

'Yeah, of course.' Tommy could see that Dean Johnson had clearly rattled his boss. Still, he kept Mad Dog holed up at the betting shop with him for added protection.

'If anything should happen to me, then I want you to go and see my brief, Bernard Cohen. He has something for you.' Pushing a scrap of paper into Tommy's hand, Davey walked away.

With a frown, Tommy looked down at the piece of paper. It was an address for Davey's solicitor. He looked back over his shoulder at his boss, before pushing the paper deep into his jeans pocket.

'Go on then, lads, get yourselves off home. If I have anything else for you, I'll give you a call.'

Not needing to be told twice, the two brothers left the betting shop, all the while, Tommy's mind was whirling. He didn't like to think of anything happening to Davey. Not only did he like his boss but he also had a lot of respect for him. His mind wandered to the scrap of paper Davey had thrust into his hand; he was intrigued as to what the solicitor could possibly have for him in the event of Davey's demise.

Returning home, both Tommy and Jimmy were in high spirits. 'Shall we go for a pint tonight?' Jimmy asked. 'It's been ages since we had a night out.'

'Yeah we could do, bruv. I'll tell Stace to get her glad rags on. We'll make a night of it. Babe, do you fancy—' The remainder of the sentence caught in his throat as Tommy stepped into the lounge.

Sitting on the sofa with his daughter in her arms, was Bethany. The colour drained from Tommy's face. What the fuck was she doing here? Instantly, he tore his eyes away from her and looked towards his wife expectantly.

'Tommy, this is my friend, Beth. Do you remember, I told you about her?'

Dumbstruck, Tommy could only nod, terrified Jimmy would recognise her from the club. He walked through to the kitchen in an attempt to compose himself. Placing his hands on the kitchen sink, he leant his weight upon them all the while taking deep breaths. He would kill her stone dead for this. Who did that bitch Bethany think she was, coming to his house and having the audacity to sit next to his wife, as though nothing had ever happened between them?

'Tommy, you're being so bloody rude. What's with you, you miserable bugger?' Stacey hissed through gritted teeth, as she busied herself refilling the kettle.

'What's she doing here?' Tommy demanded.

Stunned, Stacey turned to look at her husband. She'd never seen him behave like this before. He'd always been polite to her friends in the past. 'She came to see me. Honestly, Tommy, once you get to know her, you'll love her.'

Tommy swallowed down his irritation; that was exactly what he was afraid of. 'Tell her to go home. I'm taking you out tonight.'

'Well that's okay, Beth can come along, too. It's her day off. I'm sure she would love to come out for the night.'

Before Tommy could reply, Stacey had left the kitchen. He could hear her asking Bethany if she fancied a night out with them, and he held his breath as he waited for her to reply. He could only groan in both annoyance and fear, when she told his wife that she would love to. This was turning out to be a nightmare of epic proportions.

* * *

Standing at the bar, Tommy could feel Bethany's eyes boring into the back of his skull. He would need to get her on her own and tell her to fuck off, he decided. He certainly couldn't spend the entire night in her company, with Stacey sitting between them.

Awkwardly, he handed the two women their drinks, almost

spilling them when Bethany brushed her fingertips against his hand as he passed across her wine.

'This is nice, isn't it?' Stacey stated, oblivious to the torment going through her husband's mind.

'So, what is it you do for a living?' Bethany asked him, leaning across Stacey, a wicked grin across her face.

Cursing her, Tommy ignored the question. Enough was enough; he would definitely need to tell her to fuck off. 'I need to go for a piss,' he said, getting up from the table.

As he walked away, he could hear Stacey excusing his poor behaviour.

'I don't know what's got into him,' she said, 'he isn't usually this rude.'

He didn't need to turn his head to know that Bethany would have that same wicked smile spread across her face.

As he came out of the lavatories, Bethany was waiting for him. Astounded, Tommy glanced to where Stacey and Jimmy were sitting. Did this woman have no shame? Dragging her into the toilets, he pushed open each of the cubicles, checking that there was no one else inside to hear their conversation. Once he was sure that they were alone he rounded on her. 'What the fuck are you playing at? Why have you come here?'

'I haven't seen you at the club, so thought I'd best come to you. After what happened between us, you can't deny there isn't a spark, a connection,' Bethany answered, wrapping one arm around his neck, her free hand unbuttoning his jeans.

Detangling her arms from around him, Tommy gently pushed her away. 'I keep telling you I can't do this.' He gave the door a nervous glance. 'If Stacey walks in and catches us...'

'She won't,' Bethany purred, pressing herself against him.

'Stop,' Tommy warned. Beads of perspiration broke out across his forehead and he had to clench his fists into tight balls to stop

himself from pulling her into one of the cubicles. 'I just can't okay.'
He gave the door another glance. 'She trusts me.'

Bethany pouted. 'But what about us?'

Tommy shook his head. As far as he was concerned there was
no us. 'You need to leave.'

'You don't mean that,' she said, reaching out to catch hold of his
hand.

'Yes I do,' Tommy hissed. Was there no getting through to her?
'Look,' he said, pulling his hand free, 'I should never have even
looked at you twice let alone...' He swallowed deeply, making sure
to keep his eyes on her face. 'I made a stupid mistake, I'm sorry.'

Tears sprang to Bethany's eyes and her bottom lip trembled.

'This can't happen again; there is no you and me, we're done. I
love my wife and I won't ever walk away from her.'

There was a finality to his voice and as tears slipped freely down
her cheeks Bethany barged past him and raced from the toilets.
Massaging his temples Tommy counted to thirty then followed on
behind. As he approached the table, he felt nothing but relief to see
that his words had had the desired effect and that she'd made her
excuses and left the pub.

'Bethany had to leave,' Stacey said as he sat down beside her.
'She isn't feeling too well; a migraine.'

With a nod, Tommy clutched his wife's hand tightly in his and
closed his eyes. His stomach was tied up in knots, and he felt sick,
terrified that Stacey would find out about what he'd done. He
should never have even been tempted let alone given in to lust. He
was in over his head and could only hope and pray that this was the
last he saw of Bethany; his marriage was counting on it.

9

Dean Johnson was fuming. He'd taken one look at his daughter's tear-stricken face and wanted to kill Tommy Carter stone dead. Only Bethany's hysterical cries had stopped him from taking the gun back out of the safe where he kept it and driving towards the pub on Thames View Estate.

'Please Daddy,' she begged of him, 'don't hurt him.'

Dean hugged his daughter close, whispering into her ear that he wouldn't hurt the boy. All the while, he plotted out his revenge. Tommy Carter wouldn't get away with this. If it was the last thing he did, it would be to make sure the little bastard paid the price for hurting his daughter.

Janet Carter frowned as Stacey told her all about Tommy's behaviour the previous evening.

'It was so unlike him,' Stacey stated. 'I've never seen him behave so rudely to someone before.'

With a mug of tea in front of her, Janet had to agree it did seem odd. Her Tommy was usually friendly to everyone he met. She took a sip of the scalding liquid as she watched her daughter-in-law dress little Karen in a snow suit, ready to be taken outside.

'Do you think I should go and see Bethany and check if she's okay? I know she works in a club up Soho. Maybe Tommy could even give me a lift down there.'

'I don't think that'd be a good idea, Stace. The girl will be working, and you don't want to get her in trouble by turning up.' Janet had only met Bethany the one time, but she'd seemed friendly enough, which made Tommy's behaviour even more odd.

Stacey had to agree that Janet was right, and the last thing she wanted to do was get her new friend into trouble with her boss.

After helping Stacey out of the house with the pram, Janet stared after her daughter-in-law. She couldn't help but feel that there was a lot more to the story than met the eye.

Closing her front door, she decided she would have it out with her eldest boy. Tommy had never been able to lie to her. She had always been able to suss him out. In fact, she knew her son, all of her sons for that matter, even better than she knew herself.

As she busied herself in the kitchen Janet sighed. One way or another these sons of hers would be the death of her.

Tommy gulped down the remainder of his lager. He'd needed a pint after the night he'd had. He still felt guilty for the way he'd spoken to Bethany. He hadn't meant to come across as harsh as he did, but at the same time, he'd had to make her see he wasn't playing games, not where Stacey was concerned. If she hadn't turned up at his house, he would have remained friendly and polite with her. However, seeing her sitting there on the sofa, cradling his daughter, had been like a red rag to a bull. She'd overstepped the mark, surely she knew that.

'Davey wants us to go and collect money from the Turks restaurant.'

Tommy groaned. Not that Turkish cunt Mehmet Ali again. Did this geezer never learn?

'He's failed to make the last two payments,' Jimmy continued.

Tommy placed his empty glass on the bar. 'C'mon then, bruv. Let's get this sorted out, once and for all.'

As they left The Brewery Tap and made their way over to Tommy's car, they were blissfully unaware that they were being closely watched by Dean Johnson and his henchmen.

An hour later, he and Jimmy left Mehmet Ali's restaurant. Tommy felt no remorse for his actions. In his eyes, he was simply doing what he'd been paid to do.

'The bloke looked upset,' Jimmy stated. He would never admit it out loud, but he'd felt sorry for Mehmet.

Noting Jimmy's expression, Tommy pulled his brother to a halt. 'Don't go all soft on me, bruv. This is what Davey pays us to do.'

'Yeah, I know, but how is the bloke meant to earn any money? You heard what he said, business is slow.'

Tommy shrugged. 'Not our problem, bruv. Would you eat in there? It's a shit hole. Maybe if he smartened the place up a bit he'd actually have some customers.'

'Yeah but—'

'Enough, Jimmy,' Tommy chastised. 'You need to toughen up a bit. Fucking hell, don't go talking like this in front of Davey, otherwise you'll be out of a job.'

'I won't.' Jimmy sighed, glancing across to Mehmet's restaurant before climbing into the car. 'Won't Davey be pissed off that we didn't collect all the money?'

Tommy thought the question through. 'Nah, he knows the Turk will pay up next week. At least he should, unless he wants his legs broken next time.'

* * *

Despite Tommy's confidence, Davey wasn't happy. 'I sent you there for the money, lad. Where is it?'

Tommy sighed. 'The Turk didn't have it, so we smashed the restaurant up a little bit instead, nothing too major, a couple of chairs, a few plates. He'll pay up next week.'

'He better had, lad, otherwise me and you will fall out over this.'

'He will.'

Davey glanced across to Mad Dog, who raised his eyebrows in return. It was a well-known tactic for them to plead poverty to get out of paying, all the while, their businesses were booming.

'Trust me, I know what I'm doing, Davey.'

Davey didn't doubt that for a second, but at the end of the day, young Tommy hadn't been in the business for as long as he had, and over the years, Davey had seen every trick in the book used. 'Okay, the Turk has got one week, and then I want the cash, all of it.'

Tommy nodded. He'd learned his lesson and didn't need telling twice. 'So, where do you want us next?'

Before Davey could open his mouth to answer, the door to his office opened. Standing there with a gun in his hand was Dean Johnson.

'Tommy Carter,' Dean stated as he glared at Tommy. 'Think you can upset my little girl, do you?'

Tommy's heart was in his mouth. He glanced nervously towards Davey. What was this all about, and more to the point, who was

Dean's little girl? 'I don't know what you're talking about, mate,' he stuttered.

'Think you can use my Bethany for your own gain, then fuck her off, do you?' Dean bellowed.

Tommy's eyes widened. How the fuck was he meant to have known that Bethany was his daughter? She'd never told him that little fact. Holding up his arms, Tommy swallowed before speaking. 'Let's all calm down, eh? It wasn't like that. I told her from the off I was married, and that nothing would ever happen between us.'

'You fucking liar,' Dean spat, pointing the gun directly towards Tommy's head. 'She's told me everything; you used her, then fucked her off.'

Taking a step forward, Davey tried to calm the situation down. 'Tommy's telling the truth. He told me all about what happened, and he wanted no part in any of this.'

Dean turned on Davey. 'Are you calling my daughter a liar?'

'No, I'm saying there was a misunderstanding between your Bethany and young Tommy,' Davey stated, as he came to stand in front of Tommy, blocking him from Dean's view.

'Get out of the fucking way. This is between me and him.'

'No.' Davey stood his ground. 'This isn't about Tommy, this is about you and me.'

'I said, get out of my fucking way.' Lunging forward, Dean wrestled Davey to the ground and shoved the gun into Davey's chest. 'You've got one of two choices, Carter,' he said, looking up at Tommy. 'Either walk out of this shop with me, or this cunt here takes your place.'

'Don't do it, Tommy. If you leave this shop, he'll kill you,' Davey grunted from the floor.

Shame spread through Tommy's veins. He couldn't allow Dean to kill Davey in his place, not when he was guilty of everything he'd been accused of. He had used Bethany for his own gain; no matter how many times he'd told her that nothing could ever come of the affair he'd still taken her, still used her, and more than once.

'I'm gonna count to three, and if you haven't moved, then this cunt gets it. One... two...'

'Okay, okay!' Sweat broke out across Tommy's forehead. He grabbed hold of Jimmy's arm and gave it a squeeze. 'Look after Stace and Karen for me.'

Close to tears, Jimmy pulled on Tommy's arm. 'Don't do this, please,' he begged of his brother.

'I don't have a choice bruv.' Moving forward, Tommy resigned himself to dying. He held up his hands in surrender. 'Let Davey go then. I'll come with you.'

'Stay where you are, Tommy. Dean, get the fuck off me, and let's talk this through like fucking adults.'

His face red with anger, Dean snarled, 'Get him out of here,' to his men, nodding towards Tommy.

Writhing on the floor, Davey bucked Dean away from him, before staggering to his feet. 'Tommy, don't you dare fucking do this and that's an order. He's gonna kill you, lad.'

Dean grinned. 'That's right. I am, and I'll fucking laugh all the while I do it. Now fucking move.'

As Tommy began to move forward, a flurry of different emotions rippled through him. He would never see his Karen take her first steps, hear her first words, watch her start school, have her first boyfriend or get married. He glanced back towards Jimmy. 'Don't forget to look after them.'

'I said no.' Charging forward, Davey flung his arms around Dean's waist, knocking the man to the floor.

The explosion from the gun was loud and harsh in the small confines of Davey's betting shop. Shocked, Tommy threw himself to the floor, covering his head with his hands. His ears were ringing, and the scent of gun powder was heavy in the air.

Within seconds, it was clear to see that Davey had been hit in the crossfire. Scrambling to his feet, Tommy came and knelt beside his boss. He watched as Dean and his henchmen fled from the shop, before turning his attention back to Davey. He could see immediately that Davey was in a bad way. Blood oozed from his abdomen, staining his shirt and pooling on the threadbare carpet beside him.

Tommy placed his hands down on the wound in a bid to stem the bleeding and when he finally spoke there was panic in his voice. 'Come on, stay awake,' he pleaded.

Davey gasped for breath. He felt as weak as a kitten and so cold. He gave a shiver as his body went into shock. 'Remember what I told you, lad,' he whispered.

'No! Don't you fucking die on me,' Tommy screamed, as Davey's eyes closed and he took his final breath. Falling backwards, Tommy stared down at the blood covering his hands and the unmissable scent of iron filled his nostrils. He scrambled away and leaned his back against the wall, his eyes wide as Mad Dog took over and tried to revive Davey.

They could all see it was no use. Their boss was gone. In shock, the three men remained silent, each of them staring into space.

Finally, Mad Dog spoke. 'When the Old Bill turn up, we tell them this was an attempted robbery that went wrong.'

Numb, Tommy nodded. He was in no fit state to actually speak to anyone, let alone the Old Bill.

10

Three weeks after Davey's murder, and still Tommy hadn't been to see his former boss's brief. Tommy just couldn't stomach it. The funeral had passed by in a blur, and suited and booted, Tommy had helped carry Davey's coffin into the church, all the while wishing and praying that it wasn't true, and that Davey was somehow still alive.

He owed everything to Davey Abbott. The man had believed in him, when many others wouldn't have. He'd been a naive kid when Davey had taken him under his wing and taught him everything there was to know about the world they lived in. Davey had even given up his life for him, and for that, Tommy would always be grateful. Thanks to his former boss, he would now be able to watch his daughter grow up.

'Tommy, are you awake?' Jimmy tapped lightly on his and Stacey's bedroom door. It had gone past twelve in the afternoon, and their mum had sent him to try and get his brother up.

'It's doing him no good lying in bed all day,' she'd stated, a worried expression etched across her face.

Tommy rolled onto his side. He groaned out a reply, and Jimmy entered the room, closing the door shut firmly behind him.

'How are you doing, bruv?'

Tommy remained silent. He wasn't doing well at all, that was the truth of it. It should have been him who'd died, not Davey. After all, it was him who Dean had been after that fateful day.

'Mum wants to know if you're getting up today. She's worried about you.'

Tommy shook his head. 'I don't think I can.'

Jimmy swallowed before speaking. What he was about to say could go one of two ways. Tommy could either batter the living daylights out of him, or it could spur him into action. 'It wasn't you who died, Tommy. Davey wouldn't want to see you like this. He gave up his life, for you to live yours.'

Tears sprang to Tommy's eyes, and he swiped them away. Didn't they think he knew that? The very same thought had been going around and around, inside his head, ever since Davey had taken the bullet for him.

'Get up, Tommy. We've got things to do.' With this, Jimmy left the room.

Tommy lay contemplating his brother's words. He reached over and pulled open the drawer to his bedside cabinet and took out the scrap of paper Davey had given him. He studied the writing before forcing himself out of bed. Jimmy was right. They had things to do.

An hour later, Tommy and Jimmy had set off towards Davey's solicitors. Still, Tommy had no idea what it was Davey could have for him. After parking the car, he walked across the road towards Bernard Cohen's office with a feeling of trepidation.

'Mr Carter,' Bernard stated as he walked through to the reception area. He shook Tommy's hand and led the way towards his office at the back of the building. 'I have to say, I'd expected you a lot sooner than this, after Mr Abbott's unfortunate demise.'

Tommy didn't answer. He was here, that was the main thing. He looked around the office and took note of a tall rubber plant sitting in a large terracotta plant pot in the corner of the room, the dark green leaves shiny as though they had been polished. He tore his eyes away from the plant, sat down in the seat Bernard offered to him and pulled out the chair beside him, gesturing for Jimmy to take a seat.

Bernard began to get the paperwork on his desk in order, when Tommy interrupted him.

'So, what is all of this about? Davey said you would have something for me when, you know, he died.'

Looking up from his paperwork, Bernard was surprised. He'd thought Tommy would know why he was here. He cleared his throat. 'Mr Abbott has left all of his businesses and assets to you, Mr Carter.'

Astounded, Tommy flopped back in his seat. He turned to look across at Jimmy; the same shock he himself felt was mirrored across his brother's face. 'Can you say that again, please?'

'Mr Abbott has left his businesses and assets to you, Mr Carter. You are now a very wealthy man.'

Tommy could barely take the news in. Davey had given absolutely no indication of his intentions. To say Tommy was shocked was an understatement. 'Are you sure?' he asked. 'I mean, could there be a mistake?' Even as Tommy asked the question, his mind was whirling. What exactly did this mean? Was he rich? Was he now running Davey's firm? Nah he couldn't be could he, he'd only just turned twenty-one; he couldn't run a firm, he didn't know how to. Admittedly, Davey had made it seem easy, but then Davey had a lot of experience behind him. Not only that but men had looked up to him; he'd gained their respect and trust over the years. Who was going to look up to him? He was still a kid in the eyes of the criminal underworld; they'd laugh at him, wouldn't they, if he tried throwing his weight around.

Bernard nodded. 'It's all here in black and white. This,' he said, holding aloft several documents, 'is Mr Abbott's final will and testament. And he has you down as his only beneficiary. I'm also to give you this. Apparently, it's the key to a safe. Mr Abbott stated that you would know what to do with the contents.'

Tommy took the brass key from Bernard and turned it over in his hand. He wondered briefly what the contents of the safe could be. Surely there were no more surprises in store for him.

'If you could just sign here, please, Mr Carter.'

Signing along the dotted line, Tommy spoke. 'Is that it?'

'For the time being, yes. There are a few legalities to be taken care of, and then you will have access to Mr Abbott's businesses.'

Tommy nodded then shook Bernard's hand. 'Thank you.'

'Oh, before you go, let me give you my card. Mr Abbott used me as his solicitor for a number of years. Should the need ever arise, and you want my services, give me a call. I will be in touch with you shortly regarding the businesses.'

Tommy was in a daze as he walked back to the car. The betting shop, The Soho Club, scrap yard, and the debts all belonged to him; he couldn't get his head around any of it.

'Fuck me Tommy.' Jimmy grinned. 'Do you understand what this means? You're rich bruv.'

Tommy nodded. Leaning against the car, he took out his cigarettes; his hands were still shaking as he lit up. 'I don't understand,' he said, 'I mean why me? Why did Davey leave everything to me, why didn't he leave everything to Mad Dog?

Jimmy shrugged. 'What are you gonna do?'

'I don't know.' Tommy was thoughtful for a moment. 'Do you

think our Gary's got what it takes to work with us?' he asked, 'I mean he's nearly eighteen now isn't he, and he did all right when he helped you out that time collecting the debts didn't he?'

Jimmy shrugged. 'Yeah, he was a natural I suppose. Why?'

'And what about Sonny and Mitchel?' Tommy asked, referring to their younger twin brothers. 'They're sixteen, aren't they? When do they leave school?'

'In a couple of weeks, I think. Why, what are you thinking?'

Tommy paused for a moment. 'One thing Dad taught me is to only work with people you trust, and well, maybe other than Mad Dog, I only trust family, Jim, and I want all of us Carters working together.'

Jimmy whistled. 'Dad will go fucking ballistic! He's still going on about you and me giving up boxing; he'll go off his fucking rocker if they walk away from it as well.'

'Sod Dad. When he sees how much money we're raking in, he'll soon change his tune.'

Jimmy raised his eyebrows but decided to keep his own counsel all the same. He wasn't going to get involved, he decided. He'd leave it in Tommy's capable hands to break the news that their younger brothers were going to follow on in their footsteps.

Janet's eyes were wide. She couldn't believe the news Tommy had just given them.

'And everything belongs to you now?' Stacey gasped.

'Yep, Stace. Everything.' Tommy smiled, throwing his arms around his wife and spinning her around.

'I can't believe it.' Janet turned towards her husband and took note of his solemn expression. 'This will set you up for life, son,' she said, turning back around. 'Who'd have thought it, eh? Davey Abbott leaving you everything.'

Hearing his boss's name, Tommy stopped spinning Stacey around the room. He felt his heart sink once again. He still felt guilty and had a feeling he always would.

'Come on now, this is a time to celebrate.' Janet smiled gently, seeing Tommy's shoulders drop.

'Yeah, you're right.' Tommy hugged Stacey to him again, before whispering in her ear. 'Didn't I always say me and you would go places?'

Stacey looked up at her husband adoringly. 'You did,' she whispered back, throwing her arms around his neck.

Tommy took one look at Gary and shook his head. 'You're not coming out with me dressed like that.'

'Why not?' Gary looked down at his black and red shell suit. His outfit was the height of fashion. He'd driven his mum mad to buy him one, and all of his mates wore one, too. He happened to think he looked smart.

'Jimmy, sort him out a pair of your jeans and a shirt,' Tommy ordered.

'Yeah, but—'

'No buts, Gary! You're not wearing that.'

As Gary walked away behind Jimmy with his head down, Stacey smiled. 'I think you hurt his feelings.'

'Sod his feelings,' Tommy answered, before laughing. Today was the day he took control of the businesses, and he didn't want anything to go wrong.

Ten minutes later, Gary and Jimmy made their way down the

stairs. Casting his eyes over his younger brother, Tommy nodded. It was imperative that they looked the part; image was everything in their world. They may have been young, but he wouldn't allow them to be treated like fools, it was time to grow up; he was in charge of a firm, he had to look as though he meant business, even if he inside he felt out of his depth. 'That's better.' He grinned. 'Now you look like a Carter.'

Tommy took a deep breath before unlocking the door to the betting shop. This was the first time he'd been inside since the shooting. He glanced down at the blood stain on the carpet before averting his eyes. It would need pulling up and refitting, before they could open up for business.

As they walked around the shop, Tommy made mental notes of everything that needed doing. Other than the carpet, a lick of paint was in order to brighten the place up. He quickly calculated how much everything would cost him. He reckoned he was looking at just over one hundred pounds to get everything ship shape.

'When d'ya think it will be ready to open?'

'Hopefully in about a weeks' time,' Tommy answered thought-fully. He had a mate who was a decorator. He'd offer him the job first. 'C'mon, let's get to the clubs.'

With one last look around the betting shop, Tommy locked up and slipped the keys into his pocket. Damn, he thought to himself. He'd forgotten to check the safe. Still, it could wait he supposed, there couldn't be anything too important in there, other than maybe a bit of petty cash.

Mad Dog Harris had aged considerably since Davey's death; to be more precise, he looked as though he was carrying the world and its troubles on his shoulders. He shook their hands as the brothers entered the club, and Tommy pulled the older man into a bear hug. He knew their boss's death had hit him hard. They'd worked together for years; it was bound to be a great loss for him. The truth was, Mad Dog felt lost without Davey.

'How are things here?' Tommy asked as he glanced through the doors that led into the club.

Lillian sniffed back her tears. Like Mad Dog, she'd known Davey for a great number of years. 'Same old, same old, Tommy. Nothing changes in this place.'

Satisfied, Tommy nodded. He felt relieved to see that Bethany no longer worked here. Without even asking, he knew she would have done a disappearing act. Dean would have pulled her out of the club immediately.

He turned to look at Mad Dog. 'Can I have a quick word in private?'

Nodding, Mad Dog led the way through to the back offices.

As he followed on behind Mad Dog, Tommy looked around him. The whole place needed sprucing up. The carpeted floor was dated and sticky underneath his feet. The huge crystal chandelier installed to add a bit of grandeur above their heads did nothing to hide the chipped and peeling paintwork splashed across the tables and chairs. To put it mildly, the club was a shit hole. Tommy wanted a fresh start, he wanted to put his own stamp on the place, he wanted to make it his, wanted to show the world that he meant business. He wanted to prove that he wasn't just some kid who didn't know what he was doing; he was the boss and the businesses needed to represent him, starting with the club. It would cost him a fair bit of dough to return the club to its former glory, and he weighed this up in his mind as he walked across the dance floor.

Once they were inside the office, Tommy closed the door firmly shut behind them and rubbed at his tired eyes. 'Will you stay on and work for me?' he asked.

Mad Dog hesitated. He'd been expecting this question and was in half a mind to get out of the game. What had happened to Davey had shaken him up. He was getting on in years, and fancied retiring, now that his boss was no longer around. 'I don't know, Tommy. This is a young man's game.'

'I could really do with your help and experience, please,' Tommy said. 'You know this life like the back of your hand; I can't do it on my own. I don't know what Davey was thinking to leave it all to me,' he said, throwing up his arms. 'I can't let him down, not now. I have to start how I mean to go on, I have to step up to the plate and prove to all those fuckers out there that I mean business.'

With no family and no ties, this was the perfect opportunity for Mad Dog to get up and walk away from the line of work he was in, yet seeing Tommy's face and hearing his heartfelt request, he softened towards him. Davey had thought a lot of the boy, and for that reason alone, he knew he couldn't leave him out to dry, so to speak. 'Davey thought a lot of you, lad; he saw something in you and he believed that you have what it takes.'

Tommy gave a half laugh and slumped in the chair. 'I don't even know where to start; I mean, what do I know about running a club? I know how to order a beer and that's about it.'

There and then Mad Dog gave in. 'Where would you want me working?'

Tommy smiled, feeling as though a lead weight had been lifted off his shoulders. 'How about if you stay on at the club, run it for me. I could get one of my brothers to come in and help you out. In fact, I was thinking of having a complete overhaul in here, spruce the place up a bit. We'd have a better clientele if it looked more presentable; we could even charge for membership.'

Mad Dog nodded. Despite Tommy's reservations, he could see the lad meant business and he wouldn't be surprised if he turned the club around and made it a roaring success. 'Okay, deal. I'll stay put here and take care of everything this end. It'll do me good to be able to put me feet up for a bit.'

Happier, Tommy shook on the deal. Now that the club was sorted out, it left him the time and energy to concentrate on the other businesses.

* * *

Tommy and his brothers left the club. They were about to climb into the car when from across the street someone called his name.

Tommy's heart sank and he momentarily closed his eyes. He'd recognise the voice anywhere: Bethany Johnson.

With his brothers' eyes upon him, Tommy attempted to smile, hiding the panic coupled with rage that pounded through his veins. 'Just give me two minutes,' he said, gesturing for them to get into the car, 'I won't be long.'

Bethany gave a weak smile as he approached. 'You're okay,' she said, tears filling her eyes, 'I've been so worried.' She clutched his arm. 'My dad, he was so angry, I thought he was going to hurt you.'

Shrugging her away from him, Tommy's voice was a low growl as he spoke. 'What are you doing here?' He narrowed his eyes. 'Have you been spying on me?'

She swallowed quickly. 'I knew you would come to the club at some point; I had to see you.' Tears slipped down her cheeks. 'I love you,' she cried.

Tommy took a step away and screwed up his face. How many times had she come to the club waiting for him to show up? 'You're deluded; you don't even know me,' he spat. He glanced over his shoulder, checking that his brothers weren't watching them, then stabbed a stiff finger towards her face. 'I'm warning you, stay away from me and stay away from my wife. Have you got that?'

'But what about us?' she sobbed, reaching out for him again. 'I can't live without you, I need you.'

Anger began to get the better of him and he shoved Bethany roughly across the pavement. 'Leave me the fuck alone; there is no us, I've already told you. It was a mistake.' Shaking his head he began to walk away. 'Stay away from me, you whore,' he warned over his shoulder.

As he reached his car, Tommy willed his heart to slow down. He couldn't show his brothers that Bethany had rattled him, they would only ask questions.

'Who was that?' Jimmy asked as soon as Tommy had climbed inside the car.

'No one,' Tommy said with a glance in the rear-view mirror. To his horror she was still standing there, watching him. 'Just some dancer who Lilian gave the boot; she wants her job back.'

'You gonna give it to her?'

'Nah.' Tommy shook his head and started the ignition. 'She's done.'

* * *

That evening, Stacey cuddled into Tommy as they lay in bed. Her husband's behaviour had been worrying her over the past few weeks, ever since Davey's death, she couldn't help but feel as though he'd been on a downward spiral. But now he seemed much more like his old self.

Breathing in his familiar scent she smiled. 'I've got something to tell you, Tommy.'

With his hand behind his head, Tommy looked down at his wife as she lay next to him.

'I'm having another baby.'

Tommy smiled. 'Really?' he asked.

Stacey nodded, unsure of how he would take the news. She'd known about the pregnancy for weeks, but what with everything that had gone on, it hadn't been the right time to tell him.

Tommy turned onto his side and pulled Stacey closer towards him. 'That's the best news I've heard in ages.'

Relieved, Stacey hugged Tommy to her, a wide grin spread across her face.

'This time it will be a boy,' Tommy stated confidently. Even with the threat of Bethany looming over him, he fully believed that life was on the up. Thanks to Davey he was going to make a name for himself; he'd be able to give his wife everything she deserved and as for his kids they would want for nothing, he was determined to give them everything he hadn't been able to have as a kid.

11

Jimmy had spent the last few hours searching for his brother. As a last resort, he banged his fist on the door to the betting shop. The finishing touches were just being added to the painting. Then the new carpet would be laid in time for the grand opening in just two days' time.

Dressed in paint-splattered overalls and with a paintbrush clutched in his fist, Steven Marley pulled open the door. 'Hello, Jimmy. Are you here to see your Tommy?' he asked as he moved aside for his friend's younger brother to enter.

'Is he here?'

'He's in the office; been in there for hours, he has.' Steven nodded towards the back of the shop.

'Cheers mate.' Relieved to have finally located his brother, Jimmy walked through the shop and pushed open the door to the office without knocking.

Tommy looked up from behind the desk. 'Quick, come in and shut the door,' he said with a hint of excitement in his voice.

Jimmy frowned before taking a seat opposite his brother. He

noted that the safe was open. So, Tommy had finally got around to having a look inside.

Slamming a notebook down on the desk, Tommy nodded. 'You'll never guess what this is?'

Jimmy shrugged. 'The shop's takings?'

'Nope.' Sliding the book towards Jimmy, Tommy indicated for him to take a look through it.

After leafing through the pages, Jimmy looked up. 'Is this what I think it is?'

There was a twinkle in Tommy's eyes as he nodded. 'Davey must have had this planned out but didn't get the chance to see it through.'

In front of them were the intricate preparations of a bank robbery. Every last detail had been carefully worked out and written down, by Davey himself.

'Fucking hell, Tommy! This is mental.'

'I know.' Tommy grinned as he pulled the book back towards him.

'You're not actually thinking of following it through, are you?' There was trepidation in Jimmy's voice.

Tommy shrugged. He didn't actually know what to do with the findings of the planned robbery. The only thing he knew for certain, was that it seemed too good an opportunity to miss.

'Tommy,' Jimmy chastised. 'Please tell me you're not thinking about it?'

'Come on.' Tommy grinned. 'You know what Davey was like, he wanted me to find this, he wanted me to see this through, why else would he have given the key to the brief? He's put every little detail into the planning; it's all there in black and white.' He slid the notebook back across the table towards his brother. 'Obviously, we would have to do our own research to double check everything.'

Jimmy chewed on the inside of his cheek as he looked through the notebook. 'I dunno bruv. Haven't you got enough?' He gestured around him. 'You don't need to do this; you're loaded, and if we end up getting caught, we'll go down for it, you'll lose everything and not just this place. What about Stacey, Karen?'

'As if I'd ever let that happen.' Tommy grinned, spreading open his arms. 'Trust me bruv, Davey wanted us to do this, and I owe it to him. Look what he sacrificed for me; I'd be dead if it wasn't for him. I can't let him down, not now, not after everything he's done for me, not only that but I want to prove myself, I want to prove to all those fuckers out there that I've got what it takes, that I can step up and take over from Davey.'

Reluctantly, Jimmy nodded. He could see where his brother was coming from, but still it was a risk on their part, a huge risk, one he wasn't entirely convinced they should take.

* * *

Stacey couldn't wait for the opening of the betting shop. Tommy had bought both her and little Karen new dresses to wear, and he'd ordered in a crate of champagne to celebrate. Everyone in both of their families had been invited to attend, and he'd even joked that the mayor of Barking himself would be there to cut the ribbon. She still wasn't sure if he was telling the truth or not on that matter.

'Here, could you just take Karen for me, please, while I put my hair up?'

Not needing an excuse to hold her granddaughter, Janet smiled as she made a fuss of little Karen. She was a beautiful child, and had Tommy's piercing blue eyes, and Stacey's light brown hair. She nodded down at Stacey's bump. 'You're already showing. You haven't got two in there, have you girl?'

Stacey smiled. Twins ran in both sides of their families. It wouldn't surprise her if there were indeed two babies growing inside of her. 'It's a bit too early to tell yet. We won't know until we have the first scan.'

'You'd best prepare yourself then, son,' Janet said.

'For what?' Tommy asked, walking into the room.

Janet winked towards Stacey before answering. 'Twins.'

'Bloody hell. Don't say that Mum.' Tommy's face paled at the very thought of two babies keeping them awake at night.

'You never know, Tommy, what with your Sonny and Mitchel, and my brothers Carl and Jack, it's more than possible.'

Tommy rubbed his hand over his wife's small bump. 'As long as they're healthy, that's all that matters, eh?'

'True son. Here, take your daughter while I take these rollers out of me hair. I can't very well turn up at your grand opening looking like this, can I?' Janet giggled.

Tommy took Karen in his arms and kissed the top of his daughter's head. 'Are you really thinking it's twins?' he asked his wife, his voice low.

Stacey gave a little chuckle. 'Gawd knows, Tommy, but the rate we're going, if these are twins, then we'll end up having enough kids to make a football team.'

Tommy's mouth fell open and bursting out laughing, Stacey held onto the chair for support. 'I'm joking,' she said. 'Two kids are more than enough for me.'

'Two?' Tommy retorted, playfully slapping Stacey's backside. 'I was thinking at least four.'

It was Stacey's turn to gasp. 'It's all right for you, you don't have to give birth to them.'

'Yeah true,' Tommy agreed, 'how about we make it three then? It's not like we can't afford it now is it.'

Stacey could see his point. 'Three it is then.' She smiled.

* * *

With champagne held aloft in their hands, the newly fitted out betting shop was officially opened. They posed for photographs outside the shop, and even the local newspaper, *The Barking and Dagenham Post*, had wanted Tommy's story. The fact that he'd only just turned twenty-one and that he owned a shop, was big news apparently. They were calling him a young entrepreneur. They didn't know exactly how he'd come to own the shop, and he had a feeling they'd have a field day if the true story ever got out.

'I need to go and network.' Tommy kissed Stacey's forehead before wandering off.

'Network – hark at him.' Stacey looked across to Janet, before giving a giggle. The truth was, she was proud of Tommy and she watched as he mingled with the crowd of people who'd come to the opening. He was a natural.

Janet was also proud of her son. She glanced around at all of her boys. They were dressed in their finest clothes and were good-looking lads, each of them a clone of one another. Even her Frank had a smile on his face, which was a first.

As Tommy stopped and chatted to people and checked that their glasses were full, his thoughts turned to the notebook in the safe. Ever since he'd found it, the contents had been playing on his mind. Davey had obviously believed it could work, otherwise he wouldn't have planned everything out to the last intricate detail, and despite Jimmy's reservations, he had to see the robbery through for Davey's sake; he owed him that much at least. He wondered if Mad Dog Harris had any inclinations as to what their boss had been planning. He'd bet every penny he owned that the Scotsman knew; he was bound to have known, he'd been Davey's right-hand man. There and then he decided to pay Mad Dog a visit.

Stood in a shop doorway hidden out of sight, Bethany Johnson had watched the unveiling of the betting shop. She'd puckered her lips in disgust, as she'd watched Tommy making a fuss of his wife. Bitch, she thought to herself. Tommy should have been her man, not that bloody Stacey's.

Bethany Carter had a nice little ring to it. She repeated the name over and over in her mind. Even though she'd promised her dad she would steer clear of Tommy, she just couldn't keep away from him. She loved him, a burning love that consumed her every waking thought. In fact, she often came to watch him as he went about his business, blissfully unaware that she was near.

The moment she had read about the grand opening of Tommy's betting shop, her heart had leapt. It was the perfect opportunity to spy on him from afar. From her hiding place, Bethany took note of the comings and goings. She watched as the Carter brothers posed for photographs, and a plan formed within her mind.

It wasn't over as far as her and Tommy were concerned. In fact, he was going to wish he'd never set eyes on her.

* * *

'Here, I heard you're quite the celebrity now,' Lillian teased. 'By all accounts, you had the press interviewing you and everything.'

'It wasn't quite like that.' Tommy laughed as he leaned casually against the reception desk in The Soho Club. 'We had the local paper there doing a piece about the shop opening. That was about it in a nutshell.'

'Oh, and there was me thinking I should ask for your autograph.'

'Give over, Lil.'

'What? I'm being serious.' Lillian giggled.

With a grin across his face, Tommy shook his head at Lillian's obvious teasing. 'Is Mad Dog around?' he asked, changing the subject.

'He's in the office, darling. Do you want one of the girls to go and fetch him for you?'

'Nah, it's okay. I'll go through and see him.'

Walking through the club towards the office, Tommy took in everything around him as he weaved his way through the girls and punters on the main floor. He'd heard through Jimmy that Mad Dog was running a tight ship and that everything was in order. Apparently, the man had taken to working at the club like a duck to water.

'Hello Tommy,' Mad Dog said. He was sat behind the desk and began to stand up as Tommy walked into the office.

'Hello, mate.' Holding up his hand, Tommy indicated for Mad Dog to remain seated. He then pulled out a chair and sat down opposite him. 'So, how's everything been here?'

'All good, Tommy. No problems at all. In fact, it's better than good. Business is booming all thanks to you; you were right about sprucing this place up, we've even got a waiting list for memberships.'

Tommy smiled, then cleared his throat. He didn't want to beat around the bush. 'I opened up the safe at the betting shop last week.' He watched Mad Dog's reaction closely, on the lookout for any tell-tale signs that the older man already knew about the planned robbery.

'Oh yeah, lad?'

'Yeah. I've got to admit, I was a bit surprised by what I found.'

Mad Dog remained silent.

'I mean, I was really surprised.'

Still, Mad Dog said nothing.

Tommy began to laugh. 'Come on mate, you know what I'm talking about.'

Mad Dog shrugged. 'You tell me, lad. What did you find there?'

Tommy eyed the man suspiciously. If Mad Dog knew what was in the safe, then his expression was giving nothing away. 'The notebook.'

'Aye lad, so you found a notebook?' Mad Dog raised his eyebrows.

'Come on, you know what's in that book.'

Tommy could see Mad Dog thinking it over. He sat back in his seat, not taking his eyes off him.

'Aye, I know what's in the book, lad.'

'And?' Tommy sat up a little straighter, his eyes shining with excitement. 'Is it doable? Davey must have thought so. The details are spot on as far as I can tell.'

Mad Dog chewed on the inside of his cheek before answering. 'It's doable. We did a dry run of it, and it was perfect.'

Tommy's heart leapt. 'I knew it,' he said, punching his fist in the air. 'How many people was Davey planning to take on the job?'

'Maybe four, plus a getaway driver.'

Tommy thought this over. 'Could you get away with three doing it, plus a driver?'

'Perhaps. Look Tommy, doing that job was always going to be a big risk, so think hard on that before you even contemplate seeing this through.'

'I already have,' Tommy answered. 'I want to see this through for Davey, I owe him that much. If it wasn't for him Johnson would have killed me. But what I need is a driver.' He looked at Mad Dog expectantly.

'You don't mean me?'

'C'mon mate, you're the only person other than me brothers that I trust. I need you.'

Hesitant, Mad Dog looked Tommy in the eyes before reluctantly agreeing. 'I'll do it on one condition. You double check, then double check again, that those plans are spot on. I'm too old to end up in the nick.'

'I will do.' Tommy was deep in thought. Like Jimmy had already said, he had too much to lose to not double check them.

* * *

Sneaking into Tommy's and Stacey's bedroom, Gary headed straight for the chest of drawers where his elder brother kept his bottles of aftershave. One by one, he picked up each bottle, and after unscrewing the caps, he gave the scents a quick sniff. Gary then chose his favourite, and sprayed a generous measure over himself, before putting the bottle back exactly where he'd found it. He then raced out of the room and up the stairs to the bedroom he shared with Jimmy and his younger brothers.

He opened up his wardrobe and sorted through his clothes, before his eyes settled on his shell suit. Quickly, he dismissed the idea, and pulled out his new jeans and a white shirt. He had to look his best. He had a date tonight. Proper classy, she was, and he wanted to impress her, hence why he'd raided Tommy's aftershave collection.

Once he was dressed, Gary crept out of the house before anyone spotted him. He knew his brothers would only start teasing him if they found out he had a date.

In fact, his elder brothers would do a little bit more than tease him if they were to find out exactly who his date was.

* * *

Bethany Johnson had purposely bumped into Gary Carter a few days earlier. She'd allowed him to try and chat her up and had even laughed at his cheesy chat up lines. The fact young Gary looked like Tommy was the only thing that was going to get her through this date. In fact, Gary was nothing more than a means to an end, as far as she was concerned.

She sipped on a glass of white wine while waiting for the boy to arrive. She was in The Bull public house in Romford, far away from Tommy Carter's prying eyes. She didn't want him getting wind of the date. No doubt he would only try and put a stop to it.

'Sorry I'm late,' Gary puffed. He was out of breath after running all the way to the pub from the bus stop.

Bethany smiled. He was just a kid really. Still, every time she looked at him, she saw Tommy's face.

'It's okay, you're not late at all,' she lied. 'In fact, I've only just got here myself.'

Gary stood with his hands in his pockets. This was the first date he'd ever been on, and he was unsure of what he should do next. 'Would you like another drink?' he finally asked, nodding his head towards Bethany's empty wine glass.

'I'd love one.'

Sheepishly, Gary glanced towards the bar. His cheeks blushed red. He wasn't old enough to get served alcohol yet, he still had a couple of weeks to go before he turned eighteen and he didn't want to get turned away trying to buy them drinks, he'd end up looking like a right prick. 'Can you go up and get them, please?' He shoved his hand into his pocket, pulled out a crumpled ten-pound note, and thrust it towards her.

Snatching the money out of his hands Bethany smiled. She got up from her seat and walked to the bar. As soon as she was out of Gary's view, she rolled her eyes in irritation. She supposed she'd better buy him a lemonade too, seeing as he wasn't even eighteen yet.

* * *

Tommy sat in the office of the scrap yard. It was quiet here, and he was able to think in peace. He had Davey's notebook set out in front of him, and he'd studied it front to back so many times, he practically knew the contents off by heart.

He was waiting for Jimmy, Gary and Mad Dog Harris to arrive, so they could discuss exactly how they were going to plan the bank job out. Everything had to be just perfect. Any mistakes could very well see them all being sent down for a considerable length of time.

As Jimmy and Mad Dog arrived, Tommy looked up from behind the desk. 'Where's our Gary?'

'I thought he was here,' Jimmy said, narrowing his eyes.

Tommy shook his head. He looked past the two men towards the scrap yard itself and the metal gates beyond. He'd specifically told Gary to meet them here. He was annoyed. If he gave an order, brother or not, he expected it to be carried out.

'We'll just have to bring him up to speed when he turns up.'

'That's not good enough,' Tommy growled. He'd need to have a serious word with young Gary. Behaviour like this is what could get them caught red-handed by the Old Bill. The job in hand needed their full attention. There could be no room for sloppy mistakes. 'Okay, well we'll have to start without him I suppose. First thing's first, we need to check out this bank.'

'Aye lad, and once you've checked it out, you'll need to do your final check of the place about a month to six weeks before the job. And you need to do it casually. Just drive by the bank, checking everything's as it should be, and that's it. The last thing you want is to be recognised or caught on camera.'

'Yeah, you're right.' He began mentally working out everything they needed before counting off the items on his list out loud. 'We need a car, disguises and somewhere to store the cash afterwards.'

'For the car, we need a Granada Cosworth. Those things can fly, Tommy lad. Trust me, nothing will be able to keep up with us.'

Tommy nodded. 'Okay, that's the car sorted. What about weapons? I mean they're not just gonna hand over the cash are they? We need to look the part.'

'I can put you in touch with Freddie Smith. He'll sort you out with a gun.'

Tommy hesitated and an image of Pete with his brain spattered across the walls and ceiling flashed before his eyes. 'Do we really need a firearm? Can't we just use crowbars or something?'

Mad Dog raised his eyebrows. 'We're talking about an armed robbery lad. You can't walk in with a cosh or a bit of lead piping; they'll laugh in your face.'

Tommy thought this through. 'Yeah I suppose,' he agreed. 'All right, put me in touch with this Freddie geezer. Okay, so that leaves somewhere to hide the cash afterwards.' Referring to Davey's notebook, Tommy flicked through the pages. 'What does BP mean?' he asked, looking across to Mad Dog.

Mad Dog shrugged. 'No idea. BP garage maybe.'

Thinking it over, Tommy could think of only one BP garage that he knew of. It was situated on Ripple Road, directly opposite the cemetery.

'Burial plot.'

Both men turned towards Jimmy.

'BP could stand for burial plot,' he stated. 'Plus, the BP garage itself is opposite the cemetery.'

Tommy turned to Mad Dog. 'What do you think? Could that be what Davey was referring to?'

'Possibly, but if it does stand for that, then where is the plot, and how would Davey have pulled that off? He'd have needed an actual coffin for burial, not to mention insiders to dig the grave. Sorry, but I can't see it meaning that lads. It would mean too many people getting involved, and that wasn't Davey's style.'

Tommy sighed before banging his fist down on the desk, making both men jump. 'The BP garage is right next door to a car dealership, right?'

'And?' asked Jimmy, not sure where Tommy was going with this.

'What if Davey was planning to buy cars with the cash, then sell them on? That way the money's clean.'

'You've got a point, Tommy.' Mad Dog nodded at the idea. In fact, it made perfect sense and was exactly the type of thing Davey would have thought of.

'Right, so we need to look into buying and selling cars. Buy the Granada Cosworth and go and meet this Freddie Smith. Can I leave you in charge of arranging a meeting with him?' Tommy asked Mad Dog.

'Aye lad. I'll get on it.'

Satisfied, Tommy sat back in his seat. There was still a lot of work to do, but at least they had made a start.

* * *

Gary Carter was on cloud nine. He couldn't believe his luck when Bethany had agreed to a second date, and he'd had to pinch himself after he'd leaned in for a kiss and didn't get a slap around his face for his troubles.

A wide grin was spread across his face as he let himself into the house. Nothing and no one would be able to dampen his mood.

The hand that grabbed him around the throat and threw him against the wall had him gasping for breath.

'Where the fuck have you been?'

'What?'

'Don't give me fucking what. Where the fuck were you? You were meant to meet us at the scrap yard,' Tommy growled.

Shamefaced, Gary averted his eyes. He'd forgotten all about the meeting. 'Sorry, I forgot.'

'You fucking forgot? Is this little prick for real?' Tommy asked, glancing over his shoulder to look at Jimmy. 'Do I need to punch it into your skull next time, to remind you?'

'Leave me alone, Tommy,' Gary cried, 'I said I was sorry.'

Inching closer, Tommy sniffed the air. 'Have you got my fucking aftershave on?'

'No.' Gary's cheeks turned red.

'Yes you have. Now where've you been?'

'Nowhere,' Gary protested.

Tommy eyed his brother suspiciously. 'I reckon he's got a little bird on the go.'

Tommy burst out laughing. He could just imagine Gary wearing his shell suit out on a date, thinking he looked the dog's bollocks. 'I think it's time to have the talk with him, Jimmy.'

'Yep, I think it is, bruv.'

'What talk?' Gary's eyes were like stalks.

'The birds and the bees, Gary.' Tommy laughed. 'Just so you know what to do if you end up taking her down some back alley.'

'Give over, Tommy. I'm not a little kid.' Wrenching himself out of his brother's grasp, Gary stormed across the room and pointed his finger towards his eldest brother. 'I knew you two would be like this, that's why I never tell yous anything.'

'We're only having a laugh, Gary. Stop being so uptight. So, what's she like, your little girlfriend?'

'She's not a girl, for your information,' Gary said with a level of pride. 'She's a woman.'

This caused both Tommy and Jimmy to laugh even harder.

'What the fuck would a grown woman be doing going out with you? You're still a kid.'

'I'm not a kid. I'm eighteen in a couple of weeks.' Gary's cheeks turned red with anger. All thanks to his brothers, he was now in a foul mood. 'Just leave me alone, the pair of you.'

Tommy shrugged, before turning to Jimmy and bursting out laughing again. Young Gary had a lot to learn.

12

Freddie Smith was at the top of his game; not only did he make a great deal of money running protection rackets, but he also had a nice little side-line selling on firearms. Like most people in his line of work, Freddie Smith had heard of Tommy Carter, and the fact Davey Abbott had left everything to the lad, told Freddie everything he needed to know. He watched the boy through hooded eyes. As a favour to Mad Dog Harris, he'd agreed to the meeting, but he wouldn't fully relax until he'd sussed Tommy Carter out for himself.

Surrounded by two of his best men, Moray Garner and Danny McKay, Freddie listened intently to what Tommy was asking of him.

Tommy took a sip from his pint of lager. 'So, can you get a hold of what I need?' Despite his nerves at being in Freddie Smith's presence, outwardly he remained calm and composed. On the car journey to the pub Mad Dog had warned him not to give too much away. And under no circumstances was he to blurt out the reason why they wanted to buy the guns.

Freddie looked towards his two men before speaking. They were big lads, and more than capable of standing their ground, should Tommy Carter start getting lairy, which by all accounts, he did often, at least if Dean Johnson's version of events were to be believed.

'I can get you what you need, but it won't come cheap.' Freddie gulped down his scotch.

Noting that the man's glass was empty, Tommy indicated for Mad Dog to get them a second round of drinks, before answering. 'Like I said, money is no issue.'

Freddie raised his eyebrows. It wasn't his place to ask what the guns were for, but he took a wild guess that they would be used in some form of a robbery. Why else would the lad want four firearms? Freddie's expression was hard, as he stared at the boy in front of him. He didn't like this kid. There was something about him that grated on his nerves. The boy was too cocksure of himself. That was the problem. 'I haven't even told you how much they'll cost, boy.'

Tommy glanced towards Freddie's henchmen; their expressions were unreadable. No way was he going to humiliate himself and back down to this prick. Besides, he knew how to handle himself; years of boxing had put paid to that. He was no walkover; if the need arose just one punch would knock Freddie on his arse, and as for his henchmen they weren't much bigger than he was, and he knew for a fact that he could take them on, that he could handle whatever they threw his way. In the ring he'd fought some hefty lumps and still won; boxing was a skill, it wasn't only about power which admittedly he had in abundance, but it was about style, it was about knowing when to take that shot. 'And like I said, money is no issue.'

Freddie thought this over, business was business after all. 'Okay, six grand will get you four guns.'

Quickly swallowing his lager before he choked on it, Tommy's eyes were wide. 'Six fucking grand?' he repeated, his voice taking on an incredulous tone.

Freddie nodded. It took every ounce of his will power to keep the sly grin from his face. If the lad wanted to act the billy big bollocks in front of him, then he would have to pay more than triple the price.

'That's a bit steep, isn't it?'

'That's the price. So, take it or leave it.'

Returning with their filled drinks, Mad Dog placed the tray down on the table. 'Come on Freddie, we both know that's well over the odds. We're looking at what, two to three hundred quid for each gun? So, how the fuck are you coming up with six grand?'

'What, do you think I do this out of the kindness of my heart?' Freddie spread open his arms. 'The rest of the cash will be my cut.'

'And that's nearly five grand for your cut.' Tommy quickly did the maths.

'Like I said, take it or leave it, boy.' There was a smirk across Freddie's face. He knew they would take his deal. They had no other choice. Being new to the game, not many people would do business with Tommy, at least not until he'd gained their trust anyway.

Sitting back in the seat Tommy shook his head, his expression set like thunder. 'Nah, you can go fuck yourself, I'll take my business elsewhere.'

Freddie began to laugh. 'And who the fuck is going to deal with you, boy? You're a no one, lad.'

'Let me worry about that,' he said, getting to his feet.

As they walked from the pub an eagle-eyed Tommy noted the discreet wink that passed between Mad Dog and one of Freddie's henchmen.

* * *

'What a fucking cunt.'

Mad Dog sighed. They were sat in his car, about to make their way back towards Barking. Personally, he'd never really liked Freddie Smith himself, but in normal circumstances the man was good at what he did. It was Freddie's only saving grace, as far as he was concerned.

'Six fucking grand.' Tommy fumed. 'Is he taking the fucking piss?'

'As much as I think he's a wanker Freddie was right, you being new to the game was bound to go against you. They don't trust easily, this lot, and rightly so.'

'And what was that wink all about between you and one of the lumps?'

Mad Dog laughed. 'Young Danny's okay, as long as you stay on his good side, that is. It's him we'll be buying the guns from.'

'Do what?' Tommy's mouth fell open.

Mad Dog laughed even harder. 'Number one rule in this game is to try and not step on anyone's toes; the last thing you need this early in the life are enemies. You've shown your face in front of Freddie and kindly,' he said with a raise of his eyebrows, 'declined his offer. That means you're free to do your business elsewhere.'

Tommy took this on board. 'Can we trust this Danny?'

Mad Dog nodded. 'That just leaves the car to be bought, and then we can start planning everything out to the last detail, lad.'

Still fuming from his interaction with Freddie Smith, Tommy nodded. 'Once we have everything in place, we'll do our own dry run to double check that things are as they should be. I was thinking we should do it over the May bank holiday weekend. It'll be the perfect opportunity, and with a bit of luck, they won't even notice anything's amiss until the Tuesday.'

Mad Dog frowned. 'They'll raise the alarm before Tuesday, lad.'

'Not if they're tied up and locked in a fucking room they won't.'

* * *

Jimmy lay back on the bed with one hand behind his head, watching Gary closely. His younger brother was getting himself spruced up and ready for his date. 'Why are you keeping this bird of yours such a big secret?'

Gary ignored his brother. It had been Bethany's idea to keep their relationship quiet, and she'd made him promise that he wouldn't tell his elder brothers about the two of them.

'Well?'

'Why d'ya keep asking me the same question over and over again?'

'Because it's not like you to be so secretive,' Jimmy answered. 'You're a trappy little bastard and unless she looks like Quasimodo, I don't get why you're keeping schtum about her.'

'What would you know about it? You've never even had a bird.' It was Gary's turn to question his brother and turning around, he narrowed eyes. 'Why haven't you had a girlfriend? You're only a year younger than Tommy and he's married with a kid, and another one on the way.'

Jimmy's cheeks blushed. It was true he'd never had a girlfriend, and had no inclination to have one either, for that matter. 'Fuck off, Gary.'

'No, come on, out with it. It was all right when you were questioning me. So, now it's your turn. Why've you never had a bird? You're not a poofter are you?'

'I said fuck off, Gary.'

Gary's mouth dropped open. 'I'm right, ain't I? You fancy men.'

The unexpected punch, which connected with Gary's chin, hit him square on, causing him to collapse in a heap on the floor. 'I told you to fuck off,' Jimmy said, standing over his younger brother, his heavy fists clenched, ready to attack again. 'So, do yourself a favour, and keep that big fucking mouth of yours shut, before I end up cracking you one again.'

Dazed, Gary rubbed at his jaw and stared after Jimmy's retreating back as his brother walked out of the bedroom they shared. He couldn't get his head around this. Was Jimmy really gay? Scrambling to his feet, Gary tore out of the bedroom. Just wait until Tommy heard about this, and it would serve Jimmy right for starting on him.

* * *

Jimmy swiped at the tears in his eyes. He wanted to curse himself now. He should have kept quiet about Gary and his bird. Now, a whole can of worms had been opened up.

The truth was, he was scared of what Tommy would say when he found out he fancied men not women. Not to mention what their mum and dad would say about it. He knew, without a shadow of a doubt, they would go ballistic. Him being gay was bound to bring a slur on the family name.

Angrily, he kicked a stone from underneath his foot as he began to walk the streets on the estate where they lived. If Gary told anyone about this, then his life would be over. He knew that for a fact.

* * *

After his meeting with Freddie Smith, Tommy had asked Mad Dog to drop him off at the scrap yard. He savoured the peace and quiet whenever he was there, and the solitude gave him the perfect opportunity to think the robbery through. He wondered briefly if Davey had been planning to bring him in on the heist. It was a question he would never know the answer to.

He looked up as Jimmy entered the office. 'You okay, bruv?'

Jimmy nodded and leant against the glass window pane. 'Have you heard from our Gary?'

'No, I've only just got here. I had a meeting with that Freddie Smith. Right cunt he turned out to be and all.'

Jimmy cleared his throat. 'Something's not right with that bird of Gary's.'

'What d'ya mean?' Tommy asked, narrowing his eyes.

'Why all of the secrecy? I'm telling you, bruv, something's going on. I've just got this bad feeling about it.'

Tommy frowned. He hadn't given Gary and his girlfriend much thought, and if he was being totally honest, the robbery was the only thing on his mind. It was all consuming. 'What are you thinking then?'

'It's just a bit odd, is all I'm saying. We need to find out who she is.'

Now that he'd planted the seed of suspicion in Tommy's mind, Jimmy allowed himself to relax. Two could play at this game, and if Gary was going to tear his world apart, then he would do the same to him.

* * *

Gary was quieter than usual when he met up with Bethany that afternoon. He still couldn't believe what he'd discovered about Jimmy. The very thought of his elder brother being queer made him shudder.

'Hey what's up? You're quiet.'

Gary shrugged. How could he even tell Bethany about this? He was far too embarrassed.

'You can tell me anything, you know that.' Bethany squeezed Gary's hand in hers.

'It's me brother.'

Bethany's heart leapt. Did he mean Tommy? 'What about Tommy?'

Turning towards her, Gary narrowed his eyes. 'Not Tommy, I mean Jimmy.'

'Oh,' she said, uninterested.

'I found out something, and I don't know if I should tell anyone about it or keep it quiet.'

Bethany shrugged. 'Do whatever you think is best.'

'That's the problem,' Gary explained, 'I don't know what to do, and our Tommy will go mental when he finds out.'

Her ears picking up once again at the mention of Tommy's name, Bethany smiled gently. 'Do you want to tell me about it, and I'll let you know what I think you should do?'

Gary bit down on his lip. 'It's Jimmy... he's...'

'What?' She squeezed his hand gently in hers in a bid to hide her irritation. 'Come on, you can tell me, Jimmy's what?'

'I think he's gay.'

Bethany had to squeeze her lips together to stop her from laughing out loud. Was that it? She'd thought it was going to be something really bad, the way Gary was carrying on. 'So why would your Tommy go mad over that?'

'I dunno. It's not right, is it? It's not normal.'

Bethany shrugged. She had a few mates who were gay. It made no odds to her. Still, if it was going to cause problems between the two brothers, then young Gary should go ahead and tell Tommy everything he knew. 'I think you should tell him.'

'Really?' Gary's eyes were wide.

'Yeah, definitely. It's only right that Tommy knows something as big as this.'

Gary thought this over. If he told Tommy, it could very well end up causing a war between his elder brothers.

'I don't know,' he faltered, 'Tommy's got a temper on him and Jimmy could end up getting a dig, and it would be all my fault.'

Bethany gave him a cold stare, and when she spoke her tone was icy. 'Why bother asking for my advice if you're not going to take it? I thought you were meant to be a man, not a mouse.'

Reminded of the way Jimmy had lashed out at him just that morning, Gary rubbed at his aching jaw. Bollocks to it. Bethany was right; he was a man. And as for Jimmy, he deserved everything he had coming to him.

'Yeah, you're right,' he said, screwing up his face. 'Tommy needs to know.'

Bethany gave a smile. She had this boy wrapped around her finger, and with a little bit of luck, and her guidance, he would tear the Carters apart.

Walking towards the local parade of shops, Stacey kept her eyes peeled for Beth. She missed her mate, and hadn't seen head nor tail of her, ever since she'd left the pub feeling unwell. She had a feeling it was Tommy's rudeness that had made her leave. He must have made Beth feel uncomfortable. That was the only explanation. Why else had her friend not been in touch since then?

As she absentmindedly added items to her shopping basket, Stacey bit down on her lip. She would go and see Beth, she decided. Tomorrow morning, she would drop Karen off at her mum's house, and then she would take the train to Soho. It wouldn't take her long to find the club, she was certain of that.

Happier now that she had a plan of action, Stacey smiled to herself. She'd best keep it quiet from her husband, though. She knew he wasn't keen on her friend, even if he hadn't said as much.

And she certainly didn't want Tommy to try and talk her out of going.

* * *

Returning home that evening, Gary crept into his bedroom, took a pillow and a blanket from his bed, then made his way back down the stairs. No way was he spending the night in the same room as Jimmy.

After quickly making up a bed for himself on the sofa, he lay down and closed his eyes. His brothers hadn't returned home yet, and every little noise outside the house had him opening his eyes in anticipation. He couldn't wait to tell Tommy everything there was to know about their brother, even Bethany thought it was the right thing to do.

He drifted off to sleep, and woke with a start, as his brothers made their way through the front door.

'What are you doing down here?'

Gary could hear the confusion in Tommy's voice. 'I ain't kipping in the same room as him.'

Surprised, Tommy turned to look at Jimmy. 'What's he going on about?'

Jimmy shrugged but averted his eyes all the same. 'Fuck knows, bruv. Come on, I'm starving. I'm gonna see if Mum left us any dinner.'

As his brothers walked through to the kitchen, Gary leapt up off the sofa. 'Are you gonna tell him, or shall I?'

'Tell me what?' Stifling a yawn, Tommy sat down at the kitchen table and ripped away the tin foil covering a plate of food their mum had left out for them. He forked a boiled potato into his mouth and chewed on it before making a start on the steak and kidney pie. 'Well?' he asked, looking up.

'I gave him a whack this morning.' Jimmy spoke fast, before Gary had the chance to even open his mouth.

Turning his head, Tommy's eyes were wide. 'What the fuck are you lamping him one for?'

As casually as he could Jimmy shrugged. 'Because he's a cocky little bastard.'

Forking a piece of steak into his mouth, Tommy chewed on the meat before swallowing. 'There you go. You got a slap for being a cocky bastard, which you are most of the time,' he said, pointing his fork towards Gary.

Outraged, Gary walked farther into the room. 'Yeah, and that's not the half of it. You just wait until you hear all about him.'

Leaping to his feet, Jimmy's fists were clenched. 'Shut your mouth. I'm fucking warning you.' He left the sentence to hang heavy in the air. The anger in his voice was enough to tell Gary it was in his best interests to keep quiet.

Tommy looked at each of his brothers in turn, then shook his head. He was too tired of all this shit. Pushing the plate away from him, he stood up from the table. All he wanted to do, was climb into bed and cuddle up to his wife. 'I'm done in. Do what you want to each other, just don't go getting blood on Mum's new carpet.' With that, he left the room.

Jimmy's eyes were hard. He took a moment of satisfaction to see his younger brother turn his head away from him first.

'Just stay away from me, Jimmy.'

'Nah, you stay away from me, you sneaky little bastard,' Jimmy spat, before barging past his brother and making his way up to bed.

13

Waking early, Stacey was eager to get on with the day she'd planned out. She walked through to the kitchen and pushed her arms into her flannel dressing gown as she walked barefoot across the cold linoleum floor, before shrugging the thick material across her shoulders and wrapping it around her body, ensuring her short nightie was covered.

She flicked the switch on the kettle and set about making a pot of tea. Tommy would be awake soon, and she popped two slices of bread into the toaster for his breakfast.

'Morning, babe.' Padding across the room, Tommy planted a kiss on Stacey's cheek before taking a seat at the kitchen table.

'Did you want a couple of boiled eggs with your toast, or a bit of bacon?'

Tommy shook his head. 'Nah, I've got an early start. Toast will do.'

'Why is your Gary sleeping on the sofa?' Jerking her head towards the lounge, Stacey glanced over at her husband, before continuing to butter the toast. 'Have him and Jimmy had a row?'

'Yeah, I think so, but they'd better sort it out and quick, before I end up banging both their heads together.'

'Brothers, eh?' Stacey smiled sadly as she was reminded of her own brother, Pete.

'What have you got planned today, babe?' Still feeling guilty over his brother-in-law's death, Tommy cleared his throat, quickly changing the subject.

'I thought I might go and do some shopping, maybe treat myself to a new haircut before the baby is born.' Passing over the plate of toast, Stacey gave a small smile. She'd never been a very good liar, and she could feel her cheeks blushing at the blatant lie she'd just told.

Tommy paused while munching on his toast. 'Here, take this and treat yourself and Karen.' He handed over a wad of notes and smiled as Stacey's eyes widened.

'Tommy, this is far too much!' Stacey gasped. Without even counting the notes, she took a wild guess at what her husband had handed over, there had to be at least two hundred pounds in cash.

Popping the last piece of toast into his mouth, Tommy chewed on it, swallowed, then flashed a wide grin. 'I know, and there's plenty more where that came from, so go out and treat yourself.'

'But what about saving up for our own place? We can't keep spending money like water, Tommy, otherwise we'll never get out of this house.'

Tommy got to his feet and, leaning over the table, kissed his wife's forehead. 'I'm already earning good money Stace, in fact I thought we could start looking at places this weekend.'

Stacey's eyes widened. 'Really? You kept that quiet.'

Tommy shrugged, 'I wanted it to be a surprise. I've seen this little place in Epping, and as soon as the sale of Davey's house goes through, we'll have more than enough to buy it outright.'

Stacey bit down on her lip. The house two doors down from her parents' house was up for sale, and with three bedrooms and a lovely little garden for the kids to run around in, it would be perfect for them. She didn't want to move far away from their families; everything they needed was right here on the estate.

'Just take a look at it,' Tommy said when he sensed her reluctance. 'If you don't like it then we can look for something else.'

As her husband left the kitchen, Stacey had to pinch herself, she was so excited at the prospect of them owning their own home. In fact, she would give the estate agents a call and arrange a viewing of the house next to her parents.

After nudging Gary awake, Tommy shouted up the stairs for Jimmy to get up and get dressed. He needed his brothers to go out and collect the debts for him, whilst he drove over to Soho to pick up Mad Dog. He had a busy day set out. He had a meeting arranged with Danny McKay around lunchtime, and with a bit of luck, McKay would be a lot easier to deal with than Freddie Smith.

'I've already told you I ain't working with him,' Gary snarled.

'You don't have a choice,' Tommy growled back. 'Now get up and get dressed, you lazy little fucker.'

'Yeah, well, that's easy for you to say, you don't know what he is.'

'I don't give a shit what he is or isn't. Now, fucking move yourself, before I end up dragging you up the stairs myself.'

Gary opened his mouth to speak, before biting down on his lip. He knew better than to argue with his eldest brother. Instead, he rolled his eyes in annoyance, and made his way up the stairs.

'Oi! And take this shit up with you! It ain't Mum's job to run around after you any more.' Grabbing up the pillow and blanket, Tommy held them out to his brother.

Snatching the bedding out of Tommy's hands, Gary raced up the steps before he ended up getting a clout around his ear.

Standing at the bottom of the stairs, Tommy sighed. He could see himself losing his rag with Gary before the day was out.

The atmosphere between Jimmy and Gary was frosty to say the least. They'd jumped on a number sixty-two bus heading towards Chadwell Heath, in Romford, both of them sitting at either ends of the bus.

Ten minutes later, Jimmy jerked his head towards Gary, indicating it was time for them to get off.

They walked along the street in silence, before coming to a halt outside The White Horse public house.

'Remember, let me do the talking,' Jimmy said, his tone harsh.

Gary screwed up his face in annoyance. 'I'm not stupid. I know what I'm doing.'

'Yeah, if you say so.' Pushing open the door to the pub, Jimmy barged Gary out of the way, allowing himself to enter first. Quickly scanning the bar area, he strode purposefully towards the barman. 'Where's the guvnor, Ted Marsden?'

Aiden Coleman eyed the two men in front of him, before setting his sights on Jimmy. 'He's not in the bar today. It's his day off, but you'll more than likely find him upstairs in bed, lazy sod he is.' Coming from Cork in Ireland, he had a soft Irish lilt. He tilted his dark head towards the back staircase. 'You'll need these,' he said, holding aloft a set of keys.

As he snatched the keys out of Aiden's hand Jimmy averted his gaze. He then shoved Gary towards the door leading to the staff accommodation.

'Bent as a nine-bob note, that one,' Gary hissed, watching

Jimmy's reaction closely.

'Just fucking move yourself.'

'Do you fancy him?'

Coming to a halt, Jimmy dug his fingertips into Gary's shoulder. 'I'm seriously warning you Gaz. I've had enough of this crap from you. Now, shut your fucking mouth and move.'

Unlocking the heavy wooden door, Jimmy pushed Gary through the open doorway. With a glance over his shoulder, he caught a glimpse of the barman wiping down the bar and swallowed deeply. He could feel his cheeks begin to blush at the stirrings inside him, and he closed his eyes for a moment in a bid to clear his thoughts. He needed a clear head. Now wasn't the time to be eyeing up random men, yet despite this he couldn't stop the mixture of both fear and excitement that had begun to bubble inside of him.

* * *

Ted Marsden was in a lovely sleep, laid out on his back with his mouth wide open. He was dead to the world. His wife, Maggie, had dutifully climbed on top of him an hour earlier, and given him the ride of his life. Feeling satisfied, he'd drifted off back to sleep, blissfully unaware of the two young men making their way up the staircase towards his flat.

'Look at the state of this fat fuck.' Gary wrinkled his nose up in disgust as he stared down at the naked man.

'Oi! Wakey, wakey. Rise and shine.' Jimmy poked Ted's thick fleshy thigh with the steel-capped toe of his heavy boot.

Groggily, Ted began to stir. Opening one eye, he looked up to find Gary stood over him, and scrambled up the bed in alarm. 'What the fuck?' he began as he hastily pulled the bedsheet over his nakedness. 'Who let you in here?'

'You owe our brother money. Now, pay up.'

'Otherwise, we'll smash up your boozer. That's after we've smashed in your face, of course,' Gary added.

Dumbstruck, Ted looked from Jimmy to Gary as he tried to take in what they were saying. 'How did you get in here?'

Jimmy rolled his eyes in irritation. 'We flew through the fucking window. How the fuck do you think we got in?' Dragging the man off the bed, he curled his fist into a ball. 'This is the last time I'm gonna ask you. Where's my brother's money?'

Despite his large frame, Ted wasn't a fighting man. Clearly terrified, his body began to shake. 'It's in the safe downstairs.'

'That wasn't so hard, was it? Now, get dressed, and get the fucking cash out for us.'

'Okay, okay.' Doing as he was told Ted quickly dressed. He could feel the sweat pouring down his face, and he hastily wiped it away with the back of his hand. 'I was gonna pay Tommy the money. I swear on my life I was. There was no need for any of this.'

'It's Mr Carter to you, and you haven't paid him for the last two weeks you lying fuck. Now, fucking move yourself. We haven't got all day.'

Ted shoved his bare feet into his shoes, whilst hastily tucking his shirt into the waistband of his trousers. He hadn't moved this fast in years, and could feel his breath becoming laboured. 'Let me catch my breath first, son,' he wheezed.

Ignoring the man's plea, Jimmy roughly shoved Ted in the small of his back, pushing him out of the flat door and down the stairs. 'Pay up, and then you can go back to bed, you lazy bastard.'

Half running across the pub floor and out to the back office, Ted wheezed even harder as he knelt down onto the bare concrete floor and fumbled to open the safe. 'It's on a timer,' he explained. 'If I get this wrong, I'll have to wait another hour to try again.'

'Well, you'd best make sure you get it right then,' Gary said.

His heart in his mouth, Ted began to turn the dial on the combination lock. Sweat poured profusely from his forehead and underneath his armpits, where it had begun to pool, staining the white shirt he wore. 'You're crowding me,' he complained.

Never one to have much patience, Gary kicked out his foot. 'Stop talking and just open the fucking safe.'

Twisting the dial, Ted's mind had drawn a blank. In his terror, he could no longer remember the combination. He looked up at Jimmy, his eyes beseeching him. 'I can't remember it. I told you not to crowd me.'

'What's fucking wrong with you?' Jimmy groaned. 'Just open the poxy safe.'

Ted stared down at the lock, trying desperately to think. Was it a four or a six? With a final twist of the lock, he set it to four, and with bated breath, waited for a click signalling the safe was unlocked. There was nothing but silence.

'Well?' Jimmy demanded. 'Is it open?'

Ted shook his head, before cowering from the two young men stood over him. 'I can't remember the code.'

Throwing up his arms, Jimmy battled to keep his temper under control. 'So, now we have to wait another hour? Fucking brilliant.'

'We should batter this prick for wasting our time.'

Jimmy chewed on the inside of his cheek. Battering the bloke wasn't the answer. They needed the cash, otherwise Tommy would go ballistic. 'Okay, let's all calm down. I'll get us a drink from the bar, and you,' he said, pointing towards Ted, 'sit there and think about the combination. Once you've remembered it, write it down. Do you understand?'

Ted furiously nodded. He had no other choice but to do as they had ordered him to do.

* * *

Cold and tired, Stacey was close to tears. The small of her back had begun to ache, and she could feel blisters forming on her heels from where her new shoes were beginning to rub. She'd just about had enough and was ready to call it a day. She stopped to catch her breath, leaning her hand against the wall of a building for support. She wanted to chastise herself. How stupid she must be, to think she would easily find the club where Beth worked. Dozens of pubs and clubs she'd entered, and not one of them had had any idea of who her friend was.

Straightening up, Stacey looked up at the building in front of her, aptly named The Soho Club. She forced herself to push open the door and walk inside. This would be the last club she went into, she decided. After this one, she would make her way back to the train station. All she wanted to do was take the weight off her feet and sit down.

Looking up from behind the desk, Lillian Chambers did a double take. The young woman in front of her wasn't the usual type of girl who would totter through the doors, wearing dangerously high heels looking for work. Can I help you, darling?'

Stacey gave a small smile. The scent of stale sweat and cheap perfume hit her nostrils. She felt out of her depth, and she looked across at the blonde woman nervously. 'I'm looking for my friend, Beth. All I know is that she works in a club around here somewhere.'

Lillian gave a chuckle. 'Well, if that's all you've got to go on, darling, it'll be like finding a needle—'

'In a haystack,' Stacey interrupted, finishing off Lillian's sentence. Her mouth curled down at the corners, and she sighed, realising how stupid she must look to the older woman.

'Listen, sweetheart, half the girls in here don't even give their real names, and I don't know of any Beth working here.'

Exasperated, Stacey's shoulders dropped. 'She has long dark

hair, green eyes, and is a few inches taller than me.' She was clutching at straws, she knew that, but someone must know her friend.

Lillian pursed her lips. The only girl fitting that description was Kitty Mae, and no one had seen head nor tail of her for weeks. 'We did have a girl here. She went by the name of Kitty Mae. She had long dark hair and green eyes. It was her eyes that made me remember her. Vivid green, they were. I'm not saying it's the same girl mind, but it could be your friend.'

Stacey's heart leapt. This was the closest she'd got to anyone having any recollection of Beth. 'Do you have contact details for her?'

'These girls don't stay long enough to give out contact details, darling.' Lillian began to laugh, before stopping herself. Her heart went out to the young woman in front of her. She could see she must be at least six months into her pregnancy, if not more, and she looked done in. 'Listen, darling, you look shattered. Can I get you a drink before you leave, maybe a cup of tea?'

Stacey shook her head. 'No, thank you.' All she wanted to do was go home and put her feet up. She was half way to the door before she turned back around. 'Why did Kitty Mae leave the club? Did she give a reason?'

Lillian cleared her throat before answering. 'Let's just say she was getting a little bit too close to the boss.'

'Oh,' Stacey said. Her heart sank. Beth had never mentioned any men to her. Maybe she hadn't really known anything about her friend after all.

* * *

Jimmy walked through to the bar area and rested his forearms across the sticky wooden bar top.

'What can I get you?' Throwing down a tea towel, Aiden made his way over.

'Two pints of larger and whatever your guvnor drinks,' Jimmy answered, battling to keep his nerves at bay.

'I've seen you around, I'm sure I have.' Aiden placed the first of the pints he'd pulled in front of Jimmy.

'Nah, I don't think so. I've not been in here before.'

Aiden shrugged. 'Ah well, I never forget a face. And yours, I definitely remember.'

Jimmy ignored the remark and delved his hand into his pocket, fishing around for some loose change.

'These are on the house.' Aiden lifted up his hand, indicating for Jimmy to keep his money. 'Let that lazy fucker back there pay for them. He usually waters down the beer anyway.'

'Cheers!' Jimmy grabbed the drinks and, avoiding eye contact with Aiden, made his way back to the office.

Smiling to himself, Aiden returned to drying the glasses. Jimmy Carter was just his type, and even though he'd lied about recognising him, he certainly wouldn't forget him now.

'Well, have you remembered the combination yet?' Placing the drinks down onto the wooden desk, Jimmy passed a pint across to Gary.

Ted shook his head.

'For fuck's sake,' Jimmy groaned. By the looks of it, this was going to be a long day.

Out on the pavement, Stacey crossed over the road and began to make her way back towards the train station. On the corner of the street she eased off her shoe and lifted her foot towards her, so that she could gently rub her blistered heel. She couldn't wait to get

home and to sit in the armchair with her tired feet in a bowl of
warm water.

Slipping her shoe back on, Stacey glanced back at The Soho
Club. What a waste of a day, she sighed, and she had nothing to
show for it either. She just hoped Tommy didn't ask to see what
she'd bought with the money he'd given her earlier that morning.

She was about to begin walking once again, when a car pulling
up outside the club caught her attention. That looked like her
Tommy's car, she thought to herself. She lifted her hand towards
her face in a bid to shield the sun from her eyes. As if in slow
motion, she watched the driver's door open and a figure step out.
She gasped in astonishment. That was her Tommy.

Stunned, Stacey began to hobble towards him. She almost cried
in relief at the thought of being able to kick off her shoes and to get
a lift back home in comfort. Coming to a halt her smile froze. Wait a
minute, what was Tommy even doing here? She felt her heart sink
as she remembered he owned a club in Soho, a gentlemen's club
he'd told her.

Lillian's words echoed through Stacey's mind. 'Kitty Mae had
been getting a bit too close to the boss.' A sudden wave of sickness
spread through her body and tears sprang to her eyes.

Had him and Kitty had a fling? Was it still going on? No wonder
he'd been so off with Beth. It must have been a shock for him to
come home and find his mistress and wife sitting together.

Stacey began to run towards the train station. A hard lump
formed in her throat, making it difficult for her to swallow. What a
fool she was; Beth had never been her friend, she'd only used her to
get close to Tommy. And as for her husband, how many other lies
had he told? Angrily, she swiped away the tears that filled her eyes,
blinding her vision. She didn't want to break down, not here, not
out on the street, but it was no use. She couldn't stop the tears from
falling. She couldn't stop her heart from breaking.

14
_____

Janet Carter was horrified. She'd listened to Stacey's story about Tommy and Beth and had clasped her daughter-in-law's hand tightly in hers. She couldn't believe her son would be so stupid. He had a lovely little family. Why would he throw it all away for some little tart who worked for him at the club?

Every now and then she glanced towards the tattered suitcase Stacey had placed beside the front door and knew instinctively there would be no use trying to talk the girl out of leaving. In fact, she didn't blame Stacey at all for wanting to leave her son. If Janet were in her shoes, she would do the exact same thing.

She sniffed back the tears that threatened to glisten her eyes. Despite her earlier reservations, she had grown to love Stacey. And as for little Karen, well, she was the apple of her eye. A fresh set of tears filled her eyes and slipped down her cheeks, as she thought of her granddaughter. She would miss the little girl if Stacey left. 'I just can't believe he would be so stupid.'

'Well, obviously he is,' Stacey spat. They were sitting at the kitchen table and Stacey rubbed at her red-rimmed eyes, her voice hoarse from crying. 'I saw him with my own two eyes, and the woman who worked there, said that Kitty Mae had left because she was getting too close to the boss.'

'Well, that could mean anything, darling. You're only assuming the worst,' Janet began. She was trying to convince herself it wasn't true, but even she could see it could only mean one thing. Tommy was playing around. 'I'll bloody well batter him for this, you just see if I don't.'

Stacey nodded. She felt numb. Her whole world had crashed down around her. Even after what had happened to Pete, she'd forgiven her husband and had accepted his plea that her brother's death was nothing more than an accident. But this, she couldn't forgive. It was a step too far. How could she ever forgive him after taking another woman to bed? 'I love him so much,' she sobbed, as fresh tears sprang to her eyes.

Janet could only nod her head sadly, before pulling her daughter-in-law into her arms, and sobbing along with her.

* * *

After collecting Mad Dog from the club, Tommy had driven them straight to the meeting point where they were due to meet Danny McKay.

'Have you got the cash, lad?' It was the third time Mad Dog had asked the same question.

With a sigh, Tommy pulled down the glove box and took out a thick envelope containing the money. 'It's all there. I counted it myself.'

'Good.'

'For fuck's sake, will you relax? I'm not going to fuck this up.'

'I know lad, and I'm just warning you now to be careful. McKay's a handful and I know he may not look the type, but trust me, he can look after himself, and you don't want to get on his bad side.'

Tommy rolled his eyes in irritation. He had no intention of getting on anyone's bad side. All he wanted to do was hand over the cash, collect the guns, and get on his way.

'This looks like him now.' Mad Dog nodded towards a car pulling into the pub car park. The squelch of tyres on gravel was loud to their ears.

'Wait a minute.' Holding out his arm, Mad Dog stopped Tommy from opening the car door. Twisting in his seat, he checked that the coast was clear, then nodded. 'Okay, it's safe to go.'

Jumping out of the car, Tommy strolled over to where Danny McKay had parked. He waited for him to climb out, then shook his hand.

As he walked around to the rear of the car, Danny held out his hand for the money. 'I trust I don't need to count this?' he asked, taking the envelope from Tommy. He was a good-looking man, and as Mad Dog had pointed out, behind the façade, he was a very dangerous individual.

'It's all there.'

Depositing the money into his pocket, Danny looked around him, checking that the coast was clear, then unlocked the boot. 'There you go,' he said, glancing down at the guns.

Tommy had to stop himself from whistling through his teeth as he looked over the contents of Danny's car boot.

'You'd be better off backing the car up for the exchange,' Danny remarked.

Tommy threw the car keys towards Mad Dog and waited for him to back the car up. Quickly and efficiently, they then transferred the firearms into Tommy's car.

'Was a pleasure doing business.' There was a grin on Danny's face and Tommy couldn't help but smile, too.

'What the fuck was that all about with Freddie? Six grand for four guns?'

'What can I say?' Danny laughed. 'That's Freddie for you. He thinks you're a cocky little cunt and until you change his mind, that's how he'll treat you.'

Tommy raised his eyebrows but decided to keep schtum all the same.

'You should have bypassed Freddie and come straight to me.' Danny turned his attention to Mad Dog. 'You knew Davey only dealt with me towards the end, before he, you know...' He trailed off, leaving the sentence unsaid.

Nodding, Mad Dog was thoughtful. 'I know lad, but seeing as Tommy's new to the game, I thought it'd be best to introduce him to Freddie first, get it over and done with.'

Danny shrugged. 'Yeah, well, next time you'll know where to come.' Shaking both men's hands, he made his way around to the driver's side of the car.

Tommy watched as Danny McKay started the engine and drove out of the car park, before rounding on Mad Dog. 'Are you telling me we could have dealt with him from the off?' he asked, jerking his head in the direction of McKay's retreating car.

'Aye lad, but like I've already said, if it'd got out you'd dealt with McKay instead of Freddie, then you would have had Smith come down on you like a ton of bricks, and on top of everything else we've got going on that's aggro we don't need.'

Tommy sighed. He could see Mad Dog's point. 'You could have at least warned me,' he grumbled.

'What' – Mad Dog grinned – 'and miss the look on your face when Freddie tried to have you over? Nah Tommy lad, it was fucking priceless.'

Tommy rolled his eyes and as Mad Dog began to laugh he couldn't help but join in.

* * *

Finally, Ted Marsden had remembered the combination code and, with shaking hands, he'd written down the digits on a scrap of paper.

With the cash now tucked safely inside Jimmy's back pocket, the two brothers left the pub.

'Thought we were gonna be there all fucking day,' Gary complained.

Taking out a cigarette, Jimmy passed the box across to Gary. 'Yeah, well, we've got the cash now.'

Gary blew out a cloud of smoke. 'How come you kept going into the bar, getting us drinks?'

'Why'd you fucking think? Because I was thirsty and it was like a sauna in that office. Plus, I couldn't stand the stench of that geezer any longer and needed some air.'

Gary raised his eyebrows. 'Oh, I thought it was because you fancied the barman,' he said with a hint of sarcasm.

'Yeah, that's fucking right,' Jimmy yelled, as he grabbed hold of Gary's shirt and yanked his brother towards him so that their faces were just inches apart. He'd had just about enough of his brother's innuendos and wanted to play him at his own game. 'In fact, he gave me his phone number. Are you fucking happy now?' It was a blatant lie, but it was worth it to see the shock spread across his younger brother's face.

'I'm gonna tell our Tommy.'

'Tell who you fucking like.' With that, Jimmy walked off down the street.

Standing in the middle of Chadwell Heath High Road, Gary stared after his brother. He needed to speak to Bethany, he decided. She would know what to do.

* * *

Janet stared down at the mobile phone that Tommy had given her for her birthday. 'You have to get with the times, Mum,' he'd said, grinning. She could remember laughing and telling him she would never use it, and that the house phone was more than enough for her.

She picked the silver phone up and turned it over in her hand. She could barely remember how it worked and had only listened half-heartedly as her son had talked her through the workings of it.

Pushing the tiny button on the side, she almost jumped out of her skin as the phone came to life. She knew he'd saved his own mobile number to it, and after pushing several buttons, Tommy's name flashed up on the screen. Taking a deep breath, she pressed dial and waited for him to answer.

'Tommy, it's me, your mum.' She could imagine him smiling at that, knowing full well he would recognise her voice. 'You need to come home right now, boy. Stacey's left you.'

She didn't wait for him to reply. She switched off the call, placed the phone back onto the table, then wearily got up from her seat and walked across the kitchen. Flicking the switch for the kettle to boil, she could recall her old mum saying a cup of tea could solve everything. She shook her head sadly. The situation with her son and his wife was one problem a cup of tea couldn't solve.

Already, the house felt empty without Stacey and little Karen, and Janet dabbed a tissue at her teary eyes. As angry as she was with Tommy, she knew this would break his heart. He was only twenty-one, and already it looked as though he had a failed marriage behind him. 'Stupid, stupid boy,' she screamed at the top of her lungs before breaking down and sobbing into her hands.

* * *

Bethany Johnson lay naked across her bed. After finding it hard to get any information out of Gary, she'd had to up her game, and taking him to her bed was a sure way of making the younger man talk. In fact, he didn't only just talk, he sang like a canary. She now knew pretty much everything that went on in the Carter household.

She watched him as he began to dress and could barely keep the sly grin from her face. 'So, you'll tell your Tommy everything about Jimmy tonight?'

Reluctantly, Gary nodded. Even though he'd threatened Jimmy that he'd tell their brother, he still wasn't sure it was the right thing to do. Tommy could very well end up killing Jimmy, and he didn't want his elder brother's death on his conscience. 'I want to do it,' he whined, 'it's just... I'm scared of what Tommy will do. You don't know him like I do, and I know he's gonna go ape shit.'

Inwardly, Bethany groaned. She'd had just about enough of listening to Gary's whinging. 'Either tell or don't, but what if he finds out you knew all along and that you didn't tell him, what will he do then, eh?'

Gary shuddered. Bethany was right. If he kept schtum, Tommy could very well lay into him, too. 'Yeah, you're right. I'll tell him tonight.'

Bethany could hardly contain her excitement and she rolled onto her front to hide her grin. The Carters weren't going to know what had hit them.

Tommy's face was ashen when he burst through the front door. 'What's going on?' he demanded. 'Why has she left me?'

Janet took one look at her son and had to fight the urge not to thump him. 'Why do you fucking think?'

Taken aback, Tommy stepped away. It was the first time he'd

ever heard his mum swear, and as for the venom in her voice, it was more than enough to tell him that Stacey had left because of him, because of something he'd done. 'I don't know.' And he was telling the truth. Stacey had seemed happy that morning when he'd left for work. He'd even given her a wad of cash and told her to go out and spoil herself.

'She saw you at your club in Soho, and she also knows everything about you and your little tart Beth, or Kitty Mae, or whatever she bloody calls herself. How could you do this to her, Tommy? Heartbroken, that girl is. I've never been so bloody ashamed of you as I am now.'

Sinking into a chair, Tommy felt as though he'd been punched in the gut. As he placed his head in his hands an ice-cold shiver ran down the length of his spine. 'I haven't done anything wrong, Mum, I swear I haven't.' Even as he spoke, he could feel his cheeks blush at the blatant lie he'd just told and he kept his eyes firmly fixed on his feet, too afraid to look his mother in the eyes.

'You haven't even got the balls to look me in the eye and admit it.' The contempt in Janet's voice was enough to tell her son that she felt disgusted by his actions. 'I know you Thomas Carter, just you remember that, and I know when you're lying, I can see it, it's written all over your face.'

Tommy looked up. 'Mum, I swear to you it was nothing, I don't feel anything for her, I told her from the off that I would never leave Stace.'

Janet gave a sarcastic laugh. 'So you risked your marriage for a bit of fun, is that what your telling me?'

Swallowing deeply, Tommy shook his head. 'It wasn't like that, she's not right in the head.' He stabbed a finger against his temple to emphasise his point. 'She wouldn't leave me alone; she even came here to the house. I told her to leave me alone.'

'It's not me you should be trying to convince, is it? I bloody well knew from the start something wasn't right between you and that little tart, but not for one second did I think anything like this would be going on.'

Pale-faced, Tommy looked away. 'Don't look at me like that Mum,' he begged of her, 'I know I fucked up.'

'Fucked up,' Janet shrieked. 'You've done a lot more than just fuck up, you've broken Stacey's heart.'

Tears filled Tommy's eyes and as they rolled down his cheeks he began to sob. 'What am I gonna do? I love her.'

Sitting down opposite her son, Janet's temper relaxed. As much as she didn't want it to, her heart went out to him. 'Stacey is in a right state, and nothing you say or do will be able to make that right; you went with another woman son, there is no greater betrayal than that.'

'I've lost her, haven't I?' Tommy said, wiping the cuff of his shirt over his face.

Janet nodded and as he broke down in tears again, she wrapped her arms tightly around him and sighed. 'Why, Tommy, why did you have to do this?'

She felt him shrug. 'I don't know,' he answered truthfully. 'I didn't think Stace would ever find out I suppose.'

Janey sighed and, shaking her head, she released her arms from around him. At least he was being honest and not trying to make excuses for himself.

'Is she at her mum and dad's house?'

Janet nodded. 'I expect so.'

Wiping the tears from his eyes Tommy stood up. 'I have to talk to her; I have to try and get her to come home.'

At that moment Gary burst through the door. 'Tommy, I need to speak to you.'

'Not now, Gary.'

'Yeah, but it's important. It's about Jimmy. He's—'

'I said not fucking now.' With that, Tommy left the house.

Gary stared after his brother, his mouth wide open in shock. He looked across at his mother. 'What's up with him? I only wanted to speak to him.'

Janet patted her younger son's arm. 'When you get married, you'll understand.' She paused for a moment. 'No, for your sake son I hope that you don't.'

Gary shrugged, confused by his mother's cryptic message. It would have to wait, but he knew one thing for certain, if he didn't speak to Tommy and soon, then Bethany would go ballistic, and the last thing he wanted was for her to fall out with him.

* * *

Tommy's heart was in his mouth as he marched down the street towards his in-laws' house. Walking down the path, he paused before banging his fist on the wooden front door.

'What d'ya want?' Jack Williams flung open the door, his large frame dominating the doorway.

Peering past Jack into the house, Tommy went to take a step forward. 'I want to speak to my wife. Is she here?'

Jack shook his head. 'She's here, but she doesn't want to see or speak to you. Now, piss of before I do you some damage.'

Tommy placed his hands on either side of the door frame and bent his head. 'I just want to see my wife,' he said, looking up at Jack, his eyes beseeching.

Jack glanced behind him. He'd always liked Tommy but seeing his Stacey so distressed had been like a red rag to a bull. No one, and he meant no one, had the right to upset his little girl, and that included her husband. 'She doesn't want to see you, Tommy. Now, get yourself off home, lad. Believe me I don't want to have to give you a dig.' Jack took a menacing step forward, forcing Tommy away from the doorstep.

Rubbing his hand over his face, Tommy was distraught. 'Please Jack, I'm begging you just let me see her for one minute, then I swear I'll leave. I just want to make sure she's okay.'

'He told you to piss off.'

Surrounded by Stacey's brothers, Tommy held up his hands in surrender. 'Okay, I'm going.' He walked down the path with his head down low. His heart was breaking. Stacey meant everything to him. She had done so from the moment he'd first clapped eyes on her. He was an idiot; how could he have even thought he would get away with what he'd done? As he reached the gate, he turned to look back at the living room window. Standing there looking out at him was Stacey.

'Stace,' he called out, 'just give me five minutes to explain.'

She turned away from him and pulled across the curtains, breaking his heart all over again.

Reluctantly, Tommy began the short walk home. Swiping a stray tear from his cheek, he knew there was no one else to blame other than himself.

15

Harold Robinson had sharp eyes that never missed a trick. He walked across the floor of the Bradford & Bingley Building Society, and smiled courteously at the last customer, as they made their way out of the building.

Clicking his fingers towards the young man stood in the doorway, he indicated for him to slide the bolt across the door. He glanced down at his watch. It was dead on five o'clock, not a minute before, and not a minute after. He turned to look at his staff, then nodded. Business was over for the day.

With cold grey eyes, he watched as the clerks stood up from behind the counter and walked towards the door leading out to the staff room. It was here they would queue up, waiting for him to check that they had taken no belongings with them, mainly the customers' money.

Satisfied that everything was as it should be, one by one, he let his staff walk through to the back office to collect their bags and coats. Harold ran a tight ship and he was proud of that fact. That the staff called him a pompous old git behind his back, made no odds to him. The only thing he cared about was statistics. And the truth of the matter was none of his staff had ever got away with stealing money from the Building Society, and he planned to keep it that way.

Blissfully unaware that he was being intently watched, Harold ushered his staff out of the building and locked the thick glass door behind them. Twisting a key into a metal grid beside the door, he released a metal shutter, ensuring the Building Society was securely locked down for the night.

* * *

In a car down the street from the Bradford & Bingley, Tommy glanced at his own watch. It was now five-thirty.

'Like clockwork every single night, they lock the doors at five, and by five-thirty, they've left the premises.'

Tommy nodded. It was almost too good to be true. Unbeknownst to Harold, the fact that he ran such a tight ship had left the Building Society in a precarious position. 'Right, I reckon we should do one last check of the place over the next couple of days, and then that'll be it until the actual job next month.'

Mad Dog sucked in his cheeks as he thought over Tommy's plan. 'Sounds about right to me, lad. I'm off to look at a car tonight, and then it's only the disguises left to sort out.'

'I'll pop down to the Dagenham Sunday Market and see if they've got anything we could use. There's a stall over there that sells construction wear. They're bound to have something useful.'

'This is it then, lad. We're all ready.'

Tommy nodded. Thanks to Davey's notebook and his own plans, they were as ready as they'd ever be.

* * *

Bethany was sulking. She just couldn't understand the reluctance in Gary. All he had to do was tell Tommy about Jimmy being gay, and then she could sit back and watch the fireworks. Never send a boy to do a man's job. It was an old saying of her dad's, and more than ever, Bethany believed it to be true. She'd even contemplated sending an anonymous letter addressed to Tommy Carter but knew it would be better coming from Gary. That way, Jimmy couldn't possibly lie his way out of it. The fact that she was willing to blow apart Jimmy Carter's world, meant nothing to her. Tommy himself had blown her world apart when he had so callously told her that she meant nothing to him, other than being a whore who worked at his club.

No, she'd had enough now. She'd given young Gary an ultimatum. He either told Tommy today, or they were over. He'd actually looked as though he was going to cry when she had told him that, which only angered her even more. She'd then sent him packing and told him not to come back until the deed was done. And despite the situation she now found herself to be in, she meant every word.

Bethany glided her hand over the smooth skin stretched flat across her stomach. The fact that she had Tommy Carter's own flesh and blood growing inside of her meant absolutely nothing to her, and why should it? She wasn't even sure she wanted this baby. To be more precise, she knew for a fact she didn't want it. Let's face it. Why would she want a child who would more than likely turn out to be as weak as its father? And besides, it had always been Tommy's baby she'd wanted, not Gary's.

She poked her finger into her stomach, pushing down as hard as she could, until she cried out in pain. The quicker it, as she referred to the baby, was gone from her body, the better. Bethany gave a wicked smile as a thought came to her mind. Once she'd gotten rid of it, she could use the baby to hurt the Carters even further. Yes, she decided. It was the perfect plan, albeit an evil, spiteful one. She would pretend she was still pregnant, and then use the baby as a pawn to ensure Gary did as she bade, otherwise she would threaten to abort their child. She almost laughed out loud now. Poor Gary would end up going out of his mind with grief. In fact, the poor boy wasn't going to know what had hit him, and the beauty of it all, was she had only just begun getting her revenge on Tommy Carter. One way or another, he would rue the day he'd called her a whore.

* * *

Any other man would have wanted to know why Bethany Johnson was so hell-bent on Tommy Carter needing to know about his brother's sexual preferences. Gary, on the other hand, young and naive, was oblivious to his girlfriend's evil scheming.

Kicking a stone from underneath his shoe, Gary leant against the shutter of Tommy's betting shop in Barking and popped a cigarette into his mouth. He inhaled a lungful of smoke before blowing it out noisily. He was worried. Not only was he getting it in the neck from Bethany, but he also knew Tommy was going to go ballistic, and despite the problems he'd had with Jimmy over the past few months, they were still brothers, and he didn't want anything to happen to him.

'What are you doing here?'

Gary ignored the surprise in Tommy's voice and shrugged.

Unlocking the door to the betting shop, Tommy ushered his younger brother through the doorway, before sliding the bolt across the door behind them.

'Well, what are you doing here? It's not like you to be up and out of bed so early.'

'It's Jimmy. I tried to tell you before, but you wouldn't listen to me.'

'What about Jimmy?' Tommy raised his eyebrows.

'He's...'

'He's what? C'mon, spit it out for fuck's sake, I ain't got all day.'

'He's queer.'

Tommy's eyes were wide as he stared at Gary. 'Do what?'

'Jimmy's gay.'

Remaining silent, Tommy mindlessly picked up a stack of papers from the desk and shuffled them.

'I said he's as bent as—'

'Yeah, I know what gay means,' Tommy snapped. 'How do you know this? Did he tell you?'

'Yeah, he did.' It was a slight exaggeration. Jimmy had only referred to the barman giving him his phone number; he hadn't exactly admitted it. Gary's heart was in his mouth as he waited for Tommy to erupt. He could see the anger flash across his face and momentarily felt sorry for Jimmy. 'What are you gonna do to him?'

'What am I going to do?' Tommy's voice took on an incredulous tone as he repeated back Gary's question.

'Yeah, what are you going to do?'

Tommy slammed the stack of papers onto the desk. For a few moments he was deep in thought. 'I'm gonna go and have a chat with our brother, that's what I'm gonna do.'

Gary watched as Tommy stormed out of the shop. He was in half a mind to give Jimmy a heads up on the situation, but he knew Bethany wouldn't want him doing that. She'd already warned him that Jimmy would try and worm his way out of it if he knew Tommy was gunning for him. He sat down heavily and rested his forearms on his knees. He hoped his girlfriend was happy now, because he certainly didn't feel happy with what he'd done, not one little bit.

* * *

Tommy was furious. He pulled the car to a screeching halt outside his parents' house and climbed out. After slamming the car door shut, he stormed down the path and let himself into the house. Taking the stairs two at a time he barged into the bedroom his brothers shared. 'Get up,' he said, pushing his brother roughly in the back.

Groggily, Jimmy opened his eyes.

'Get up and get dressed. I need to have a word with you.' Tommy's voice brooked no arguments and walking from the room he made his way back down the stairs.

'What are you doing here? I thought you'd gone to work,' Janet said, surprised.

'Yeah, I did. I came back to collect Jimmy.'

'Jimmy, get up now,' Janet bellowed at the top of her voice, before turning to look at her eldest son as he stared out of kitchen window.

After a few seconds, Tommy walked out to the hallway impatiently and called up the stairs, 'Jimmy, move yourself. I'll be in the car waiting for you.'

* * *

Shrugging on his jacket, Jimmy closed the front door behind him, and walked down the path towards his brother's car.

'What's all this about?' he asked, opening the car door. 'Is it to do with the bank job?'

'Just get in,' Tommy ordered. He started the engine and eased the car into first gear. He'd barely got halfway down the road, when he saw his wife walking down the street towards him. He was in two minds to pull the motor over and speak to her. Against his better judgement, he carried on driving, frequently checking her retreating back in the rear-view mirror as he did so.

'Well, are you gonna tell me what's going on, or am I supposed to guess?'

Remaining silent, Tommy pulled into the scrap yard, switched off the engine and climbed out of the car. Jimmy opened the car door and followed suit.

Hastily unlocking the office door, Tommy indicated for Jimmy to enter, then followed, firmly closing the door shut behind them.

'Well?' Jimmy sat down. 'What the fuck is going on?'

Tommy sighed. 'Do you know what, I've been asking myself the exact same question.'

Confused, Jimmy screwed up his face. He couldn't for the life of him think of what he'd done wrong.

'I spoke to Gary. We had a nice little chat about you.'

Jimmy's heart plummeted. Now everything made sense. This could only mean one thing: Gary had followed through with his threat and told Tommy everything. Looking down at his feet, he averted his eyes. He didn't want to see the disgust spread across his elder brother's face.

'So, you told Gary?'

'What?' A cold shiver of fear ran down the length of Jimmy's spine and he wiped the sweat away from his forehead with the back of his hand. 'I told Gary what?'

Tommy struggled to keep his temper in check. 'You know fucking what. Don't play games with me, bruv. You told Gary you're gay, but you couldn't tell me?'

Jimmy's mouth fell open. 'I...' he began. Unable to find the right words, he held his head in his hands and sobbed.

'Did you honestly think that I hadn't already guessed? That I didn't know?' Tommy's voice was gentle.

Jimmy looked up, tears slipping down his cheeks.

'I know you as well as I know myself. There's only eleven months between us and we're not just brothers, we're best mates, ain't we?'

Swiping at his tears, Jimmy nodded. He was unable to speak, the lump in his throat choking him.

'So, why tell Gary and not me?'

'I don't know. I was scared, I suppose.' Jimmy answered, his voice was hoarse.

'Why the fuck would you be scared?' Screwing up his face there was genuine confusion in Tommy's voice.

'I don't know, and I didn't tell Gary, he guessed, and has threatened me with it ever since.'

'That fucking Gary. I'll kill him,' Tommy spat.

'So, what happens now?' Jimmy's heart was in his mouth as he looked towards his brother warily. More than anything, he was afraid that despite Tommy's words, this would change everything between them.

Tommy took a few moments to think. He knew for a fact this meant Jimmy wouldn't have an easy time of it, once word got out that he fancied men and not women. However, being his brother, he'd always watch out for him and have his back if need be, not that Jimmy needed his protection. He was more than capable of taking care of himself. 'Nothing happens. You're my brother and nothing changes that fact. We carry on as we always have.'

Jimmy gave a half smile and wiped the tears from his eyes.

'Come on.' Tommy reassuringly gripped Jimmy's shoulder, before pulling him to his feet. 'We've got work to do, and don't think this will get you a day off either, because it won't.'

Jimmy laughed. He felt as though a weight had been lifted off his shoulders. In a roundabout way he had Tommy's approval. It was just their parents who needed to be told now.

As if reading his brother's mind, Tommy spoke. 'If you want me to tell Mum and the old man for you, I will.'

Jimmy smiled his gratitude. 'Thanks, bruv.' Instinctively, he knew it would be better coming from Tommy.

* * *

Bethany was livid and felt like screaming in frustration. She'd fully expected Tommy to want to bash Jimmy's head in. Instead, it had transpired that he'd always known his brother was gay and was just waiting for Jimmy to tell him. She looked across at Gary and had to hide the anger she felt. Sporting a blackened eye and a split lip, he was feeling sorry for himself. Well, if he was looking for sympathy, he'd come to the wrong place.

'See, I told you me brother would be like this.' Gary gingerly touched his eye. 'Battered me, Tommy did, for threatening our Jimmy.'

'Oh, just fuck off, Gary.'

'What have I done wrong now?' Gary's eyes widened in alarm.

'You can't do anything right, can you? One thing I wanted you to do and even that you fucked up. Now piss off,' she screamed, dragging Gary to his feet and pushing him out of her bedroom.

Slamming the door closed in Gary's face, Bethany threw herself onto the bed. She needed to think. She had to up her game. That was exactly what she needed to do. She climbed back off the bed and raced out of her room. 'Gary, I'm sorry.' She purred as she tore after him. 'I didn't mean what I said. In fact, I think it's time we made it official and I met your family.'

* * *

Jimmy looked down at his watch. It was dead on five-thirty.

Sat forward in his seat, Tommy rested his arms over the steering wheel. 'See, what did I tell you? Like fucking clockwork every single night.' The two brothers were sat in Tommy's car down the street from the Building Society.

Jimmy whistled through his teeth. 'This is gonna be like taking candy from a baby.'

'You can say that again, bruv.' He started the ignition and began to drive forward. 'Look, can you see? There's three cameras: one pointing to the left, one to the right, and one that points directly down from above the door. There is fuck all pointing straight ahead, and that is the way we'll be going in and out.'

Jimmy nodded. He could see exactly what Tommy was referring to. The Bradford & Bingley was situated on the corner of the street, and there was a vast area the cameras failed to pick up on. As far as Jimmy could tell, this job was easy pickings and theirs for the taking. 'What if someone out on the street spots us going in though? Won't we look out of place if we turn up in boiler suits and balaclavas?'

'Nah.' Tommy shook his head. 'I've already sussed that out. We're going in suited and booted, and once in, we've got thirty minutes to do the job. We need to be out of there by five-thirty, and trust me, when we walk out of that place, we're gonna look like any other average Joe bank clerk locking the place up for the night.'

'We ain't gonna hurt anyone though, are we?' Jimmy's eyes were narrowed as he glanced across at his brother. It was the first time he'd asked the one question that had been troubling him ever since Tommy had decided to see the robbery through.

'What do you take me for? As long as they cooperate, no one will get hurt.'

Jimmy swallowed deeply. That was exactly what he was afraid of. Tommy had a short temper at the best of times.

* * *

Stacey grimaced as a pain shot through her back. She shifted her weight as she sat on the sofa beside her mum. It was too early for her to go into labour; she had at least another five weeks to go before the baby was due. She bit down on her lip to stop herself from crying out loud. She wanted the contractions to stop, but instead, they were coming faster and stronger.

'Stace.' There was alarm in Mary Williams' voice. 'What's wrong?'

'It's the baby,' Stacey gasped, as another contraction ripped through her body. 'I think it's coming.'

'But it's too early.' Mary jumped up from the sofa. 'Where the bloody hell is your dad when I need him?' She already knew the answer. Jack was down the pub, propping up the bar, same as he did every night.

'It's getting worse, Mum,' Stacey cried.

Mary pursed her lips. 'I'm gonna have to go and fetch Janet and Tommy.' She held up her hand to cut off Stacey's protests. 'I know you don't want him here, but as the father, it's his right.' She slipped her feet into her slippers and pulled her woollen cardigan around her shoulders. She'd already discussed it with Janet. When the time came, whether Stacey liked it or not, Tommy would be there.

Crying out, Stacey gripped hold of the cushion. 'Just hurry up, Mum.'

Putting her front door on the latch, Mary ran down the road towards the Carters' house. She was out of breath by the time she banged her fist on the wooden door.

'The baby's coming,' she quickly explained to a wide-eyed Janet, as the door was flung open.

'Bleeding hell, it's too soon. Tommy, come on,' Janet yelled. 'The baby's on its way.'

* * *

Tommy felt as though he were on cloud nine as he and his brothers went out to wet the baby's head. Despite being born early, the baby, a boy whom they had decided to name Peter after Stacey's brother, was doing well.

'To the next generation of Carters!' Tommy raised his glass in the air.

'He's half Williams, don't you forget that.' Jack Williams staggered up to the bar. His cheeks were ruddy, he stunk of booze, and unless Tommy was very much mistaken, spoiling for a fight.

Tommy nodded. 'So he is.' He raised his pint glass into the air a second time. 'To the next generation of Carters and Williamses.' He watched as Jack sauntered off towards the far end of the pub with his cronies, then raised his eyebrows towards Jimmy.

'Why'd you back down like that? He'll always be a Carter, through and through.'

'Because, Jimmy, his daughter happens to be my wife, and I want her back, and if that means backing down to that old bastard, then I'm more than prepared to do just that.'

Jimmy nodded. He could see Tommy's point. 'Here, what's up with him?' He jerked his head in the direction of Gary. 'He's had a face like a smacked arse all day.'

'He's probably still sulking because I gave him a dig. You all right, Gaz?'

Gary nodded. He had something on his mind. The truth of the matter was, he was in a lot of bother, and couldn't for the life of him think of a way out of it.

'Well, fucking smile then. We're meant to be celebrating the birth of my son, and by the way, it's your round.' Tommy gave a cheeky grin as he pushed Gary towards the bar.

As he ordered the round of drinks, Gary ignored his mobile

phone vibrating in his jacket pocket. He knew who it would be: Bethany. Just that morning, his girlfriend had dropped a bombshell on him. She was pregnant. He wiped his hand across his clammy forehead. Just thinking about the terrifying situation he now found himself to be in, was enough to bring him out in a cold sweat.

Tommy raised his freshly filled pint glass in the air. 'To us Carters!' He took a sip from his pint of larger. 'This time next month, we'll be raking it in.' He pointed towards his brothers. 'And I don't want any distractions right, from either of you. This job needs our full attention.'

Gary lowered his eyes. How was he meant to keep his attention on the job now? Bethany was doing his head in, and he had a feeling it was going to get a lot worse.

16

With balaclavas resting on top of their heads, Tommy, Jimmy, and Gary were waiting with bated breath for the last remaining customer to make their way out of the Building Society.

'Fucking move yourself,' Tommy muttered from inside the car. His hand was firmly clutched around the car door handle, as he waited on tenterhooks to fling it open and jump out. 'Get ready,' he warned his two brothers. 'And remember, as soon as we get near to the door, pull the balaclavas down.'

Jimmy swallowed deeply. To say he was nervous was an under-statement. 'What's taking them so long? If they don't hurry up, they're gonna end up locking the doors behind them as they leave, and then we're fucked.'

'He's got a point, Tommy.' Mad Dog glanced down at his watch. 'Four minutes to go before they're locked.'

'Fuck it, we go now.' Flinging open the car door, Tommy jumped out, with his two brothers hot on his tail. 'Remember what I said. Cover your faces as soon as we reach the door.'

They moved quickly. To all intent and purposes, they looked like any other business men, even down to the fact that they were carrying briefcases. The only difference being they had balaclavas perched on top of their heads and guns hidden inside their jackets.

Pushing through the door, Tommy took the lead. Pulling out the gun, he pointed it towards the young open-mouthed clerk's head as he stood quivering beside the glass door, ready and waiting to slide the heavy bolt across. 'You,' he shouted towards Harold. 'Throw me over the keys now. And the rest of you, I want you around this side of the counter. If any of you even think about doing something stupid, then sunshine here gets a bullet through his head.'

As his two brothers stood brandishing the guns, Jimmy slid the bolt across the door and then snapped off the overhead lights, ensuring they couldn't be seen from outside.

Stunned, Harold stared at the three men who'd burst into the Building Society, his Building Society. 'This is absurd,' he began, before snapping shut his mouth and throwing across the keys. 'You won't get away with this. I can assure you of that.'

In deathly silence, Tommy threw the keys across to Jimmy, indicating for him to open up the staff area. He'd fully expected the staff to scream, shout, or at least do something to try and stop them. Instead, all he saw was their panic-stricken faces staring back at him as he ushered them out towards the back of the building.

Unlocking the door to the staff room, Jimmy stepped aside as his brothers pushed the staff and last remaining customer forwards into the windowless room.

'Right then. This is how it's gonna be. As long as you all cooperate, no one will get hurt,' Tommy stated once they were all inside the room. He opened up the briefcase he'd been carrying and took out a roll of duct tape and a handful of cable ties. 'Tie them up,' he instructed his brothers.

Silently, Jimmy and Gary used the cable ties and duct tape to bind together the hands and feet of the terrified hostages, all the while underneath the watchful eye of Tommy. Once satisfied they would not be able to escape and raise the alarm, he pushed Harold out of the room. 'Now, you are gonna show me exactly where the money is kept. And remember, if you even think about doing something stupid, then people are gonna get hurt.'

Clearly terrified, Harold nodded. He stumbled forwards and clutched at his chest as Tommy roughly shoved him in the back. 'Fucking move. We ain't got all day.' Glancing down at his watch, Tommy's heart beat wildly in his chest. They had just fifteen minutes left to get the cash from the safe and then get out of the building.

With the safe open, Tommy frogmarched Harold back to the staff room. 'Tie him up with the others, and be quick about it,' he ordered, tapping his watching, indicating they were running out of time.

Swiftly, Jimmy bound the bank manager's hands and feet together. Satisfied he would be unable to escape, he then backed up towards the door, and after ushering Gary out of the room, he locked the staff room door firmly shut behind them.

'We've got eight minutes to go.' Tommy's voice was low.

Quickly and efficiently, they began filling the briefcases with the cash. 'Two minutes to go.' Tommy glanced at his watch. 'That's it, times up. We leave now.'

'What about the rest of the cash?' Gary's eyes were wide as he looked from Tommy to the remaining notes in the safe.

'Leave it. We stick to the plan and time's up. We go now.'

Shrugging, Gary snapped the briefcase he'd been carrying closed.

Quickly, they walked across the Building Society floor, pausing briefly to cut through the phone cables and remove the video cassettes from the cameras. As if on cue, in the time it had taken them to walk towards the glass door, Mad Dog had reversed the silver Cosworth up to the entrance. In a casual manner, the brothers walked out. With the set of keys in his gloved hand, Tommy locked the glass door behind them, then stood back slightly to release the metal shutter.

Just as Tommy, and Davey before him, had stated it would be, the robbery was a piece of cake.

'We fucking did it! What did I tell you?' Pulling off the balaclava covering his face, Tommy's cheeks were flushed as he turned in his seat and grinned at his brothers. 'Didn't I tell you it was ours for the taking?'

'Were there any problems, lad?'

Tommy turned in his seat. 'It was like taking candy from a fucking baby.'

'I thought that old geezer was gonna have a heart attack at one point,' Jimmy said.

'Fuck him. The silly old bastard... It ain't even his money.'

'Yeah, I know, but still.'

Tommy threw his younger brother a look of warning. 'You're too fucking soft, Jimmy, that's your trouble. Anyways, forget about him now, and just think about all of that lovely dough we've got.'

'How much do you reckon you got away with, lad?'

Tommy blew out his cheeks and glanced at his brothers before answering. 'What do you reckon, seventy grand?'

'If not more,' Gary chirped in. 'And we even left some behind because we ran out of time.'

'Not bad for thirty minutes graft, eh?' Tommy grinned.

Mad Dog laughed. 'Aye a good day's work then, lads.'

* * *

Pulling into the scrap yard, Mad Dog switched off the ignition.

'Right, let's get these hidden away,' Tommy said, nodding towards the briefcases. 'Mad Dog, you'll get rid of the car, and then we carry on as we normally do, okay? We don't touch this money for at least two months, maybe even three.'

They all nodded in agreement. As they climbed out of the Cosworth, Tommy pulled Mad Dog back towards him. 'What are you going to do with the car?'

'I'll take it down to silver town, lad, burn the bugger out. Nothing will come back to us.'

'You're certain of that?'

Mad Dog raised his eyebrows. 'I was working for Davey long before you were even a twinkle in your old man's eye. It's not the first car I've had to get rid of, Tommy.'

Tommy chuckled. 'I know, it's just...' He glanced towards his brothers. 'You know what I mean.'

'I do, lad. You want to protect those two and trust me, there will be nothing left of the car. There'll be no comebacks. Your main concern should be making sure those two over there' – he jerked his head towards Jimmy and Gary – 'can keep quiet about it.'

Tommy chewed on the inside of his cheek. Jimmy, he knew he could trust with his own life. It was Gary who concerned him the most. 'They'll keep quiet.'

'Let's hope they do, lad, for all of our sakes.'

* * *

Janet was just about to dish up the sausages when her sons burst through the front door. 'You're just in time,' she shouted out, 'and look who's here having their tea with us.'

Scooping Karen into his arms, Tommy grinned. 'How are they?' he asked, bending down to kiss the top of his son's head as he lay in Stacey's arms.

'They're both fine.'

Tommy nodded before gently squeezing his wife's shoulder. 'Are you having your dinner with Daddy?' he asked, turning his atten-tion to Karen, and walking across the kitchen towards the cooker.

'Tommy, get out of the bleeding way. How am I supposed to dish up with the two of yous in front of me?'

Tommy chuckled. 'Come on, we'd better get out of Nanny's way.' He took a seat next to Stacey at the table. 'When are you coming home?' he asked, his voice low. 'I miss you.'

Stunned, Stacey turned in her seat to face her husband, not sure if she'd heard him right.

'Well?' Tommy raised his eyebrows. 'I want you to come home, all three of you.'

'I...' Before she could answer, Janet had placed a steaming plate in front of her, and the rest of the family had scrambled to the table. 'We'll talk about it later,' she whispered.

As usual, meal times were loud in the Carter household, each of them trying to out talk the other. Tommy tapped his knife against the side of the plate to get everyone's attention. 'Seeing as all the Carters are here tonight,' he said, glancing across to Stacey, 'I think we should have a little toast, to us.'

Raising their glasses in the air, they shouted out, 'To us Carters!'

With so much chaos around them, no one noticed how quiet Gary was, and had been for the last few weeks.

* * *

'Come on, Stace, just come home.'

'It's not as easy as that, is it? I'm not so sure I could trust you again.'

Tommy swallowed deeply, and as a pink tinge crept up his neck, he spoke fast. 'I swear to you babe, I didn't touch her. Nothing happened between me and Bethany. She's deluded, obsessed, you know she is. This is what she wanted; right from the start, she wanted to cause problems between me and you.' His heart hammered inside his chest so hard and so fast that he was sure Stacey would be able to hear it. As he reached out to grasp her hand in his, he willed himself not to give the game away. Stacey could never know the truth, she could never know that he'd betrayed her, that he'd broken their marriage vows. 'I won't give up darling, I can't, I love you. Please come home.'

Tommy watched as Stacey hesitated. She hadn't said no, not directly anyway. That had to be a good sign, didn't it?

'Look, we've been getting on really well lately, and I want you back. I want all three of you to come home. I'll even sort out a place of our own for us to live. Anywhere you want, just let me know and I'll buy it,' he said.

'I know you won't bloody give up.' Stacey laughed.

'Well then, what do you say?' Ever hopeful, there was a twinkle in Tommy's eye.

Stacey glanced towards the house. She could see Janet through the kitchen window as she did the washing up, and knew her mother-in-law, despite being up to her elbows in soapy suds, would be listening in on the conversation. 'Do you really mean it? That we can get our own place, anywhere I want?'

Tommy's heart leapt. 'Anywhere, Stace. You just name it, and it's yours.'

'Okay.' She sighed. 'I'll come home on the one condition you give me your word you will never see or speak to that woman again. I mean it Tommy; this is your one and only chance.'

'On my life Stace, I promise. You won't regret it,' he said, lifting her up and kissing her on the lips.

Janet jumped up and down with joy. She'd already guessed that Stacey was coming home before they'd even had the chance to break the news. 'You and our Tommy were made for each other,' she told her daughter-in-law later that evening.

'I know,' was all Stacey needed to say. The huge grin spread across her face said it all.

* * *

'I've done things, Stace. Bad things.'

They were lying in bed. Puzzled, Stacey turned onto her side to look at her husband. 'What do you mean?'

Tommy sighed. 'I don't want any more secrets between us. I know I messed up, but I don't ever want to lose you again.'

Swallowing deeply, Stacey sighed.

'I've hurt people, Stace, and I don't mean when I was boxing. I mean since then, since I started working for Davey. I went off the rails for a bit I suppose, and I liked it, I liked the power it gave me.'

'Why are you telling me this?' There was alarm in Stacey's voice and Tommy pulled her closer.

'Because, I want you to know everything there is to know about me. That way, nothing'll shock you if it ever comes out.'

With her head on Tommy's chest, Stacey closed her eyes tightly. 'I don't care about what you've done. It's in the past now, isn't it?'

Tommy remained silent. It wasn't in the past though, was it? And let's face it, that was half the problem. The bank job just that morning had given him such a high. In fact, it had given him one of the biggest adrenalin rushes he'd ever experienced and he wanted to do it again. Not only that, but he was good at it, and couldn't wait to begin planning out the next robbery. He'd actually found something he excelled in, and he wasn't ready to put a stop to it, not yet anyway. 'I did something today that could have put me away for a very long time if I'd been caught.'

Stacey's heart began to beat faster. She placed her finger against his lips. 'Don't tell me, Tommy. I don't wanna hear what you did.

The less I know, the less I can repeat. Just promise me you'll be careful if you ever do it again.'

In the darkened room, Tommy nodded. He planned on being careful. He wasn't looking to get his collar felt anytime soon. He had a wife and two kids to look after.

* * *

Gary sat on the edge of Bethany's bed. 'Are you sure you want to do this?'

'Yes.' Moving forwards, Bethany wrapped her arms around him.

'You want us to tell everyone you're pregnant at Peter's christening?'

Irritated, Bethany closed her eyes. 'Yes, I want to announce it at the bloody christening, how many times do we have to go over this?'

'But my family have never even met you. Don't you think we should wait until they've got to know you first?'

Pushing herself away from him, Bethany crossed her arms over her chest. 'Well, if you don't want this baby, Gary, we can soon get rid of it.'

Alarmed, Gary turned to face her. 'Okay, I'm sorry. We'll announce it at the christening.'

'Good.' Feeling smug, Bethany began planning out her outfit. She needed to make sure she looked stunning when she stood beside Stacey. And more than anything, she needed to make sure Tommy wouldn't be able to take his eyes off her.

17

Stacey was adding the finishing touches to the finger buffet. The church service was at ten, and then everyone they knew had been invited to the christening party in Tommy's parents' back garden.

With her hair in rollers, Stacey had had to slap Tommy's hand away from the buffet on more than one occasion. 'Leave it out,' she scolded. 'There'll be nothing left for the guests at this rate.'

Laughing, Tommy swept his gaze across the table laden with food. 'Stace, you've got enough here to feed hundreds of people. One sausage roll isn't going to hurt, is it?'

Despite her stern expression, Stacey couldn't help but laugh along. Tommy was right. There was more than enough food to go around. 'I just want everything to be perfect, that's all.'

'And it will be, so stop worrying.' He pulled her into his arms. 'Well, Mrs Carter, you'd best get yourself ready. It's nearly time to leave.'

Patting the rollers in her hair, Stacey gasped. 'I forgot I had these in. Give me five minutes to take them out, and then we can leave.'

Tommy rolled his eyes towards Jimmy. 'Women, bruv. Which

reminds me, Gary's bringing his little bird along today.' He popped a sausage roll into his mouth and chewed on it before swallowing. 'Look at him, he looks like he's shitting bricks.'

Jimmy looked across to Gary and began to laugh. Their younger brother looked as though he had the weight of the world on his shoulders. 'She probably looks like Quasimodo, that's why he's shitting it. Why else has no one even met her yet? He hasn't even told us her name.'

'True, bruv. Hey, Gary! What's your girlfriend's name?' Tommy called out.

Ignoring the question, Gary wandered back into the house, leaving his two elder brothers to laugh even harder. 'Fucking hell. Young love, eh?'

* * *

Dressed to impress, Bethany added a spritz of perfume to her neck and wrists. It was an expensive fragrance and had cost her dad a small fortune. She stood back now and admired herself in the full-length mirror. After much deliberation, she had chosen a long, tight-fitting black dress and a cropped white denim jacket. She turned sideways. She wasn't showing yet, and the material clung to her curves in all the right places. She slid her feet into a pretty pair of diamante sandals. The diamantes matched the diamond necklace she wore around her neck. As a finishing touch, she placed a pair of sunglasses on top of her head. They would give her the perfect opportunity to watch Tommy from afar, without anyone else knowing she only had eyes for him.

A shiver of anticipation ran down her spine. Today would be the first time she had seen him since she'd stood spying on him that day he'd reopened the betting shop. It felt like a lifetime ago.

She glanced down at her watch. Just an hour to go before Gary came to meet her, and then she would drive them to the party in her brand-new Mini Cooper, yet another gift from her father. She smirked to herself. She couldn't wait to see their faces when Gary told them she was having a baby. Of course, she wasn't keeping it. She'd have to think of something when the time came and she'd gotten rid of it. Maybe a miscarriage. She began to laugh out loud. Poor Gary. The silly sod really believed he was about to become a father.

* * *

The christening had gone like a dream. Little Peter had cried in all the right places, and then slept for the remainder of the service. Proud as punch, Stacey and Tommy had posed for photographs with their little family.

Janet held onto Frank's arm as they walked through the church-yard back to their car. 'Such a lovely service,' she said, smiling, 'and little Peter was a star today.'

'He's a Carter, all right. I've got high hopes for that boy. Once he's old enough, I'll put him into the ring.'

'You and your bloody boxing. You'll do no such thing. It'll be up to Tommy and Stacey what he does.'

Frank screwed up his face. 'If it's left up to Tommy, the boy will end up collecting debts.'

'And would that be such a bad thing?' Janet implored. All of her sons, with the exception of young Jonny, worked for Tommy now, and they were all doing well for themselves.

Frank shrugged, not answering. In that instant, Janet's heart went out to her husband. She'd always known how much he'd wanted a boxing champion in the family, and she patted his arm. 'Let's just see what the future brings, eh? Besides, you've got six sons to give you grandchildren.'

She took note of the glare from her husband, and bit down on her lip. She'd forgotten about Jimmy. When Tommy had told them about Jimmy's sexual preference, she'd tried to convince herself that Jimmy just hadn't met the right girl yet. But in her heart she knew it was true. She'd always known, how could she not? Jimmy was her son; she'd birthed him, raised him, she knew him as well as she knew herself.

'Five sons,' she corrected, before changing the subject.

* * *

With the drinks flowing and music blaring from the stereo they had set up in the garden, the party was underway. Stacey smiled as her friends oohed and aahed over both the baby and little Karen, who looked adorable in her new party dress.

'Tommy.'

The alarm in Janet's voice made both Tommy and Stacey snap their heads towards her.

His face drained of all colour, Tommy turned to look at his wife. 'I'll take care of this, okay? Don't let it spoil the day.' Anger began to bubble inside of him. He'd only just managed to win Stacey back, and now Bethany had turned up. If he wasn't careful, she would fuck everything up again and he would be back to square one; what if she blurted out all the gory details of what they had got up to?

'Don't let it spoil the day?' Stacey's voice began to rise as she repeated back Tommy's words, causing a few of the guests to turn their heads to see what the commotion was. 'I'm not having this. Who fucking invited her?' Standing with her hands on her hips she looked around her. 'I said, who fucking invited her?'

Tommy swallowed deeply. He had no idea what was going on. 'I don't know, Stace. Let me go and sort it out.'

Stacey shrugged him away from her, and marched towards

Bethany and a startled Gary, who was standing beside her. 'You dare even look at my husband, and I'll scratch your fucking eyes out.'

Shocked, Tommy tore after his wife with Jimmy following close behind. 'What's she fucking doing here?' Jimmy hissed.

Shrugging, Tommy pulled on Stacey's arm. 'Babe, let me deal with it.'

'No,' Stacey answered, shrugging her husband away from her. 'I'll deal with this.' Her cheeks were flushed as she looked Bethany up and down. As always, her former friend looked stunning and Stacey had to hide the jealousy and insecurity that began to ripple through her; she was still carrying her baby weight and even though Tommy had promised her over and over that it didn't bother him she couldn't help but feel like a frump compared to Bethany. 'Why are you here?' she demanded. 'And I'm warning you now, lady, keep your eyes off my Tommy. You're not wanted here, so go on, fuck off back to wherever you came from.'

Standing with his mouth wide open, Gary looked from Bethany to Stacey. 'Don't talk to her like that.'

Stacey laughed; she could feel the hysteria begin to rise within her. 'Do yourself a favour, Gary. Fuck off and take this whore with you.'

Gently pushing his wife out of the way, Tommy grasped hold of both Bethany's and Gary's arms in a vice-like grip and dragged them through the house. Once outside, he rounded on his brother. 'Why the fuck did you bring her here?'

'Why wouldn't I? This is my girlfriend.' Gary's eyes were wide; he had no idea of what was going on, or why Bethany had caused such a reaction from his brother and sister-in-law.

Feeling smug, Bethany pressed her lips together in an attempt to hide her sly grin. 'Tell him the rest.'

Tommy turned towards Bethany, hatred clearly evident across his face. How he could have even contemplated sleeping with her he had no idea, she was poisonous, and to think he'd risked his marriage for her. 'What?' he demanded of Gary.

Gary kicked a stone from underneath his foot. She's...'

'For fuck's sake, spit it out!' Tommy could feel the anger rise within him. He was scared and panicking, that was the truth of the matter, scared that he'd lose Stacey all over again.

'I'm pregnant! Congratulations, you're going to be an uncle.' And there it was, spread across her face, that wicked grin Tommy had grown to despise.

Stunned, Tommy stared hard at Bethany and then at his brother. 'You're what?'

'I'm having a baby. Gary's baby.'

Tommy shook his head. For the life of him, he couldn't get his head around what they were saying. He clenched his fists, wanting to wipe the smug grin off her face. Instead, he lunged towards Gary. 'Are you that fucking stupid? That you'd knock up this spiteful bitch. Don't you know who she is?' He then turned his attention to Bethany. 'He's only just turned eighteen. Are you sick and twisted in the head?' He stabbed his finger towards his temple to emphasise his point. 'Is that what this is all about? You couldn't have me, so you went for Gary instead?'

Crocodile tears sprang to Bethany's eyes and she looked towards Gary. 'Are you going to let him speak to me like this?'

Gary could only look down at the floor. There was no way he was going to go up against his elder brother. Tommy would wipe the floor with him.

'There's your answer. Now, fuck off away from me and my family.' Grabbing hold of her arm Tommy began to drag her down the street.

Struggling to break free, a terrified Bethany screamed out in fright, 'Ow, you're hurting me.'

Out of earshot, Tommy pulled her to halt. 'Get fucking rid of it. That kid will never be a Carter. Do you hear me? Get rid of it.'

Anger spread across Bethany's face. 'Do you really think I want to keep it? Look at him,' she spat, glaring towards Gary. 'He's fucking weak, and this,' she said, poking her finger into her stomach, 'will end up just like him.'

His expression one of pure disgust, Tommy snarled, 'And God forbid it turns out like you. Get rid of it and stay away from me and my family.'

'What have you told her about all of us?' Tommy's hand was grasped tightly around his younger brother's throat. His free hand was curled into a fist, ready and waiting to smash into Gary's face.

'Nothing.' Clearly terrified, Gary blinked rapidly as he cowered from his brother. 'I ain't said nothing.'

'You're fucking lying.' Tommy's anger was so strong, he could practically taste it. 'Just one word from her, and we're finished. How much have you told her? Does she know about the robbery?'

Gary began to stutter. The truth was, Bethany knew everything there was to know about them all.

'Stop muttering and fucking stuttering, answer the fucking question. I'm warning you, don't play fucking games with me. What does she know?'

Stepping in, Jimmy grasped Tommy's shoulder. They would get nowhere like this. 'Gaz, we can't sort this out unless you tell us what she knows.' His voice was strong, but not as irate as Tommy's. And just like Tommy, he knew exactly what the implications meant for them if Gary had told her about the robbery.

'I...'

Tommy had had enough and he drove his fist into Gary's stomach. As his brother dropped to the floor, he kicked out towards his head. 'I know you've fucking told her.'

'Enough, Tommy. Not here, not in front of everyone, today of all days.' Jimmy's voice was low as he glanced sideways at the guests who'd begun to congregate outside the house.

Looking up, Tommy wiped his hand over his face. He had to calm down, he knew that. Now wasn't the time to lay into Gary. 'Show's over,' he stated, as he began to usher the guests back inside the house. 'And as for you,' he said, stabbing his finger towards Gary. 'I'll deal with you later.'

Gary swallowed deeply. To say he was scared was an understatement. He staggered to his feet, his hand clutching at his aching stomach. He wished he'd never opened his mouth now. He knew for a fact Tommy hadn't even started with him yet.

* * *

Tommy pulled Stacey into his arms, the colour returning to his cheeks. 'Fucking hell, Stace, you're a Carter all right. I thought you were going to swing for her.'

Stacey's expression was stony as she looked up at her husband. 'I may be a Carter now, but don't you forget I was a Williams first, and I ain't taking no shit from anyone, Tommy.'

Tommy nodded. He didn't answer her, he didn't need to. She'd made her point, one he wouldn't forget in a hurry.

* * *

Just as she always had in the past, Bethany ran straight to her father. Wrapped up in a duvet, she lay on the sofa with her legs tucked underneath her. Feeling sorry for herself, she sobbed her heart out. It was more the fact that she knew Tommy Carter would never be hers that was making her so upset, not the fact that she had a tiny life growing inside of her, who was unwanted by both its mother's and father's family.

'You're keeping it.' Raised as a catholic, Dean Johnson's word was final. He looked over at his daughter and felt nothing but anger. How could she be so careless and become pregnant by a Carter? For the life of him, he couldn't understand. 'The child will be a Johnson, and that's it. No arguments.' There was absolutely no way he would ever accept a grandchild with the Carter surname into the family.

Bethany looked up at her father and gasped. 'But Daddy, I don't want to keep it.'

'Then you should have kept your fucking legs closed.' He took a step towards her, the anger he felt evident across his face. 'Everything you've ever wanted, I gave you, and you repay me like this?'

Bethany sobbed even harder. 'Please don't make me have it, Daddy. I don't want a baby,' she begged him.

'You're fucking having it!' Dean roared. He looked around him at the vast room his late wife, Bethany's mother, had decorated to the highest of standards. The pristine glass cabinets, which held the crystal glassware, glistened in the afternoon sun. The crystals reflected off the walls, creating light shadows, the purity mocking him. He now knew for a fact he had raised a whore. In that instant, he threw open the cabinets, and with one arm he swiped the contents to the floor. Picking up the unbroken pieces, he hurled them through the air towards the glass patio doors.

The sound of smashing glass caused Bethany to dive underneath the duvet for protection. Her body shook as she cried in fear. Never had her father been so angry with her.

Yanking off the duvet, Dean pulled Bethany to her feet and dragged her towards the mirror above the fireplace, and with his hand grasped around her chin, he forced her to look at her reflection. 'Look at yourself. You're nothing but a whore.'

In horror, Bethany closed her eyes tightly. She could barely breathe, the terror she felt was so strong.

'A fucking whore is what I've raised.' Dean threw his daughter away from him and felt nothing as she collapsed in a heap on the floor at his feet. He crouched down beside her. 'Get upstairs and pack a bag of clothes. We go to Spain tonight, where I can keep you under lock and key in the villa until that baby is born.'

Gingerly, Bethany staggered to her feet. Silently, she walked from the room, oblivious to the shards of glass which sliced into her bare feet.

Placing his hands on either side of the mantelpiece, Dean bowed his head. He would give anything for his wife, Maggie, to be here now. She would have known exactly how to handle the situation. He looked up at his own reflection and shook his head sadly. Of all the men in the world, it had to be a fucking Carter, he thought to himself bitterly.

'She's not even fucking keeping it. Are you that much of an idiot that you really believe someone like her could love anything other than herself?' In frustration, Tommy kicked the door of the scrap yard office closed. For the life of him, he couldn't get his head around how stupid and naive his brother could be. He was meant to be a Carter, not some dim-witted fool.

Tears sprang to Gary's eyes. Bethany wouldn't get rid of their baby, he knew she wouldn't. Tommy didn't know her like he did.

'Are you even listening to me?' Tommy took a menacing step closer. 'She told me herself she's getting rid of it.'

'You're lying.' Gary glared at his brother.

'I'm warning you, Gaz. Look at me once more like that, and I'll bite your fucking nose off.'

'Why are you doing this to me?' Gary cried, swiping the tears away from his cheeks. 'Ain't it enough that you've driven her away?'

Tommy threw up his arms and looked across to Jimmy. 'Talk to him, will you? Knock some sense into that thick skull of his, before I end up losing my rag with him again.'

'Gaz.' Jimmy shook his head. Already, bruising was beginning to form across their younger brother's cheeks, after he'd had to pull Tommy off him just moments earlier. 'She ain't keeping it, so stop trying to protect her. Now, tell us exactly what you've told her about all of us. Does she know about the bank job?'

Gary gulped down the lump in his throat. He watched through narrowed eyes as Tommy paced the floor of the office and felt nothing but hatred towards him. 'She knows everything. Are you happy now? And I hope she does go to the Old Bill. It's what you deserve for what you've done to me. You've ruined my life.'

Springing forward, Tommy knocked over the chairs, in his haste to get to his younger brother. Slamming himself heavily into Gary's body, they both tumbled to the floor, bringing the desk and stacks of paperwork down on top of them.

Punch after punch, Tommy pummelled his fists into Gary, despite Jimmy's best efforts to pull him off.

'Stop! Enough!' Jimmy roared as he slung his arms around Tommy's waist in a final attempt to pull him away. 'He's had enough.'

Falling across Jimmy, Tommy kicked out at Gary one last time for good measure. He blew out his cheeks. The exertion had caused his heart to beat wildly in his chest. His dark hair was wet with sweat and plastered to his forehead as he fell onto his side and pushed himself into a sitting position, whilst Jimmy scrambled up from underneath him.

'Fucking hell, Tommy, what have you done?' Jimmy's eyes were wide as he looked over his shoulder at his brother.

Tommy remained silent. He sat with his head bowed, waiting for his heart to once again reach a steady rhythm.

'Tommy.' Jimmy's heart was in his mouth. 'What have you done to him?'

Looking up, Tommy looked from Jimmy to his younger brother's broken body. Finally, he forced himself to speak. 'Is he...?' He left the sentence unsaid.

Crouching down, Jimmy pressed his fingers to Gary's neck, checking for a pulse.

'Well?' Tommy's voice began to rise; what was taking Jimmy so long? How hard could it be to tell if someone was breathing? He crawled across the strewn paperwork, stopping just inches away from Gary's lifeless body. 'Is he alive?'

'I don't know!' Panic swept within Jimmy as he tried to shake Gary awake. 'I can't fucking tell. Do something! You have a look. Is he breathing?'

Tommy pushed Jimmy aside. He brought his ear to Gary's face. Breathe, he silently begged of his brother. As much as he was angry with Gary, he hadn't meant to kill him. He pushed his ear down even farther, and almost cried with relief when he could feel Gary's laboured breath against his cheek. 'He's alive.'

'Will he be all right?' Jimmy let out a shaky breath.

'Do I look like a fucking doctor? How would I know? Pass me a phone.'

Digging his hand into his trouser pocket, Jimmy passed across his mobile phone.

Tommy tapped in a number, brought the phone to his ear and

waited for it to be answered. 'Mad Dog,' he said into the mouth
piece. 'We've got a problem. I need your help.'

* * *

Mad Dog Harris took one look at Gary and shook his head. 'Fuck
me, lad, what have you done to him?'

Tommy looked down at the floor as shame flooded through
him. 'It just got out of hand.'

'Out of hand?' Mad Dog remarked. 'This is a bit more than out
of hand, Tommy lad. You've battered him to within an inch of his
life.'

'Can you sort him out? Take him to yours for a bit, even if it's
just for a few weeks? I can't let me mum see him like this. Here, take
this and get him something from the chemist shop. Buy him whatever he needs.' Tommy thrust a handful of crisp ten-pound notes
into the older man's hand.

'Fuck me, Tommy. He needs a bit more than a bottle of paracetamol. He needs to go to the hospital, lad.' Mad Dog stood
thinking for a few moments. 'How about I drop him off at the
nearest accident and emergency department and let them deal with
him? I could say I found him on the roadside?'

Rubbing at his temples, Tommy leant back against the wooden
desk. His shoulders drooped as despair flooded through him. Gary
was his own brother and he'd tried to decimate him. Even when
he'd been boxing he'd never attacked anyone with the same brute
force, he'd always been in control, had always known exactly what
he was doing, but this was different, it was as though a red mist had
descended over him. He felt sickened to the core and was thoroughly ashamed of himself. He was like an animal; he was out of
control. 'We can't do that. They'll phone the Old Bill. Please mate,
take him to yours and sort him out for me.'

'How do you expect me to sort this out? I'm not a miracle worker. What the fuck am I supposed to do with him?' As he peered down at Gary, Mad Dog's voice began to rise. 'Is he even breathing?'

'He groaned just before you got here,' Jimmy answered, looking down at his brother. 'But that's about it. He hasn't moved or opened his eyes at all.'

Against his better judgement, Mad Dog nodded. 'I'm warning you now though, Tommy. This'll be on your head if it all goes wrong. I don't want you coming down on me like a ton of bricks; don't say that I didn't warn you that he needs medical help.'

'I know and I won't. This is my call.'

'Come on then, lads, give me a hand getting him up.'

With difficulty, the three men hauled Gary up from the floor. Still unconscious, Gary's head fell onto his chest. He was a dead weight and as they moved forward, Gary's feet dragged behind him. 'This ain't gonna work,' Tommy stated, out of breath. 'Jimmy, you'll have to get his feet. I'll take the top half.'

Finally, they managed to negotiate their way out of the office, side stepping the broken chair and strewn contents of the desk. 'I'm telling you, Tommy, if he croaks it, we're done for.'

'Don't you think I already know that?' Tommy hissed, once they had managed to push and pull Gary into the car. 'Jimmy, you'll have to go with Mad Dog and help get him out. I'll stay here. We need to make things look normal, otherwise Mum and Stace will get suspicious if all three of us go on the missing list.' Both men agreed. 'Don't forget to let me know what happens, no matter how bad it is.'

Tommy gave his brother one final glance, before banging his fist on the car roof, indicating for Mad Dog to drive away. With just his thoughts for company Tommy stood in the middle of the scrap yard alone. Jimmy had told him months ago that something wasn't right with Gary. He should have taken heed of the warning, he realised that now. He looked up at the night sky and felt like crying. What a fucking mess everything was, and there was just one person at the centre of it all: Bethany fucking Johnson.

Wandering back inside the office, he looked around him at the chaos he'd created and had to resist the urge to not finish what he'd started, and smash the entire office to smithereens. Instead, he took deep breaths, sat down on the floor, and held his head in his hands. He was scared all right, scared that Gary wouldn't wake up, scared he'd have to tell their mum Gary was dead, scared Stacey would leave him all over again. His eyes began to glisten with tears, and he let them fall freely onto his cheeks. With his head bent, he sat for hours contemplating how he could get out of the situation he was in, only to realise there was no solution. His only saving grace would be for Gary to not only wake up, but to wake up with no permanent damage. It was a scary thought.

* * *

As the plane began to climb in the night sky, Bethany Johnson looked across at her father. He hadn't said a single word to her for hours. His lips were set in a tight line, his expression hard.

She had never been scared of her daddy before. She had never seen him for the hard man that he was. He had only ever been gentle with her. She swallowed deeply, before turning her head and looking out the window at the tiny lights from streetlamps, houses and cars below. She wanted to cry but couldn't. All she felt was numbness. It was the shock of seeing her father's rage, it had to be, she told herself.

Instinctively, Bethany knew that nothing would ever be the same between them again. The fact that she had a Carter growing inside her was enough to tell her that. Her father would always remember what she was: a whore.

Her thoughts went to her unborn child. She didn't want it; she would never want it. The hatred she felt for her own flesh and blood was so strong, she could feel it ooze out of her pores. She blamed the child for Tommy's own hatred of her. If only the child didn't exist, if only it hadn't been conceived, she may still have been able to win him over. In fact, she knew she would have been able to. Even after all this time, Bethany was still in denial. Her obsession with Tommy Carter was all consuming. It ate away at her like a cancer. She was nothing without him; she was an empty shell that only he could fill.

With his mobile phone clutched in his hand, Tommy chewed nervously on his thumb nail. For all intents and purposes, he looked outwardly calm. His mind, however, was in turmoil. Every few minutes, he glanced down at the phone, waiting with bated breath for news on his brother's condition. How he managed to smile and hold a conversation with his wife and family, he had no idea.

Leaping up from his position on the sofa, Tommy raced out of the house and made his way towards the end of the back garden. Nervously he glanced back towards the house. In the kitchen his mum was busying herself making a pot of tea, and he turned his back to her, hoping and praying the call was about to bring him good news. His heart beat wildly in his chest, as he looked down to see Jimmy's name flashing up on the mobile screen.

'Jimmy,' he said, answering the call. He could feel a tightening at the back of his throat as he began to pace backwards and forwards. 'How is he?' he asked, his breath coming in short, sharp bursts. As Jimmy spoke, Tommy sank to his knees and clawed at a handful of grass. The evening dew left his hand and his jeans wet, but he didn't care. All he felt was a sense of relief flood through him. Gary was awake and had spoken; there was no brain damage. Gary was going to make it. He looked up at the sky. He'd never been a religious man, but he thanked everyone he could think of for making everything turn out okay.

18

The Ilford Palais, in Ilford, Essex, was where the twins, Sonny and Mitchel, were hosting their eighteenth birthday.

After paying their five-pound admittance fee, with a confident air, all five of the elder Carter brothers strolled into the venue. They were good-looking men and dressed impeccably. The fact that they had money, and a lot of money at that, oozed out of them. They attracted admiring glances from the flocks of women who were standing around in groups, waiting to catch the eye of a man, in the hopes of getting their drinks paid for. And if they were really lucky, a quick cop off or a shag around the back of the club, would be the highlight of their night.

The brothers made their way towards the bar. The dated, patterned carpet was sticky underneath their feet. Taking out his wallet, Tommy waited in line to be served. 'This place is a fucking shit hole,' he stated, looking around him at the grimy club. 'Didn't I say we should have gone to The Soho Club instead? Look at them.' He nodded towards the revellers on the dance floor. 'They've shovelled that many pills down their neck, most of 'em are out of their fucking nut.'

Jimmy shrugged. 'It's where the twins wanted to go, bruv. Who are we to argue with that?'

Tommy screwed up his face. 'Fuck me! Even the khazis in my club are better than this dump. Oi.' Never one to have much patience, he shouted over to the barman, 'We're still waiting to get fucking served over here.'

Aiden Coleman made his way down the bar. 'What can I get you?' he shouted above the music, turning his ear towards Tommy so he could hear him better.

Nudging Jimmy in his side, Tommy forced his brother to turn and face him. 'What does everyone want?'

'Five bottles of Bud.' The words caught in Jimmy's throat. He recognised the barman immediately and turned back to the dance floor to compose himself.

Tommy passed across a twenty-pound note and handed the bottles out to his brothers. 'Here.' He nudged Jimmy again. Even in the dimly lit club, he could see that Jimmy's cheeks were flushed. He eyed his brother suspiciously. 'What's up with you?'

'Nothing.'

Tommy held his hand out for his change. His eyes missed nothing and he noted the barman's eyes flick towards Jimmy. 'Do you know him?' he asked his brother, jerking his head in Aiden's direction.

'Nah.' Sipping at his beer Jimmy shook his head. He knew him all right. It was the very same barman who'd worked in The White Horse when he and Gary had gone to collect a debt from Ted Marsden.

Shrugging, Tommy gulped down his beer. The club was heaving with punters and the dance floor vibrated underneath their feet from the heavy base of the music system.

Thirty minutes later, Tommy was back at the bar. As he waited in line, he watched as a man he assumed was the manager, flanked with a heavy at his side, emptied out the cash from the tills. He chewed on the inside of his cheek as he stood watching their every move. 'Jimmy,' he called out with a jerk of his head, indicating for his brother to join him.

Pushing his way through the crowd of revellers on the dance floor, Jimmy lifted his eyebrows. 'What's up?'

'Look,' Tommy said, nodding his head towards the manager. 'This place must rake in a fortune.'

Jimmy looked around him. 'You'd think they'd spruce the place up a bit then, wouldn't you? Look at the fucking carpet. I'm sure Nan and Grandad had the same one, and that was back in the seventies.'

Tommy rolled his eyes. 'Forget the fucking carpet, look,' he stated, nodding his head towards the manager again. He kept his voice low. 'That's the third till they've emptied and there's another bar upstairs.'

'Yeah, and?'

Tommy grinned and glanced around him before answering. 'There's a lot of dough in this place, and trust me, bruv, it's ours for the taking.'

Jimmy began to laugh. 'Does your brain never switch off?'

'Nope.' Tommy winked. He went back to watching the manager and the heavy, the idea of the next robbery now planted firmly in his mind.

* * *

Despite taking the contraceptive pill, Stacey had fallen pregnant for a third time. Clasping the pregnancy test in her hand Stacey had turned towards her husband. 'This is it now, Tommy, no more kids. There's only one thing for it. You'll have to have a vasectomy.'

Jerking his head towards her, Tommy's eyes had been wide. 'Like fuck I am.'

Stacey burst out laughing. She'd already known exactly what his answer would be. 'It's all right for you, you don't have to give birth. But seriously, Tommy, we'll have to think of something. Three is definitely enough for us.'

As much as the third pregnancy was a welcome surprise, she was right. Three kids were more than enough for them. 'We'll sort it out, Stace. Don't worry, babe.'

With two kids under the age of three and another one on the way Stacey sighed as she pushed yet another load of dirty clothes into the washing machine.

Leaning against the door frame, Stacey watched as Karen and Peter played in the back garden. As usual, Karen took charge of their games, while little Peter tottered on behind her. 'Play nicely,' she called out to them.

They were now living in their own home. As Tommy had promised, he'd bought her the house she'd wanted, the one which had been up for sale just two doors down from her mum and dad's.

She heard him now, padding down the stairs, and glanced at her watch. 'So, you've finally risen then? You do know it's nearly lunchtime!'

Tommy groaned and brought his hand up to his head. 'Don't start, Stace, I've got a headache.'

'Hangover, more like, you mean.' There was a hint of humour in Stacey's voice. 'The bleeding racket you made coming in last night, I'm surprised you didn't wake the kids up.'

'Where are they?' Taking a seat at the kitchen table he held his head in his hands. 'Have we got any painkillers?'

Shaking her head at her husband's antics, Stacey walked across the kitchen and took a bottle of paracetamol from the cupboard. 'They're playing in the garden.' She handed over two tablets and a glass of water. 'As usual, your daughter is bossing Peter around.'

Swallowing down the tablets, Tommy grinned. 'She takes after her mother.'

'Oi!' Playfully, Stacey slapped her husband around the back of the head. 'Less of your cheek, Tommy Carter. I was thinking we could go over to your mum and dad's tonight, treat them to a take-away, what do you reckon?'

Tommy shook his head. 'I can't tonight. I need to work.' He noted the glance Stacey gave him and explained himself further. 'I've got a meeting tonight, but if it ends early, then we'll go over to me mum and dad's, okay?'

Stacey raised her eyebrows. 'Are you even going to be in a fit state to go to work?'

Tommy nodded. There was nothing like planning a robbery to cure his hangover.

* * *

'No.' Mad Dog held up his hands, cutting Tommy off. 'No way, Tommy. Not there. Not the Ilford Palais, lad.'

Throwing up his arms, Tommy leant back in his seat. 'Why the fuck not?' He glanced across to his brothers as they stood leaning against the walls of the scrap yard office. The place is heaving with customers. They're raking it in. We were there last night, tell him Jimmy.'

Jimmy nodded. 'He's right, the place is heaving.'

Mad Dog sat forward in his seat. 'Freddie Smith runs the doors there, and that's aggro we don't need.'

'Fuck Freddie Smith.' Tommy spat. 'That cunt tried to tuck me up and you know he did, and I ain't gonna forget something like that in a hurry.'

Exasperated, Mad Dog blew out his cheeks. 'Are you trying to start a fucking war? Because that's exactly what'll happen. I'm telling you now, lad, if you follow this through, Smith won't let it lie. He'll hunt you fucking down, and then what are you gonna fucking do, eh? There's what, five of you, six if you include me? How the fuck are you going to go up against him and his firm?'

'Let him.'

'What?' Mad Dog's eyes widened. 'What the fuck is that supposed to mean, let him?'

Tommy sat forwards in his seat. Exactly what I said, let him try and find out who robbed the club. Why would he even think it's anything to do with us?' He looked around at his brothers. 'We're not the only ones out there capable of robbing a venue, are we? So, why would our names even come in to the equation.'

'Tommy lad, you're not listening to me. If you do this, then Smith will not rest until he's found whoever it is responsible, and believe me, this will be one war you won't win.'

'And like I said, let him fucking try. We're doing it.' Tommy's mind was already made up, and nothing Mad Dog said to him was going to change that fact.

* * *

With the meeting over, Tommy dismissed his brothers. As they filed out of the office, he held out his hand towards Jimmy. 'Hold on, bruv, I want a word in private.'

Jimmy took a seat. He kicked out his legs in front of him as he waited for his elder brother to close the office door. 'What's up?'

Tommy paused. 'I may be out of line here, but I know you knew that barman last night, the Irish one.'

'Nah, I didn't.'

Tommy raised his eyebrows. 'C'mon, bruv, it's me you're talking to. Do you know him or not?'

Jimmy sighed. 'I've met him once before, when me and Gary went to The White Horse to collect a debt.' He paused.

'What?'

'Nothing.' He could hardly tell Tommy that he'd been attracted to the Irishman.

'No, c'mon, what is it?'

'He was working there behind the bar. It was just something Gary said about him being, you know, gay.' Jimmy looked to the floor. 'That's it.'

'Right.' Tommy was thoughtful. 'If he works at the club, then obviously he is gonna have inside knowledge. I need you to go and see him and find out the score. I don't care how you do it, but you need to make him talk.'

'Leave it out Tommy. No fucking way! I'm not doing that.' Jimmy shook his head.

'Come on, Jimmy. We need to know when they take the cash to the bank. For all we know, they could keep up to a week's worth of takings in there.'

Jimmy shook his head. 'Why me? Why can't one of the others do it?'

'Because he fucking knows you, that's why.' Tommy smiled, taking the edge off his words, and placed his hands on Jimmy's shoulders. 'C'mon, bruv. I need you to do this for me, please. There isn't anyone else I can ask, is there?'

Reluctantly, Jimmy nodded. 'Okay, I'll do it.'

'Good.' Tommy made his way across the office.

Remaining seated, Jimmy looked towards the door, where his younger brothers and Mad Dog had exited just moments earlier. Tommy's plan for the Ilford Palais was troubling him. 'Listen

Tommy, are you sure this is such a good idea? What Mad Dog said about Freddie Smith... how are we gonna take on a firm if they come after us?' He held up his hand before his brother could answer him. 'I know what you're gonna say, and yeah, thanks to our old man, we can fight, but that's about it, Tommy. We ain't gonna win if we have to go up against him, are we? You're not thinking logically. There's only five of us, and Smith has got a lot of muscle behind him.'

With his back to his brother, Tommy stared out of the office window towards the scrap yard. 'Then we make sure we stay one step ahead of him.' He turned around. 'We box clever,' he said with a grin. 'That's one thing we do know how to do. Trust me, we can do this, Jimmy.'

Jimmy sighed. 'I hope you know what you're doing, bruv.'

'Of course I fucking do,' Tommy replied.

* * *

Aiden Coleman smiled as he made his way down the bar. He'd recognised Jimmy the moment he'd laid eyes on him the previous weekend. 'What can I get you?'

Jimmy looked across the bar. He took in the various bottles of alcohol against the far wall, before nodding his head towards the fridge holding the bottled beers. 'I'll have a Bud.' He paid for his beer, then smiled. 'It's quiet in here tonight.'

'It's still early.' Aiden raised his eyebrows. 'We've met before, haven't we? You came into The White Horse when I was working there. You had a problem with the guvnor. He owed you money or something like that.'

'Yeah.' Jimmy nodded. He could feel his cheeks blush; he was out of his depth, that was the problem, and wanted to curse Tommy for making him come here tonight.

'I remember.'

Jimmy smiled. He didn't know what to say in return and gulped at his beer to hide his nerves.

'So, are you on your own tonight?'

'My brother is meeting me here later.' It was a blatant lie. Tommy had taken Stacey out for the evening.

There was a twinkle in Aiden's eyes. 'So, they were your brothers with you last week?'

Jimmy bit down on his lip before answering. The action couldn't have been more seductive in Aiden's eyes. 'Yeah.' He moved away slightly from the bar. 'I'll see you later.' He gave a wink and walked away. He'd done his part and made contact with the Irishman. He'd got the man's attention, he knew that with a certainty. He placed the bottle, still half full, on a table and left the club.

Freddie Smith was the Top Dog of the East End. He took a sip of his brandy, his narrowed eyes watching everything around him over the rim of the glass.

Snapping his fingers at the younger man who stood behind him, he waited for him to bend forwards, so that he could speak privately in his ear.

After listening intently to what the older man had to say, Danny McKay straightened up. He strode purposefully towards a group of men across the bar. Without warning, he pulled back his fist and knocked one of them to the floor. 'You were fucking barred last week, now piss off.' He shook out the tension in his hand as he watched the man scramble to his feet and dart out of the bar, before walking back towards the table where his boss was sitting.

Freddie Smith gave a small nod of his head, satisfied. He allowed no one to get one over on him, and it was this fact that had kept him at the top of his game for so many years. He leant forward in his seat. A snarl spread across his face and he crooked his finger towards Danny for a second time. 'Keep an eye on that cocky little bastard.' Freddie nodded towards a man and woman who had just walked through the door.

Looking up, Danny took note of Tommy and Stacey as they entered the bar. 'Do you want me to have a quiet word with him?'

Freddie shook his head. 'No, just watch the cocky little cunt and make sure he doesn't start getting lairy. I don't trust him. He's a jumped up prick.'

Danny shrugged. He had no problems with Tommy and had, in fact, been dealing with him behind Freddie's back for quite some time.

* * *

Tommy smiled as he ordered his and Stacey's drinks. The fact that Freddie Smith was sitting just across the bar meant nothing to him. He'd already known that Freddie would be here. He glanced across at the older man and held his pint glass aloft in the air. 'Drink, Freddie?' he called out.

He grinned as Freddie nodded. 'A round of drinks for that lot over there,' he instructed the barman.

Tommy continued sipping at his beer. 'Just give me two minutes, Stace. I need to go and have a quick word with a business acquaintance.' He nodded towards Freddie.

'Don't be bleeding long. I'm gonna look like a right lemon sitting here on my own,' she answered, planting a kiss on her husband's cheek.

'Two minutes, I promise.' He placed his glass down on the bar and made his way through the crowd towards the older man. 'Freddie, Danny.' He smiled in a greeting. 'How's tricks?'

'Tommy.' Freddie nodded. 'This is not your usual manor, is it?'

He looked around him, emphasising his point. 'I thought you only crawled around on that shit hole of an estate that you call home?'

Tommy laughed. 'Yeah, well I thought it'd be nice to show the missus how the other half lives for once, and I must say Freddie, it doesn't live up to expectations. Still stinks of the same old shit, present company the exception of course.'

Danny raised his eyebrows, silently warning Tommy to back off.

Tommy took heed of the warning and smiled to take the edge off his words. 'You never know. I might even become a regular here.' He looked around him at the upmarket bar. In actual fact, the bar wasn't his cup of tea. It was too poncy, and full of city blokes wearing suits.

'What the fuck do you want, Carter?' Freddie snarled, his patience wearing thin. 'Is there an actual purpose to you being here, other than trying to wind me the fuck up?'

Tommy shook his head. 'Just a friendly hello, mate, that's all.'

'Well, you've said hello, now you can fuck off.'

Tommy laughed and held his hands up in surrender. 'I'm going.' He began to walk away.

'That's right, fuck off. You might be the kingpin on that estate of yours, but out here in the real world, you're fuck all.'

Tommy stopped dead in his tracks. He could feel his temper begin to rise. The smile slipped from his face and was quickly replaced with an expression of contempt. He bit back a retort, closed his eyes, and counted to three, before moving forward a few paces. Only when he'd composed himself, did he continue to walk towards his wife. Once he'd reached the bar, he gulped down his beer and glared towards Freddie. The exchange with the old bastard had made him even more determined than he already was to rob the club.

* * *

Mad Dog Harris was concerned. He lay on the bed staring up at the ceiling. Beside him, lay Lillian Chambers. Throwing the duvet away from him, he sat on the edge of the bed.

'What's wrong?' Lillian turned onto her side to face him and reached out to touch his back, her fingertips caressing the smoothness of his skin. 'You know you can tell me anything.'

Mad Dog glanced over his shoulder and sighed. 'I'll give you three guesses.'

Lillian gave a small smile. 'Tommy?'

'Aye hen, got it in one.' He stood up and pushed his hand through his hair. 'He's getting in over his head and won't take heed of mine or anyone else's warnings.'

Lillian was thoughtful. She was fond of Tommy; he'd only ever been kind to her. 'Maybe he needs to figure it out by himself. Let him make his own mistakes. It's the only way he'll learn.'

Mad Dog nodded. That was exactly what he was afraid of. Young Tommy would learn all right. Freddie Smith could very well end up ordering his heavies to kill him. He'd need to have another word with the boy, he decided. He owed that to Davey at least.

'Are you not content with having the Old Bill two steps behind you, you want Freddie Smith on your back as well?'

Tommy rolled his eyes. For over an hour, Mad Dog had been trying to convince him to change his mind about the robbery. 'Freddie Smith can go fuck himself.'

Following Tommy through the betting shop, Mad Dog threw up his arms. 'Tell me, Tommy, is this about honouring Davey, or is this about you getting one over on Smith? Because from where I'm standing, it looks like all you want to do is get one over on Freddie Smith.'

Anger flashed across Tommy's face. 'What do you fucking take me for? Of course it's to honour Davey, that's the only reason we do this.'

'Look lad, forget about this job. You know Smith is going to hunt you down. Have you even got any idea of what he does to people who annoy him, let alone rob from him?'

'No.' Tommy shrugged, unconcerned. He picked up a stack of paperwork and flicked through it. 'Look, I know what I'm doing. This isn't the first job I've done, is it?' he said, turning to face Mad Dog. 'You know me. I'll plan it all out, I always do, so what's the problem?'

'The problem, lad, is Smith will end up killing you over this and I don't want your death on my conscience.'

Tommy grinned. 'Maybe that's the key to it all.' He tapped the side of his nose. 'Freddie Smith isn't the one who does the actual killing, is he?'

Mad Dog was confused. 'And how exactly is that going to help you?'

'Like I keep on saying, let me deal with this. I know what I'm doing.' Patting Mad Dog on the shoulder, Tommy walked away from him.

As Tommy made his way out of the shop, Mad Dog sank into the nearest chair and wiped his hand across the stubble covering his jaw. He'd done all he could. There was nothing else he could say. There was no getting through to the lad.

* * *

Danny McKay took a sip of his brandy. 'So, what can I do for you, Tommy? Same as usual, is it?'

Tommy looked around him before answering. Despite choosing a quiet corner in the Becton Arms public house, there were one too many customers around for his liking. He waited for a couple to pass by their table, then sat forward in his seat. 'No, I'm after sawn-offs this time.'

Danny's eyes widened. 'You want a sawn-off shotgun?'

Tommy shook his head, annoyed. 'Fuck me is there an echo in here? Yes, I want a sawn-off.' He paused. 'In fact, I want five.'

Immediately suspicious, Danny silently studied Tommy. What was the little fucker up to this time? He knew one thing for sure. Whatever it was Tommy Carter was involved in, he obviously meant business. The fact that he was taking sawn-off shotguns with him, was more than enough to prove that point. 'You're going up in the world a bit, aren't you? What are you planning this time?'

'What's with all the fucking questions?' Tommy's voice began to rise, and he looked around him, checking that no one else was within earshot.

Danny held up his hands. 'I'm just concerned, mate, and to be honest, I'm more than a bit surprised. This is not what you usually buy from me, so obviously this must be a big job you're planning on doing.'

Tommy shrugged. Danny would find out soon enough what the job entailed. 'Let's just say, this job comes with more risk than usual.'

Danny raised his eyebrows.

Tommy took note of the questioning look Danny gave him, and he sank back in his seat. He was getting sick and tired of having to explain himself. 'I know what I'm doing, so spare me the concern. Can you get me them or not? Or do I need to take my business elsewhere?'

Danny exhaled heavily. 'Yeah, I can get what you need.'

'Good.' It was exactly what Tommy had expected him to say, and he gave a satisfied smile. His plan was falling into place nicely.

* * *

'Right, so that's the guns taken care of.' Tommy looked around at his brothers as they lined the walls of the scrap yard office, and his eyes settled on Jimmy. 'How's it going with the barman?'

A snigger came from where his younger brothers were standing and snapping his head around Tommy glared at the culprit. 'You got something to say, Mitch?'

The smile quickly slipped from Mitchel's face and he pressed his lips together, his cheeks flushing pink.

'Well?' Tommy stood up and pointed his finger towards his brothers, the authority in his voice stopping them dead in their tracks. 'If any of you have something to say, then you'd best say it now. So, come on Mitchel, what's so fucking funny?'

'Nothing.' Looking down at the floor Mitchel averted his gaze.

For a few moments Tommy glared at his younger brother. 'So,' he said, tearing his attention away from Mitchel and back to Jimmy. 'Have you found anything out?'

Jimmy glanced nervously at his brothers before speaking. 'From what I can gather, they're a bit erratic. Sometimes they'll cash the takings on a Monday morning, other times it's been as late as on a Thursday afternoon.'

Tommy was thoughtful. 'So, I was right. They keep up to a weeks' worth of takings in there, if not more.'

'It looks that way.' Jimmy nodded.

'Okay, well, see what else you can find out. And the rest of you, back to work.' As his brothers filed out of the office, Tommy put out his arm, bringing Gary to a halt. 'You all right, Gaz? What are your thoughts on us doing this job? You've not really said too much about it.'

'What do you want me to say?' Gary barked.

Tommy was taken aback. Even after all these months there was still conflict between them. 'I don't know, I just wanted your thoughts on it, I suppose?'

Gary gave a bitter laugh. 'And when have you ever valued any of our opinions? If it's not done your way, you don't want to know.' He took a step closer to his brother and looked him in the eyes. 'You've already made your mind up about this job, and that's it as far as you're concerned. All we are to you are your puppets: do this, do that. You control everything we do. Look at Jimmy, he didn't even want to get involved with that barman, but you made him.'

Tommy's eyes widened. 'Is that what you think? Is that what you all think about me?'

Gary stared at his brother. 'Work it out for yourself, Tommy. You're a fucking joke, mate, a complete and utter fucking joke, and the only reason they all follow you around, is because they're too scared not to.'

Open-mouthed, Tommy watched as his brother walked out of the office and turned towards Jimmy. 'Leave him, let him go.' He held his hand out, stopping Jimmy from charging after their younger brother. In a way, Gary was right. It was his way or no way, it always had been. But, in his defence, someone had to take charge, someone had to do the thinking, someone had to be the one to keep them all from ending up behind bars, and that person happened to be him. 'He'll come around,' he said quietly, speaking to no one in particular. He'd been saying the same thing for months, and still they were no nearer to ironing out their differences. 'He'll come around, he just needs a bit more time,' he said, turning to face Jimmy, forcing his voice to sound a lot more confident than he actually felt.

Jimmy gave a small smile. They both knew that was never going to happen. Bethany had well and truly got her claws into their little brother, and in the process, had completely and utterly fucked up his head.

Gary climbed into his car, the grey leather cool against his back. It had been a bribe from Tommy to keep his mouth shut about the beating, and as much as he'd wanted to tell his brother to stick the car up his arse, he wasn't going to turn down a free motor. His eyes flashed menacingly; the hatred he felt for his eldest brother was still as strong as it had been the day he'd driven Bethany away from him. He would have been a father by now. Sometimes, he imagined his and Bethany's child. Would it have been a boy or a girl? He shook his head sadly. He would never know the answer.

All thanks to Tommy, there was no child. It wouldn't surprise him if he'd been the one who'd forced Bethany to get rid of their baby. He wouldn't put anything past his brother.

He started the ignition and skidded out of the scrap yard. Fuck Tommy, fuck Jimmy, fuck all of them.

* * *

Sipping on a glass of iced water, Bethany lay back on a sun lounger. She placed the glass down beside her and closed her eyes. More than anything else, she wanted to drown out her son's screams. 'Will you just shut up?' she hissed.

Six-month-old Cameron looked up at his mother, his brown eyes wide, his arms outstretched.

Sick of the sight of her own child, Bethany sighed. He was such a needy baby, always wanting her attention, always wanting to cuddle her, always crying. She snarled at him. The hatred she felt for her own flesh and blood clearly evident across her face. She couldn't bear to touch him; he made her skin crawl. If he'd looked like Tommy, she may have been able to feel something for him. She may have even been able to love him, but instead, he looked like her father, even down to his hazel eyes and light brown hair. There was absolutely nothing of Tommy in him.

'Hey, what's all this?' Dean scooped his grandson into his arms.

Bethany pushed herself into a sitting position. 'He's just woken up,' she stated. 'You know how grumpy he gets.' The lie easily tripped off her tongue.

Oblivious to his daughter's hatred for her child, Dean hugged the little boy to him. 'It's okay,' he soothed, 'Grandad's here.'

Bethany rolled her eyes. The boy was spoiled, that was the problem. No wonder he was always crying. The fact her son cried because he craved his mother's attention, didn't even enter her head.

As she lay back down on the sun lounger Bethany closed her eyes. She hated her life, hated the fact she was kept a prisoner in the villa. It wasn't as though she hadn't done her bit; she'd given birth to the little brat, she'd given her father a grandson, what more did he want from her? Her mind wandered to Tommy Carter. The love she'd once felt for him had long since turned to hatred. He'd ruined her life; it was because of him she was being kept under lock and key, it was because of him she was forced to touch the one thing in the world she despised more than anything else, her son. There and then she vowed that she would one day make him pay; no matter how long it took, she would have her revenge.

19

'What the fuck is this?' Tommy's eyes were wide as he looked over the van Sonny had acquired for the robbery.

'Fuck me, where did you find this heap of shit?' Jimmy laughed as he walked around the vehicle.

'What?'

'What do you mean, what?' Tommy's voice took on an incredulous tone as he began to walk around the van. The driver's side had been spray-painted white, the passenger side black, and the bonnet green. 'Please tell me this is some kind of a wind up, Sonny, because I'm telling you now, I'm not driving around in this monstrosity.'

Sonny grinned as he followed his elder brothers around the van. 'It's genius, ain't it? Just think of how much this'll confuse anyone who sees us.'

'It's confusing me, let alone any witnesses. We're gonna stick out like sore a thumb in this.' Tommy shook his head and began to laugh. 'Where the fuck did you even get it from?'

'The Isle of Sheppey. Me and Mitchel went over there to buy it.'

'And you actually paid for this?' Jimmy asked.

'Yeah. We only paid five hundred quid for it.'

'Five hundred quid?' Tommy choked on his words. 'Fuck me, they should have been paying you to take this piece of shit away.' He knelt down beside the wheel arch, tugged at the rusting body work, and shook his head. 'Look.' Dried flakes of rust crumbled away into his hand. 'They must have seen you fucking coming, bruv. It's falling apart. There's only one place this shit heap should be heading to, and that's a scrap yard.'

'Well, at least it's in the right place,' Jimmy said, laughing at his own wit.

Tommy rolled his eyes. 'Cheers for that, bruv.' Getting to his feet he kicked out at the front tyre. 'The fucking tyre's flat, how did you even manage to drive this back?' He shook his head as he moved around the van to inspect the rest of the tyres. 'What the fuck is wrong with you, Sonny? Why would you even contemplate buying this, let alone actually go through with it?'

'Don't you like it?' Sonny's shoulders dropped.

'What's to like about it? It's gonna cost me at least another hundred quid just to sort the tyres out.' Tommy blew out his cheeks as he gave the van a final once over. 'You'd better hope and pray this lump of shit doesn't die on us when we make our getaway, otherwise there'll be hell to pay,' he said, jumping behind the wheel.

Sonny grimaced as his brother turned the key in the ignition. Please start, please start, he repeated over and over again in his mind like a mantra.

Turning his head Tommy glared when the engine failed to start.

'Just give it one more try,' Sonny said, already backing away.

Twisting the key, the engine finally spluttered into life.

'See I told you.' Sonny beamed. 'It just needs a bit of TLC.'

'TLC!' Tommy laughed, incredulous. 'I'm warning you now, if this heap of shit is the cause of us getting caught, I'll fucking muller you.'

'It won't,' Sonny replied, sounding a lot more confident than he actually felt. 'It'll be fine, trust me,' he muttered, unsure if he was trying to convince his elder brothers or himself.

* * *

Pushing his legs into a navy-blue cotton boiler suit, Jimmy glanced across at his brothers as they too began to dress in the crowded scrap yard office. He pulled the suit up his body, then pushed his arms through the sleeves. Perched upon his head sat a thick woollen black balaclava.

Beads of sweat had already begun to break out across Jimmy's forehead. No matter how much planning Tommy did beforehand, the fear of the unknown and the terrifying thought of the robbery going wrong, always brought him out in a cold sweat.

'Here, take these and make sure you put them on before you even think about touching those guns.' Tommy looked at each of his brothers in turn as he handed out four sets of thin black leather gloves.

Jimmy pushed his fingers into the gloves and leant towards his elder brother. 'Are you sure about this, Tommy?' It was a question he asked before every job they did, but tonight he felt even more uneasy than usual. Tonight, they wouldn't be dealing with bank clerks, or the general Joe Public. Tonight, they would be dealing with Freddie Smith's henchmen, the majority of them hardened criminals.

Tommy nodded. 'We've been over this time and time again, haven't we? So stop worrying.' He patted Jimmy's shoulder. 'Trust me, I know what I'm doing, and as long as we stick to the plan, nothing will come back to us. I've sorted everything out.'

Jimmy gave a small nod. He hoped Tommy was right about this. As his younger brothers silently filed out of the office and made their way towards the van, he could feel his heart begin to beat wildly in his chest, and he wished more than ever that Tommy would change his mind.

'Are you sure you won't come with us?' Tommy asked, turning to look at Mad Dog.

'No lad. This is one job I won't get involved with, and I wish you'd change your mind about it.' He watched as Tommy began to climb onto the battered and torn driver's seat. Even as he said the words, he knew he wouldn't be able to change Tommy's mind. 'Just be careful, okay. I'll be here waiting for you all to get back. I'll make sure I have a small fire burning to burn those boiler suits. The less evidence there is lying around the better.'

Tommy nodded. He gave a small smile, then slammed the driver's door shut.

'You all know what to do, right?' Tommy pushed the key in the ignition, then glanced over his shoulder at his brothers in the back of the van. He waited for them to nod their heads in acknowledgment, then eased the gear into first. Beside him in the passenger seat, Jimmy adjusted his balaclava. The two brothers locked eyes. They didn't need to speak; instinctively they knew what the other was thinking. Releasing the handbrake, Tommy pushed his foot down on the accelerator. This was it. He swallowed deeply; nerves were beginning to get the better of him, he needed to get a grip on himself and fast. 'It's going to be okay.' His voice was low, the words he spoke were not only for Jimmy's ears, but his too, as he tried to convince himself that everything would go to plan.

* * *

On a side street in Ilford, Tommy parked the van. It was just before seven, and only two hours before the club opened up to the general public, giving them at least an hour to get the job done and then get back out. He took a deep breath, looking around him. 'Let's go.'

The brothers piled out of the van. As always, Tommy took the lead as they began the short walk towards the club. As the cold evening air hit his body, his breath streamed out ahead of him, not that his brain registered this fact – pure adrenalin flooded through him. They reached the corner of the side street, and Tommy pulled down the balaclava, ensuring his face was covered. He pointed his finger towards his brothers, indicating they do the same.

Bypassing the main doors, they made their way towards the side entrance. Even from the outside, the venue looked exactly what it was: a shit hole. He pointed his finger up towards where the security alarm was situated. They would need to get inside the offices above the alarm in double quick time to disable it.

Down the side alley, Tommy paused in front of the fire escape doors. 'Gary, Mitchel... I want the pair of you to get up in the offices and sort out that alarm. The rest of you stay with me, right.'

They nodded, and Tommy took this as his cue to begin kicking at the doors. With relative ease, they burst inwards, leaving shards of splintered wood hanging from the door frame. They waited for the shrill of the alarm and were met with only silence. 'It ain't even connected,' Tommy stated, his voice incredulous.

Steven Coulson made his way across the dance floor, his large frame slowing him down. He tugged at the black jacket across his chest and stomach and unbuttoning the top and middle buttons, he let out a long sigh, thankful for the instant relief. His wife was right, he needed to shift some weight and fast.

A loud crash from behind him stopped him dead in his tracks. 'Who's there?' he called out. He was met with silence. For a few moments he stood listening, his ears straining, before shrugging his shoulders and continuing on his way. He wasn't overly concerned; it was more than likely just some piss head outside in the alley.

Steven had only walked a few steps when the sound of move-ment made him spin around. 'I said, who's fucking there?' He peered across the dimly lit club and wanted to curse himself for not switching on the main lights – he could see fuck all. 'Stop playing games, who's there?' His heart began to pound inside his chest. Again, he was met with silence and he almost laughed out loud; his mind was obviously playing tricks on him.

He'd barely turned his head, when a rush of black figures was upon him.

'Where's the fucking safe?'

Shocked, Steven stumbled backwards, his arms flying out as he battled to regain his balance. In the time it took him to grab onto the bar top and pull himself into a standing position, he'd assessed the situation and as the figures advanced towards him, he roared at the top of his lungs, 'We're being turned over.'

Tommy thrust the shotgun out in front of him, bringing Steven to a halt. 'Don't do anything stupid,' he screamed. 'Don't try to be a hero, otherwise you'll end up getting hurt.'

The overhead light snapped on, causing Tommy to blink his eyes rapidly. Momentarily blinded, he adjusted his vision to the sudden light. Turning his head from left to right, heavies ran towards them from out of nowhere. Stunned, Tommy felt his brothers stiffen beside him. They were surrounded. Not for one moment had he expected this many of Freddie Smith's henchmen to be at the club. There had to be at least twelve of them, if not more. What the fuck were they all doing here? He took a step forward, the gun pointing straight ahead of him. 'Where's the fucking safe?' He had to take control of the situation and fast, and the fact he was brandishing a sawn-off shotgun had to give him the advantage, surely.

Tommy watched as the men faltered and he took a step closer. 'Don't make me fucking shoot you. Now, where is the safe?' Met with silence, he watched as one of the heavies made a small inclination of his head towards another of Freddie's henchmen. The action was so slight, many people would have missed it, only Tommy's eagle eyes missed nothing. 'Don't fucking nod your head at him.' He could feel the heavies begin to crowd forward; they were practically on top of them and they had no means of escape. Taking the situation into his own hands, Tommy had no other choice but to squeeze his finger on the trigger.

The gunshot was deafening, and as the scent of gun powder filled the air Freddie's henchmen ducked for cover. The mirrored wall behind the bar took the impact and as bottles once full of alcohol were obliterated, no further proof was needed to show just how much damage the shotgun was capable of causing, as plaster, dust, and glass flew out in all directions.

Taking this as his chance to get the situation under control Tommy sprang forward and pushed the gun into the side of Steven's head. 'Unless you want to die, you'd best start fucking talking.'

'Okay, okay.' Steven held up his hands. As sweat began to trickle down his forehead he spoke fast, his voice high. 'I'll show you where the safe is,' he cried, slowly pulling himself up from the floor, his hands above his head in surrender.

Tommy nodded. 'Now, we're all going to calm the fuck down and then no one will get hurt.' He watched as his brothers rounded the men up and pushed them into the far corner of the club. Satisfied that his brothers had the heavies under control, Tommy jerked his head towards Jimmy and Sonny, indicating for them to follow him. 'You two wait here, and watch this fucking lot,' he ordered his two remaining brothers. 'If they start getting lairy, shoot the fuckers.'

As they followed Steven up a flight of stairs Tommy slammed the barrel of the gun into the small of his back. Their bodies were tense and alert as they took each step, fully expecting heavies to be lurking around every corner. Finally, Steven led them down a corridor; the bare concrete floor was loud and harsh underneath their feet, the plastered walls above the chipped wooden skirting boards cracked and crumbling.

'This is it,' Steven said as he came to a halt.

'Well, unlock it then.'

'I haven't got a key,' Steven answered, licking at his dry lips.

Tommy swallowed down the irritation. 'Then how the fuck are we going to get into the safe, if you haven't got a key?' he growled.

Steven shrugged; he didn't have the answers. Only Freddie Smith had a key to the room and safe.

'Kick the fucking door in,' Tommy ordered Jimmy.

Within moments, they were inside the room and pushing Steven forward. Tommy turned his attention to Sonny. 'Watch him, and if he moves, shoot the bastard.'

Sonny nodded. Brandishing the gun towards Steven, he backed him into a corner.

'How are we gonna fucking do this?' Tommy asked, his voice low.

Jimmy chewed on his lip. 'Shoot at the fucking safe, that's all we can do. Blast the fucking thing wide open.'

Tommy thought the dilemma through. 'Open them up first and see if there's anything worth taking.' He jerked his head towards five large navy-blue holdalls lined up against the wall beside the safe.

Jimmy did as his brother asked and, kneeling down beside the first of the bags, he pulled across the zip and almost fell backwards in shock. 'Fuck me, get a load of this,' he said, letting out a soft whistle.

'What?' Tommy turned his head and did a double take. He locked eyes with Jimmy, his heart beating wildly inside his chest. 'Open the rest,' he urged him, not taking his eyes away from the bags.

With all of the bags opened, Tommy stared down at the haul. Each bag had been crammed full of gold bars, and he took a wild guess as to where they had come from. This had to be the stolen gold from a recent robbery over in Deptford. He clasped his hand on Jimmy's shoulder, a wide grin spread across his face and a twinkle in his blue eyes. 'You'd better go and get the van. It's fucking pay day for us.'

Danny McKay pushed through the doors of the Ilford Palais and as he strode across the dance floor he quickened his pace. With the main lights on, the club showed up every imperfection. The dated threadbare carpet and peeling paintwork were further proof that the club needed a bit more than a lick of paint to bring it up to standard.

'What the fuck happened?' he asked.

Looking over his shoulder, Freddie snarled, 'They've taken everything: the gold, the cash, the fucking lot. The no-good cunts. I want these bastards found and brought to me. Someone out there will know about this.' Freddie's heart beat wildly in his chest. He'd only been looking after the gold until Mark Hopper, an armed robber with the mentality of a complete and utter lunatic, could ship it abroad to be melted down. In his naivety, he'd believed the run-down club would be the perfect place to stash it. Who in their right mind would even contemplate robbing the venue? It was a shithole. He wiped his hand across his face as the severity of the situation hit home. 'Hopper will fucking kill all of us over this.'

'Who was on the doors?' Danny tore his attention away from Freddie and nodded towards the heavies as they crowded around the bar area. 'How the fuck could you have let this happen? Did it not cross your fucking minds to try and stop them? There were more than enough of you here.'

'They had guns, mate. Nearly took my fucking head clean off one of them did, look.' Steven Wright jerked his thumb behind him at the gaping hole in the wall. 'I'm lucky to be still standing here. I'm telling you, Danny, they meant fucking business. How the fuck were we meant to stop them, when they were pointing sawn-offs at us?'

Danny narrowed his eyes, momentarily taken aback. 'Sawn-offs?' This was the first anyone had mentioned sawn-offs being used in the robbery.

'Yes fucking sawn-offs. You try stopping five blokes pointing them at your head. I thought me days were numbered, I can tell you.'

The colour drained from Danny's face. Immediately, his thoughts turned to Tommy Carter. No, he wouldn't dare, or would he? No. He shook his head. It couldn't have been Tommy, surely fucking not, he wasn't that stupid to take Freddie on, was he? He wiped his hand over his face, smearing the cold sweat that had begun to break out across his clammy forehead. His heart was beating so hard and so fast that he could barely hear what was going on around him let alone think. The last conversation he'd had with Tommy sprang to his mind and he inwardly groaned. *Let's just say this job has more risk than usual.*

Realisation took hold. It had to be Tommy Carter. How the fuck had he even known about the gold? They hadn't exactly made it common knowledge. 'I...' He battled to regain his composure. 'I can't fucking believe it. Someone must have talked.' His voice sounded a lot higher than usual to his ears, and he cleared his throat, turning his back on the rest of the firm as he tried to get his head around what had just taken place.

'Well, obviously someone has been talking. Doesn't take a genius to work that out, does it? How else would they have known about the gold?' Moray Garner was thoughtful for a few moments. 'Let's face it, someone has opened their mouth, and those guns had to have come from somewhere. I reckon that's where we should start looking. Find out who supplied them.'

Freddie nodded, his lips set in a straight line. 'Start asking around then. I want every supplier brought to me. I'll find these fuckers, if it's the last thing I do.' He wiped his hand across his face. He needed the gold back, and the quicker, the better. Otherwise, Mark Hopper, the lunatic, would kill them all stone dead, of that he was certain.

Danny turned to look at Moray. They'd been best mates ever since they had started working for Freddie as kids. Moray was right, of course he was. Find out whoever had supplied the guns, and then the culprits responsible for the robbery would be revealed. An ice-cold shiver ran down the length of his spine and he averted his eyes. Problem was, if Tommy Carter was indeed guilty then he knew for a fact it was him who'd supplied those guns. Five sawn-off shotguns Tommy Carter had bought from him, and five shotguns had been used in the robbery. He'd bet his life on it that they were the very same guns.

* * *

'Fucking hell, Tommy.' Jimmy pulled the balaclava off his head, leaving his hair damp with sweat. 'That was fucking close.'

'Tell me about it.' Tommy was driving the van back towards the scrap yard. Frequently, he checked the rear-view mirror, making sure they weren't being followed. He wiped his hand across his forehead, pushing his dark hair out of his eyes, his skin hot and clammy. 'I nearly shot that bloke. Could've ended up taking his head off his fucking shoulders. I reckon I would've done and all, if he hadn't ducked out of the way.' He turned to look at his brother. 'Fuck me, Jimmy, I wasn't expecting all of that gold. No wonder they had so many heavies in there.'

Jimmy nodded. He was just as stunned as Tommy. 'What the fuck are we meant to do with it now though?'

Tommy shrugged and, pulling into the scrap yard, looked around him, before giving the all clear for his brothers to climb out.

Mad Dog Harris made his way out of the office. He took one look at their faces and raised his eyebrows, concerned. 'What happened?'

Tommy made his way around the van. 'It was a fucking nightmare from start to finish.' He began unloading the bags of cash, passing them across to his younger brothers. 'There were more of them than we were expecting. They came out of fucking nowhere.'

'None of you were hurt though?' Mad Dog asked, looking the brothers over.

Tommy shook his head. 'Just shook us up a bit, that's all. We weren't expecting that many heavies to be in there.'

'Well, the main thing is you're all okay.' He peered inside the van, his eyes widening. 'What's this, lad?' he asked, staring down at the holdalls containing the gold bars. 'Where the fuck did they come from?'

'Believe me, we were just as fucking shocked,' he answered, hauling the holdalls out of the van. 'We opened up the room where the safe is, and they were sitting there.'

'What do mean, they were sitting there?'

'Exactly what I said. We opened the door and there they were.

The place is such a shit hole, they probably thought that no one would even contemplate robbing it.'

Mad Dog blew out his cheeks. 'This isn't Freddie's style. He runs doors, amongst other things. What he doesn't do is commit robberies.' He looked across at Tommy. 'You should have left the gold, lad. You've got yourself involved in a situation you have no right to be in.'

Hauling out the last holdall Tommy shrugged. 'Yeah, well, it's a bit too fucking late now, ain't it? We can hardly take them back.' He wiped the sweat from his face, his cheeks red from the exertion of moving the heavy bags. 'This has to be the gold from that robbery over in Deptford.'

'Aye lad, I reckon so.' Mad Dog nodded. 'What the fuck are you going to do with it, Tommy? This is too big, even for us.'

'I'll think of something.'

Mad Dog watched as the younger man walked towards the office. 'And where are you going to stash this lot?' he called after him. 'You know your name will be the first out of a lot of people's mouths. You can't just chuck them in the office, and hope no one turns up looking for them.'

Tommy paused. He looked around him at the broken scrapped cars piled on top of one another. 'For tonight, they can be stored in them.' He gestured towards the cars. 'Tomorrow, I'll think of something better.'

'Aye lad.' He followed Tommy into the office. 'Come on, you all need to move fast. You have to get yourselves over to the pub.' He chewed on the inside of his cheek. 'Now, more than ever, you all need to be seen in there.'

* * *

Changed into fresh clothes, the brothers made their way into The Short Blue public house. They needed watertight alibis, should Freddie Smith start asking questions. Indicating for his brothers to go through, Tommy glanced nervously around him as he brought Jimmy to a halt beside him.

'What's up?' Jimmy narrowed his eyes, the cold night air causing his breath to mist.

Tommy swallowed deeply before answering. 'Danny McKay will come here for me tonight.'

Jimmy's eyes widened. 'What? You said everything was sorted out. Nothing would come back to us, you said.'

'It is sorted out.' Tommy sighed. 'When he comes for me, don't get involved, I need you to keep the others away, too. Promise me, Jimmy.'

'You can't ask that of me, Tommy. I ain't gonna let McKay barge in and cause fucking ructions, am I? You're my brother, I can't do that.'

Tommy grasped his brother's arm in a vice-like grip. It was imperative he understood. 'You can and you will. I need to be on my own with him, I mean it, Jimmy. Promise me you won't get involved.'

Jimmy looked to the floor, thinking it over, then gave a nod. He had no other choice but to do as Tommy asked.

The public house was busy and Tommy gulped down the beer that had been placed before him. Around him he blocked out the conversations, his head bowed, waiting for McKay to make his grand entrance, and he knew it would only be a matter of time before he caught up with him. More than anything, he needed time to think. With the gold in their possession, now more than ever, he had to have everything clear in his mind. He had to know what to say to the man.

'Tommy fucking Carter.'

Tommy could hear the rage in Danny McKay's voice, and he inwardly groaned as he took in the man's stance; it was enough to tell him and everyone else standing in close proximity that trouble was brewing, and a lot of trouble at that. As he got to his feet Tommy could feel his brothers' eyes on him. He didn't speak. He didn't even glance in their direction. Instead, he followed Danny out of the pub with as much dignity as he could muster. He'd long resigned himself to the fact that he could very well be in for a beating. In fact, all along he'd known this moment would be coming.

They had barely made it out of the door, when Danny slammed him up against the wall, his fist connecting with the side of Tommy's face, his free hand firmly clutching at the front of Tommy's shirt.

'You fucking bastard; it was you.'

The unexpected punch to the side of his head left Tommy feeling momentarily dazed.

'It was fucking you. You were the one who robbed the Ilford Palais.' Danny's breath came out in short, sharp bursts and he smashed his fist into the side of Tommy's face for a second time. 'I swear to God, I will fucking kill you over this. We need that gold back. Do you fucking hear me?'

Tommy swallowed deeply, the side of his eye already beginning to swell. 'What gold?'

'Don't play fucking games with me,' Danny warned, curling his fist into a ball, ready to strike out again.

'I don't know what you're talking about,' Tommy said, sidestepping out of the way of Danny's fist, years of semi-professional boxing giving him the advantage. 'Don't try and mug me off, Danny, you've swung for me twice. Do it again, and I'll bounce you across this fucking car park.'

Danny's face reddened, the anger he felt seeping out of him. Snarling, he threw a third punch. 'I should fucking haul you in front of Freddie and let him deal with you.'

'You should, but you won't.' Tommy battled to regain his composure. He twisted his body around and shoved Danny up against the wall. His forearm slammed against his chest, restraining him. 'You won't because you can't, can you? Not without incriminating yourself.'

'What?' Danny shook his head as he tried to take in Tommy's words. 'What the fuck are you talking about?'

'Don't try and play innocent. I buy guns from you Danny, therefore you're up to your neck in this as much as I am, and I don't think Freddie will be too happy when he finds out about our business arrangement.'

Danny's mouth fell open. He tried to speak but was lost for words. Tommy Carter had well and truly tucked him up, and he hadn't even seen it coming. He threw Tommy away from him, brought his fingers up to his temples, and rubbed at his throbbing head. Finally, he spoke. 'Are you trying to fucking blackmail me? Because trust me, I will bury you.' He threw Tommy a cold stare. 'We need that gold back, otherwise there'll be murders. I know it was you. Five sawn-offs I sold you, and five shotguns were used in that robbery. Do you really think I'm that fucking stupid that I wouldn't connect the dots?'

'It wasn't me.'

His green eyes flashing dangerously, Danny stabbed his finger in Tommy's face. 'This ain't even about Freddie any more. We're not dealing with Mickey fucking Mouse here, this is Mark Hopper I'm talking about, and believe me, he'd eat you for breakfast and spit you out for lunch. The man is a fucking psycho.'

'I've already told you I don't know anything about any gold.'

Danny shook his head. He could feel his blood pressure rising, could hear his heart drum loudly in his ears. 'I'm fucking warning you—'

'I've already told you,' Tommy interrupted, 'I haven't got your gold, and let's face it, you haven't got any proof that I have. I'm not the only person out there capable of a robbery, am I?'

Danny snarled, 'I sold you those guns, I know it was you.'

Tommy battled to remain composed. He took a step towards Danny, his body tensing. 'So what? You sold me guns, that doesn't mean I had anything to do with the robbery. We both know you can't go to Freddie without incriminating yourself, and I'm pretty certain Freddie isn't going to go to the Old Bill, is he? So come on, Danny, what exactly are you gonna fucking do, eh?'

Pulling back his fist, Danny took a step forward, his temper beginning to get the better of him. 'I'm gonna tell you one last time...'

'And I've already told you, try and smash me again, and I'm gonna bounce you across this fucking car park, so do yourself a favour and fuck off.'

Danny flopped back against the wall and brought his hands up to his head in defeat. To say Mark Hopper was going to go ape shit was an understatement. He exhaled loudly, struggling to catch his breath. 'I swear to God, if I find out this was something to do with you, then I'm gonna break every bone in your fucking body.'

Glancing over his shoulder, Tommy began backing away. 'Bit of advice for you: if I was you, I'd start covering my tracks. I don't think Freddie is gonna be happy when he finds out you're a supplier, and that you've been dealing with me behind his back all this time.'

Dumbstruck, Danny stared after Tommy's retreating back; the slippery fucker had well and truly fucked him over. His thoughts immediately went to Moray; he needed to speak to him and fast. He was going to need all the help he could get to find a way out of the situation he'd stupidly landed himself in. There would be murders committed before the week was out; all he could do was hope and pray it wouldn't be his own death he was predicting.

As soon as he re-entered the pub, Tommy took a deep breath, his heart beating ten to the dozen. Hastily he composed himself and as he reached the table where his brothers were sitting, he locked eyes with Jimmy. 'We need to move that gold,' he said simply.

20

Jimmy was incensed. After spending the past thirty minutes hauling the bags of gold over the cemetery railings and across the grave stones, he and Tommy had finally reached Davey's burial plot.

He took the shovel Tommy handed him, slammed it into the hard ground, and leant against it. 'So, what am I supposed to tell him then?' he said, spitting out the words, his cheeks red and his eyes flashing dangerously.

Tommy shrugged. 'I dunno, just spin him a load of old shit.'

With only the moon to illuminate Tommy's face, Jimmy could tell by his brother's nonchalant attitude that he really didn't give a toss about the predicament Aiden Coleman found himself in. Earlier that morning, the Irishman had come to the betting shop, terrified. In fact he'd stood in front of Jimmy a quivering wreck. The cause of his fear was Freddie Smith. 'I can't do that, can I? We made him a part of this by getting him to give out information on the club, and you know Smith is gonna kill him if he gets wind of that.'

Tommy sighed. 'Well, I dunno. I'll throw some cash at him, and he can fuck off someplace instead then, can't he?'

'What d'ya mean, you'll throw some cash at him and he can fuck off? He might not want to fuck off, have you even thought about that?' And more to the point, Jimmy didn't want the Irishman to go anywhere, he'd grown fond of him in recent weeks.

'Fucking hell, Jimmy. What exactly do you want me to do? He's your friend, and I use that term loosely. So, come on, you tell me, because I'm all ears. What do you want me to do?'

Jimmy was quiet. The truth of the matter was, he really didn't know how to help Aiden, he'd been hoping that Tommy would have the answers. He shrugged in defeat. 'I don't know, but all I'm saying is that thanks to us, he's in a right state.'

'Well, there you go then. I'll chuck him a couple of grand and he can fuck off back to Ireland.'

'A couple of grand, is that it? You've torn his fucking life apart. He's shit scared of what Smith is going to do to him, and you're going to give him two grand as compensation?'

'Jimmy.' Tommy shook his head. 'I didn't hold a gun to his head and make him talk, did I? He did that all by himself. So yeah, two grand is all he's gonna get from me, and believe me, that's me being generous.' He began digging at the hard earth. 'Like I said, tell him to go back to Ireland, and he'll have a couple of grand in his back pocket for his troubles. Everyone's a winner.'

'You really don't care, do you? He can't go back to his family, they're fucking catholic and don't know he's, you know... gay.'

Tommy stopped digging and blew out his cheeks. 'Fuck me, Jimmy. Don't you think I've got enough troubles of my own, without your boyfriend adding to them? I've not only got Freddie Smith, but I've also got Danny McKay, Moray Garner, and more than likely the whole of Freddie's firm, ready and waiting to rip my fucking head off if they get wind of my involvement in all of this. Not to mention Mark Hopper, who apparently is a fucking psychopath, so excuse me for not jumping through hoops to help the Irish bloke out. Fuck me, as much as I love you, Jimmy, you're really starting to do my nut in. If you wanna help him so much, put your hand in your own pocket and help him, but leave me fucking out of it.'

Jimmy raised his eyebrows. It was the first time Tommy had referred to Aiden as his boyfriend and in that instant, his mood softened towards his brother. 'Are you really that worried?'

'What do you fucking think?' Tommy crouched down and wiped his hand over the rough stubble covering his jaw. 'I'm this close to being hauled in front of Freddie Smith.' He placed his thumb and forefinger an inch apart to emphasise his point. 'I need to be able to think, bruv. I need to sort this out, otherwise we are all in a lot of fucking shit. And I'm sorry, but the Irishman isn't my top priority at the moment. I have to keep you lot safe, my wife and kids safe, myself safe.'

'Tell me what I can do to help.'

Tommy shook his head. 'There ain't nothing you can do, bruv.' He stood up and resumed digging the grave all the while wishing that he'd taken Mad Dog's advice and steered clear of robbing the club. It wasn't even himself he was worried about; he could take care of himself if and when the need arose but should anything happen to his brothers or Stacey and his kids he would never forgive himself. 'Right now, we just need to get this gold hidden away, that's our top priority. As long as they can't find it, then I can carry on telling them it was nothing to do with me, and that's gotta be a big bonus for us, hasn't it? Because the minute they find it, we are all dead.'

'I've never seen you this worried.' There was concern in Jimmy's voice.

Tommy sighed. 'That's because I've never been this worried. Mad Dog was right; we should have left the gold where it was. To be perfectly honest, bruv, I think we've bitten off more than we can chew, and I don't know if I'm coming or going with it all.'

Jimmy clasped his brother's shoulder and resumed digging the grave. It wasn't like Tommy to make such an epic fuck up. He blew out his cheeks from the exertion. He had a feeling this was only the start of their troubles.

* * *

As Tommy had predicted, it didn't take long for his name to come up on Freddie Smith's radar and just days later Moray Garner and Danny McKay hauled him out of the scrap yard office and threw him across the back seat of Moray's car. The scent of the highly polished leather seats hit Tommy's nostrils, filling him with dread. Sitting quietly with his head bowed, Tommy wracked his brain as he tried to think of a way out of the situation. After a few moments his stomach churned, as realisation took hold; there was no way out, he was as guilty as sin. All he could do was deny all involvement, and hope and pray Freddie believed him.

Moray pulled the car to a halt outside the Ilford Palais, and Tommy looked out of the window towards the scene of his crime. 'Why've you brought me here?' He looked across at the two men. He had to play the game. 'What's this all about? Why does Freddie want to have a word with me?'

The two men remained silent. Moray switched off the engine and opened the car door. He climbed out and began to walk around the car, to where Tommy was sitting on the back seat.

'He's got nothing on you.' Staring straight ahead of him Danny spoke quietly.

Tommy's heart leapt. 'Then why the fuck, have you brought me here?'

'Just get out of the fucking motor and do us both a favour and keep your mouth closed. Whatever you do, don't start getting lairy with him, you know what he's like; as it is he's waiting for excuse to take you down.'

Feeling a lot more confident, Tommy climbed out of the car before they had the chance to drag him out. Flanked on either side by McKay and Garner, he walked inside the club. He was taken up a staircase, leading to where the offices were situated and they made their way along the same corridor Tommy had walked just days earlier. Keeping his head pointing forward, Tommy resisted the urge to glance inside the room where the safe was kept. Instinctively he knew that just a flick of his head in that direction would give the game away.

They brought him to a halt outside a room at the far end of the corridor. Taking a deep breath, Tommy battled to regain his composure as Moray rapped his knuckles on the wooden door. It took just a few moments for the door to be flung open, and with a sharp shove in the small of his back, Tommy was pushed inside the room.

Sitting behind the desk, as large as life, was Freddie Smith. 'Well, well, well,' he growled, 'look who it is: Tommy fucking Carter. Where is the gold?'

Before Tommy could answer, he was slammed down into a chair in front of the desk. 'What gold?' he asked, shifting his weight to make himself more comfortable.

'The gold you fucking stole you no good bastard.' Freddie's face was almost purple with rage.

Tommy shrugged. 'I dunno what you're talking about.'

'We both know you do. Five geezers. Actually, to be more precise, five cunts, stole the gold from my club. This very club,' he spat. 'And there just so happens to be five Carter brothers. Bit of a coincidence that, isn't it?'

'Actually there's six of us. I think you missed out my little brother, or are you accusing him in this conspiracy of yours as well?'

Freddie snarled; he was done playing games. 'Do I need my lads to rough you up a bit? Maybe even cut you open? Is that what it's gonna take to make you start talking?' He stabbed his finger across the desk. 'Because believe me, there is nothing that would give me greater pleasure, than to see you bleeding out like a pig on the floor.'

'I haven't got your gold.' Tommy gave a carefree shrug, his voice strong, unwavering.

Freddie sighed. He gave a nonchalant flick of his hand. 'Smash him up.'

'Whoa, whoa.' Tommy held up his hands. 'There's no need for that Freddie, is there? Come on, what more do you want me to say? I don't know anything about your gold. I swear to you, it wasn't me.'

Freddie sat back in the seat, his fingers steepled in front of him. 'It'd be a shame if anything was to happen to that little brother of yours. What's his name?' He clicked his finger several times as though the action would somehow refresh his memory. 'That's it, Jonny. From my understanding he has a promising career in front of him. In fact' – he smirked – 'it was only yesterday I went to watch him train at Gold's Gym. Your old man is a hard task master, I'll give him that; he really put him through his paces and by all accounts the boy is good, almost as good as you were, so I'm told.'

'What?' The hairs on the back of Tommy's neck stood to attention and an ice-cold shiver ran down the length of his spine. 'What's my brother got to do with this?'

Freddie shrugged. 'Like I said, it'd be a shame if anything was to happen to him, or if that pretty little face of his became disfigured in some way. So, this is how we are going to play this out; you've got forty-eight hours to give that gold back, otherwise' – he gave a mock wave – 'bye bye Jonny. Now, get him fucking out of here.'

Shrugging Danny and Moray away from him, Tommy snarled, 'You are one fucking cunt.' He spat out each word. All he wanted to do was wipe the smug grin from Freddie's face and he prepared himself to launch across the desk, his fists curled into tight balls. Just one punch – that was all it would take to put Freddie on his arse, just one punch to wipe the sickening smirk from the bastard's face.

Unconcerned, Freddie glanced down at his watch. 'Forty-eight hours Carter, and time's ticking.'

With as much dignity as he could muster, Tommy walked from the room, slamming the door closed behind him. Out in the corridor, he brought his hands up to his head. He felt sick to his stomach and he took deep breaths in a bid to quash the sickening waves that began to ripple through his body.

He glanced back towards the door, resisting the urge to smash it down and batter Freddie Smith to within an inch of his life. Instead, and against his better judgement, Tommy tore down the corridor, picking up speed as he descended the stairs. He had to get out of the club, and more than anything else, he needed to breathe air into his lungs.

Out on the street, Tommy placed his hands on his thighs and lent his weight upon them. Hunched over, he gasped for breath. Noting a taxi rank ahead of him he sprinted across the street. 'I need a taxi,' he shouted, thumping his fist upon the glass partition. 'I need to get to Gold's Gym in Barking, as quick as you can.'

The familiar scent of sweat hit Tommy as soon as he pushed through the gym door. It had been years since he'd stepped inside the place, and in that instant, he realised just how much he missed it. He recalled the hours of training he'd put in over the years, all that hard work that eventually had led to nothing, all because he'd seen a future with Davey Abbott instead of a career in boxing. If

only he could turn back time, he could have been fighting profes-
sionally by now.

Even above the consistent pounding of leather against leather,
as men swung their gloved fists at punching bags, Tommy could
hear his father's voice from across the gym. He recalled a time when
he had lived and breathed boxing, and it had been him listening to
the familiar orders Frank barked out.

Moving towards the ring, where his youngest brother was spar-
ring, he held back slightly, not wanting to get too close. He felt like
an outsider, which he supposed in a way he was. He had no right to
be in the gym; he'd not only turned his back on the life but had also
shattered his dad's dreams in the process. 'He's good.' Feeling
awkward, Tommy shoved his hands into his pockets.

Frank Carter glanced behind him, his body immediately tensing. 'Yeah well, you were better.'

Tommy gave a small smile. He could still sense the tension
between them. Frank had never fully forgiven him for quitting the
ring and Tommy had a feeling that he never would, and who could
blame him? He'd let his dad down, he'd even let the sponsors down,
leaving Frank to deal with the aftermath of him selfishly walking
away.

As the baby of the family, fifteen-year-old Jonny threw a succes-
sion of quick jabs. Tommy listened to the instructions Frank gave.
He had to give credit where it was due; his dad was a good trainer.
'He's got a fight coming up, hasn't he?'

Frank turned to face his son. 'What is it you want, Tommy?
We're busy here unless it's escaped your notice.'

Tommy shrugged. 'I just wanted to see how he's getting on,
that's all.'

'Well, you've seen how he's his doing, now you can leave.' Frank
turned his attention back to his youngest son. Pausing, he spun
around. 'You're not taking another one of my boys,' he said, stab-

bing his finger forward. 'You've already taken the other four. Jonny is the only one I've got left, the only one who's still interested in the business.'

'I wouldn't.' Shaking his head at the accusation, Tommy lowered his eyes. His father's words stung a lot more than he ever thought they would. He had no intention of trying to steal Jonny away; the last thing he wanted was for his youngest brother to follow on in his footsteps. He wanted his brother to have a crack at boxing, he wanted Jonny to make it as a professional, he wanted to watch him lift a title belt in the air; if nothing else they owed that to Frank at least. 'I just wanted a quick chat with Jonny, that's all, I wanted to wish him well for the fight, I hardly see him any more.'

'What do you expect?' Frank growled. 'He's in training; something you've obviously forgotten about. Now if you don't mind you can wait outside, you've no business in here.' Frank gave a sharp nod of his head towards the exit, then turned his back on his eldest son.

Tommy's cheeks flushed pink and he glanced around him to see if anyone else had heard the dismissal. 'Okay, I'll be out there.' Dejected, he jerked his thumb towards the doors, not that anyone was paying him any attention, including his father. Giving Jonny one last glance, he walked across the gym floor, his head down, his shoulders slumped.

Glancing over his shoulder, Frank watched his son leave. Tommy was a fool. He'd had a natural talent that his younger brothers could only have hoped to emulate; he could have made something of his life, he could have been up there with the greats of the boxing world, but all that talent had been thrown away as though the god given skill he'd been gifted meant nothing. He shook his head sadly, then turned his attention back to Jonny, the only son he had left interested in boxing. If only Jonny had half the

power and skill his eldest brother had had, then Frank would have
been a happy man.

* * *

An hour later, Frank and Jonny emerged from the gym. Tommy
smiled as his youngest brother walked towards him. Jonny's cheeks
were flushed pink and his hair in disarray, still damp after his
shower. It was an image Tommy instantly recognised, having seen
himself and his brothers each emerge from the gym looking the
exact same way.

'Did you come to watch me, Tommy?'

Tommy smiled. 'Yeah, you did good.'

A wide grin spread across Jonny's face at the praise his elder
brother gave him. He held his fists up and bounced on his feet. 'I've
got a fight coming up in a couple of days.'

'I know.' Tommy nodded as he glanced anxiously towards their
father. 'Listen Jonny, I want you to do me a favour. I don't want you
to go out with your mates for a few days.' He could see the confusion in his brother's eyes and resisted the urge to pull him into his
arms, to wrap him up, and keep him safe. 'Just stay at home with
Mum and Dad for a couple of days, okay?'

'Why?' Standing stock still, Jonny narrowed his eyes, his forehead furrowed. 'Why can't I go out?'

Tommy blew out his cheeks. How was he supposed to tell his
baby brother that his life was in danger, that Freddie Smith was
capable of causing him serious damage? 'There's some things going
on with my work, and I need you to stay at home, just for a couple
of day so that I know you're safe.'

'Have I done something wrong? Am I in trouble?'

'No.' Tommy gave a laugh that sounded hollow to his ears. He
was terrified that Smith would follow through with his threat; that

Jonny, his baby brother would be harmed. 'No of course not, this is to do with me, not you.' Placing his hands on his brother's shoulders, Tommy swallowed down the hard lump in his throat. 'Promise me Jonny, you'll stay at home, just until you've had your fight.'

Jonny shrugged, blissfully unaware of just how much danger he was in. 'Okay.' He smiled up at his brother.

'Good.' Tommy looked across to Frank. 'Go on, you'd best go. Dad's waiting for you. And I'll be there to watch you fight. We all will.' He raised his fists. 'You're gonna smash it, bruv. It'll be a win for us Carters.'

'Thanks, Tommy.' Jonny eyes shone with excitement. He couldn't wait to add a trophy or two of his own to the cabinets that held his elder brothers' trophies. 'Dad reckons I'm nearly as good as you were; he thinks I've got what it takes to make it as a pro.'

'I don't doubt that for a second.' Tommy grinned, pulling Jonny into a bear hug and ruffling his dark hair. 'Go on, Dad's waiting.'

As Jonny ran across the car park, Tommy couldn't help but feel as though a lead weight had been lifted off his shoulders, all he could do was hope and pray that he'd done enough to keep his youngest brother safe.

Stacey was worried. Her Tommy had been so quiet, even the kids hadn't been able to lift his mood. 'Are you okay, babe?' she asked as she leant against the door frame leading into the lounge.

Tommy nodded. Absentmindedly he watched as Karen and Peter played; he may have been there in body, may have nodded and smiled at all the right times, but in his mind he couldn't have been further away. Maybe he should send Stacey and the kids away on a holiday. It would be one way of keeping them safe. Who knew what Freddie was capable of, or how far he was willing to go to destroy him. Would he come after one of his kids next? Not to mention what Mark Hopper would do to his family, when he found out he'd taken the gold. He'd heard more than one or two rumours that Hopper was hiding out abroad, and due back in England at any time. The very thought was enough to bring him out in a cold sweat.

Chewing on his thumb nail he turned towards Stacey. 'Why don't you take the kids to see your nan and grandad in Norfolk for a few days?'

Stacey narrowed her eyes, surprise etched across her face. 'Why?' she asked, screwing up her face. 'Why would you even suggest that?'

'I just thought you might want a little break.'

'What's going on, Tommy? You've never suggested anything like this before.' She glanced down at their children and lowered her voice. 'Are you in trouble, are we in danger?'

Tommy gave a dry laugh. 'No, of course not. It was just a suggestion, that's all.'

'I'll think about it, okay?' She gave a small smile then left the room. In the kitchen Stacey bit down on her lip and took her mobile phone out of her handbag. Tommy had her worried all right; something wasn't quite right with her husband. Scrolling through her contact list, her finger hovered over Jimmy's phone number, and with a quick glance towards the door, to make sure she wasn't being overheard, she pressed dial.

After one or two moments the call was answered. 'Jimmy, it's me,' Stacey said, her voice hushed. 'I need you to come and see your brother; I'm worried about him.'

* * *

Within thirty minutes, Jimmy had arrived. Letting her brother-in-law into the house, Stacey motioned for him to go through to the lounge. 'Find out what's going on,' she whispered.

Walking into the room, Jimmy jerked his head towards his brother. 'What's going on bruv?'

Tommy looked up, his eyebrows raised. 'What are you doing here?'

'Stacey called me, she's worried about you.'

Picking up the remote control, Tommy switched the television off, then slumped back against the plump cushions. 'I was taken to see Freddie Smith today.'

Shocked, Jimmy's eyes widened. He looked his brother over, on the lookout for any visible injuries. 'And you didn't think to tell me something like that?'

Tommy shook his head, dismissing his brother's words. 'If we don't give the gold back within forty-eight hours, he's coming after Jonny.'

'Do fucking what?' Jimmy's mouth fell open. 'Then we give it back. It's a no-brainer, as far as I'm concerned. We take the fucking lot of it and dump it outside the club if we have to.'

Tommy nodded, thoughtful for a few moments. 'They're scared.'

'Who's scared?' Jimmy stared at his brother, waiting for him to answer. 'Who's scared, Tommy?' he repeated when it became clear that Tommy wasn't going to elaborate.

'That lot, Smith, McKay, and Garner. They're scared of Hopper and what he'll do when he gets back and finds there's no gold.'

'From what I've heard about the bloke, they've every right to be scared. He's a fucking lunatic.'

'Yeah, I know. It's just, I can't help but keep thinking, what if there was no Hopper?'

Jimmy shook his head, confused. 'What are you talking about?'

He watched his brother closely, not taking his eyes off him. 'What is that supposed to mean, if there was no Hopper?'

Tommy leant forward in his seat, looking Jimmy in the eyes. 'What if Hopper was no longer on the scene? What if he ceased to exist?'

'And how the fuck is that gonna happen? And even more importantly, how the fuck is that gonna help the situation? No, Tommy, we're giving the gold back. I don't want something happening to Jonny on my conscience.'

'I've told Jonny to stay at home for a couple of days, and as long as he does as he's told, he'll be safe.'

Jimmy threw up his hands. 'Are we seriously having this conversation? You want to put our little brother's life at risk?'

'All I'm saying is, what if, and it is only a what if, Hopper was to disappear, and as far as Freddie Smith was concerned, he'd taken the gold with him.'

'I can't believe I'm hearing this! What the fuck is wrong with you?' Jimmy's voice began to rise. Aware that Stacey was only in the room next door, he sucked in his bottom lip while he composed himself. 'What the fuck is wrong with you?' he asked again, lowering his voice. 'Is your brain working all right?' He stabbed his finger against Tommy's temple to emphasise his point. 'This is our little brother we're talking about, not some stranger you've just met down the boozer. Are you seriously willing to risk his life, all because you're too fucking stubborn to give the gold back?'

'No, of course I'm fucking not.'

'Well, that's sorted then. We give the gold back.'

Tommy nodded if for no other reason but to pacify his brother. How could they give the gold back without implicating themselves? Either way they were fucked and once the gold had been retrieved there was nothing stopping Freddie from going after Jonny out of revenge, to make an example of them. In fact, they would be playing straight into Smith's hands. The seed of a plan had begun to grow in Tommy's mind, and he knew just the man to help him to follow it through.

* * *

Danny McKay watched as Tommy parked his car beside him. They were in secluded car park across from Epping Forest. 'You'd better have a good reason for dragging me out here,' he growled once Tommy had climbed out.

Nodding, Tommy lit a cigarette and inhaled the smoke deep into his lungs. 'You told me that Freddie had nothing on me, so what the fuck was that all about yesterday?'

Danny sighed. He took note of how drawn and tired Tommy looked. It was clear to see the man hadn't had a wink of sleep, maybe for days if the dark rims under his eyes were anything to go by. 'He hasn't got anything on you, and how was I supposed to know he would come out with that about your brother? I'm not a fucking mind reader.'

Tommy didn't answer and coming to stand beside Danny, he leant against the car, staring straight ahead.

'Hopper is due back in England today.'

Tommy nodded. 'I know. I heard.'

'It's only a matter of time before he comes looking for that gold.'

Tommy nodded again, taking a deep breath. What he was about to say, could go one of two ways. McKay could either batter the life out of him and haul him once again in front of Freddie, or he could listen to what he had to say and see what a fantastic opportunity he was offering. 'What would you do if I said I had the gold?'

Danny jerked his head around, his eyes widening. 'And have you got it?' he asked.

Tommy ignored the question. 'What would you say if I said I

had a proposition for you, something that could make you very rich?'

Danny turned back to look at the forest. He thought the question over and swallowed before answering. 'Okay, I'm all ears. What's on your mind?'

'If something were to happen to Hopper, then there would be no one to collect the gold, would there?'

Danny narrowed his eyes. 'Where are you going with this?'

Tommy cleared his throat. 'As far as Freddie needs to know, Hopper took the gold, and then fucked off abroad with the haul.'

'And how exactly is that going to happen? This is Hopper we're talking about. He's got more lives than a fucking cat. Do you even realise how many attempts he's had on his life? I seriously don't know how the fucker is still standing.'

Tommy gave Danny a sidelong glance. Instinct told him that he had the man's interest. Mark Hopper was a thorn in a lot of people's sides, and he knew for a fact there would be many sighs of relief the day Hopper took his last breath. 'He's just used up his last life. Together, me and you, we kill him and this time we make sure we do the job properly.'

21

Mark Hopper walked around the pool, soaking up the last of the early evening sun, before he departed for England. The heat felt good on his back and was just one of the many things he would miss when he left sunny Spain. He was a stout man, with a thick neck, and dark receding hair. Though many would say he wasn't attractive, he had a memorable appearance, which made him stick out in a crowd. Most people instantly remembered his slack lips and expressionless brown eyes that instantly became black whenever he was angry, which just so happened to be often. He was a nasty piece of work, who revelled in intimidating others.

He shoved his hands into his trousers pockets as he watched the woman stretch out on the sun lounger opposite from where he stood, her dark hair tumbling around her shoulders. He was thankful for the sunglasses he wore. The dark lenses gave him the perfect opportunity to watch her from afar, without her being aware of his stares. The truth was, he'd always had a soft spot for this woman. Ever since they were kids, it had only ever been her who could fire up the longing inside of him.

He tore his eyes away from her and turned around as her father approached.

'The taxi is on its way.'

Mark nodded. 'Cheers, mate.'

'Have a safe journey, and don't forget, if you come across one of those Carters, mainly Tommy Carter, give him a dig from me.'

'I will do, and it'll be a fucking pleasure and all.' He glanced across to the woman he had loved for the majority of his life. He still couldn't believe she was actually a mother now. What a shock that had been for him, when he'd turned up at the villa and seen her son cradled in Dean Johnson's arms. 'I'm actually looking forward to a run-in with one of the no-good cunts. See you soon, darling,' he called out to Bethany.

'So, I should expect to see you back here in about a week's time?'

'Yeah give me a week, two at the most.' Mark slung the handle of a navy-blue holdall over his shoulder. 'As soon as I've collected the gold, I'll start planning the journey to bring it over here. Have a meeting with your contact and be ready and waiting for when I return.'

Dean Johnson nodded, more than satisfied with the plan.

As the taxi pulled up at the front of the villa, Mark shoved out his hand. 'Thanks again, mate, and I'll see you next week.'

On the front step Dean watched as the vehicle began to move away from the kerb. Already, he'd begun planning out what he was going spend his cut of the robbery on. He'd build an extension, he decided, and maybe even a games room for his grandson to play in. Only the best would do for the apple of his eye, Cameron. Dean conveniently chose to forget the child was also Tommy Carter's nephew.

* * *

Danny remained quiet as he tried to get his head around the proposition Tommy had put to him. Faced with a dilemma, he knew for a fact that if Tommy Carter was hauled in front of Freddie for a second time, then his own name would more than likely come up in their enquiries. It was bound to; after all, Carter would hardly keep that little gem to himself, would he?

After what seemed an age, Danny spoke. 'If I do this, and it is a big if, then I'm bringing someone in with me.' He took note of the sideways glance Tommy threw him. 'What?' he asked. 'Did you actually think I would trust you to have my back?'

It was a fair comment, and Tommy shrugged.

'You tucked me up, remember?' Danny stabbed his finger forward, his expression a mask of anger. 'Believe me, I'm not going to forget that in a hurry. So, how would you suggest we play this out?'

Tommy was thoughtful. 'My brother has a fight coming up in a couple of days. D'ya reckon you could get Hopper there?'

Danny gave a long sigh. 'Perhaps, if I told him the gold was there, I dunno though.' He rubbed his head and looked into the distance. 'I'm not sure if he'd buy it, to be honest. Would you if it was your gold that you'd come to collect? Because I know I wouldn't. He's bound to think it's suspect.'

'If it had been me, I wouldn't have been so fucking stupid, as to trust someone to look after it in the first place.'

'Yeah, well, this is Hopper we're talking about. Who in their right mind would try to tuck him up or steal the gold from him? Only a fucking imbecile would give it a second thought.'

Tommy gave a small laugh. 'That'd be me, I suppose.'

'Yeah, well you said it. And what about Freddie? He's expecting Hopper to go and see him. How do we get out of that one?'

'You could always tell Smith that you've sorted it all out with

Hopper. I dunno, you could say you heard a rumour, went to check it, found the gold and took it straight to him.'

Danny gave a hollow laugh. 'This is Freddie we're talking about, he won't fall for that old bollocks.'

Tommy sighed. 'Well have you got a better idea?'

After thinking it through, Danny shook his head in defeat.

'Come on, Freddie trusts you, can't you just tell him that Hopper took the gold and fucked off abroad with it?'

'There seems to be a lot of stuff that I have to do here. What are you actually going to do in all of this?'

'I'll get my hands dirty, don't you worry about that,' Tommy replied.

Danny raised his eyebrows. Tommy had to be out of his mind if he thought his little plan would work. Freddie trusted no one; it was this that had kept him at the top of his game for so long. 'Right, well I'll let you know if I decide to go through with it.'

Tommy nodded. He shook Danny's hand and walked around to the driver's side of his car. 'Don't forget, the fight is in two days' time,' he said as he slipped behind the wheel. 'Everything will need to be sorted out by then.'

* * *

'Are you out of your fucking mind?' As he walked across the dance floor of the Ilford Palais, Moray Garner fingered the six-inch scar that ran down the side of his cheek. The thick, pale-pink puckered line was a stark contrast against his brown skin.

'This is a good opportunity for us.'

'No, Danny, it's not. Now, we know that Carter has the gold. We go straight to Freddie, no fucking around. Let him deal with the little bastard. He's given us untold grief this past week and deserves everything he gets coming to him.'

'Yeah, I know he does, but let's be honest here, you've been saying for a while that you want to break away from Freddie and run your own doors. And this would be your perfect opportunity to do just that.'

'Yeah, until Hopper ends up killing us or Freddie finds out, and we end up being fed to the pigs, or thrown in the Thames. Either way, we'd still be dead. You can't pull off something like this, mate. It's too big.'

'I think we could do it, and Tommy Carter thinks we could do it too.'

Moray burst out laughing. 'I should have fucking known his name would come up. Of course he thinks we can do it; he wants the gold. What the fuck is wrong with you, Danny? Can't you see what's going on right underneath your nose, or are you actually on a death wish or something?'

Danny shook his head. 'Of course I fucking ain't. C'mon, Moray, I need you in on this.'

'What do you need me for? You've got your pal Tommy Carter to help you out.' There was a hint of sarcasm in Moray's voice.

'C'mon, Moray. I trust you. Carter on the other hand, I do not.'

'Then why the fuck, are you dealing with him?' Moray held up his arms, exasperated. 'Surely your gut instinct has gotta tell you something? You know what my motto is? Trust no one; even the devil himself...'

'Was an angel once,' Danny finished off Moray's sentence and sighed.

'Got it in one.'

'I know. It's just, this would be the perfect opportunity to get rid of Hopper. You know what my thoughts are when it comes to that cunt.'

'Yeah, I do,' Moray answered as he thought through Danny's request. There was no love lost between his best mate and Hopper,

and it had almost come to blows between them on numerous occa-
sions. He shook his head and continued on his way towards Freddie's office. 'I'm sorry, mate,' he said, holding up his hand, 'It's too
much of a big ask.'

Danny took a deep breath. He closed his eyes for a moment,
then spoke. 'If you go to Freddie, and him and Hopper look into
where those guns really came from, I'm dead anyway.'

Stopping dead in his tracks, Moray slowly turned to face Danny,
his eyebrows raised. 'What do you mean by that?'

'It was me. I supplied them to Carter, but I swear I didn't know
he was planning on robbing this place.'

Moray cocked his head to the side, unsure if he'd heard the man
right. 'You sold them to Carter?' There was more than a hint of
surprise in his voice and taking a step forward he stabbed his finger
in Danny's direction. 'You were the one who sold him the guns, and
you've just watched me travel half the fucking country looking for
the supplier?'

'What was I supposed to do? I've been trying to get the gold
back.'

'I missed my son's birthday, because I was sent on a wild fucking
goose chase, and you knew all along it was you?' There was disbelief in Moray's voice. 'You're un-fucking-believable, do you know
that?' He gave Danny a cold stare. 'I can't fucking believe this! I can't
believe what I'm hearing. What the fuck is wrong with you, eh?' He
took a step forward, the anger inside him bubbling to the surface.
'Why the fuck are you even dealing behind Freddie's back?' Moray
spat.

Shamefaced, Danny looked to the floor. 'I'm sorry about your
boy's birthday, I really am, but I was desperate. I was trying to cover
my tracks, and I wasn't even 100 per cent certain it was Carter until
today.'

'Let me get this straight.' Moray rubbed at his scar. 'You thought it could be Carter, have I got that much right? And you still watched me drive all the way to fucking Manchester, putting my own life at risk in the process, for fuck all.'

Danny looked around him, checking that there was no one else within earshot to hear their conversation. He could feel Moray's anger seeping out of him, and he put his hand up in a bid to calm his mate down. 'I'm sorry, mate, but you know Freddie as well as I do. And you know he would have put a fucking price on my head, if he'd found out it was me. Without a second thought or a backward glance, he would have had me finished off. And do you wanna know what's even more fucked up about all of this? He would have ordered you to do it. That's how sick in the head he is. The twisted bastard would have got a kick out of it, and we both know it.'

Despite his anger, Moray nodded. Danny was right. They both knew Freddie well, having worked for him since they were seventeen. Without a shadow of a doubt, he knew the older man would have put a price on his best mate's head. No matter how valuable they were to their boss, they weren't indispensable. He sighed as he gave a little shake of his head. 'Tell me what I have to do, but I'm warning you now, if this backfires on us, I'll come after you myself. Freddie and Hopper won't even get a look in, am I making myself clear?'

'Crystal clear and cheers, mate. I owe you one,' Danny said, his shoulders sagging with relief.

Reluctantly, and against his better judgement, Moray nodded. 'Yeah, you fucking do, so you better hope and pray this goes to plan.'

If it had been any other man who'd spoke to him the way Moray had then, Danny would have buried them long ago, bringing further proof of their closeness. He clapped his hand on Moray's shoulder. 'I'd best arrange a meeting with Carter then, eh?'

'Yeah, you do that.' Moray sighed. One way or another, Danny McKay would be the death of him, of that Moray was certain.

* * *

Mark Hopper walked out of Gatwick Airport with a wide grin spread across his face. He made his way towards a black Sierra parked outside the arrivals entrance and shook hands with the owner.

'Hello, mate, long time no see. Did you have any problems getting through security?' Jason Moore asked.

'Nah, was a piece of fucking piss.'

Mark threw his holdall on the backseat, climbed into the passenger seat and lit a cigarette.

'So, where to first?'

Mark was thoughtful. 'Do you know of a Carter family? They come from over Barking way?'

'Yeah, a boxing family, good little fighters they are and all. I've seen them fight a few times.'

'What about the eldest one, Tommy Carter?'

'Yeah, I know who he is. Fuck me that boy could box I can tell ya. I'm surprised he didn't make it as a professional; threw it all away apparently. He took over from Davey Abbott when he kicked the bucket.' He flicked the switch on the indicator and eased out of the parking space.

'Where can I find him?'

Jason shrugged. 'I haven't seen him around for a while. Keeps himself to himself, does Tommy. I'm not even sure if the family still lives in Barking.'

Mark thought this through. 'I need to see him. Can you set up a meeting?'

'Yeah, no problem, I'll ask around. Shouldn't be too difficult. Like I said, they're well known in the boxing circle.'

Mark gave a satisfied grin. He couldn't wait to get his hands on Tommy Carter.

* * *

Ushering his brothers out of the Portakabin, Tommy watched as Danny McKay drove on to the forecourt. 'All of you, out,' he shouted. 'And that includes you, Jimmy.'

Jimmy narrowed his eyes and, lounging back on a leather sofa, he screwed up his face. 'What the fuck is going on?' he hissed. 'What are they doing here? I'm telling you, Tommy, this better not be what I think it is.'

'It's not.' Tommy swallowed deeply. It wasn't often he lied to his younger brother and he averted his gaze, his cheeks flushing pink, knowing for a fact, Jimmy would only try to throw a spanner in the works. 'It's to do with Smith, and when he hauled me in the other day.'

Jimmy made a show of making himself comfortable, his chin pointing upwards in defiance. 'Well, in that case, I'd best stick around and make sure they don't try anything on.'

'They won't.' Pulling on his brother's arm, Tommy glanced over his shoulder. It was too late, McKay and Garner were already approaching the door. With no time to evict Jimmy, Tommy welcomed the two men into the office, his teeth gritted as he raised his eyebrows in a warning to his brother to keep his mouth shut. 'You both remember me brother, Jimmy.'

The two men nodded.

Taking the seat offered to him, Moray sat down, and steepled his long fingers across his chest. 'Before we begin, let me get something

straight, I'm here because of him,' he said, jerking his thumb towards
Danny. 'Now, I don't trust you, either of you,' he said, 'so, let me tell you
now, everything you do, I will be watching, and believe me, the very
second I feel that something isn't right, there's gonna be hell to pay.'

Tommy nodded. 'Likewise. So, are you in or not?'

Danny McKay cleared his throat. 'We're in. We want Hopper
disposed of, and then all profit from the gold will be split fifty-fifty.
I'll sort Moray out from my cut, and you can deal your brothers in
with your cut.'

'Deal.' Tommy thrust out his hand. He could feel Jimmy's eyes
on him, and he deliberately avoided making eye contact.

'Whoa, hold up a minute.' Jimmy held up his hands, his voice
incredulous. 'What the fuck is going on here?'

All eyes fell upon Tommy and underneath their hard stares he
groaned. Flopping down into a chair, he looked across at his
brother wearily. 'We're gonna kill Hopper and split the proceeds of
the gold.' There, he'd said it, and now Jimmy knew the score.

Jimmy narrowed his eyes. 'And when were you gonna tell us
about this? You know, us, as in your brothers.'

Tommy sighed. 'I was gonna tell you once the deed was done.
The less you lot knew about it, the better.'

'So, you were willing to put Jonny's life at risk after all?' Jimmy
spat out the words, as further proof to just how angry he was.

'I've already told you he isn't in danger. I've sorted it out.'
Tommy kept his voice low, embarrassed to have to explain himself
in front of McKay and Garner.

Shaking his head, Jimmy turned to stare out the window. The
atmosphere in the room had turned decidedly frosty.

'Is there a problem here?' Danny wagged his finger between the
two brothers.

'Nah.' Tommy gave a nonchalant shake of his head. 'My brother
knows the score, and I run things around here, ain't that right?'

Tommy said, looking at Jimmy. His eyes flashed dangerously, silently warning his brother to back off.

Jimmy gave a small nod of his head and pursed his lips. To say he was angry was an understatement, and he stood quietly brooding on the deal Tommy had made. The fact that Tommy was willing to put Jonny's life at risk had shocked him to the core. So much for his brother's code of practice that family always came first.

* * *

Once the two men had left the office, Jimmy rounded on his brother. 'You really are a piece of work, Tommy, do you know that?'

Tommy sighed and rubbed at his temples. 'Don't fucking start, bruv, you're giving me a headache.'

'I'm giving you a headache?' Jimmy began to laugh at the accusation. 'Let me tell you now, if anything happens to our brother, you'll have more than just a headache to deal with.'

'Nothing's gonna happen to him. You've just heard the plan for yourself. Once Hopper arrives on the premise of collecting the gold, we do him over. Job done.'

Jimmy sat forward in his seat. 'Yeah, and your last plan worked out so well, didn't it? That's why were in this mess.'

'I'm only human,' Tommy said and held up his arms. 'I am allowed to fuck up every now and again.'

'Yeah, a fuck up of epic proportions. You always seem to be at the centre of everything that goes fucking wrong.'

'What's that supposed to mean?'

Realising he'd gone too far, Jimmy quickly changed the subject. 'And since when did you become a cold-hearted killer, eh? We rob banks for fuck's sake. We're not hitmen.'

'No back up. What did you mean by I'm at the centre of every-thing that goes wrong?'

Standing up, Jimmy looked his brother in the eyes. 'All right, if you want me to be honest, I will be.' He began ticking off the list on his fingers. 'Pete Williams; Davey Abbott; you half beating our Gary to death; Bethany fucking Johnson; and now you want to kill Mark Hopper. Do I need to continue?'

'That's not fair, Jimmy.' Tommy swallowed deeply; he wasn't afraid to admit that the truthfulness in Jimmy's words stung. 'You know I was more than willing to give myself up, when Davey was killed.'

Jimmy nodded, recalling the moment. 'Yeah, I know, I remember. I'm sorry, okay.' He sighed.

'And as for Bethany Johnson, well she's a fucking nut job, and we both know it,' he said, walking across the office.

Again, Jimmy nodded in agreement. 'I just don't like this deal you've made, bruv. It's too risky.'

'It's a lot better than the alternative. Did you really believe Smith and Hopper would let us go on our merry way, once we'd given back the gold?'

'Well, yeah. Why wouldn't they?'

'Do me a favour, you need to wise up. It must be so nice to live in that head of yours,' Tommy said with a half smile, to take the edge off his words. 'As soon as they'd got the gold back, they would have killed us, all of us. Do you really think Smith would have let us off with what we did?'

'I dunno, I thought' – Jimmy shivered as ice-cold fear trickled down his spine – 'I thought once we'd given it back, that'd be it.'

'No, Jimmy. That wouldn't be it.' Tommy looked his brother in the eyes. Jimmy's naivety worried him at times, he was too nice for his own good. 'Don't worry. It'll be okay, and like I keep saying over and over again, I've sorted it out.' Tommy took a seat behind the desk. He pushed a stack of paperwork away from him, knocking several biro pens to the floor. He rested his forearms across the wooden table top. The plan had to work, he was counting on it, and if it didn't, well the consequences didn't bear thinking about. The only thing he knew for sure was that Freddie would take great pleasure in bringing him down, and that included his brothers, all of his brothers, young Jonny included. 'The worst that'll happen is that McKay and Garner could end up double-crossing us.'

Jimmy's eyes widened and, putting up his hand, Tommy gave a small smile. 'Don't worry, bruv. Trust me, if the worst comes to the worst, then they can keep the fucking gold, okay? I'm only doing this deal to get Smith and Hopper off our backs. So yeah, as far as I'm concerned, Jonny's safety does come first. In fact, it's paramount to me, the gold doesn't even come into it. I couldn't give a rats arse about it, and that's the truth of the matter.'

Jimmy looked to the floor, shame flooding through him. He should never have doubted his brother. All along he should have known, Tommy wouldn't have put their baby brother at risk.

Jason Moore made his way into Gold's Gym and watched as men of all ages swung their gloved fists at punching bags. Spotting Frank Carter across the gym, he slowly made his way towards him, navigating around the busy room.

He came to a stop in front of the boxing ring. 'Frank Carter, isn't it?' he asked, shoving his hand forward.

Frank turned around. 'Yeah.' He shook the proffered hand, recognising Jason from previous fights he'd been to.

Jason smiled. 'I think I've seen all of your boys fight, apart from this one,' he said, nodding his head towards Jonny.

'He's got his first fight tomorrow night.' Frank turned his attention back to his youngest son.

'How's your eldest boy, Tommy, doing?'

Frank glanced over his shoulder. 'He's doing okay.' He narrowed his eyes, immediately suspicious. 'What is it you want? It should only be fighters and trainers in here.'

Jason stroked his chin. 'Have you got a contact number for Tommy, or know where I can find him?'

Frank shook his head. 'No.'

Unsure if Frank was telling the truth or not, Jason studied him for a few moments. 'Okay.' He glanced back at Jonny. 'Let's hope he gets a win tomorrow night.' With that, Jason walked out of the gym. In the foyer, he stopped to look at the posters on the wall promoting the upcoming fights. Snatching up a flyer, he shoved it into his jacket pocket, and walked out.

Climbing into his car, Jason passed the flyer across to Mark Hopper. 'The youngest Carter has a fight tomorrow night. Tommy Carter is bound to be there to watch his brother.'

As his eyes skimmed over the leaflet, a wide grin spread across Mark's face. 'Of course, he'll fucking be there.'

Jason chewed on the inside of his cheek. 'What is it you want to see Tommy about?'

Mark tapped the side of his nose. 'That's my business.'

Nodding, Jason had a feeling it wouldn't be a friendly visit. Nothing with Mark ever was. He started the ignition and swung on to the road. He wouldn't get involved, he decided. He'd learnt long ago, that when it came to Mark Hopper, it was best to keep your own counsel – and for your own safety, your nose well and truly out of the man's business.

* * *

'Come on! Behave yourselves, otherwise there will be no chocolate cake at Nanny's house.' Stacey's words had the desired effect and, taking a deep breath, she gathered her children by their hands. With difficulty, Stacey navigated her way out of the front door. Her cheeks were red by the time she met Tommy at the car, and she rolled her eyes at her husband, flustered.

'What's going on?' Tommy couldn't help but smile as he climbed out of the car to help put the children on to the backseat.

'One day, Tommy, for just one day, you are going to stay at home and look after this lot. And then, you'll understand.' She planted a kiss on her husband's cheek, then climbed onto the front seat.

'And breathe.' Tommy spoke slowly, emphasising his words, hiding the smile that threatened to spill across his face.

'I mean it, Tommy. I'll make you do it one day,' she said, as she glanced over her shoulder at their children and burst out laughing. The moment Tommy appeared, they always turned into angels. She shook her head. 'This lot will be the death of me, I swear they will.'

'You don't want another one once this baby is born then?' It was said tongue-in-cheek.

Stacey's eyes shot towards her husband. 'No, I bleeding well don't,' she said, rubbing her hand over her bump. 'These three will keep me on my toes as it is.'

Tommy laughed. 'Come on, we'd best get cracking,' he said, starting the ignition. 'Me mum will be having kittens if we're late.'

* * *

Janet Carter welcomed her son and his family into the house with open arms.

'Oh Tommy,' she said as she helped the children out of their coats, 'your dad wants a word with you.'

Rolling his eyes Tommy winked across at Stacey, before making his way into the living room. As he entered Frank was sitting in the chair beside the fire. 'Mum said you wanted a word.'

Frank looked up. He placed the latest issue of a boxing magazine he'd been reading onto the floor beside his feet and gave a nod. 'Close the door.'

Doing as he was asked Tommy closed the door then took a seat on the sofa opposite his father. 'What's up?'

'A bloke came into the gym today, asked me how he could contact you.' Frank pursed his lips.

'What bloke?' Tommy frowned.

'I dunno. I've seen him around before though, at a couple of fights. Jason something or other.'

'What did he look like?'

Frank shrugged. 'Average-looking I suppose, mousey-coloured hair, and no, he didn't look like Old Bill, before you ask.'

'Did you give him my number?'

'No.'

Tommy bit down on his lip. 'Good,' he said, getting to his feet.

'What are you getting my boys involved with this time, Tommy? That fella must have wanted you for something, and seeing as you're involved, I'm guessing it wasn't a friendly visit.'

Taken aback, Tommy sunk down on the sofa and rested his elbows on his knees. 'What do you mean?'

'You!' Frank waved his hand towards his son. 'You've always had an eye for trouble, and you've taken my sons along for the ride with you.'

Tommy leant towards his father. He battled to keep his temper under control. 'I know I let you down by walking away from the ring, but I am still your son.'

Frank narrowed his eyes.

'All I ever hear from you is… my boys this, my boys fucking that,'

Tommy spat. 'Well, what about me, eh? Whether you like it or not, I am still one of your boys.'

Frank swallowed before answering. He could feel his cheeks redden at Tommy's words. His son, the one he'd had such high hopes for, had given him a few home truths on fatherhood and it was true, he couldn't deny the fact that he'd pushed his eldest boy out of his life. Ever since Tommy had quit the ring, he'd practically ignored him. 'Yeah, you're right. You are still my son.' Shame flooded through him. 'So, who is he, this Jason bloke?'

Tommy sighed. 'I don't know. He could be anyone.' And he was telling the truth. As far as he was aware, he'd never dealt with a Jason before.

Frank stared at his son. 'Be truthful with me, Tommy. Have you got yourself into trouble? First of all, you turn up at the gym, wanting to speak to our Jonny. And then, this bloke comes looking for you.'

Shaking his head, Tommy averted his eyes. How could he tell his dad the truth? The mess he'd got himself into was so much worse than Frank could even begin to imagine. 'Of course not, Dad, you know me. I only do a bit of ducking and diving to make a bit of cash, nothing heavy.'

Frank studied his son. 'As long as that's all it is, Tommy.' He watched as his eldest boy nodded. 'Then, in that case, if this bloke turns up again, I'll tell him to sling his hook.'

Tommy remained silent. His old man had got him thinking as to who this Jason bloke could be. He sat back in his seat and chewed on the inside of his cheek as he tried to rack his brains. He couldn't recall any Jason from when he'd been boxing.

'Dinner's ready!' Stacey popped her head around the living room door. She smiled at her husband. 'What are you two up to? It's quiet in here.'

'Just having a little chat, that's all.' Tommy smiled, masking the worry that rippled through him. What with everything going on with Freddie Smith and Mark Hopper, he was starting to feel paranoid, and he couldn't shake the feeling that this Jason bloke was somehow involved, he had to be. Getting up from the sofa, he sighed. It would all come out in the wash. It was an old saying of his gran's, and if Tommy was being totally truthful, that was exactly what he was afraid of. Not for the first time did he wish that he could turn back time; he would have steered clear of the Ilford Palais that was for sure. He should have listened to Mad Dog and Jimmy; they'd both tried to warn him that he was biting off more than he could chew but being the stubborn bugger he was he hadn't wanted to listen.

22

'I don't think he's gonna buy it.'

Danny turned to face Moray. 'He has to, for this to work. So, we need to be convincing, right?'

They were sat in Danny's car, outside the Ilford Palais, looking up at the venue. Moray sighed. 'You know what he's like. He'd question Jesus Christ twice, and even then, he'd think he was trying to get one over on him.'

'Yeah, I suppose.'

'No suppose about it. I can guarantee he'll question us.'

Danny began tapping his thumb against the steering wheel. After a few moments, he shifted his weight in his seat. 'Come on, let's get this over and done with.' He opened the car door and climbed out.

'Remember we're off to Birmingham, not Manchester or Liverpool. It's Birmingham. We have to at least get the destination right.' They began walking towards the club.

'Yeah, I know. We'll just tell him some cock and bull story. We've had a tip off that the gold is in Birmingham, and we're driving there now.' Danny paused on the steps leading inside the club. He lifted his eyebrows upwards. 'Are you ready?'

Moray mirrored the action. 'As I'll ever be.'

They pushed through the doors and made their way across the dance floor. Together, they made a formidable team, both over six feet tall, broad shouldered, and muscular. They took the stairs two at a time, then walked along the upper corridor towards Freddie's office. Pausing, Danny took a deep breath before rapping his knuckles against the wooden door.

'Come in,' Freddie's booming husky voice called out.

Pushing open the door, Danny and Moray walked through. 'Boss.'

Freddie looked up from behind the desk. 'Have you found the gold? I've heard rumours Hopper is back in England.'

Danny glanced towards Moray, before speaking. 'We've had a tip off it's in Birmingham.'

'Birmingham?' There was surprise in Freddie's voice. 'What the fuck is it doing in Birmingham?'

Moray gave a shrug of his shoulders. 'Fuck knows, but we're going to drive there now and see what's going on.'

Freddie was thoughtful. 'I don't understand.' His forehead furrowed. 'How would someone in Birmingham know about the gold?' He scowled across at the two men in front of him. 'Who has links to Birmingham?' he demanded.

Both men shrugged and Danny cleared his throat before speaking. 'Beats me, but I've had a very good tip off. A little firm in Brum has been opening their mouths, stating they have the gold. It seems the real deal to me.'

'Do you need more muscle?'

Opening out his arms Danny's heart began to beat faster. Having other heavies tagging along with them was the last thing they needed. 'What the fuck for?' He glanced across to Moray. 'It's a little firm in Brummie land. We can take care of it.'

Freddie nodded. He didn't doubt them for a second. Both men were lumps and faces in their own right. McKay was a loose cannon, and Garner, a bare-knuckle prize fighter. 'Okay, well, keep me updated.' He stabbed his finger forward. 'Let me know as soon as you have that gold.'

As they turned towards the door, Moray nudged Danny in the ribs, raising his eyebrows towards him.

'Oh.' Danny turned back around. 'Maybe we should take the gold straight to Hopper once we've recovered it.'

Freddie narrowed his eyes, a quizzical expression passing over his face.

'Just in case he turns up here looking for it. I could give him a call and tell him I'm off to collect it now.'

'And what if it isn't in Birmingham?'

'I'm pretty sure it is. Like I said, my tip off was a dead cert.'

Freddie nodded. The mere thought of Hopper turning up looking for the gold was enough to bring him out in a cold sweat. 'Okay, don't forget to keep me updated.' He waved his hand, dismissing them.

Outside in the corridor, Danny blew out his cheeks, and raised his eyebrows. 'That was fucking close,' he said, his voice low.

'Come on.' With a backwards glance towards Freddie's office, the two men made their way back to Danny's car.

'By the way, you can call Hopper. There's no point in me doing it. That wanker hates me as much as I hate him.'

Moray groaned. He should've known this one was coming. 'Give me his phone number,' he growled.

* * *

Mark Hopper ended the call and smiled. 'Looks like I'm gonna be killing two birds with one stone.'

Jason glanced sideways, waiting for the man to elaborate.

'Not only will Tommy Carter be at the fight, but my gold's gonna be brought there.' He rubbed his hands together. 'What a fucking touch.'

Jason remained quiet. He concentrated on the road ahead of him. He wasn't keen on Hopper and didn't trust the man as far as he could throw him. One minute, he could smile at you, the next, he'd plunge a knife deep into your chest. Jason knew this for a fact, because he'd seen it happen before his own eyes. Silently, he counted off the days until Hopper fucked off back to Spain. In fact, the only reason he was driving Hopper around, was as a favour to his boss, Dean Johnson.

'Pull over.'

The authority in Mark's voice caused Jason to immediately swerve the car over to the kerb. He'd barely pushed his foot on the brake when the man leapt out of the car and bounded across the road. From his position in the driver's seat, Jason watched as Mark had some unsuspecting victim up against the wall by the throat. He groaned inwardly. Today was going to be one of those days, he could feel it.

Aiden Coleman smiled as he watched Jimmy begin to dress. 'Do you know what we should do?'

Jimmy turned his head. A slow grin began to spread across his face. He loved Aiden's accent. The soft Irish lilt was like music to his ears. 'What's that?'

'We should go on holiday.' He stretched out across the flowered bedspread. 'Somewhere sunny, like Spain. Somewhere no one knows us.' He tilted his head upwards. 'Some place where we don't need to hide away from your brothers.'

Jimmy took note of the way Aiden raised his eyebrows at the mention of his brothers. 'Yeah, we should do that.' He was thoughtful for a moment. In fact, he fancied a little break and to have the chance to let off a bit of steam, and a change of scenery sounded like heaven. Besides, Tommy had already asked him if he would be willing to travel to Spain and meet a contact there who was in the business of melting down gold. He may as well kill two birds with one stone. 'All right, yeah, we'll do it.'

Jumping up off the bed, a smile spread across Aiden's face. 'I'll get some brochures from the travel agents then.'

Jimmy nodded. All that was needed first, was for Mark Hopper to be disposed of, and then he was free to take a little holiday. He just had to hope and pray Aiden wouldn't go into a strop every time he disappeared off to do business for Tommy. He looked across at the man, watching as he began sorting through his wardrobe, pulling out shorts and T-shirts. He had a feeling it wasn't going to go down too well. He turned his head away. Bollocks to him. He was a Carter first and foremost. This was family business, and that would always be his top priority.

* * *

Climbing out of the bath, Tommy stood on the bathmat. Trickles of water ran down his body, pooling at his feet. It wasn't every day that he planned on killing a man. He studied his reflection in the mirror. He looked tired. He closed his eyes briefly, before grabbing up a bath towel. Beginning to dry himself, Tommy looked down at the towel in his hands, before tossing it into the sink, and placing his hands upon the wall, his head bowed. Jimmy was right. He was an armed robber, not an ice-cold killer. Nerves were beginning to get the better of him. Could he really go through with it and kill Hopper? Could he really take a man's life? His thoughts went to his youngest brother. He couldn't turn back the clock; he would see it through. He had no other choice; he had to do this not only for Jonny's sake, but for all of their sakes.

After spraying a generous amount of deodorant underneath his arms, Tommy began to dress. He dismissed the fact from his mind that Hopper was a psychopathic lunatic, who would more than likely kill him in the blink of an eye. He knew for a fact he would need to be ready and waiting to attack hard and fast, if there was any chance of the hit being successful. He turned towards the sink, the towel he'd tossed there saturated from the running tap. 'Fuck it,' he mumbled. He pulled up his sleeves and yanked the sodden material out of the sink. He noted the weight of the wet towel in his hands, before wringing it out and dumping it into the bath and walking out of the bathroom.

Deep in thought Tommy made his way downstairs. He would need McKay and Garner to entice Hopper into one of the changing rooms used by the boxers. It was there that the crime needed to take place, far away from any witnesses.

He came to stand inside the living room doorway. From his position, he watched as Stacey and the children played. His wife caught his eye and gave him a smile. She had no idea of what he was planning, or for that matter, what he was capable of. Tommy walked into the room and kissed the top of her head. More than anything, he planned on keeping it that way. He had promised Stacey long ago there would be no more secrets between them, but this was something he could never tell her. How would he even begin to find the right words?

'I'm off now. I'll see you tonight.'

Stacey looked up. 'Where are you off to?'

'Jonny's fight.'

'Oh yeah, I'd completely forgotten all about it. Tell him to break a leg.' Stacey paused, and leaning back against the leather sofa, she twirled a strand of dark hair around her finger. 'Can you say that to boxers, or is it just actors?' She gave a small smile. 'I hope I haven't just jinxed him.'

'Nah, it's fine, I'll tell him. Right.' He ruffled her dark hair, the silky strands soft beneath his fingertips. 'I have to go. Don't wait up for me.'

'I won't.' She began to laugh. 'Besides, it's bound to get messy.'

'Huh?' Tommy snapped his head towards her, and his heart began to beat faster. What did she mean by that? Did she know what he was planning? He raised his eyebrows questioningly. 'What do you mean?'

'You out with your brothers. There's bound to be alcohol involved somehow.' She tilted her head to the side, narrowing her eyes. 'What did you think I meant?'

Tommy laughed, hiding the fear he'd felt. All of this creeping around was making him paranoid. 'Nothing. I'll see you tonight.' He walked from the room, aware of Stacey's gaze following his retreating back. He wanted to kick himself; of course he should have known what she'd meant.

'Why do I have a horrible feeling of déjà-vu? I feel like we've been in this position before,' Moray said. They were sat in Danny's car outside the Barking Assembly Hall in Barking, Essex. It was here Jonny Carter was due to fight.

Danny continued staring straight ahead, out of the car windscreen. Immediately, he knew what Moray was referring to. 'This is different.'

Moray shifted in his seat. 'Is it? Feels the same to me.' He fingered the scar across his cheek, a constant reminder of a crime they'd committed as teenagers. 'We were sitting in a car waiting then as well.' He looked around him at the Mercedes' plush interior. The grey carpets in the foot well were spotless. There was no denying his mate kept the motor spick and span. 'Granted, it was a shittier model back then, but it was still a car.'

'For fuck's sake, Moray, is there an actual point to this? It's done, dusted, forgotten. Enough now, eh?'

Moray raised his eyebrows. He knew when to keep schtum. He began looking out the car window towards the people making their way inside the venue. 'It wasn't as busy as this then though, was it?' He nodded towards the hall, unable to stop himself from saying what was on his mind.

Danny threw up his arms. 'Fuck me! What's got into you? Thanks for the trip down memory lane, but I'd rather stay in the present, if you don't mind. I already know what we did, where we did it, and why we did it, so let's leave it at that.' Danny turned his head to look out the side window. The truth was, he still felt guilt from what they'd done. Not the murder itself, no, that cunt had deserved everything he'd had coming to him. It was what they had done afterwards that was causing his guilt. Planting the evidence on an innocent man and watching him go down for life, was something that still lay heavy on his conscience.

'That's Hopper over there, ain't it?'

Danny turned his head to follow Moray's eyeline, thankful for the change of conversation. 'Yeah, that's him, the fucking cunt. I'd recognise that bastard's cocky swagger a mile away.'

'Wait for Carter to show up,' Moray stated, 'and then we'll follow him inside. The last thing we want, is to actually be seen going in with Hopper.'

* * *

Tommy banged his fist against the steering wheel. He'd been stuck in traffic for more than twenty minutes. It was always the same whenever he tried to get off the estate in rush hour. No matter which direction he drove in, the roads were chocka block. It was the A13 which was causing the delay, and seeing as he needed to drive across it, he had no other choice but to sit there and curse anything and everything around him.

By the time he pulled into the car park adjoining the assembly hall, he was ready to go ape shit. He'd planned on having a quick word with McKay and Garner, and now, all thanks to the poxy traffic, he couldn't. His old man was already parked up and had begun unloading the boot. Realising the moment was lost, Tommy inwardly groaned. It would have to wait. He couldn't be seen chatting to the men, especially not by his father or brothers. They would only get suspicious. He switched off the engine and climbed out of the motor in time to watch his younger brothers begin piling out of Gary's car. He raised his hand in a greeting and walked over to Frank's car.

Pulling Jonny into a bear hug, Tommy grinned. 'Here he is... our champ.' He swung his arm around his brother's neck, ruffling his dark hair.

'Hey, cut that out, he's got a fight,' Frank warned. 'You should know better than that, Tommy.'

Immediately Tommy released his brother and rolled his eyes. Frank had always had a knack of making him feel like a naughty school boy. 'I told you we'd all come to watch you, didn't I?'

Jonny nodded, biting down on his thumb nail, his eyes wide.

'And you're gonna smash this, bruv.'

'Do you think so?' Jonny asked.

'Yeah, of course you are. You're a Carter, boxing's in your blood. Besides, you've only got to fight for three rounds. You could do that with your eyes closed.'

'It's four rounds he's fighting.'

Tommy raised his eyebrows, clearly impressed. Most juniors only fought three rounds. 'There you go, four rounds. That's eight minutes to show them you've got what it takes.'

Jonny moved his head from side to side, easing out the tension in his neck. As he looked up at the venue, he felt sick to his stomach.

'Come on.' Tommy gave a small laugh as he slung his arm across his youngest brother's shoulders. They had all been in Jonny's shoes at one point or another over the years. 'Stop thinking about it, and just get in there and do it.'

Once inside the foyer, they waited for Frank to sign Jonny in. Already, the venue was beginning to fill, and an excited hush could be heard from the main hall, as they walked down a set of corridors. Tommy looked around him, getting his bearings, and took note of the exits. It was imperative that they knew how to slip out unseen. The hard part would be getting Hopper's body out after the deed. He forced the dilemma to the back of his mind. He, McKay, and Garner, would have to work it out when the time came.

He fell into step beside Jimmy, making sure to keep his voice low. 'Stay with Dad and the others tonight. This could get dangerous, and I don't want you there.'

'That ain't your choice to make.'

'Yeah, it is,' Tommy answered, staring straight ahead of him. 'I've already made my decision, and I don't want you there. And unless you want me and you to fall out, you'd better do as I say.'

Jimmy took heed of his brother's warning. Having been on the receiving end of Tommy's temper in the past, he took his brother's words seriously. He swallowed down a retort and nodded. 'Just be careful, okay? And don't forget, this is Hopper you're dealing with.'

'Don't worry bruv, I won't.' Tommy forced his voice to sound a lot more confident than he actually felt.

* * *

Mark Hopper walked inside the assembly hall. He looked around him. Already, the hall was beginning to fill up as people, mainly men, took their seats. That cunt Tommy Carter had to be somewhere. He turned his head sideways. 'Is he here?' he asked Jason Moore. 'Can you see him?'

Jason shook his head, breathing a sigh of relief. The last thing he actually wanted to do, was cause trouble for Tommy Carter. He was a nice kid, from what he could remember of him. 'Nah, I can't see him. I can't see any of the Carters, come to think of it. They've got to be backstage still.'

'Go and have a butcher's then and come straight back to me if you see him.'

Inwardly, Jason groaned. He didn't like what was being asked of him, not one little bit. 'I don't think they'll let me back there, Mark. I haven't got a pass or anything, have I?'

'Just go and fucking do it.'

Jason shoved his hands into his jeans pockets and wandered off towards the back of the hall. To his surprise, he had no trouble getting backstage. He wandered down the corridors, keeping his eyes peeled for the changing rooms. He could hear voices coming from along the corridor, and he darted behind a doorway, pressing his back up against the wall. It was the Carters.

Casually, and from a safe distance, Jason followed, watching which changing room they entered. With a heavy heart, he made his way back to the main hall to relay the information back to Mark Hopper.

* * *

Frank Carter began to wrap Jonny's hands. He secured the cotton bindings with tape and instructed his son to clench and unclench his fist. 'They feeling okay?'

Jonny threw a succession of punches into the air and nodded. All he wanted to do was to get into the ring and get the fight over and done with.

Sitting back on the wooden bench, Frank looked up at his elder sons. 'Come on, you lot out, give your brother some breathing space, and go and get in your seats.'

The brothers did as their father bade, wishing their brother luck on their way out of the changing room.

Tommy pulled Jimmy aside. 'I'm gonna go and look for McKay and Garner. Save me a seat, yeah?'

Don't be long, otherwise they'll start asking questions.' He nodded ahead to their younger brothers. 'And I can only give them excuses as to where you are for so long, before they start getting suspicious.'

* * *

Mark Hopper's lips were set in a straight line. He nodded as Jason spoke privately into his ear.

'He's wearing a white shirt, dark hair.'

'Wait here for me, and make sure you've got your phone switched on. When I ring you, go and get the car, and then come straight back for me. I'm gonna need help carrying the bags.' Mark's dark, emotionless eyes bore into Jason's skull, as he waited for the man to nod his head in agreement.

Satisfied, he swaggered in the direction of the changing rooms. In his pocket he felt around for his mobile phone and taking it out, he scrolled down to his incoming calls and pressed dial. 'Hello, it's Mark Hopper,' he said, his voice gruff. 'Meet me where the changing rooms are, and make sure you have my gold with you, no fucking about. I've got some business I need to take care of first.'

He switched off the call and looked up to see someone fitting Tommy Carter's description walking towards him. Slipping his phone back into his jacket pocket he held out his arms, blocking the man from passing him by. 'You Tommy Carter?'

Tommy stopped abruptly, his eyebrows raised. There was trepidation in his voice as he answered, 'Yeah.'

Mark's arm shot out and, grabbing Tommy around the throat, he shoved him inside the nearest changing room. Luckily for him, it was empty, not that it would have mattered if it had been occupied, he would have soon told them to fuck off out of it.

'Do you know who I am?'

With great difficulty Tommy nodded. Of course he knew who he was, he had to be Mark Hopper.

'Yeah, well, I've got a message for you from a very good pal of mine.' He drove his fist in to Tommy's stomach. 'That's from Dean Johnson.'

His grip tightened around Tommy's throat and he pushed him across the changing room, slamming him up against the metal lockers. 'And this is from me.' Using his full strength, he drove his fist forward a second time.

23

Moray and Danny walked into the changing room, in time to see Tommy being slammed up against the lockers, Mark's hand grasped tightly around Tommy's throat. They shared a glance before simultaneously stepping forward.

'What's going on here?' Making sure to keep his voice light Moray nudged Danny in the ribs. This wasn't exactly how they had expected events to pan out. Shouldn't it have been Mark being slammed against the wall?

'Fucking hell, put him down, will you? People will start talking.'

Mark turned his head. 'Well, well, look who it is. Bill and fucking Ben.' Releasing his grip from around Tommy's throat, a snarl spread across Mark face. 'What did you bring this prick with you for?' he asked, giving Moray a cold stare.

'Who are you calling a prick?' Danny's green eyes flashed dangerously. His body immediately became tense, his muscles straining against the cotton shirt he wore.

'So, Freddie's finally let you out to play, has he?' He threw Tommy away from him, and turned to face Danny, the corners of his lips curling into a smirk. Arrogance seeped out of his pores as he took a step closer. 'And what are you gonna do about it, eh?' he asked, looking Danny up and down. 'Well, come on, I'm waiting. If you wanna act the big man, go ahead and take a shot.'

Moray slammed his arm across Danny's body, restraining him. 'Leave him,' he said, gritting his teeth. 'He ain't worth it.'

Mark raised his eyebrows and began to laugh. 'Bottle gone has it, prick?' he goaded. 'In fact, you look like you've just fucking shit yourself.'

Danny curled his fists into tight balls and mumbled underneath his breath. 'Just let me crack him one, just once, and then I'll walk away.'

Moray shook his head. He had no concerns for his mate's safety where Mark was concerned. Danny could look after himself, and he better than anyone knew that to be a fact.

Mark began to laugh. 'Yeah, I thought as much.' He began waving his arms in and out, mimicking those of a chicken. 'Lost your bottle now, ain't you? Watch out, I think he's gonna cry.'

'Leave it,' Moray warned, pushing Danny away from the situation. He stabbed his finger towards Mark. 'If he goes for you, then believe me when I say this: I'm not interfering, you fucking asked for it.'

Laughing, Mark took a step away. He screwed up his eyes, staring at the two men intently. He'd had his fun, and now it was time to get back to business. 'So, where is it then?' he asked, looking around him, his eyes narrowed. 'Where's the gold.'

It was Moray's turn to grin. 'Do you want the good news, or bad news first?'

Mark lunged forward. His face reddening, spittle gathered at the corners of his snarled lips. 'Where's my fucking gold?'

* * *

After rubbing at his throat where Hopper had dug his thumbs into the flesh of his neck, Tommy staggered towards the adjacent shower room, coughing and gasping for air. Each time he swallowed, he felt as though his throat was on fire. Leaning back against the tiled walls to steady himself, Tommy took a deep breath. He could feel his erratic heart begin to slow back down to its normal rhythm, and he was thankful for the familiar thumping inside his chest. He wiped his hand across his face, his fingertips gliding across his cold and clammy skin.

For a few moments, he closed his eyes in a bid to regain his composure, then he pushed himself away from the wall. He was about to walk back inside the changing room, when he stopped abruptly. From the corner of his eye he took note of a white cotton bath towel that had been thrown carelessly into the corner of the shower room. Picking the towel up, he walked over to the sink, twisted open the hot tap, and watched as the steaming water saturated the thick cotton. With the material pulled taut between his fists, he was oblivious to the water that dripped down his wrists, soaking the cuffs of his shirt. Now that he was ready, he walked calmly back to the changing room.

Stepping out from around the doorway, Tommy heard Mark's irate shouts before he saw him. As far as he was concerned, there were no exceptions, this cunt had to go. He took a step closer. Mark's back was towards him and he crept further into the room. With as much force as he could physically muster, Tommy leapt forwards, and threw the steaming hot towel over Marks head, ensuring his face was covered and pulled hard, twisting the towel in his fists. He could sense Mark's shock, and twisted even harder, as the man's hands desperately clawed at the saturated thick material covering his face.

Mark's knees began to buckle as he fought for his life. Tommy battled to keep his grip. He couldn't fuck this up, not now; he needed to finish what he'd started. He pulled on the towel harder. He could hear muffled groans, could hear and feel the panic, as Mark struggled to breathe, the hot, thick, heavy, wet cotton towel suffocating him. The man dropped to his knees and, pushing his foot against Mark's back, Tommy pulled even harder. Using all of his strength, he pulled and twisted the towel until he could sense the man's life slowly begin to ebb away. Only when Mark fell to the floor, did Tommy collapse in a heap beside him.

His cheeks scarlet from the exertion, Tommy panted for breath, his lungs screaming out for much needed air. Taking the hand Danny offered out to him, he was hauled to his feet. He didn't need to ask if Mark was dead, just one glance at his red and purple mottled complexion, his bulging eyes, and the thick tongue, which protruded out from his slack blue lips, was enough to tell him that Mark Hopper was a goner.

* * *

'Right, well, now that this cunt is brown bread, what now?'

All eyes turned to Moray and both Tommy and Danny shrugged. 'We need to get him out of here,' Tommy said.

'No shit, Sherlock. There are no flies on you, are there? Fucking hell, I know we need to get him out of here.' Moray rolled his eyes. 'My point is, how exactly are we going to get him out? There's at least five hundred people through that door.' He looked towards the two men expectantly, before holding up his hand. 'Please tell me you actually have a plan.'

Tommy and Danny shook their heads, and Moray threw up his hands. 'Homework, Danny, fucking homework. This should have been one of the first things you pair of soppy bollocks thought through,' he said, shaking his head at his best mate's care-lessness.

'Homework? We're not at fucking school,' Danny snapped back. 'We'll think of something.'

'Well, you'd better think fast!' Muffled cheers echoed off the main hall and he jerked his thumb towards the door. 'That lot will be on us at any minute, and then the shit really will hit the fan.'

Looking around him, Tommy nodded towards a black holdall. He sized it up. It could easily fit a body inside, albeit it might be a tight squeeze. He walked towards the bag and began emptying it out, tossing the contents across the room. 'Stuff him in this. It's the only way we're gonna get him out unseen.'

'And then what, eh? Come on, Einstein, what do we do with him afterwards?'

'I don't fucking know. I thought you two would know what to do with him.'

'And why exactly would we know what to do with him? Killing people and disposing of their bodies isn't our day job, you know. Fuck me, Carter! Who do you think we are, the Mexican cartel or something?'

'I dunno, I just thought you'd know.'

'Well, you thought fucking wrong.' Moray shook his head. He watched as Tommy threw the holdall towards Mark's body, and he glared across at Danny. 'You pair of muppets.' He crouched down, lifting up Mark's feet. 'Well, come on then, help me get him into the bag, or are you both just going to stand there watching me?'

A few minutes later, with the bag now firmly encasing Mark's body, Tommy nodded. 'There you go. I told you he'd fit inside. No one would even be able to guess what's in it.'

'No one would guess what's in it?' There was disbelief in Moray's voice. 'Are you for fucking real? Look at it! It looks exactly what it is: a fucking body in a bag. What the fuck is wrong with you?'

Tommy's cheeks flushed. 'It's not that obvious.' He turned his head from side to side, inspecting the makeshift body bag.

'Right.' Moray stood back, looking down at their handiwork, his arms crossed over his chest. 'The way I see it, we've got one of three options. One, we throw him in the Thames and hope the cunt sinks to the bottom. Two, we take him out to Epping Forest and bury him. And three, we take him over to the farm in Brentwood and feed him to the pigs. The choice is yours.'

Danny chewed on the inside of his cheek. He looked across to Tommy. 'It's your call. What do you wanna do with him?' He looked down at the bag. 'What do you reckon?'

Tommy rubbed his fingers across his neck where Mark had tried to throttle him. 'Feed him to the fucking pigs.'

Danny tilted his head towards Moray. 'There you go, you heard the man. We feed him to the pigs.'

'Now, we're starting to get somewhere. Danny, you grab one end, and Einstein there can grab the other end. I'll be lookout.'

Hauling the bag several inches off the floor, they navigated their way out of the changing room, and moved down the corridor towards the nearest exit. 'He's a fucking dead weight,' Danny complained.

'What did you expect? He's dead. Stands to reason he'd be a dead weight.' Moray rolled his eyes. They were starting to jar his nerves with their stupidity. He pushed open the fire exit door, stepping aside, so the two men could manoeuvre out of the door. 'Wait here. I'll get the car.' He held out his hand for Danny's car keys.

Dumping his end of the bag onto the concrete steps, Danny dug deep into his denim pockets and passed across the keys. He glanced around him. 'Just hurry up,' he hissed. 'The last thing we want is to be caught red-handed with this,' he said, nodding down at the holdall.

* * *

With the body safely concealed in the boot of Danny's car, Tommy shoved his hands nervously into his pockets. He glanced behind him at the fire exit door. He was eager to get back inside the hall. He needed an alibi, and even more than that, he didn't trust McKay and Garner not to decide to dispose of him while they were at it. After all, why stop at one body? Throwing a second to the pigs would be no hardship on their part. He stood back slightly, watching as the two men began to climb into the car.

'Well?' Danny raised his eyebrows towards him. 'What are you waiting for? Are you getting in the motor or what?'

'I dunno, is it wise that we all go? I mean, shouldn't I stay here and show my face in there?' Tommy jerked his thumb behind him.

'Yeah, just leave us to do all the hard work, why don't you.' Moray blew out his cheeks. Carter was starting to take the piss now.

'You do the hard work?' Tommy poked his finger into his chest. 'It was me who did the hard work. I didn't see either of you two get your hands dirty; you didn't even lift a hand to help me.' He began to walk down the steps. 'Hopper would still be alive if I hadn't done him in.'

'And if we hadn't turned up when we did, it would have been you in the fucking boot of a car, instead of Hopper. Don't forget that.'

Danny held up his hand. 'Enough! This ain't gonna get us anywhere, is it? Tommy's right, we can't all go. It's gonna look a bit suspect if he goes on the missing list as well. No one even knows he had a meet with Hopper, so if he isn't in that hall, people will start asking questions.' Danny was thoughtful. He bit down on his lip before speaking. 'Yeah, you stay here. Me and Moray will take care of the situation. But I am gonna be coming for you tomorrow to sort out that gold.' He stabbed his finger towards Tommy.

Relieved, Tommy nodded. He walked back up the steps and turned to watch as the car pulled away from the kerb. He waited until the motor was out of sight, then made his way back inside the venue.

* * *

Tommy entered the main hall in time to see Jonny climb out of the ring.

'Where the fuck have you been? You missed the fight.' Gary eyed his brother suspiciously.

'I had some business to take care of.' He could feel Jimmy's eyes on him, and he gave a small nod to confirm that the deed was done. Mark Hopper was dead.

'Yeah, well, he won, not that you've even asked or likely to even care come to that.'

Tommy tore his eyes away from Jimmy to look at Gary, the contempt for himself written across his brother's face angering him. 'Of course I fucking care. So he won did he?' He forced a wide grin to spread across his face and clasped his hand on Jonny's shoulder. 'See, I told you, you'd win.'

'Yeah.' Jonny beamed. 'Done him in the third round. You should have seen it, Tommy, he went down like a sack of shit.' He felt exuberant and couldn't contain his excitement at winning his first fight.

Frank bounded behind his youngest son. 'Come on,' he barked, pushing Jonny forward. 'Where were you?' he spat, giving Tommy a cold stare. 'Your brother's big night, and you were nowhere to be seen.'

'I...' Tommy could feel shame flood through him. He could hardly tell his dad he'd missed the fight because he'd just killed a man. 'I had something I had to do.'

'Something more important than your brother's first fight?' Frank shook his head, disgust clearly evident across his face. 'Exactly what I would have expected from you. All you've ever done is think of yourself. Shame on you, Tommy.'

Tommy stepped aside as his father barged past him and ushered Jonny away. He could feel his brothers' eyes on him, and he swallowed down his embarrassment. He looked to Jimmy and shook his head sadly. The relationship he had with his father was beyond repair, he knew that now. Frank would never forgive him for quitting the ring, and he had a feeling that missing Jonny's fight may well be the final nail in the coffin as far as Frank was concerned.

As he walked towards his car, Tommy's head was bowed. All he wanted to do was to go home. He'd had a gutful. No matter what he did, he was always in the wrong.

* * *

Jason Moore looked down at his phone. Mark had been gone for well over an hour, and he still hadn't given him a call. He'd spotted the Carters, including Tommy, inside the hall, so where the hell was Mark?

Unsure of what he should do next, he poked his head around the door leading out to the corridor where the changing rooms were. Nothing. Hopper was nowhere to be seen. Wandering back to the main hall, Jason took out his phone and dialled Mark's number. It rang off.

'We're closing up now.'

Jason stuck his thumb up in the air. 'Cheers, mate.' He dialled Mark's number a second time, and again it rang off. With one last glance around him, Jason made his way to the exit. Outside on the concrete steps, he shrugged. Mark Hopper had, for all intents and purposes, disappeared.

* * *

In the pitch-black darkness, Danny and Moray hauled the holdall containing Mark Hopper's body across a wet and muddy field. 'Are you sure we're even going in the right direction?' Heaving up his end of the bag, Moray blew out his cheeks. With each step they took, the bag seemed to get heavier.

'Yeah, it can't be much further. I can fucking smell them from here. Either that, or Hopper is starting to stink already.'

Moray pushed his nose towards the bag. 'It's not him. We must be close.'

They continued walking. 'See, what did I tell you? I said we were going the right way,' Danny said. Up ahead, they could just make out the outline of the farm.

'We're gonna have to strip him.' They dumped the bag on the ground and began the grisly task of stripping Mark Hopper of his clothes and belongings.

Careful of where they trod, they manoeuvred the body through the dense slippery earth. 'Talk about pig in shit,' Danny groaned as they made their way towards the nearest pigsty. 'Fuck me, they don't half stink.' He wrinkled up his nose, then held his breath, not wanting to breathe in the foul stench of pig excrement. 'We're gonna stink of pig shit after this.'

'They say it takes a pig eight minutes to get through a body.'

About to launch himself over the fence, Danny placed his foot back on the ground. 'Cheers for that. I'll bear it in mind. Right, well in that case, we'll have to just chuck him over. I'm not getting in there with that lot now. Fuck that.'

Moray laughed. 'What's fucking wrong with you? They're pigs not lions.' They hauled up Mark's body and pushed him over the fence, jumping backwards as he fell to the ground with a loud squelch.

The splash of the body hitting the mud caused the pigs to squeal and run in all directions. Conscious of being seen, Danny glanced around him, then nodded down at the body. 'Shouldn't they be eating him by now?'

'How the fuck would I know? I'm not a pig farmer, am I? Get in there and push the pigs towards him.'

Danny's eyes widened. 'You can fuck right off! You get in there.'

Moray was thoughtful. He began searching on the ground for something he could throw at the pigs. Picking up a small rock, he aimed it forward, launching it into the air. 'Go on, go that way,' he shouted, trying to shoo the pigs towards the body.

The pigs squealed even louder. 'For fuck's sake, Moray, leave it out, will you? You're making them go Garrity.'

'Well, what do you suggest we do, eh?' Moray ran his hand through his hair. 'Maybe they're not hungry?'

'They're fucking pigs. They're always hungry, ain't they?'

Moray shrugged. 'I dunno.'

'Well, I ain't sticking around to find out. Come on, let's go.' Danny bent down to collect up the holdall and Mark's belongings.

'And what if they don't eat him?' Moray glanced behind him at the pigsty.

Danny sighed. 'Surely, by the time morning comes around, they will have. We can't sit here all night waiting for them to tuck in, can we?'

'Nah, I suppose not.' They began walking back across the field towards Danny's car.

'Look at the state of me,' Danny grumbled. He looked down at his jeans and boots. They were ankle deep in mud. 'I only bought these boots last week, and now they're fucked.'

'We've got to get in the motor like this yet.' Knowing just how particular his mate was about his car, Moray gave a small grin. 'Your boots are the least of your worries, mate.'

Danny groaned. 'Fucking Mark Hopper. Even when he's dead, he's giving me grief.'

Moray began to laugh. 'No wonder them pigs didn't wanna go near him.'

* * *

Stacey was in the kitchen, ironing. Beside her sat a small, plastic basket full of freshly washed clothes. The steam iron hissed as she ran it over one of Tommy's shirts. Unlike some women, she didn't find ironing a chore. There was something therapeutic about watching the creases disappear in front of her eyes, as she ran the hot iron over them. She heard a key turn in the lock and looked up at the clock on the wall. It was barely ten o'clock. 'Tommy is that you?' she called out.

As he entered the kitchen Tommy threw his keys onto the table and pulled out a chair, the wooden legs scraping against the lino.

'What are you doing back so early?'

'I didn't fancy it tonight.' Tommy sighed.

'Are you all right, babe?' Stacey peered closely at her husband; she couldn't help but noticed how shattered he looked. With a sigh she placed the iron in its holder, walked across the kitchen, and took a seat opposite him. 'What's wrong? And don't tell me nothing, because I know you, and I can tell when something's on your mind.'

Tommy shook his head. 'I just wanted to be on my own, away from everything, that's all.'

'What? Even away from me?'

Tommy could hear the hurt in his wife's voice and he reached across the wooden table to hold her hand. 'Course not.' He gave her a small smile. 'You and the kids are the only ones keeping me sane at the moment.'

'Do you want to tell me what's wrong?'

Tommy shook his head. How could he tell her? He knew the moment he opened his mouth, he would see disgust written across her face. He'd not only put his family's lives in danger but he'd also killed a man. 'It's just my dad. You know what he's like.'

Stacey gave a small smile. Tommy was right, she knew full well what Frank was like. Ever since he'd quit boxing, her husband and father-in-law had had a volatile relationship, and that was putting it mildly. 'Would you like a cuppa?' Stacey stood up and walked across to the kettle, flicking on the switch. She set out two mugs on the worktop and began spooning sugar into them. 'You can't change what's already happened, Tommy. You just have to get on with things. You had your reasons for what you did, and your dad's gonna have to accept that. Don't let him get you down.'

Tommy nodded. Without realising it, her words had hit the nail on the head. He'd had no other choice, but to kill Mark Hopper, and now that he was dead, he could get on with the rest of his life without having to look over his shoulder, or worry about keeping everyone he loved safe. A smile spread across his face. 'Come here,' he said, holding out his arms.

Stacey fell into her husband's arms. Pushing herself further towards him, she breathed in the familiar scent of his aftershave. She kissed the top of his head and smiled. 'Everything will work out okay. You just watch and see.'

24

Dean Johnson stepped off the plane at Gatwick Airport. This was the first time he'd set foot on British soil in over a year. He took a deep breath, inhaling the familiar scents deep into his lungs. How he missed good, old Blighty.

Walking through arrivals, Dean headed straight outside the airport. He was a man on a mission, and God help anyone who got in his way. Frankie Sullivan was standing beside his car waiting for his boss.

The two men shook hands, and with his lips set in a straight line, Dean spoke. 'Where the fuck is Hopper?'

Frankie had been expecting the question, and he gave a small shrug, his mouth opening and closing as he chewed on a piece of gum. 'I dunno, boss. He's disappeared off the face of the earth. No one has seen head nor tail of him.'

It wasn't the answer Dean had wanted to hear. He handed Frankie his suitcase and climbed into the front passenger seat. With every passing second, it was becoming clearer, that where the gold was concerned Hopper had had him over. He waited for Frankie to climb into the driver's seat, before speaking. 'Tell me everything. I wanna know where Hopper went, and who he spoke to while he was here. Who was the last person to see him?'

Frankie glanced towards his boss. 'That would be Jason Moore, and he's just as stumped as we are.'

Dean turned in his seat to look at Frankie. The constant smacking of Frankie's jaws as he chewed on the gum, was already beginning to grate on his nerves. 'Right, take me straight to Jason Moore; he'd better have some answers for me. And for fuck's sake, stop smacking your lips together.'

'Sorry, boss.' His cheeks reddening, Frankie nodded, wound down the window and spat out the gum. He knew better than to antagonise Dean Johnson.

As Dean was entering Britain, Jimmy and Aiden were leaving. Earlier that day Tommy had dropped them off at Stanstead Airport, in the heart of Essex.

'Here take this,' he'd told Jimmy, thrusting a scrap of paper containing the address of an acquaintance in the business of melting down gold, into his hand. 'Don't forget to go and see him while you're there. It's important, Jimmy.' He glanced over at Aiden. 'And make sure you go on your own. Don't take him with you whatever you do. This is family business.'

'Yeah, I know, and I won't.'

As he pulled away from the kerb Tommy leant across the passenger seat and shouted through the window. 'Don't forget, Jimmy. I'm counting on you.'

Jimmy raised his hand in acknowledgement.

'What was that all about?'

'Nothing.' Jimmy remained tight-lipped. He could feel Aiden's eyes on him and sighed. 'Just something I have to do for me brother while we're away. Family stuff.'

'What, while we're in Spain?'

Jimmy could hear the confusion in Aiden's voice and nodded. 'Yeah, it shouldn't take me long to do though. Hopefully just one or two days.'

Aiden placed his suitcase on the floor. 'So,' he hissed as he processed what Jimmy had told him. 'This was never about us spending quality time together. This was an excuse for you to go to Spain, and do work for that brother of yours?'

Jimmy rolled his eyes. The last thing he needed was for him and Aiden to fall out. They hadn't even stepped foot on the plane yet. 'Of course I want us to spend time together,' he said, placating the man. 'It's just, while I'm there, I need to go and do something, that's all.'

'And what am I supposed to do when you're flaunting off to do this family stuff, huh?'

'Sunbathe, get pissed, do some shopping, I don't know.' Jimmy shrugged. 'Do whatever you want.'

Aiden puffed out his cheeks. 'You better make this up to me,' he sulked.

'Yeah, I will,' Jimmy answered. Not for the first time in his life did he want to curse his brother. He had a nasty feeling that trying to make it up to the Irishman was going to somehow cost him dearly.

* * *

Dean Johnson climbed out of Frankie's car. They were in Dean's old neighbourhood. Born and bred in Dagenham, one of England's largest council estates, he stood outside Jason's house and looked around him. The place never seemed to change, only the people changed, as the previous residents moved out of the area trying to better themselves, not realising that no matter how far they moved away from the place, their Dagenham roots would never leave them. The two men walked down the path and, reaching the front door, Dean thumped his fist against it.

Cautiously, Jason inched open the door. He'd left the chain across as a precaution and peered out. 'Yeah?' he enquired.

'It's Dean Johnson. Open the fucking door.'

Sliding back the chain, Jason sighed with relief. 'Fuck me! You've got a knock like a copper.' He ushered the two men inside and, steering them through to the lounge, Jason indicated for them to take a seat. Quickly, he swept aside the discarded newspaper and empty crisp packets from the sofa. He was the first to hold his hand up and admit that his house was a shit hole; over-filled ashtrays and stained coffee mugs littered the small table. Empty cigarette packets had been crumpled and thrown into the corner of the room. And that was without the smell omitting from the over-used cat tray. Even he could smell it, and his nose had become accustomed to the stench. Cleaning had never been his missus' strong point, and shame flooded through him as he watched the men wrinkle their noses. He'd need to have a serious word with his wife when she came back from bingo. They couldn't go on like this. He gave her more than enough money each week, and she never seemed to be without a spray tan. The least she could do, was buy a can of polish and a duster.

Jason pushed his hands into his trousers pockets. 'What can I do for you, Dean? Can I get you a drink or something?'

Swiping crisp crumbs to the floor, Dean shook his head as he cautiously took a seat, declining the offer of a beverage. From the state of the lounge and the stained mugs, he didn't fancy taking a chance on a drink. 'Let's cut to the chase. Where the fuck is Mark Hopper? Frankie here tells me you were the last one to see him.'

Jason gulped. He had nothing to hide as far as Hopper was concerned, but still, he could feel his hands begin to tremble. 'I don't know.' He swallowed deeply. 'He went into the hall and never back came out.'

'What the fuck do you mean, he never came back out? He couldn't have just disappeared.' Dean spat out his words, anger clearly evident across his face.

Jason spoke fast. Dean Johnson was an intimidating individual, and that was on a good day. 'He went into the Barking Assembly Hall, and he didn't come back out. I looked everywhere for him. He must have slipped out of one of the side doors.'

'What did he go there for?'

'The gold. He said someone was bringing the gold to him.'

Dean looked to Jason expectantly. He lifted his arms in the air. 'Well, who was bringing the fucking gold?' He was losing his patience and couldn't help but feel as though he may well have been talking to a brick wall.

'I dunno.' Jason shrugged, looking from Dean to Frankie.

'Well, didn't you ask him?'

Jason shook his head.

'To be fair, boss,' Frankie cut in, 'Hopper isn't exactly the type of bloke you question, is he?'

Dean sighed. They had a point. It wouldn't have been in Jason's best interests to ask the man too many questions. Everyone knew what a loose cannon Hopper was, and to be on the receiving end of that temper of his, was not only dangerous, but terrifying. He stood up and began to make his way to the front door. Clearly, he would get no answers here.

'Oh.' Jason chewed on the inside of his cheek. He cocked his head to one side. 'He did go and have a chat with someone backstage, but I saw the man in question afterwards in the hall, and Hopper wasn't with him.'

'Who?' Coming to an abrupt halt, Dean turned around.

'Tommy Carter. He used to be a boxer and well, his younger brother was boxing there that night. Mark was keen to have a word with him, and so he went off looking for Tommy. That was the last time I saw him, but like I said, I saw Tommy in the hall afterwards, and Hopper wasn't with him.'

Tommy fucking Carter. Dean should have known his name would come up in his enquiries.

Once outside, Dean rested his arms on the car roof while he thought through the situation. He wished now that he'd asked Hopper where he'd stashed the gold. He had a feeling that could well be the missing piece of the puzzle. He slapped his hand on the roof, and opened the car door, climbing inside.

'Where to now, boss?'

Dean sighed. 'Just take me home.' He wasn't getting any younger and needed to recharge his batteries. More than anything, he needed to think. He knew he had a huge task ahead of him. He'd have to go right back to the beginning, and piece everything together. It was the only thing he could do, if he wanted to find Hopper, and more importantly, find the missing gold.

* * *

Jimmy squinted up at the bar, the sun blinding his vision. It wasn't a huge property. It had a small bar area and dance floor, with six tables and chairs positioned outside, and despite the low price tag, it had been nicely decorated and furnished.

'It also comes with a nice two-bedroom flat upstairs.'

Jimmy tore his eyes away from the building to look at the estate agent. Beside him Aiden was squirming with excitement.

'Just think, Jimmy, our own little piece of heaven.' A wide grin was spread across Aiden's face and he clicked his fingers 'That's what we could call it: Heaven's.'

Chewing on the inside of his cheek, Jimmy was unsure. It was a huge commitment and him and Aiden hadn't even been together that long, not to mention, he had a life back home in England.

Roger Draper smiled at the two men before him. He couldn't quite work them out. The Irish one, he'd bet every peseta in his bank account, was gay. But the tall, broad-shouldered, dark-haired fella, he wasn't so sure about. 'Would you like a few moments alone to think about it?'

Aiden nodded, before looking up at Jimmy, his eyes wide and almost pleading. 'This could be a new start for us.' He gave a cheeky grin, knowing full well Jimmy would cave in.

'Go on then mate.' Jimmy turned to the estate agent. 'We'll take it.' Beside him, Aiden jumped up and down with joy.

'I just need your details, and the name of your mortgage provider.' Roger gave a wide smile.

'Mortgage provider?' Jimmy frowned. 'I'm gonna pay in cash, mate.'

Roger raised his eyebrows, hiding his surprise, as Jimmy signed along the dotted line. It wasn't often people paid in cash, unless they were, how could he put it, unsavoury characters, or criminals and the like. He shook both men's hands, promising to return the following morning with the keys, before retreating back to the safety of his car.

'This is it, Jimmy,' Aiden smiled. 'Our very own place in the sun.'

Jimmy nodded, knowing full well this was an impulse purchase, but as he looked up at the bar he now owned, he couldn't help but feel a flutter of excitement in his belly. The only fly in the ointment was Tommy. He wasn't sure how his brother was going to take the news. He had an inkling it wouldn't go down too well, though.

* * *

Mad Dog Harris busied himself making a cup of tea. He glanced across to Tommy. 'Are you sure you won't have one, lad?'

Tommy shook his head. He leant back in the chair, kicking his legs up onto the desk, making himself comfortable. 'I'd rather have a beer.' He glanced up at the clock hanging by a nail precariously on the wall of the scrap yard office. Even by his standards, he knew it was too early for alcohol.

Mad Dog raised his eyebrows but kept schtum all the same. It hadn't slipped his notice that young Tommy had been drinking a lot more than usual of late.

'Any news from Jimmy?'

'Yeah, he rang me last night. He's made contact with the gold dealer. All we need to do is ship the gold over, and he'll take care of the rest. Apparently, it's a piece of cake.' He was thoughtful for a few moments. 'He said he has something to tell me when he gets back.' He looked across to the older man now. 'I mean, Jimmy. He's got something to tell me.'

Mad Dog pondered over Tommy's words. 'Not trouble, I hope.'

'Nah, I doubt it. He probably wants to shack up with this bloke of his.' Sighing, Tommy balled a scrap of paper in his hand and threw it in the direction of the waste bin, before massaging his closed eyes.

Mad Dog watched him intently. 'What's wrong, lad?'

Tommy shrugged. 'I dunno.' He bit down on his lip and glanced up at the clock, wondering if the pub was open yet.

'Drink isn't the answer son, trust me, I know. Been there, done it, got the bloody T-shirt, lad. And in the long run, it doesn't help.'

'Yeah, I know.' He sighed. 'I just feel like me head's gonna explode with it all, d'ya know what I mean?'

Mad Dog nodded. 'Aye, lad.' He sat forward in his seat. 'But once this gold's been taken care of, things will calm back down.'

Tommy remained silent. He just had a sinking feeling he couldn't shift. 'Yeah, I suppose so.'

'It will. How about that cup of tea now?'

Tommy gave a small smile. 'Go on then.' He may as well. After all, the pub didn't open for another hour.

* * *

Dean Johnson woke early. He'd always been an early riser, going right back to when he and Davey Abbott used to rob the lorries coming over from France at Tilbury docks. He thought of Davey now. It wasn't often he thought about him, admittedly. There had been too much bad blood between them in the later years leading up to when he'd taken the man's life. It was hard to recall the times when they had been more like brothers than business partners and mates. He sighed and pushed Davey to the back of his mind. What's done is done. There was no point brooding over it.

He wandered through the empty house. At one point, it had been full of laughter. He could still hear the giggles from his wife and little Bethany, whenever they had tried to prank him. He smiled at the memory. Where had it all gone wrong? He knew the answers lay with himself. After Maggie's death, he'd spoiled his daughter trying to overcompensate the loss of her mother. As a result, he'd raised a monster – a selfish, heartless woman. He was no fool. He knew Bethany had no maternal feelings when it came to his grandson, little Cameron. Wrongly, he blamed Tommy Carter for that. In his opinion the man had ruined his daughter, why else would she have grown so cold, what other reason could there be for the fact that she couldn't find it in her heart to love her own child? Her obsession with Carter was all consuming. She had no room inside of her to love anyone else.

Dean took a sip of his coffee and threw open the patio doors. He walked outside to the garden. Really, he should sell the place. It was highly unlikely they would ever move back to England. How could they? He couldn't risk his daughter being in close proximity to Carter. Again, he wrongly blamed Tommy Carter for this. He walked across the lawn, inspecting the roses. His Maggie had loved the house. He glanced back at his home. It was only bricks and mortar, he told himself, so why was he so reluctant to sell up? From inside the house the phone began to ring and making his way inside, he crossed over to the mantelpiece and lifted the phone off the cradle. 'Hello.' He listened for a few moments and nodded. 'Yeah, you'd better come and see me.'

* * *

Frankie Sullivan took a seat on Dean's plush velvet sofa. He almost had to stop himself from whistling out loud. The sofa alone must have cost a couple of grand. That was without the rest of the contents in the sitting room; from the stereo unit to the television set, there was a fair few bob in this house.

'Well?' Dean looked from the man to his companion, who was sitting silently beside him.

Frankie cleared his throat. 'Shawn here dropped Hopper off to see Freddie Smith. This was the day before he, you know...' he said, giving a little wink, 'did that job.'

Dean turned to look at Shawn. He was a gaunt man with a long, skinny face, and thin, straggly, greasy hair. He couldn't help but notice he had an ear lobe missing. He tore his eyes away from the missing lobe. 'What did he go and see Smith about?'

Shawn lifted his arms. A strong, foul, pungent scent of body odour wafted out from him. 'Dunno. He didn't say.' As he spoke, a remnant of food flew out of his mouth down onto Dean's carpet.

Feeling sickened, Dean averted his gaze and nodded. He weighed up whether it was worth paying Smith a visit. The likelihood was that Hopper could have gone to see the man about anything, not necessarily the gold. 'Okay...' He spoke slowly, as he tried to think. 'Looks like a visit to Smith is in order then.' He gathered up his jacket. 'Well, come on,' he barked. 'There's work to do.'

* * *

Freddie Smith, flanked by Danny and Moray, strolled inside the Ilford Palais. Now that the gold had been retrieved, he didn't have a care in the world. As the Top Dog of the East End, it was his given right that people spoke to him with the respect he deserved; whether they were young or old, if they didn't tip him his due, they would soon feel the back of his hand.

To his surprise Dean Johnson and his heavy were helping themselves to a bottle of brandy. Freddie narrowed his eyes. 'What's going on here?'

Dean Johnson held his glass aloft, inspecting the colour of the alcohol. 'Is this watered down?'

Freddie shook his head, too stunned to speak.

'That old trick is it then?' He pointed his finger towards Freddie. 'You've poured cheap brandy into an expensive brandy bottle; that way you can charge over the odds for it, am I right?'

Freddie nodded, causing Dean to laugh. 'They're probably too pissed to even notice the difference.' He placed his glass on the bar and walked towards Freddie, slinging his arm across the man's shoulder. 'Me and you need to have a little chat about a mutual friend of ours.'

Inwardly, Freddie groaned. It had to be something to do with Mark Hopper. If there was so much as a gold bar missing, he'd come down on McKay and Garner like a ton of bricks. Too wrapped

up in himself, Freddie failed to notice the startled glance shared
between his two heavies.

* * *

Stacey pushed open the door to The Short Blue public house and
marched across the floor towards the bar. Little Peter was nestled
on her hip. 'So, this is where you've been all afternoon is it, propping up the bar?' She spat out her words, disgusted by her
husband's behaviour. 'How could you, Tommy?'

Tommy placed his pint glass down on the bar and groaned,
barely even turning his head to look at his wife. 'What have I
done now? Did I forget to put the milk back in the fridge this
morning or something?' He gave a grin and resumed downing his
pint.

Stacey shook her head, her heart sinking; he'd been drinking a
lot more than usual of late and if she didn't like it one little bit. 'You
missed your daughter's nursery play. You know, Karen, your daughter? You must remember her, that little girl who happens to call you
Daddy.'

Anger flashed across Tommy's blue eyes. In that instant, he
looked menacing and Stacey took a step away and gulped. She'd
never been scared of her husband before. Tommy had never given
her any reason to be, but in that moment, she saw him as others
did: dangerous.

As quick as it came, the anger was gone. 'I'm sorry, okay?' he
groaned. 'I completely forgot it was today. I've had a lot on my
mind, Stace.'

'No, it's not okay. I reminded you this morning, before you left
for work, that the play was this afternoon. What's got into you,
Tommy? This isn't like you.' She pointed her finger towards him.
'And you can be the one to explain to our Karen why you weren't

there to watch her. Her little face, Tommy, looking for you in the audience, it broke my heart. You promised her you'd be there.'

Tommy closed his eyes, then placed his hand on the sticky bar. As much as he loved his daughter, Karen's school play was the least of his problems. 'I know I did, and I've said I'm sorry. What more do you want me to say?'

Taking a step closer, Stacey placed her hand on her husband's back, the anger within her ebbing away. 'What is going on, Tommy?' She watched as he ordered another beer and shook her head. 'Please, will you just come home and talk to me?'

'I will do when I've finished this one.'

Stacey sighed. Her Tommy was on a downwards spiral and she could see it happening before her own eyes. In a quandary, she didn't know what to do for the best. She didn't trust him to come home of his own accord if she left the pub without him. 'Okay, well, I'm going to sit over there and wait for you.' She gestured to a table in the corner.

Rolling his eyes, Tommy continued drinking. Women, he thought. He gulped at his beer. All he wanted to do was get plastered. He'd had enough of everyone and everything around him and getting pissed was the only sure way of blocking everything out.

Taking a seat, Freddie Smith swallowed deeply. 'So, what is this all about?'

Dean lit a cigar and as an afterthought he held up his hand. 'You don't mind, do you?' he asked, indicating towards the smoking cigar. 'Where's my manners, eh? That's always been my trouble, I do things without thinking of the consequences. It used to drive my late wife mad.' He gave a grin, showing perfect white teeth, then puffed contentedly on the cigar before getting down to business. 'Mark Hopper.'

Freddie could feel his face pale and he battled to regain his composure. He knew it; those thieving bastards had taken a gold bar. 'Yeah, what about him?' There was caution in Freddie's voice.

'I've heard a rumour that he came to see you a while back.'

Freddie narrowed his eyes. 'Yeah?' He couldn't see where Dean was going with the conversation.

Dean spread out his arms. 'So, what did he want to see you about?'

'Shouldn't you be asking Mark that question?'

Dean smiled. 'I would if I knew where to find him.' He banged his fist down on the desk, his voice rising. 'Now, I'm gonna ask you one last time before I end up losing my temper.' He gave a little grin, chilling Freddie to the bone. 'And trust me, you don't want that to happen, not unless you want this lovely club of yours to burn down to the ground with you inside it. Now, what did he come to see you about?'

Freddie shrank back in his seat, weighing up his options. Between Hopper and Dean Johnson, he wasn't so sure which one out of the two was worse. Finally, he spoke. 'The gold. He wanted me to stash it away for him.'

'And did you?'

Freddie nodded and swallowed. Did they know someone had gotten into the club and stolen it?

'Well?' Dean spread out his arms. 'What happened next?'

'Hopper brought it here, and then he collected it from two of my men.'

Dean was thoughtful. He stared at Freddie through hooded eyes. 'So, where did he go? Where did he take the gold?'

Freddie shrugged. 'No idea. Look, what's this all about?'

Dean ignored the question. So, Mark did have the gold. He

tapped his fingers against the arm of the chair. 'Have you heard from him since he took the gold?'

'No.' Freddie gave a little shake of his head.

Standing up, Dean walked towards the door. His hand on the door handle, he paused. 'Do you know Tommy Carter?'

A snarl spread across Freddie's face. 'Yeah.'

Gauging by Freddie's reaction, the two men weren't on friendly terms. 'He isn't a friend of yours I take it?'

'Can't stand the jumped-up prick. Why? Has he got something to do with this?'

Dean shrugged. 'Perhaps.' He walked out of Freddie's office. For all intents and purposes, it seemed to be the case that Tommy Carter was the last person to see Mark Hopper.

* * *

Shooing the children into the living room, Stacey quickly switched on the television set. She gave the children a biscuit each, and told them to be good, while she had a little chat with Daddy.

With the children now settled, Stacey walked through to the kitchen. 'Talk to me,' she pleaded to her husband.

Tommy sat down heavily at the table. He wasn't happy that he'd been dragged out of the pub. He was a grown man, not a school boy. 'What do you want me to say?'

Close to tears, Stacey wiped her fingers across her eyes, angrily. 'You,' she stated. 'Something's not right. You can't see it, but I can. I know you.'

'You don't wanna know, Stace. Trust me on this.'

Open-mouthed, Stacey stared at her husband. 'So, I'm right. Something is wrong.' She took a seat and reached out to grab his hand. He snatched it away, and she almost gasped in shock.

'I feel like I'm talking to a brick wall,' Tommy snapped. 'I keep telling you I've got a lot going on with work, amongst other things. I just need to let off a bit of steam, that's all. I'm sorry about Karen's play, okay? I genuinely forgot. I don't know why you're making such a drama out of it.'

Stacey's voice was small as she replied, 'Because, I'm worried about you.'

Tommy shook his head. 'Just do me a favour, and leave me alone, Stace, please. Let me deal with things my own way.' He stood up from the table, scraping the chair across the lino.

'Where are you going?'

'Out.' Snatching up his keys, Tommy left the house, leaving his wife to sit at the table with tears rolling down her cheeks.

* * *

It was Mad Dog who picked Jimmy up from the airport. Surprised, Jimmy's eyes were wide. 'Where's Tommy?'

'We'll talk about that later, lad.' Mad Dog gave a small nod of his head towards Aiden. 'So, how was the holiday?'

With half an ear, Mad Dog listened to what they had to say. He could sense Jimmy was quieter than usual, and he knew he'd worried the lad. He was worried himself, and if he was being truthful, he was glad to have young Jimmy back home. Maybe he would be able to get through to his brother, where the others hadn't.

They dropped Aiden off at his flat, and as soon as the door was closed, Jimmy turned in his seat. 'What the hell is going on?'

Mad Dog puffed out his cheeks. 'I was hoping you would be able to tell me, lad. Tommy's not been himself, drinking a lot, arguing with his missus, ready to bite everyone's head off.'

'Why? I don't understand. He was fine before I left.'

'Was he?' Mad Dog glanced sideways. 'He hasn't been right since that job at the Ilford Palais. Now, I don't know what went on, and I don't need to know, but whatever it is, it's taking its toll on him.'

Jimmy remained silent. Tommy would bounce back, he always did. 'I'll speak to him,' he answered confidently.

* * *

Tommy was sitting alone in the scrap yard office when Mad Dog pulled the car to a halt on the forecourt. Jumping out of his seat, Tommy flung the door open and pulled Jimmy into his arms, holding on for dear life.

'Am I glad to see you!' Tommy grinned. 'I've missed you, bruv.'

Jimmy smiled. He took note of Tommy's appearance. Other than looking a bit tired, he looked the same as usual. 'Same here! So, what's been going on?' He looked his brother in the eyes, not giving him the chance to look away.

Tommy shook his head. He didn't even know where to start. He could feel a hard lump form in his throat and he sat back down. 'All of this,' he said.

'What?' Jimmy shrugged.

Taking a deep breath, Tommy continued trying to explain himself. 'The gold, Hopper. It's doing me head in, Jimmy.' He paused. 'I feel like I have to be a step ahead of everything, d'ya know what I mean?'

Jimmy shook his head, still unable to understand where his brother was coming from. 'You've always been a step ahead of everything.'

'It's like...' Tommy paused, trying to find the right words. 'I wouldn't be bothered if this was to do with me. You know me, and I don't give a shit about anyone. I can fight my own battles. But when it comes to you lot – my family, my kids – I can't deal with it.' He held his head in his hands.

Alarmed, Jimmy moved forward. He'd never seen his brother in such a state before. Even when Stacey had left him, he hadn't been this bad. 'Come on, bruv. We've taken care of Hopper and the gold's being sorted out. You've got Freddie Smith off your back as well. As far as he knows, Hopper has the gold.'

'I know.' Tommy looked up. 'But if something goes wrong, it's on my head. I started all of this.'

'Nothing's gonna go wrong, you know that. Everything's been taken care of, you've said as much yourself. Am I right, or am I wrong?'

Tommy nodded. He gave a small smile, feeling his cheeks flush with embarrassment. 'So, what was it you wanted to tell me?' he asked, changing the subject.

Jimmy paused. Now wasn't really the time to give his brother his news. 'It can wait. You know what you need, bruv? You need to get back in the gym. Either that or have a tear up. It'll do you the world of good.'

Tommy laughed. 'Yeah, you're probably right… it would.' He wiped his hand across his face. 'C'mon spill the beans, I wanna know your news. It'll take my mind off all this other shit.'

'I…' For the first time since he'd arrived, Jimmy looked away.

'What?'

'I bought a bar, in Spain.'

'What?' Tommy's mouth fell open. 'What do you mean you bought a bar?'

'Me and Aiden. We bought this bar, and we're gonna run it together.'

Tommy shook his head, trying to get his head around his brother's words. 'I don't understand.' He paused. 'Does this mean you're leaving? You're going to go and live in Spain? Is that what you're trying to tell me?'

'Not exactly. I'm planning to spend a few weeks there, and a few weeks here.' He averted his eyes. 'Or something like that.'

'So, you are, you're leaving?' Tommy felt as though he'd been kicked in the stomach. He couldn't recall a time when Jimmy hadn't been there. With only eleven months between them, it had always been the two of them together, until their younger brothers had started coming along of course.

'Nothing's final yet.'

Looking his brother over, Tommy nodded. 'Yes it is. You just don't wanna tell me.' He threw up his hands in disbelief. 'Just when I need you the most, you're leaving.'

'That's not fair, bruv.'

Deep down, Tommy knew he was being unreasonable. Jimmy was his own man, and he needed to do what was right for him, but knowing all of that, still didn't make it any easier. He shook his head, unable to get his head around Jimmy's news. 'I'm going down the pub. D'ya wanna come, or do you need to go home and pack for your new life?' There was more than a hint of sarcasm in his voice.

Jimmy shook his head sadly. 'I'll go and see Mum and Dad first, then I'll come over there.'

'Suit yourself.' Tommy shrugged.

Sitting back in his seat, Jimmy blew out his cheeks. He'd fully expected his brother to be annoyed. He just hoped, once he'd calmed down, he'd see what a great opportunity the bar was.

Pint after pint Tommy had sunk and by the time Jimmy entered the pub he was stumbling around, unsteady on his feet. 'Here he is: my brother,' Tommy shouted at the top of his lungs.

Embarrassed, Jimmy wiped his hand across his face. 'Leave it out, bruv.' He smiled, taking the edge off his words.

Tommy placed his hand on his brother's arm to steady himself. 'I'm sorry, okay,' he slurred, 'I was bang out of order for having a dig at you. It was a bit of a shock, that's all.'

Jimmy nodded. 'Okay, apology accepted, and from what I've heard, you also need to apologise to your wife.'

'I know, and I will do. Come on, get the drinks in.'

'One more drink, and then I'm taking you home, okay?'

Tommy nodded. 'Come on then, get to the bar.'

Paying for the drinks, Jimmy slipped his change into his pocket. He took the filled glasses over to a corner table, placing the beer in front of his brother. 'This needs to stop, Tommy. This isn't you.'

Taking a sip from his pint, Tommy gave a slight nod. 'Yeah, I know, and I will.'

Jimmy eyed his brother over the rim of his glass, not quite believing him. 'Say something did happen. Say Smith came here right now. You'd be in no fit state to help anyone.'

Jimmy's words instantly sobered his brother up and, looking towards the door, Tommy could see Jimmy's point. His brother was right. He wouldn't be in a fit state to help anyone. He could barely even think straight.

'Right, like I said, after this drink you're going home to sleep it off, bruv. Tomorrow's a new day. We'll sort it all out.'

Taking one look at her husband, Stacey rolled her eyes. 'Look at the state of him,' she complained. 'That's the third time this week he's come home like this, stinking of booze.'

Jimmy smiled apologetically. 'I'm sorry, Stace. Where shall I put him?'

Stacey motioned towards the living room. 'Put him in there. He can sleep on the sofa tonight.' She watched as her brother-in-law half dragged Tommy towards the sofa and shook her head. 'What's got into him?'

'He's got a lot on his mind Stace,' Jimmy answered as he swung his brother's legs up onto the sofa. 'We'll sort it out. I've already told him this has to stop.'

'It's all right telling him to stop, but is he gonna listen? This is Tommy we're taking about, don't forget,' she said, raising her eyebrows.

'Yeah, he'll listen all right. He has to.'

They walked out of the room, closing the door behind them. Wandering through to the kitchen, Stacey walked towards the sink. Leaning her back against it, she faced Jimmy. As always, the kitchen was pristine, not a cup out of place. She opened the cupboard and took out two mugs, before flicking the switch on the kettle. 'Tea?' she asked as an afterthought, unsure if Jimmy wanted to get straight off or stick around for a bit.

'Yeah, go on.' He studied Stacey. He could see that his brother's behaviour was taking its toll on her. She didn't look her usual happy self and had dark circles underneath her eyes. He watched as her shoulders began to heave, and it was only when she brought her hands up to her face, that he realised she was crying. 'Hey, what's all this?' Alarmed, he stood up and walked towards her.

Stacey wiped at her eyes. 'It's him,' she spat, before breaking down for a second time.

Jimmy's heart sank as he led his sister-in-law to a chair. 'It's gonna be okay, Stace,' he said, kneeling down in front of her and clutching her hand in his.

'Will it?' She sniffed back her tears. 'I'm scared, Jimmy. I don't know what's going on in that head of his any more. He doesn't talk to me. He isn't even interested in the kids. All he wants to do is go out and get pissed.'

Jimmy closed his eyes, unsure of what he was meant to say to her. 'I know. Look, it's nothing personal, Stace. He really does have a lot on his mind, and I'm not making excuses for him. Some stuff happened at work, and he's trying to deal with it, albeit he's going about it the wrong way.' He gave a half smile, trying to lighten the mood. 'He'll fight back, he has to, and I've given him a right bollocking tonight. I think I've knocked some sense into him. You just wait and see. Everything will be okay.'

* * *

The next morning, Tommy woke early. He rolled over and immediately clutched at his head. Never again was he going to drink. The fact that he'd already thought that to himself three times that week alone, was erased from his mind. Sheepishly, he wandered through to the kitchen. 'Sorry, Stace.' He shoved his hands into his pockets, waiting for a backlash from his wife.

Turning to face her husband, Stacey sighed. 'I suppose you want some painkillers?'

Tommy nodded. 'Yes, please.' He sat down at the table and placed his aching head into his hands.

'Here.' Stacey held out two paracetamol and a tumbler of water.

Taking the painkillers, Tommy quickly swallowed them down. 'I mean it. I am sorry. I've been a bastard to live with, I know that.'

Stacey nodded. 'Jimmy told me you had some problems.' She pulled out a chair, easing her body down onto the seat. 'Just don't block us out, Tommy. We need you, too.'

'I know and I won't. I'm gonna take care of it, Stace, and I'm gonna sort myself out while I'm at it,' he groaned as he clutched at his head. 'Just as soon as this hangover has gone.' He gave a small smile and was relieved to see his wife smile back at him.

25

Dean Johnson's mind was going into overdrive. From what he could puzzle together, Mark had collected the gold, slipped out of the Barking Assembly Hall, and then disappeared into the night. An idea popped into his head. In fact, he was surprised he hadn't thought of it sooner. Mark's old mum still lived in Forest Gate, East London. There was no way he would have left the country without saying goodbye to her. Knowing just how close the two were, he wouldn't be shocked to learn that Mark was, in actual fact, hiding out at her house.

Taking out his mobile phone, he dialled a number, then brought the device up to his ear. 'I need you to drive me somewhere, now.' He waited for the man to answer, then switched off the phone. If anyone knew where Hopper was, it was bound to be his old mum.

* * *

Shirley Hopper was a frail woman with greying hair and a hooked bent nose, which had been broken more than once by the heavy fists of her ex-husband, Mark's dad. She'd had a hard life and had worked two to three jobs at a time when Mark had been a young boy, just to make ends meet. She opened the front door and peered out. 'Yes, can I help you?'

Dean Johnson smiled. 'Mrs Hopper, I'm a friend of Mark's. May I come in?'

At the mention of her only child's name, Shirley's eyes lit up. 'Yes, dear, come on through.' She walked ahead of Dean, leaving behind her a wake of flowery perfume. 'Come in.' She smiled, gesturing for Dean to walk through to the lounge.

Dean walked through and was instantly taken aback. Aside from the overly stuffed armchairs, two sideboards, and a small television set sitting proudly in the corner of the room, every visible surface held a photograph of Mark.

'Please, take a seat.'

Dean did as the woman bade and smiled, wondering briefly how such a mild-mannered, polite woman could have birthed someone like Mark Hopper.

'Would you like some tea?'

Her words broke Dean's thoughts, and he shook his head, declining the offer. 'Mrs Hopper,' he began.

Shirley held up her hand. 'Please, call me Shirley. I don't like to be called Mrs Hopper, it brings back too many memories of Mark's father, you see. Awful, wicked man.'

Dean smiled gently and began again. 'Shirley, have you seen much of Mark lately?'

'Oh yes.' She gave a wide smile.

'And when did you last see him?'

Shirley screwed up her face as she tried to think. 'Well, it must have been Tuesday.'

'You mean yesterday?' There was hope in Dean's voice.

'Oh no, dear, I mean last Tuesday. It was definitely over a week ago. I know that, because Mark was here when the man came to clean the windows, and he comes fortnightly.'

Dean's heart sank. 'Do you know where he went, or where he's been living?'

'No.' She paused for a moment. 'He said he was going to go on holiday and visit his friend.' She put her fingers to her lips as she tried to think. 'Dean, that was his name. He's got such a lovely house in Spain, and Mark was going to stay there for a few weeks. I think he's taken a shining to a young lady over there.' She gave a little giggle. 'I do hope it works out for him. That's what he needs... a nice lady friend, maybe he'll even get married and have a couple of children.'

Dean nodded. Well, Mark definitely hadn't returned back to the villa. 'Thank you.' He stood up. 'If you hear from Mark, could you give him my telephone number? It's important I speak to him.'

'Of course!' She lifted up her handbag and looked inside for a scrap of paper. 'There you go, dear. You'll find a pen on the sideboard beside you.'

Dean wrote down his telephone number and passed the paper back across. He smiled as he watched her tuck it away safely in the zipped compartment of her bag. 'Well, thank you for your time. Please don't get up, I'll see myself out.'

Outside on the street, Dean blew out his cheeks. He'd been dead certain that he'd find Mark hiding out at his mum's address, and the fact that she hadn't heard from him in over a week, despite their closeness, was somewhat disturbing. He looked back towards the house and wondered briefly if Mark could have stashed the gold there and was just lying low elsewhere for a bit. No, Mark wouldn't put his old mum at risk, he loved the bones of her. He walked towards the car, chewing on the inside of his cheek.

'No joy, boss?'

Dean shook his head. It just didn't make sense to him. Why

would Mark just disappear? It wasn't as though he wouldn't have got enough from his share of the gold.

'So where to now, boss?' Frankie asked.

'Take me to Ripple Road Cemetery.' He wanted to lay some flowers on his brother Chrissy's grave. He hadn't been for a long time and felt the need to pay his respects. He still missed his brother, even after all these years. He supposed that he always would.

Within the hour, they were at the cemetery. On the way in, Dean bought a bunch of flowers from the flower stall outside the gates – mainly carnations, with a couple of roses, and some green foliage thrown in. He instructed Frankie to wait in the car while he visited the grave. Walking across the grass, he reached Chrissy's burial plot. Laying down the flowers, he tidied up the grave, emptying out the dead flowers from a vase beside the headstone.

'Hello, mate.' He always spoke to his brother when he came. It made him feel as though Chrissy was still around. 'Brought you some flowers,' he continued, telling his brother his news, before filling the vase with the fresh flowers. He bent down to kiss the headstone, then straightened up. 'See you soon, Chrissy. I'll come and visit you before I go back to Spain.' Dean began to walk back towards the car, before slowing down his pace. He turned and walked in the opposite direction, stopping beside Davey's graveside. 'Hello, you old bastard, bet you didn't expect me to pay you a visit.' He smiled to himself. Knowing Davey, he would probably turn in his grave. Dean read out the inscription on the headstone and sighed, before shoving his hands into his coat pockets and walking away. Unbeknownst to him, he'd been standing just feet away from the missing gold he'd been searching for.

* * *

Tommy had rounded his brothers up and summoned them to the scrap yard office for a meeting. With just a small leather sofa and two chairs, it was standing room only, and so they lined the walls of the cramped space, talking amongst themselves while they waited for Tommy to begin. Despite being reluctant at first, Tommy had decided to take Jimmy's advice. Their brothers needed to know the score, and he needed to have some of the responsibility taken off his shoulders.

Tommy waited for Mad Dog to take a seat before speaking. More than anything, he wanted their full attention. 'Okay, so this is how it is. After we robbed the Ilford Palais, I was hauled in front of Freddie Smith.' He gauged their surprised reactions before continuing. 'Freddie gave me an ultimatum. If we didn't give back the gold, he was going to come after Jonny.' This time an angry buzz went around the Portakabin, and Tommy held up his hand to quieten them down. 'Now, obviously I took this threat very seriously, and I wasn't prepared to let anything happen to our brother.' He paused. 'What I'm about to say next must go no further than this room. I need your word on that.' Tommy waited for his brothers and Mad Dog to nod their heads, knowing without a doubt they wouldn't repeat what he told them. 'So, on the night of Jonny's fight, I killed Mark Hopper.' He heard them gasp. 'As far as Freddie knows, Hopper fucked off with the gold. So, hopefully that'll be the end of it, but there's always a chance this could still go wrong, and so I need you all to be vigilant; don't take any risks and if you're out collecting debts then go out in pairs.'

'I knew there was something wrong, lad, but have to admit, I hadn't expected it to be so bad. Hopper's really dead?' Mad Dog asked, his voice low.

'Yep.' Tommy nodded. He leant forward in his seat so that they could speak privately. 'The problem is, I don't know who else is involved. Now, as for Freddie Smith, he believes Hopper took the gold and fucked off, but I'm guessing Hopper had backing.'

'In other words, people could still be expecting that gold,' Mad Dog said, scratching at his chin.

'Yeah, and that's what worries me. They could start digging around, or they may just believe Freddie Smith's version of events, I don't know.' He shrugged.

'Other than us, does anyone else know?'

'Yeah.' He took note of Mad Dog's raised eyebrows and gave a small smile. 'Danny McKay and Moray Garner. They disposed of Hopper's body.'

'Well, you have no worries with those two.' Mad Dog let out a sigh of relief. 'And do you think Freddie believes Hopper fucked off with the gold?'

Tommy shrugged. 'I don't know, but what I do know, is that he believes McKay and Garner took the gold to him.'

'Well, that's a start, and at least it came from his own men.'

'Exactly.' Tommy raised his eyebrows.

'So, just how much danger are we all in?' This came from Gary and as he always did, he looked over at Tommy with contempt in his eyes.

Tommy sighed. 'I don't know, and that's the truth. No one knew I met with Hopper, so, as far as I'm aware, my name is being kept out of it.'

'So, what are we all meant to do now?'

'Just be careful; watch who is around you.'

'And what about our Jonny? Is he safe now?' Mitchel asked.

'Yeah, for the time being, and for as long as Smith thinks that Hopper has the gold. But remember, Jonny doesn't know anything about this, so keep your mouths closed, okay?' He gave them a smile, then clapped his hands together. 'Okay, back to work, and remember, be careful.'

The brothers and Mad Dog filed out of the office, leaving Jimmy and Tommy alone. 'You did the right thing, bruv. You couldn't go on bottling it all up, trying to deal with it all by yourself. Besides, if they're old enough to go out collecting debts, then they're old enough to know the score, and look out for themselves.'

'Yeah, you're right.' Tommy clasped his brother's shoulder. Jimmy was right; he felt an instant relief to have got it all off his chest.

'So, no more boozing your days away?'

Tommy shook his head and turned his face away, not wanting Jimmy to see him blush. 'I'm gonna sort myself out. I promised Stacey that I would.'

'Good. I don't wanna see you going down that road, bruv. It's hard to get off once you're on it.'

'Yeah, I know. Right, well, we'd best get back to work ourselves.' He collected up his car keys. 'Let's get it over and done with and meet with McKay.'

* * *

Danny McKay placed two pints of beer down onto a small round rickety table. He pulled out a wooden chair and sat down. Once seated, he took a sip of his own drink, enjoying the kick to the back of his throat the brandy gave him.

Tommy leaned forward in his seat. He studied the man in front of him. 'So?' he enquired. 'What's the latest?'

Danny smacked his lips together. 'Someone came looking for Hopper, enquiring about the gold.'

'Who?'

'Dean Johnson.'

Tommy felt the familiar stirrings of anger at the mention of Johnson's name. He looked up, watching as an elderly gentleman wearing a flat cap and a grey, zipped-up cardigan walked through the doors of the Becton Arms. Quickly assessing that he posed no threat to them, he leant forward. 'How does that old cunt know about the gold?'

'How should I know?' Danny gave a small shrug. 'The main point is, he does know about it, and according to Freddie, he's on the war path looking for Hopper. He thinks he's had him over.'

'Well, that's got to be good for us, hasn't it?' Tommy glanced across at Jimmy for confirmation. 'If he thinks that Hopper's done him over and fucked off with the gold, then that's got to take the heat away from us?'

'Yeah, true, but the fact he is asking questions is a worry. I mean' – Danny lowered his voice – 'who else has he spoken to?' He raised his eyebrows. 'How long before he actually comes looking to speak to me or Moray, and who else knew Hopper was looking for you? They're valid questions, Tommy, and we need to know the answers.'

Tommy sat back in his seat pondering over Danny's words. 'Other than you and Moray, I doubt anyone knew he was looking for me.'

'What did he want from you anyway?' Danny raised his eyebrows questioningly over the rim of his glass.

'I'm not sure, to be honest. He smashed me one in the gut, and said it was from Dean Johnson.' His voice tapered off, realising what he'd said. 'Dean Johnson.'

'There you go!' Danny leant back in his seat. 'Johnson knew that Hopper was planning to meet you.'

'Nah, doesn't necessarily mean anything, does it?'

'I dunno, but one thing I do know, is we need to start moving that gold abroad.'

'Yeah, I know and Jimmy's made contact with a fella in the gold business over in Spain.' Tommy motioned for his brother to fill Danny in.

'Yeah.' Jimmy cleared his throat. 'He said all we need to do is get the gold to him, and he'll take care of everything else. He said he's gonna mix it with copper and brass, so that it looks like scrap gold. That's the only way you can get it back onto the market. Reckons it'll be a piece of cake.'

'Do you trust this bloke?'

'He was a business associate of Davey's. Mad Dog has vouched for him, so yeah, I trust him.'

'And how exactly are we gonna get it over there?' Danny picked up a food menu and studied the contents, recalling he hadn't eaten yet.

'Tommy's got a plan. Tell him.' Jimmy nudged his brother.

'Well, we can either get the ferry across to Northern Spain, but that obviously comes with a lot of risk, mainly being caught red-handed with the gold. Or' – he paused – 'I've got a mate who regularly sails to Spain and France as a courier. He's, as you can imagine, a bit dodgy, but I trust him not to have us over. That way, we can fly over and meet him there. It's more or less risk free. Now, Jimmy here, has just bought a bar in Spain, so I was thinking, get all the family to go over to Spain for the opening night, and that'll make it seem like we have a legit reason to travel there.'

Danny narrowed his eyes. 'Still sounds a bit risky though.' He tossed the menu back onto the table. 'If anything goes wrong, it'll put us in the same country as the gold. So, how much do you trust this bloke?'

'I trust him 100 per cent. His old man was one of my first trainers. He's as sweet as a nut.'

'Okay.' Danny nodded. 'We go with the second plan then. Let's face it, the less risk involved, the better.'

'Exactly.' Tommy grinned.

Downing the last of his brandy, Danny stood up, bumping back his chair. 'Another round?' He nodded down at Tommy's full glass. 'Are you not drinking that?'

'Nah, I'm off the drink for a bit. I'll have a coke.'

'And I'll have his.' Jimmy picked up Tommy's glass and placed it down on the table in front of himself.

Shrugging, Danny walked across to the bar.

Once McKay was out of earshot, Jimmy turned to his brother. 'You do realise Johnson is gonna come looking for you, don't you?'

'Yeah, and I'll be fucking ready for him. I've been waiting for that cunt, after what he did to Davey, not to mention that psycho bitch daughter of his.'

Jimmy nodded. He'd already known what Tommy's answer would be, and he had a feeling it may well be just what his brother needed – the perfect excuse to let off a bit of steam.

Dean walked into the reception area of The Soho Club with an arrogant air. He glanced around him and wrinkled his nose with distaste. He'd never seen the attraction himself, of having a semi-clad woman dancing in front of you with her tits hanging out. He would much rather have had his wife cuddled up beside him on the sofa.

'Evening, gents.' Lillian smiled at them from behind the counter. 'It's a ten-pound, per person, admission fee. We're open until 3 a.m., and we only have one rule: no touching the girls.'

Turning to face the woman, Dean looked her up and down. The disgust he felt was clearly evident across his face. 'Excuse me?'

'I said, it's a ten-pound admittance fee.'

'Yeah, I heard what you said.' Dean cut her off. 'I want to speak to the boss. Where is he?'

Lillian frowned. She glanced towards the main doors. 'Can I ask what this is about? Only, if it's a complaint you want to make, we have a form down here.' She reached underneath the counter, pulling out a pad of paper.

'No, like I said, I want to speak to the boss.'

'Okay, I'll call Mr Harris and see if he's available to speak to you.' Lillian picked up the phone.

'No.' Dean took the phone out of Lillian's hand and placed it back onto its cradle. 'You're not listening to me. I want to speak to the organ grinder, not the monkey. Now, where is Tommy Carter?'

'Tommy!' Lillian exclaimed. 'He doesn't work here, darling. Mr Harris runs the club.'

Dean gave a small nod. 'But he does own' – he looked around him slowly, trying to find the right words – 'this shit hole of a club.'

'Well, yes.' Taken aback, Lillian glanced nervously once again towards the main doors. Where the hell was Mad Dog when she needed him? 'But he isn't here.'

As Dean smiled, the two heavies beside him pulled out baseball bats from underneath their coats. They began to smash the glass display boards, which contained posters of the girls alongside upcoming events that the club offered. 'Well, make sure you tell him that Dean Johnson paid him a visit. Can you do that for me?'

Horrified, Lillian's eyes widened and her body began to tremble. 'Yes, yes, I'll tell him.'

'Good.' With that, Dean, followed by his heavies, turned on their heels and left the premises.

Still shaking, Lillian placed her hand across her racing heart. She waited until the men had left the building, and then without a backward glance, she ran through the club towards Mad Dog's office.

* * *

Tommy was incensed. He stormed through the club with Jimmy by his side. 'I'll fucking kill him,' he growled.

He pushed open the door to the office and took in the scene before him. Lillian was sat beside the desk, her face deathly white, sipping on a large brandy to calm her nerves. Tommy walked straight towards her and put his arm around her shoulders in a bid to offer comfort. 'Are you okay, Lil? He didn't hurt you, did he?' he asked, his voice gentle.

Still shaking, Lillian shook her head. 'No, just shook me up a bit, Tommy, that's all.'

He turned to Mad Dog. 'Was it definitely Dean Johnson?'

'Aye lad. It's all on camera.'

'What's he fucking playing at, eh?' He began to pace the small office. 'I'll kill him, I'll fucking kill him for this.' Tommy's voice began to rise, his eyes flashing dangerously. 'Give me an address for him,' he said, stabbing his finger towards Mad Dog.

Mad Dog hesitated, knowing full well that if he handed over Dean's address, then a war would more than likely be on the cards, just as there had been between Davey and Dean, and they all knew the outcome of that.

'Mad Dog?' Tommy demanded. 'I'm waiting.'

Mad Dog raised his eyebrows. 'Come on, lad. Is that wise? Hasn't enough damage already been done?'

'You want to talk about damage?' Tommy roared. 'Look what he's done to my club, what he did to Davey, what his bastard of a daughter has done to my brother! That slag has fucked him up in the head, and you know she has.' He spat out the words, pressing his finger against his temple to emphasise his point. As much as they pretended that Gary was okay, deep down they all knew that he wasn't. 'And you wanna sit there, questioning me about damage? Because I haven't even started on that cunt yet.'

Mad Dog held up his hands. 'Okay, fair point, lad.'

Tommy held out his hand. 'Are you going to give it to me, or not?'

Reluctantly, Mad Dog quickly jotted down the address on a piece of paper. Snatching it out of the older man's hand, Tommy studied the address, estimating it would take him roughly thirty minutes to drive to Epping from Soho if he put his foot down. 'You can either stay here or go home.' Tommy turned to look across at Jimmy.

'What?'

'You heard what I said, I'm doing this alone.'

'Hold on a minute bruv,' Jimmy began. 'You don't know what'll be waiting for you at that house.'

'Yeah, I do. Dean fucking Johnson.' Tommy's eyes were cold. 'I'm warning you Jimmy you either stay here or you go home.'

Looking from Mad Dog to Tommy, Jimmy's shoulders dropped. 'I'll wait here.'

Tommy nodded, satisfied. Leaving the office, he marched through the club, his lips set in a straight line. In the reception area, he paused beside the desk and reached underneath to grab the baseball bat. He inspected the wooden baton in his hand, before turning to look at the damage Dean Johnson's heavies had caused. Well, two could play at that game. With one final glance at the smashed display cabinets, Tommy left the club.

26

Every evening at eight o'clock, Dean called his daughter. More often than not, the telephone was answered by his housekeeper, telling him Bethany couldn't come to the phone – she was sleeping, or in the bath, or drying her hair. He wasn't stupid, he knew the truth; his daughter didn't want to speak to him. He asked after his grandson and smiled as he was told that Cameron was thriving. Placing the phone back onto the cradle, Dean took his glass of brandy and sat on the sofa. Kicking out his legs in front of him as he relaxed, he closed his eyes, listening to the jazz CD he'd put on the stereo. There was just something about jazz that he'd always loved. As far he was concerned, you just couldn't beat it. The kids of today could keep their music, house music or something or other they called it. Whatever it was called, it sounded like a load of old tosh to him. He sipped at his brandy, enjoying the way the instruments dropped in and out, creating a masterpiece.

The sound of footsteps caused him to open his eyes in alarm. He blinked rapidly. Standing in front of him was Tommy Carter. He peered beyond the man, noting that the patio door was ajar. He must have left it unlocked. 'What are you doing here?' He pulled in his legs and pushed himself up off the sofa.

Tommy took a step closer. He brought the baseball bat up in front of him. 'You wanted to see me, so here I am.'

Dean tore his eyes away from Tommy to look at the bat. It had always been his policy not to have heavies inside his home. Safe in the knowledge that he could take care of himself, he had never needed anyone to fight his battles, and sure to God, didn't need anyone now. He began to laugh. 'Am I supposed to be scared?' He sniggered. 'Because let me tell you now boy, I was out there scrapping long before you were even a twinkle in your old man's eye.'

Tommy snarled. 'And is that supposed to scare me?' He took a step closer, slapping the bat against his open palm. 'I've been waiting a long time for this moment to come. The destruction you and yours have caused ends today.' He spat out his words with a confident air, causing Dean to erupt with fury.

Charging forward, Dean's fists were curled into tight balls. He swung them towards Tommy, his heavy knuckles catching the younger man's lip. He felt just a moment of euphoria, until the baseball bat crashed against the side of his skull and brought him to his knees. As blood sprayed out from an inch-long split across the side of Dean's head, he sunk forwards, bringing his hand up towards the oozing wound, feeling both dazed and defeated.

With his opponent down on the floor, Tommy took a moment to bring his finger up towards his lip. He looked down to see a droplet of blood smeared there. Bringing the baseball bat up above his head, he swung it towards Dean, feeling nothing but satisfaction as each crashing swing hit its target. The sickening crunch of bone fracturing, as the bat crashed methodically against the older man's flesh, spurred Tommy on. Months and months of pent-up rage flooded through him. He wouldn't stop. He couldn't stop, not until he was spent – not until Dean Johnson's lifeless body lay in front of him.

Battered, bruised, and bleeding, Dean fell onto his side. His mouth was swollen. He could feel his teeth dislodged from his split gums, he could feel them wobble with every heavy intake of breath he took. He spat out a mouthful of blood, not surprised to see a tooth fall to the floor. He brought his hand up towards his battered face; one eyelid was swollen shut, and he tried to focus on Tommy with the remaining sight he had. 'Enough,' he groaned, his loosened teeth causing him to lisp. He put out his hand in a bid to stop the attack. He had clearly underestimated the man in front of him. 'The boy needs me.'

About to swing the bat again, Tommy stopped dead in his tracks, his forehead furrowed. He breathed deeply, exhaling noisily though his flared nostrils.

'Without me, he has no one.'

'Who?' Tommy demanded, the bat raised above his head ready to be swung downwards.

With great difficulty, Dean spoke. 'My grandson; your nephew.'

Despite being taken aback, outwardly Tommy showed no emotion. 'Not my problem,' he spat, bringing the bat down heavily against Dean's kneecap. From the loud crack, he knew he'd broken a bone. He brought the bat up above his head, in preparation to crash it down for a second time.

'She doesn't love him. She'll never love him. He was fathered by the wrong Carter.' Dean's voice took on a pleading tone. Despite the agony he was in, his mind was alert. He began to speak to Tommy as though he were a fellow conspirator. 'The boy, Cameron, he needs me, he's only a baby.'

Tommy paused, giving Dean enough time to begin to crawl away, leaving a trail of blood across the polished wooden floorboards behind him. Immediately, Tommy's thoughts went to his brother, Gary. He'd always believed, as they all had, that there was no child, that Bethany had terminated the pregnancy. He swallowed deeply, unable to get his head around this revelation. Crouching down, he leant his weight against the bat using it as a crutch. 'A boy?' His voice was low. 'She told me she was getting rid of it.'

'I wouldn't let her. He was born in Spain.'

'My brother has a son.' Tommy spoke to know one in particular, merely trying to take in the fact that Gary was a father, and he himself, was an uncle.

Dean coughed. He spat out a mouthful of blood onto a black and cream, swirling patterned rug that he'd paid a small fortune for. The rug was the least of his problems. He'd bet his life on having more than one broken rib, and a broken knee cap, if he wasn't mistaken. He was only thankful to still be alive, and that it hadn't been a shotgun used. That was usually the weapon of choice for men like them. 'Yes, a boy, Cameron.' He closed his eyes, the exertion of speaking wearing him out.

Tommy got to his feet. The fight had left him now; the urge to kill was gone. He looked around him. Dean Johnson's blood splatter covered almost every surface. The room resembled a blood bath. He breathed heavily, pointing the bat towards the older man. 'You go back to Spain, and you stay there. I don't care what you have to do but make sure you keep your daughter away from me and my brother. Am I making myself understood?'

Slowly, Dean nodded, thoroughly understanding the threat. In order to save his own life, he had unwittingly given away his only weakness, Cameron. After this, he had no intention of getting in Tommy Carter's way ever again, and his thoughts briefly went to Mark Hopper. The fact he'd originally planned to question Carter over Hopper's disappearance was gone from his mind, and the knowledge that little Cameron needed his grandad was more than enough to ensure it stayed that way. 'I swear to you on my grandson's life, I will not come near you or yours ever again. This feud of ours, it ends now, today.'

They stared across the room at each other, with both mutual hatred and a new-found respect. Satisfied, Tommy gave a nod of his head. He walked from the house and breathed in a lungful of fresh air. He could still smell the unmistakable scent of blood, and looked down at his stained hands, further proof of just how close he had come to killing the man. It was over; there would be no comebacks where the gold was concerned. With a backwards glance towards the house, Tommy walked across the mowed lawn. He pulled up the hood of his jacket and scaled over the fence into the night.

* * *

Within days, Dean Johnson had left England. 'A car crash,' he told the worried air steward, as a way of explaining away his bruised and battered face, as he boarded the flight back to Spain. Taking his seat beside the window he was still struggling to breathe through his nose and the pounding inside his head was tremendous. Quickly he swallowed down some painkillers before the plane took off. As the plane began to power down the runway, he closed his eyes; he'd already decided that he would give Bethany the same explanation. To be perfectly honest, he doubted she would even care. More than anything, he needed to save face. No one could ever know the truth. No one must ever know that Tommy Carter had got one over on him.

* * *

With more hands on deck, the gold had easily been retrieved from its hiding place. Danny McKay shook his head. 'You are one slippery bastard, Carter. I would never have thought of looking for it here.'

Tommy had shrugged. In actual fact, he was glad to be shot of it. The gold had caused him nothing but grief. If he hadn't known better, or had been a superstitious man, he would have claimed the haul to be cursed.

They'd waved goodbye to the gold at Tilbury docks, estimating it would take Tommy's friend just a few days to reach Spain.

Shoving his hands into his coat pockets, Danny walked towards his car. 'I'll see you over in Spain in a couple of days.' They'd decided between them it was safer and a lot less suspect to travel separately.

Tommy nodded. 'Yeah, see you there, mate.' He watched as Danny drove away, then flashed Jimmy a smile. 'I can't bloody wait to just get away for a few days, bruv.' He pulled his jacket collar up around his neck in a bid to keep out the bitter wind. 'It'll be nice just to feel the sun on my back.'

Jimmy smiled. 'Are you sure you're okay with all of this? I mean, me buying the bar with Aiden. You know it's gonna mean me spending weeks away at a time.'

'Course I am. You're your own man, you have to do what's right for you. Besides, I think I've dragged you around with me for long enough, haven't I?' He gave a wide grin, proving he had no hard feelings towards his brother. 'It just means Gary, Sonny and Mitchel will have to step up to the plate. Well, Sonny and Mitchel anyway. Gary's a lost cause.'

Both brothers grinned sadly. 'She ruined him, you know that, don't you? He's not right up here.' Tommy pointed to his head, his tone serious.

'Yeah, she did,' Jimmy agreed, recalling how their younger brother had been before Bethany Johnson had entered his life. 'We can't change what's done though, so no point dwelling on it.'

'Yeah, you're right.' Tommy stared into the distance; it was on the tip of his tongue to blurt out that Gary had a son. 'Come on, let's head back,' he said, deciding to keep quiet about the revelation Dean Johnson had dropped on him. 'It's bloody cold, and like a pair of fucking lemons, we're standing on the docks freezing our bollocks off.'

* * *

To say Janet was stressed out would be an understatement. She counted out the passports in her hand for the third time in the past ten minutes alone, before placing them inside her flight bag.

'They're all there,' Stacey said with a laugh.

'What if one's missing?' Janet pulled the bundle out of her flight bag once again.

'I've just watched you count them at least twice, and they are definitely all there.'

'Have you got your passports?'

Stacey nodded. 'Right here.' She patted her handbag.

Janet couldn't help but giggle. 'Oh, I'm so excited, Stace.' She linked her arm through her daughter-in-law's. 'Who'd have thought it, eh? My Jimmy, owning a bar in Spain? And when we get there I'm going to have the largest glass of sangria you've ever seen.' She gave a giggle. 'I've never even tried it before. I hope I bleedin' well like it.'

'I know, it's so exciting, and I'm pleased for him. He deserves this.' She paused, checking that her husband wasn't within earshot. 'And what do you think of Aiden?' She nodded towards the man in question, a cheeky smile plastered across her face.

'Oh, he's a handsome devil, isn't he? My Jimmy's obviously got good taste.'

Stacey nodded, smiling. 'I wouldn't say no.'

'Stace!' Janet cried, her mouth falling open in shock.

Stacey laughed out loud. 'I'm only joking. You know I only have eyes for my Tommy.'

'I know you do, darling.' Janet hugged her daughter-in-law to her.

The beep of a car horn outside the house threw Janet into further panic. 'It's here! Come on everyone, the minibus is here.'

'Right, have we got everything?' Stacey gathered her children together, while the men carried the suitcases out to the minibus.

'Yeah, that's everything, come on.' Tommy ushered his mum and Stacey out of the house. This was to be the first family holiday abroad they had all been on together. And the fact that he and Jimmy would be mixing both pleasure with business, remained at the forefront of his mind. He was under no illusions that this trip to Spain was all about the gold and ensuring it was melted down with minimum of risk to themselves.

The family walked out of the house, leaving Tommy to lock the front door behind him. He took note of Gary just ahead of him and pulled on his brother's arm. 'Gaz.'

Turning around, Gary did nothing to hide his irritation. 'What?' he said, spitting out the word.

Tommy swallowed deeply; the knowledge of his brother's son lay heavy on his mind. Ever since Dean Johnson had blurted out that Gary had a child, Tommy had felt nothing but turmoil inside of him. He just didn't know what to do for the best and hadn't even told Jimmy about this turn of events. The dilemma he faced was all to do with Gary's state of mind. Should he tell him he had a son, or was it best left unsaid?

'Well, what do you want?'

Tommy could see the hatred in Gary's eyes. Maybe now wasn't the best time to tell him about Cameron, not when they were actually going to Spain, and would be putting themselves in the same country as the Johnsons. He shook his head. It could wait. After all, Gary had already waited all these months. Another couple of weeks of waiting wouldn't hurt. Once they were safely back in England, he would tell his brother everything there was to know. 'Nothing. It doesn't matter.'

'Can I go now?' Gary sighed, tapping his foot impatiently.

'Yeah.' With a heavy heart, Tommy watched as his brother rolled his eyes, before walking away from him. He gave the house one final glance, then locked the front door.

'Come on!' Janet called out. 'We don't want to miss the flight.'

Walking down the path towards the minibus, a huge grin spread across Tommy's face. What with the fortune they would make from the gold, not to mention his other businesses, and now this little holiday to Spain, life really couldn't get any better than it already was. Hadn't he always said it to anyone who would listen? The Carters were going places, and with him in charge, he was more than certain that this was only the start for them.

MORE FROM KERRY KAYA

We hope you enjoyed reading *Under Dog*. If you did, please leave a review.

If you'd like to gift a copy, this book is also available as an ebook, digital audio download and audiobook CD.

Sign up to Kerry Kaya's mailing list for news, competitions and updates on future books.

http://bit.ly/KerryKayaNewsletter

Another gripping gangland read from Kerry Kaya, *The Price*, is available now.

ABOUT THE AUTHOR

Kerry Kaya is the hugely popular author of Essex based gritty gangland thrillers with strong family dynamics. She grew up on one of the largest council estates in the UK, where she sets her novels. She also works full-time in a busy maternity department for the NHS.

Follow Kerry on social media:

 twitter.com/KerryKayaWriter

 instagram.com/kerry_kaya_writer

 facebook.com/kerry.bryant.58

ABOUT BOLDWOOD BOOKS

Boldwood Books is a fiction publishing company seeking out the best stories from around the world.

Find out more at www.boldwoodbooks.com

Sign up to the Book and Tonic newsletter for news, offers and competitions from Boldwood Books!

http://www.bit.ly/bookandtonic

We'd love to hear from you, follow us on social media:

facebook.com/BookandTonic

twitter.com/BoldwoodBooks

instagram.com/BookandTonic

Printed in Great Britain
by Amazon

28607305R00185